This spellbinding novel brings to life an epoch lost in time, recreating compelling history as it might have been, portraying passionate men and women who move us with their dreams—never ceasing to remind us of the timeless longings of the human heart.

"Wolf has obviously studied up on her Jean Auel, mastered some of the mega-seller's lessons, and even bettered her in some vital areas . . . its characters and themes are sharper—making it an exceedingly strong contender on the prehistoric fiction front." —*Kirkus Reviews*

"RICHLY TEXTURED . . . COMPELLING . . . SATISFYING . . . Wolf has done her homework." —*Rocky Mountain News*

"EXCELLENT . . . A quick-moving, enchanting tale . . . which holds a powerful modern message concerning the battle of the sexes and the masculine/feminine faces of God." —*Booklist*

"A satisfying and broadly accessible prehistoric drama." —*Publishers Weekly*

Ⓢ **SIGNET BOOKS** (0451)

SUPERB TALES OF ROMANCE
AND HISTORY
BY JOAN WOLF

☐ **THE ROAD TO AVALON.** Shimmering with pageantry, intrigue and all the magic of Camelot, here is the epic story of Arthur—the conqueror, the once and future king who vanquished the Saxons and loved but one woman, the beautiful Morgan of Avalon. (401387—$4.50)

☐ **BORN OF THE SUN.** This compelling saga about a beautiful Celtic princess who gives her heart to a Saxon prince explodes with the passions of love and war. "Triumphant ... majestic ... a grand adventure!"—Booklist
(402252—$5.50)

☐ **THE EDGE OF LIGHT.** Two headstrong lovers vow to fight to change the world rather than forfeit their passion—in the magnificent tale of Alfred the Great and the woman he could not help but love. (402863—$5.99)

Prices slightly higher in Canada

Daughter of the Red Deer

Joan Wolf

AN ONYX BOOK

ONYX
Published by the Penguin Group
Penguin Books USA Inc., 375 Hudson Street,
New York, New York 10014, U.S.A.
Penguin Books Ltd, 27 Wrights Lane, London W8 5TZ, England
Penguin Books Australia Ltd, Ringwood, Victoria, Australia
Penguin Books Canada Ltd, 10 Alcorn Avenue,
Toronto, Ontario, Canada M4V 3B2
Penguin Books (N.Z.) Ltd, 182–190 Wairau Road, Auckland 10, New Zealand

Penguin Books Ltd, Registered Offices:
Harmondsworth, Middlesex, England

Published by Onyx, an imprint of New American Library,
a division of Penguin Books USA Inc. Previously published in a Dutton edition.

First Onyx Printing, November, 1992
10 9 8 7 6 5 4 3 2 1

For my brown-eyed children, Jay and Pam

AUTHOR'S NOTE

Daughter of the Red Deer is a fable about how men and women might have lived together fourteen thousand years ago in the Vézère Valley of France. The people in the novel belong to the specific Cro-Magnon culture which scientists have called the Magdelenian, a culture which flourished from the Dordogne to the Pyrenees during the Upper Paleolithic, the period of the last ice age.

The sculptures and engravings and paintings produced by the Magdelenians are the creations of enormously talented and observant artists. The technology of the Magdelenians was equally astonishing. With only the very basic raw materials of stone, bone, and antler, they made all of the tools necessary to secure life in a cold, relatively inhospitable climate. Further, they made decorations and ornaments, to beautify life as well as simply to survive it.

In regard to *Daughter of the Red Deer,* what is fact and what is fiction?

All of the paintings, tools, and weapons described in the book are based on actual artifacts left by early man. Specifically, the description of the sacred cave of the Red Deer is based on the cave of le Tuc d'Audoubert in the Pyrenees at Montesquieu-Avantes. The famous sculptures in the sanctuary of Le Tuc d'Audoubert are of bison, however, not of deer. And the sacred cave of the Tribe of the Horse is, of course, the famous cave of Lascaux, in the Vézère Valley of the Dordogne.

Outside of what the Magdelenians left in paint, stone, bone, and antler, almost everything postulated about their way of life (by scientists as well as by novelists) is speculation.

It is pretty well agreed upon that the Magdelenians must have had a fully articulate language, but of course that language has been completely lost. In writing this book, I decided to go ahead and use relatively sophisticated English words and not overly worry about "realism." Obviously the characters are supposed to be speaking their own language and not modern English, so, since we are pretending, why not pretend that they would have had a word to express the concept of *fastidious* or *religious*?

An issue of some controversy is whether or not the Magdelenians would have understood the relationship between copulation and pregnancy. While it is true that many primitive peoples do not, it seemed to me that one does not necessarily have to draw the same conclusion about the Magdelenians. These were extremely observant people, who were very attuned to the animal world (the cave paintings are certainly worthy to be ranked among the most expressive of mankind's artistic works). Even if the Magdelenians did not herd and breed animals, they were surrounded by wild animals whose habits they obviously observed closely. There are also many signs drawn in the caves and shelters that can be interpreted as fertility symbols: triangles to signify the vulva, loops to signify the phallus, etc. Under the circumstances, it does not seem to me unlikely that the Magdelenians would have understood this most basic fact of human life.

There is also some disagreement as to whether or not the Magdelenians had pottery. They most probably did not know how to fire pots (there are none extant), but it is not unreasonable to speculate that such a versatile people would have known how to make pots from sun-baked clay.

Out of all the extensive reading I did on the subject of the Magdelenians and their artifacts, the book I found most illuminating was Alexander Marshack's *The Roots Of Civilization*. I recommend it to anyone interested in this subject.

ACKNOWLEDGEMENTS

I must offer thanks to my long-time editor, Hilary Ross, for first suggesting to me that I write a book about pre-history, and then for doggedly refusing to give up on the idea. If it weren't for her, this novel would not exist.

Thanks also to my agent, Olga Wieser, for her unfailing support of all my projects.

And last, but most certainly not least, truckloads of gratitude to my friend Edith Layton Felber, whose sympathetic ear and unfailingly good advice are one of the greatest comforts in the life of this harried writer.

PART ONE

The Autumn

Prologue

The hunters burst silently out of the trees and ran along the narrow trail that led beside the shore of the small mountain spring. They ran lightly, with a long and bounding stride, their spears held securely in their right hands, their bows slung over their left shoulders. They were deadly quiet: the small animals scurrying underfoot on the forest floor did not hear their steps as they went by.

It was not just the spears and bows that marked these ten as hunters. They wore red ochre on their faces, in the hunter's distinctive markings, and they were dressed in undecorated deerskin shirts and trousers, the traditional hunting garb of the Tribe of the Red Deer. Behind them followed two large hunting dogs, as silent and as light-footed as the boys they shadowed.

For they could only be boys, these ten. The bodies under the deerskin clothing were too slender to belong to grown men. Boys, then: perhaps a hunting pack not yet initiated into Tribal manhood, out to bring down a Great Stag and thus prove to the tribe their worthiness for initiation.

Only when the line stopped, and the leader bent to examine the spoor on the path, did the image of boyhood shift. A clear bell-like voice said, "They are just ahead of us." The leader straightened and, in silhouette, the curve of breasts under the deerskin shirt was faintly evident.

The hunters raised the traditional chant: "Let us run

with the deer! The deer in the forest, the deer on the mountain, let us run with them, oh Mother! Swift and strong, let us run with the deer!''

The voices were pure, high, and unmistakably feminine.

Then, as swiftly and silently as they had come, the line of hunters vanished into the forest.

It was ten minutes before the two young men who had been watching them came out from their hiding places. They stood for a long silent moment, looking up the trail along which the girls had gone.

Then, ''Are you thinking what I am thinking?'' the smaller, black-haired man said in a soft voice to his companion.

''Sa,'' came the equally soft reply. White teeth showed in a summer-brown face. ''Tane, I believe we are in luck.''

The black-haired man let out his breath in a long, reverent sigh. ''All those girls,'' he said. ''And they are out in the forest alone!''

''Easy game for an ambush.'' The big blond man threw up his head, and his white grin flashed wider. ''It is in my heart that the men of the Horse will not be sleeping alone for many more moons.''

The two young men looked once more up the game trail. A brown rabbit hopped out of the woods, hopped across the trail, and disappeared into the trees on the other side.

''We'll stay in the area for a while,'' the blond finally said. ''We need to learn more about their habits. Then, when we come back with the rest of the men, we'll know what we must do.''

''Sa.'' The man called Tane nodded his dark head in approval. Then both men turned and, with the long loping gait of the hunter, they vanished down the trail in the opposite direction from the one the girls had taken.

One

"Alin. I have been looking for you."

The girl's head tilted, but otherwise she remained perfectly still, gazing at a rock in the rushing stream before her as the man approached across the clearing.

"The Mistress wants you," he said when he came to a halt beside her. He glanced at the stream also, and his lips curled in a small, wry smile. "She is beginning to be annoyed, so I thought perhaps it was time that someone found you."

Alin's gaze veered to the face of the man beside her, and then slowly returned to the large rock jutting up aggressively in the midst of the mountain stream. She said, "How did you know I would be here?"

He answered, "I used to come here when I was a boy and I wanted to be alone." Once again he gave that small, wry smile.

Alin did not reply, but her brown eyes, the same color and shape as the man's, were thoughtful.

"The time of Winter Fires will soon be here," the man said. He looked at the almost-bare birch trees that lined the stream as it wound its way up the mountainside. "The stags are rutting; the leaves are falling. Soon the snow will be here."

"Sa." And the girl crossed her arms over her breasts, as if his words had brought with them a blast of winter cold.

The man asked, "Will Lana be making the Sacred Marriage at Winter Fires this year?"

There was a long silence. As he waited, the girl's profile was very still, very remote. Finally she said, "This year it will be for me to do. The Mistress is beyond the bearing of children, she says. It will be for me to make the Sacred Marriage for the life of the tribe."

He raised one thin, strong hand, looked at it thoughtfully, then flexed it. "So the talk then is true."

"What talk?" Her head swung around; her clear, bell-like voice was suddenly sharp.

The man shrugged, his eyes still on his hand. "Even the men's cave hears gossip. There has been talk, that is all." He dropped his hand and his large dark eyes moved to her face. "It is time, after all. The Mistress is no longer young."

Alin's brown eyes looked back at the man who had fathered her.

"Tor . . ." The word was long and drawn out, sounding as if it were strange to her tongue.

"Sa?"

There was a moment of hesitation. Then she said, "I have been thinking of whom I should choose."

He nodded, his eyes still on her face. "It was in my heart that that might be what had brought you here." The hand he had been flexing moved slightly to reach out to her, and then it stilled. He said softly, "Whom does Lana say you should choose?"

"Jus."

Tor looked away from her toward the rock in the midst of the stream. "Na," he said. The word was final, though he spoke softly still. "Not Jus."

"Why not?" Alin asked.

"Jus is Lana's man. He will always be Lana's man, Alin. Take a man who will be loyal to you."

"There is no rivalry between me and my mother, Tor!" The words were sharp, almost frightened.

"I know that," he said. He looked down at her gravely. He was a tall man, and he had given his height to her as well as his eyes. "Take one of the younger boys," he said. "One of the boys you know and like."

She did not reply.

"Ban is a nice lad," he said.

Still she said nothing.

He sighed. "The Mistress rules the Tribe, Alin. She may have grown too old to bear, but she has not grown too old to rule. She will not give over any of her power to you. So take a boy you will like. It is Lana's man who will be chief of the men, no matter whom you choose. Leave Jus to her. Take one of the boys."

Alin drew in a long deep breath. Then she said, her voice carefully expressionless, "I was thinking the same thoughts. That is why I came out here."

He nodded as if he perfectly understood.

"Tor," she said, and frowned as she heard the note that had come into her voice. She raised her chin. "How did you know?" she asked. "We have seen so little of each other. How did you know what I was feeling?"

He looked away from her. He said, "You are the Mistress's daughter, Alin. You belong to her. Without her there would be no children for the Tribe, no fawns for the deer." He shrugged, a graceful gesture that Alin herself often made. "I am only a man. It is not for me to meddle with what is hers." Then he reached out and took her chin into his hand. "But I care for you, my daughter," he said, "and so I tell you: Do not take Jus."

Alin did not try to pull away from his hold and the two pairs of brown eyes met and held. "Did you seek me out today only to tell me this?" Alin asked at last.

"Sa," he said. "I did."

There was a thoughtful silence. Then Alin said, "It will be Ban, I think."

Tor nodded and let go her chin. "Ban." He turned and looked toward the path he had come by. "Come now, before the Mistress begins to be angry."

In silence, without touching, father and daughter returned through the forest.

The caves belonging to the Tribe of the Red Deer lay in the chain of mountains that would one day be called the Pyrenees. There were a number of other tribes dwelling in this area, as the mountains here were riddled with caves that for thousands of years had served as dwelling places and religious sanctuaries to the tribes of men. They were hunting tribes and, as the game was generally plentiful, for the most part they lived with one another in peace.

The Tribe of the Red Deer belonged to the grouping of people who called themselves the Kindred. These tribes covered the land between the mountains, where the people of the Red Deer dwelled; to the sea to the west and the great river valleys to the north. The tribes of the Kindred spoke the same language, lived mainly in the caves or rock shelters that were so plentiful, and met together each spring and autumn at tribal Gatherings, where they traded for goods and wives.

The Tribe of the Red Deer differed from most of the other tribes of the Kindred in one important respect: the people of the Red Deer still followed the Way of the Mother, while long ago their neighboring tribes had learned to follow the male God of the Sky.

The home of the Tribe of the Red Deer was located in the valley of the Greatfish River, and the scene that greeted Alin and Tor as they came into the settlement was both peaceful and pleasantly domestic. The two large caves used by the tribe as communal dwellings lay at the level of the valley floor. Above them towered the dark stone of the mountains and the deep crystal blue of the sky. Winding through the center of the valley was the Greatfish River itself, at this time of year lower and less rapidly flowing than it would be in the spring, but still a plentiful source of fish and of clear water.

Covering part of the valley floor were the huts within which most of the tribe lived. These huts were round in shape, and the main support of each was a tree trunk in the center; saplings dug into the earth leaned against the central tree to make a frame. Smaller boughs were interlaced between the saplings, and then the whole was covered by animal skins.

The married couples of the tribe lived in these huts along with their very young children. The unmarried girls and women lived in the women's cave, under the rule of the Mistress. The unmarried boys and men lived in the Men's Cave, under the rule of whichever man the Mistress had chosen that year to be her mate.

For in this tribe dedicated to worship of the Great Earth Mother, it was the chief priestess, or Mistress of the Mother, who ruled, whereas in the tribes who worshipped Sky God, the ruler was the male who was chosen to be chief. Because the Tribe of the Red Deer was so different from most of its neighbors in this regard, it held itself aloof, rarely attending the seasonal Gatherings, choosing instead to make its marriages within the tribe when possible, seeking mates from without from the few individual tribes near them with which they were on good terms. The rest of their commerce was limited to the occasional peddlers who came to trade their shells and furs for the beautifully soft deerskins the Tribe of the Red Deer excelled in producing.

As Alin and Tor came up the valley, they could see the smoke from the hearth fires spiraling out of the smoke holes in the roofs of the huts. Fires were burning too in the openings of the two dwelling caves. Alin and Tor parted without further speech, Tor to go to the hut he shared with his wife and younger children, and Alin to go to the women's cave, which lay the greatest distance from the river and in front of which only a single hut was pitched.

Three girls were standing just outside the cave opening, laying the small fire of sticks that would be the evening's cookfire. They looked up as Alin approached.

"Alin," one of the girls said with a small frown, "where have you been? The Mistress has been looking for you."

"I did not know," Alin returned. "I came as soon as I heard." But instead of moving away, she stood for a moment and watched as one of the girls lifted a cut branch and thrust it into the large fire that had been lit at the edge of the cave opening for warmth.

The girl who had first spoken said again, "The Mistress has been looking for you."

Alin met her best friend's eyes. She smiled wryly, a smile that suddenly made her look very like her father, and said, "All right, Jes. I am going."

A fire blazed in the circle of stones that formed the hearthplace of the Mistress's large hut, and the smoke

from it stung Alin's eyes as she came in through the flap
in the skins. She blinked and then she saw Lana, half
reclining on a pile of deerskins. The air in the hut was
dense and warm after the brisk autumn chill outside. Alin
said, "You wanted me, Mother?"

"Sa." The woman on the pile of deerskins did not
move; even so, she managed to give the distinct impression of coming to attention. "Where have you been?"
she asked her daughter calmly. "I have been wanting you
since midday."

"I am sorry," Alin said. "I did not know." She knelt
on the edge of the deerskins, sitting back on her heels so
she could look directly into her mother's face. "How
may I serve you, Mistress?" she asked, reverting to her
mother's formal title.

A short silence fell as the two women regarded each
other. Lana's light blond hair had been arranged with
bone hairpins into an intricate knot at the back of her
head. Its paleness almost hid the faint streaks of gray.
Her eyes were long, faintly slanted, and blue-gray in
color. She was not a tall woman, but the sense of power
that emanated from her small, almost-plump person was
one of the most striking things about her. She wore a
necklace of golden shells around her still-firm neck, and
bracelets of ivory adorned her wrists and arms.

The faintly irritated expression faded from Lana's face
as she smiled at her daughter and held out her hand. "I
wish to make final arrangements for Winter Fires," she
said. "Leaf Fall Moon is past the three-quarter phase, so
it is time."

Alin felt a flicker of apprehension. She knew her
mother would not like her choosing Ban. "As you will,
Mistress," she said, her face perfectly composed, and
she put her hand into her mother's.

Lana sighed. "How well I remember the first time I
made the Sacred Marriage," she said. "I have been sitting here all day, remembering and feeling old."

Alin squeezed the small capable hand that reposed
within her own long narrow grasp. "You will never be
old," she said.

Lana smiled faintly. Then she sighed again. "I can no

longer bear children, however. Last year, at Spring Fires, I was not sure. But it is certain now." She compressed her lips. "All those sons! So many years, and I have only one daughter to offer to the goddess. And now, to know that there is no chance of any others . . ." Her lips pinched together even more tightly.

Alin remained silent, holding her mother's hand and watching her face. It was still a remarkably youthful face, wider at the brow and eyes than it was long from brow to chin. A cat's face, Alin had often thought. A cat's face, with slanted cat's eyes. A striking face. Almost, a beautiful face.

Lana had not borne a child in over seven years.

Sensing her daughter's thoughts, Lana straightened her spine and crisply removed her hand from Alin's. "Your hands are all callused," she complained. "I do not understand this insistence of yours upon hunting. The men are perfectly capable of doing the hunting. You are the only Daughter the Mother has given to the tribe. If you are killed, where shall we be then?"

"The Mother holds all things in her hands, Mistress," Alin replied, her voice quiet yet firm. "What she wills to pass, will pass. Nothing that I can do will change her will. If I am marked to die, it will happen one way or another."

"You are not marked to die, my daughter." Lana was staring now into the fire. "You are marked to be Mistress of the Tribe after I am gone. I saw that in you when you were still a child. You are beloved of the Mother." She flashed a faint, nostalgic smile. "The night you were conceived, I knew."

There was a pause. "And yet . . ." Alin hesitated, and then asked the question that had puzzled her for years, one she had never dared to ask before. "You never again picked Tor to be your mate, Mother. Yet it was he who gave you your only daughter."

Lana's eyes swung back to her daughter's face. The smoke drifted between them, veiling each other's face. Lana said at last, "Listen now to what I tell you, Alin. Never choose a man you cannot control. That is how Sky God came to rule so many of the tribes of the Kindred.

The mistresses were weak and let the control slip away from their hands. Most men are safe, are properly respectful, spill their sap and worship the Mother who will bring forth life out of it. But every once in a while there is a man who challenges that. . . ."

"Tor does not challenge the Mother!" Alin protested before she had time to consider the wisdom of doing so.

Frowning Lana leaned forward to see Alin better through the smoke. "There are men whose very being is a challenge to the Mother," she said, her voice hard. "Tor is one of those men, my daughter." Lana's eyes had turned the same color as the smoke, Alin thought as she stared back into the cat-slanted gaze of the Mistress. Lana sat back a little, and the hard note left her voice. "He served his purpose," she said. "He gave the tribe a Daughter. It would have been dangerous to allow him to continue for more than a year as chief. Under him the men were . . . different."

Alin did not answer. Her mother's gaze did not drop.

"Do you understand what I am telling you?" Lana asked softly.

"Sa," Alin said. She stared, mesmerized, into her mother's blue-gray eyes. "I do."

"See that you do not forget it." And Lana leaned back on her pile of skins, releasing Alin from the hold of her eyes. "I know that you are old to be a maiden still, my daughter. Fifteen winters is a long time to wait. I know that it must have been hard for you, to watch the other girls at Spring and Winter Fires, but it was proper for you to save your maidenhood for the first time you made the Sacred Marriage. It will be stronger so; a more powerful mating for the tribe."

Alin nodded.

"Has it been hard for you, my daughter, the waiting?"

It is a little late to ask me that now, Mother, Alin thought, dropping her eyes to the hands clasped together upon her knees.

"Alin." It was the voice of authority, the voice that no one in the tribe ever disobeyed. "I am asking if the waiting has been hard for you."

"Na," Alin answered, speaking the truth. She looked

up from her deerskin-covered knees. "It is true that I have watched the other girls at the Fires, and I have wondered. But . . . I have not yet felt the call, Mother. I think Earth Mother has been waiting also."

Lana's slanted eyes scrutinized Alin's grave face. Then she said softly, "When the time comes, and the spirit of Earth Mother fills your womb, then you will feel the call."

Alin's brown head nodded in serene understanding. "Sa," she said. "It will be so."

Lana sighed. "It will hurt," she warned. "It always does the first time. The barrier must be broken. And a man is not gentle when his blood is pounding with the drums of the Fires."

"I am not afraid," Alin said.

Lana said, "You will be a worthy successor to me, my daughter. So. Then I shall send for Jus."

"Na," Alin said quickly. She saw the surprise spring into Lana's eyes, and looked away before she could also see the anger certain to follow. "Jus is *your* mate, Mother. He will still be chief of the men, no matter whom I choose. I understand that. All the Men's Cave will understand that. I do not need to choose him as mate for him to continue in his office."

"*I* am the one who does not understand, Alin." All the tenderness had left Lana's voice. "Of course it must be Jus," she said. "The mate of the Mother is chief of the men. That is the law."

"*You* are Earth Mother, Mistress," Alin said. "My making the Sacred Marriage will not change that."

"Of course it will not change that," Lana snapped. "Nevertheless, the man who makes the Sacred Marriage is always the chief of the men. It has always been so."

Alin felt her heart pounding in her chest, and she drew a long, steadying breath. "But always before it was the Mistress who made the Sacred Marriage," she said. "This time it will be different. I know, all the tribe knows, that you are the Mistress, and your mate will continue to be chief of the men. My mate will be merely . . . the god at Winter Fires."

"And who is to be your mate?" Lana asked in her

hardest voice. "Who is so much more to your taste than Jus?"

Alin swallowed. "Ban," she said.

The fair, faintly graying eyebrows rose. "Ban? Ban is just a boy."

"And I am just a maiden, Mother. I will choose Ban."

Lana leaned back upon one elbow. She said thoughtfully, "Jus frightens you, Alin?"

Na, Alin thought. He does not frighten me. But Tor is right. I want a man who will be loyal to me. She could not say that to her mother, though.

"You can control him," Lana was saying. "He is like the bull: strong and of the earth. He is not one of those men I warned you about."

"I know," Alin replied. "It is not that."

"What then?"

What to say? Alin thought back on Lana's words, saw the way. "I am thinking that perhaps he is too much like the bull for me, Mother," she said. "Perhaps he does frighten me a little."

A small, secret smile pulled at the corner of Lana's mouth. She said, "When once you have felt the fire of Earth Mother in your loins, then a man like Jus will not frighten you. But you are a maiden. Perhaps you are right, Alin. Perhaps for your first time Ban will be best. He is a boy, but he is man enough to make the Sacred Marriage with you. He may even be man enough to get you with child. Sometimes it is the young ones who can best do that."

Alin bowed her head and did not reply.

"All right," Lana said with sudden decision. "Then I shall send for Ban."

"Winter Fires! Winter Fires!" The words were ringing around the tribe. "The Mistress has called for Winter Fires!"

Again and again, as the news circulated from the Men's and the Women's Caves to the married folks' huts, the same question was asked again and again: "Who is to make the Sacred Marriage this year?"

And the answer, which was always given with a lilt of

excitement in the voice, was: "Alin. Alin is to be the goddess this year. And she has named Ban to be the god!"

For twenty years it had been Lana. For all those years had the tribe sung and danced while Lana and her chosen mate made the Sacred Marriage to ensure the fertility of the tribe and the herds. For the last three years, since Alin had reached womanhood, the tribe had expected to hear that Lana had resigned her role to the younger woman. For the last three years they had been disappointed.

"It is time," they said around their hearth fires as the night closed in and they felt the cold of the coming winter creeping into their huts and swirling around the stone floors of their caves. "There must be youth and fire in order for the beasts to bear. Lana will still be Mistress, but it is right that Alin should make the Sacred Marriage."

In the men's cave the hunters were congratulating the young dark-haired boy who had been chosen by Earth Mother to give his sap to the ritual mating that would ensure the continued fertility of the animals they all lived upon.

Ban laughed, his dark eyes glowing with pleasure, his blood running hot at the very thought of what was to happen. He and Alin were of an age, and together they had learned how to hunt under the tutelage of old Lar. Of necessity, there had always been a distance between them. He, after all, was only a boy, and she was the Chosen One of the Mother. But in an unspoken way, they had been friends. That was why she had chosen him, he thought, as finally he lay down in the skins of his sleeping place in the men's cave and tried to compose himself for rest.

Usually he fell asleep as soon as his head touched the warmth of his skins, but tonight he lay awake long after the heavy breathing of the other men told him they were asleep. He lay awake, in an almost trancelike state, staring into the flames of the fire. In his mind's eye he was seeing Alin, seeing the lithe slimness of her, the sweet curves of her breasts and hips, the warm brown of her

hair that was so unusually streaked with threads of gold,
the huge long-lashed brown of her eyes. He felt his phallus stir and become erect at his thoughts. His heart
pounded.

The Mother would approve, he thought, as he felt his
manhood rise hard and taut with life. The Mother would
say Alin had chosen well.

She was so beautiful, Alin. He had always thought so. And
soon . . . soon would come the drums and the flutes and the
dance of the mating beasts. Soon it would be he who was the
one to follow Earth Mother deep into the recesses of her
sacred cave. At the thought he felt the hair on the back of his
neck stand up as straight as his phallus.

Deep, deep he would go, into the bowels of the earth
with her, and there they would make the Sacred Marriage
together, his sap waking her womb with life for the tribe,
life for the herds, life for the world of men.

He quivered and shook. It was almost too much, the mystery of it, the sensation.

The man who had been appointed fire guard for the
night stirred and went to throw on another log. The
movement between him and the leaping flames broke
Ban's trance. He blinked, turned over, and willed himself
to go to sleep.

Two

The band of young men encamped on the shore of the small river were eating the smoked buffalo meat they had carried with them and looking at the mountains to the south.

"How much longer do you reckon, Mar?" one asked as he bit off a piece from the strip of cured meat in his hand and began to chew it.

"Two days," the big, golden-haired man replied, holding up the appropriate number of fingers. He counted: "Two days to reach the tribe's home ground; two or three days to lay the trap"; more fingers were held up, "then two handfuls of days on the road back. A half moon from now, and we should be home again."

"With women!" At those words a low murmur of excitement broke out around the campfires.

"How many do you think we might take?" This time the question came from the far side of the second fire.

The man called Mar shrugged. "If we capture the hunting party, then it will be two handfuls. It is the young girls who go hunting, and it is the young girls we want."

"I still find it hard to believe that women go out on the hunting trail," said another. "The men of this tribe must be bloodless weaklings, to allow their women to face the dangers of the hunt."

"The men hunt, too," Mar said. "Tane and I saw them when we were here in the summer weather. But they do not hunt with the girls. When the girls hunt, they hunt alone." There was the flash of very white teeth in the growing dark. "That is to our advantage. As I told you before, if they are out hunting we can capture them with little trouble. And by the time the rest of the tribe realizes they are missing, we will be gone."

"It would be good if we could take more than two handfuls," a brown-haired boy said.

"We shall take what we can take easily, Melior," Mar said. "I do not want any fighting."

"We men of the Horse are fine fighters," Melior replied, putting up his chin. "We are not afraid of a fight."

"We number but three handfuls," Mar said. "There are many more men than that in the Tribe of the Red Deer." Mar looked at the circle of faces around the fire. "It is in my heart that nothing would make Altan and the nirum happier than to see the young men of the initiates' cave killed on this expedition," he said.

There was a startled silence.

"Dhu!" said a very blond boy. "Do you think so, Mar?"

Mar shrugged his big shoulders. He said easily, "Why do you think the chief allowed me to bring only the initiates on this raid?"

The blond boy, who was called Dale, looked around at his fellows. "I did not think about that," he confessed.

Mar grinned. "I must confess, perhaps I . . . misled . . . Altan a little about the difficulties involved in the raid."

An appreciative chuckle ran around the fire.

Mar sobered. "I do not think we will have much difficulty taking these girls," he told his followers. "Tane and I watched them for the passing of the moon. We know their hunting runs. We will know where to lay the trap. But we cannot be greedy. We must take what we can take quickly, and then get away."

"Sa, sa," the men replied. "We hear you, Mar."

Mar nodded. "It is time to get some sleep. We leave tomorrow with the dawn."

When the new moon of Winter Fires was first sighted, a pale, thin crescent hovering over the western sunset, the women of the Tribe of the Red Deer knew that the

time had come for them to go to their sacred cave in order
to make ready for the tribe's great semiannual fertility
rite.

The next morning, the matriarchs and the unmarried
girls of the tribe began winding their way up the mountainside to the sacred cave of the Mother. All that day
they would celebrate the ritual's prescribed preparatory
rites.

There were thirty women in the procession, which took
the narrow uphill path along the shore of the Greatfish
River that clear autumn morning: the young and the old
women of the tribe. Those who were with child or were
mothers of small children would come tomorrow, with
the men, and the official ceremony of Winter Fires would
begin.

There had already been snow in the higher reaches of
the mountains, but below, on the slopes that the women
of the Red Deer were climbing, the weather was cool
and sunny and dry. After a two-hour walk, the procession
reached the Volp, a stream that tumbled swiftly along its
boulder-strewn bed. The girls and the women turned to
follow the stream, which led them toward the stone cliff
of the hillside. And then, abruptly, the stream disappeared.

The cave opening out of which the rushing waters of
the stream flowed was a wide low arch of rock. In past
years, the Tribe of the Red Deer had cleared the undergrowth in front and on this cleared land the women put
down their sleeping rolls and knelt to extract from them
flat stone saucers filled with animal fat. Carrying these,
the women of the tribe gathered around Lana, their Mistress, who was waiting for them near the cave entrance.

As the women approached her one by one, Lana took
the live coal she had carried just for this purpose, and lit
the moss wick in each of the saucers. The passages of the
sacred cave went deep into the mountain, and there would
be no natural light once they got beyond the entrance
chamber.

The depth of the Volp was shallow at the threshold of
the cave, though it grew considerably deeper along the
length of the river's subterranean course. This time of the

year the Volp was relatively low, and by walking along
the gravel bed beside it, it was possible to enter the first
chamber of the cave on foot. In the spring, at the rites of
Spring Fires, the river was in flood and the gravel was
completely covered. At that time they had to take a small
boat through the entrance passage in order to gain access
to the first hall.

Carefully carrying their stone lamps, the thirty women
followed the stream into the blackness of the cave, tread-
ing carefully along the extremely narrow path that went
between the cave's wall and the dark, rushing water. After a little while the stone walls of the cave began to
widen, and the stream flowed into a large chamber whose
walls were decorated with the engraved pictures of animals: buffalo, reindeer, and horses. There were shamans, too, men who wore the masks of beasts. And,
most important, the sign of the Mother, the *P*,
danced before them in the shadowy light.

The river passed through this chamber, and then disappeared into a dark pit, its channel taking it ever deeper
and lower into the mountainside.

This decorated chamber, however, was far from their
destination, and the women did not pause. Instead they
bore to the left, away from the path of the Volp, down a
small gallery that led them into yet another chamber, this
one vast and white and hung all over the ceiling and the
floor with glorious milky white stalactites and stalag-
mites. This glittering chamber was utterly silent save for
a ghostly drip-drip of underground water somewhere in
the distance.

Lana, who was in the lead of the long single-file procession, did not linger to regard the startling beauty of
the White Chamber. Purposefully she crossed the glittering white floor to an opening in the rock in the far end
that led into what seemed to be a narrow chimney. Turning sideways, she slid into the opening. One by one, the
women slipped into the opening after her, and then
climbed up the ladder of woven sinew that the tribe always left hanging inside the small, high hole.

Alin stood at the top of the ladder, in a dark, narrow
passage, and watched as the glowing stone lamps ap-

peared at the top of the chimney one after the other. The air here was cold, for the temperature rarely varied so deep within the mountain.

Once they were all assembled in the passage, Lana turned to the wall on her left and held her stone lamp high. Alin, with the same ceremonial gesture as her mother, also raised her lamp, so that all could clearly see the picture that was engraved there upon the wall.

Two grotesque, fantastical animals leaped into being under the glow of the lamps: the Guardians of the Sanctuary of the Sacred Cave, engraved on this wall by an unknown hand unknown numbers of years earlier. The one on top had a horrible head with a single short horn, flanked behind by a wide ear. Its thin neck supported the heavy head with a rippling outline. The prominent muzzle was rounded and the jaws were open. The withers were sunken, the head and body were marked with vertical and oblique lines, and the slender long forelegs ended in long claws. The animal beneath was reduced to a grotesque head, like the preceding one, crowned by two small ears.

The women looked. For a long moment, it seemed as if even their breathing stopped. *Let no unsanctified soul pass here,* said the silent fantastical beasts keeping vigil on the wall of the passageway.

The women solemnly followed Lana down the gallery; through other passageways that were so low they had to crawl; through gallerys that still bore witness to the cave bears that at one time had made these passages their home; past a silent underground lake, a black, solid, unmoving mass of water; until at last, after over an hour of underground travel, they came to the place that was the heart of the sacred mystery.

It was a long, low chamber, and set in the midst of it, sculpted from golden clay and leaning against a natural block of rock, were the statues of two red deer, a male and a female, so beautifully modeled they could almost have been real.

The female deer, which was finer in form, had her neck stretched forward and her tail raised, in the position of the doe awaiting the stag. The male deer was posi-

tioned directly behind her, more robust and less fine in
form. He was on the point of mounting the female, already raised on his hind legs, his tail pressed tight between his thighs in the effort.

A long, wordless sigh ran through the group of women.

This, then, was the purpose of the sacred cave: copulation, the perpetuation of the life of the deer and the life
of the tribe that bore its name.

Ever since Alin had first come here, for her initiation
into womanhood, she had felt the power of Earth Mother
pulsing in the still cold air of the sanctuary. Tomorrow,
she thought, her eyes on the beautiful sculptures of the
deer, tomorrow the power would come through her. She
would be the instrument. At last she would come into her
heritage.

On the clay floor of the sanctuary were the heel marks
of all the previous dancers who had made the fertility
dance in this sacred place. On the walls were engraved
the signs of the phallus, the male symbol of fecundity
and the beginning of life.

Alin felt a tightness, a throbbing, in her loins. For
three years she had looked upon these symbols of generation and had known it was not yet her time. The shiver
that suddenly shook her had nothing to do with the chill
damp of the sanctuary.

Truly, she thought, it is as the Mistress had said: When
the spirit of Earth Mother fills your womb, you will feel
the call.

It is so, Alin thought, in wonder and in exultation. It
is so.

The women were stripping off their clothes, getting
ready to don the bell-shaped ritual skirts they had carried, preparing for the ceremony of purification.

All this part of the cave belonged to the women. The
only man who was ever allowed to penetrate into the
deepest chambers of the sacred cave was the one chosen
to make the Sacred Marriage. He would be brought to
look at the deer, he would see what few others of his
kind had seen, he would lie with the Mother upon a bed
of soft skins, and serve her, and in so doing he would

ensure the fertility of the tribe and of the beasts that fed the tribe.

Alin drummed her heels and sang with her sisters as the skin drums beat for them in time. She could feel the blood flowing strong and steady in her veins. Mother, she thought, I am ready.

They slept that night outside the cave, under the autumn stars. The night air was chill but very dry; the stars overhead were brilliant, undimmed by the pale scimitar of the new moon. Having packed away their ritual skirts until the morrow, the women lay down to rest, dressed in long-sleeved shirts and soft deerskin trousers.

Alin did not fall to sleep right away. Her mind was too full of what was going to happen the next day, of the mysteries of nature and fertility and birth. She lay on her back under the warmth of her skins and gazed, wide-eyed, up at the stars. There was darkness all around her, but up there in the sky the stars were bright. She felt open to them, felt their pure keen light pouring into her, exalting her, filling her with the potency of their power.

Tomorrow night, she thought, she would lie deep in the heart of the sacred cave. Ban would lie with her, but it would be the power of the stars that would be entering the fertile darkness of her womb. It would not be a single man, but all of nature she would embrace when she lay tomorrow night with Ban.

Alin lay awake for a long time, looking up at the bright heavens. Then she fell into a deep and dreamless sleep, and when she awoke the stars had faded and the darkness of night was beginning to glimmer with the light of morning. A breeze was blowing off the river, and with it was coming the pale light of dawn. As Alin lay still, watching the sky, the light grew stronger, and then, over the whiteness swept a glorious flush of rose.

The sun was rising. The light shifted, the rose began to shimmer and turn to yellow, and the young flaming ball of the sun pushed its way up from beneath the earth to begin its daily journey across the sky.

Alin's soul quivered with ecstasy.

It was then that they came. One moment all was bright

and perfect, and then the next the day was shattered by the aggressive noise of men and of dogs. Instantly Alin sat upright. She reached for her javelin and spearthrower, which were not there. She flung up her head and there, at a distance of less than three feet, she saw the spear pointed straight at her heart. She froze. Then, very slowly, she raised her eyes. A man stood there, holding the big spear and looking back at her. Even in her fear and confusion, Alin noticed the blue of his eyes.

All around her the women of the Tribe of the Red Deer were scrambling to their feet, their voices raised in a babble of protest. Alin slowly rose as well and, wrenching her eyes away from that blue stare, she looked around.

The ambush had been neatly done, she thought with bitter recognition. The captive women, now on their feet, were securely surrounded by a barrier of men and spears and dogs. Their own weapons were out of reach, having been piled for the night in a place close by the fire.

Abruptly one of the older women spun around and began to run toward the trees that were directly behind them. A deep voice said a single word, and suddenly a dog was in her way. The dog's lips drew back; he snarled, low and menacing. The woman stopped dead.

The silence was intense. Then another male voice said two words that sounded like: "Got them!"

At that, the huddle of women parted a little, and Lana stepped forward. "Who are you and what do you want here?" Her voice was cold and sharp as an icicle; every inch of her small frame blazed command. She sounded furious, and not at all afraid. Pride in her mother surged through Alin.

The blue-eyed man was the one to answer. He spoke the language of the Kindred, although with a strange accent. "We have come to take your girls," he said. "We have need of women in our tribe." There was a heartbeat of appalled silence. Then he added, "We want only the young ones; the old mothers can stay."

A clamor of feminine voices rose to the heavens.

"*Silence!*" Lana no longer looked small and plump; she seemed to have grown inches since the man had first begun to speak. The Mistress stared coldly at the blue-

eyed giant who had addressed her. Her words were clear
and distinct, pronounced so that he would be sure to understand every syllable. "Do you know with whom you
meddle? We are here on the Mother's business, and you
violate her sanctuary. Perhaps if you go away immediately you will not suffer overmuch for your blasphemy.
But if you try to take our girls, the curse of the Mother
will fall upon you all."

Alin felt a shiver go up and down her spine. Lana
sounded so menacing! Alin looked to the man whom her
mother had threatened, fully expecting to find him ready
to retreat. In all of her years on this earth, Alin had never
yet seen a man stand up to the Mistress when she spoke
in that voice.

This man laughed. No words could have made his answer more petrifying. He glanced at the slim black-haired
man beside him and said, "Separate the girls out, Tane.
I do not want to tarry. We do not know when their men
might be coming."

Who were these men? Alin stared in shocked disbelief
as a group of the invaders, accompanied by the dogs,
began to advance toward the women trapped within their
circle of spears.

"Take your sleeping rolls with you," the blue-eyed
man who was obviously their leader ordered. "We have
a long journey to make, and the sleeping will be cold and
hard if you must lie unprotected on the ground." The
words he used were familiar; it was the intonation that
made them sound so strange. He broadened some of the
sounds and clipped short others.

Where did these men come from? Alin thought with a
mixture of fear and bewilderment.

Now the slim black-haired man was standing beside
her. "You," he said. "Pick up your skins and come."

"No!" The voice was Lana's, imperious yet also filled
with anguish. "You cannot take her! She is the Chosen
One, the Daughter of the Mother! You will be cursed
forever if you take the Chosen One from her place by the
Mother's side."

The man paused and turned to look at his leader. Alin
held her breath.

"Do not worry," the blue-eyed man answered Lana. He actually sounded amused. "Your Chosen One will be about the Mother's business all right. We shall see to that."

The rest of the men laughed, and the man who was standing beside Alin put his hand upon her arm. "Come," he said. "Over there."

She tensed her muscles, contemplating resistance. The man was not that much taller than she, and she was strong, with muscles trained in the discipline of the hunt. The man must have felt her thought, for he lowered his voice and said quietly, "You will only be hurt if you try to run. Be sensible, girl, and come with me."

Alin turned, looked into a pair of black-lashed green eyes. "We will not harm you," he said.

Alin looked beyond his shoulder to where Lana stood. "We have no choice, Mother," she said.

The Mistress's face was a mask. She said to Alin, "You are the life of the tribe, my daughter. Remember that and be watchful of your safety." There was a beat of silence. Lana looked, narrow-eyed, at the tall leader of the kidnappers, and then she said to Alin, "I shall find you. Be sure of that."

The eyes of mother and daughter met. Then Alin nodded, once. She bent to pick up her skins and crossed to where the men were holding the girls they had separated out from the larger group.

Sixteen girls between the ages of twelve and fifteen were marched at spearhead away from the sacred cave that perfect autumn morning. The older women, the tribal matriarchs, had been left behind, bound hand and foot with leather thongs, to await rescue by the men of the tribe who would be coming to the cave at midday.

Half of the kidnapping men were in front of the girls, with the other half behind, and the dogs roamed freely back and forth. Alin walked in the midst of the girls, with her closest friend at her side. They were going eastward, she noted, along a track she knew from her hunting expeditions. Next to her, Jes voiced out loud the thought that was in all the girls' minds. "Who *are* these men? Where can they have come from?"

The girls in front and the girls behind all looked to Alin for an answer. She said, "They speak the language of the Kindred so they cannot be reindeer hunters from the north, or mammoth hunters from the steppes to the east."

"Sa. Sa. That is so." The girls all nodded their heads in agreement.

Elen said, "If they are of the Kindred, then they will not be beyond the reach of the Mistress."

Just then a dog came cantering past them at the very edge of the track. Alin watched it go by, then she said very softly, "The Tribe of the Red Deer has dogs also."

There was the flash of teeth as the girls around her smiled.

"Did you count their number?" Elen asked next.

"Sa. Not quite four handfuls," Alin answered.

"The Mistress will call out the whole tribe," Jes said. "All the men and the boys. The dogs will find us, and then these," she flicked a hand in disparagement toward the men striding before them, "these will fall like deer beneath the flying spear."

"Liniut can track anything," Elen said.

They all pictured the great wolf-like dog who belonged to Tor. They exchanged glances and satisfied nods.

"The men will bring Ban to the sacred cave at midday," Alin said. "Then they will have to go home again for the dogs."

"We will not be celebrating Winter Fires tonight," Elen said regretfully.

"Na," said Sana. "But perhaps tomorrow night we will be."

"Walk more slowly," Alin suggested. "Let us do what we can to delay."

Alin was surprised by the ease with which these strangers zigzagged their way through the hills. For how long, she wondered, had they been planning this raid?

The spirits of the girls remained high for the first two hours of the march. And then they came to a stream that cut across the track, and the blue-eyed man ordered them to bear right, wade in, and follow the water.

The girls looked at each other.

"Why?" Alin demanded. "I know of a hunting track we can easily take if that is the direction you wish to go in. We shall get our moccasins and trousers wet if we wade through the stream, and it will make walking both cold and uncomfortable. It is not necessary to go through the water."

"I did not ask you, girl," came the deceptively pleasant-voiced reply. "I told you. Everyone into the water. We will follow the streambed for a while."

Alin looked up at the man who had come to stand beside her. He was a full head taller than she, with great broad shoulders under his buffalo skin vest. His hair was the color of the sun. He held a large spear in one hand, and a tall well-muscled dog shadowed his heels.

Alin said, "I do not like to be wet. I will walk along the stream's edge."

The man's eyes, bluer than any eyes she had ever seen, glinted at her. "I suppose I could carry you," he said, "but I am not inclined to do so." He handed his spear to the black-haired man who usually walked beside him, lifted her by her elbows, walked to the stream, and plunked her down in the water. "Now walk," he said, and went back to retrieve his spear.

The water was freezing. All around her the men were urging the girls into the stream. A dog nipped at someone's heels and a girl yelped.

May his spear shatter when he needs it most, Alin thought viciously as the icy water lapped against her shins and she felt the hard rocks of the streambed dig into the soles of her wet moccasins. He was drowning their scent.

No matter, she thought as she waded miserably through the freezing water with the other girls. The men of the Red Deer would know what had happened when their scent disappeared at the stream. The dogs would simply follow the stream and pick up the scent wherever they exited. That blue-eyed son of a hyena could not keep them walking in the stream forever, after all.

He kept them walking for much longer than was comfortable, however. The girls slogged along, heads down-cast, teeth set to keep them from chattering with the cold. After a while Alin's feet turned numb, and she stumbled over stones she could hardly feel. She knew the way they were going, and so she did not look up until the men in front of her finally turned to climb out of the water.

Then Alin looked at Jes, who was walking beside her. Neither of them spoke, but followed the men up the stone bank with alacrity.

They went along a wild pig track for a while, and now the girls walked with their heads up, looking around, taking care to rub here and there against a tree in order to leave their scent. Then, abruptly, the men in front stopped.

"Now we turn around," said the deep authoritative voice Alin was coming to detest.

Alin and Jes looked at each other again. "Turn around?" Alin raised her voice challengingly. "What do you mean, turn around?"

The leader was coming toward her. "You are a hunter, girl," he answered as he came up to her. "I've seen you and your pack out after the deer. I think you understand very well what I'm doing." He came to a halt directly before her. "If anyone following you has the sense to follow this stream, the dogs will pick up your scent at the place where we came out, and follow the trail you have so carefully laid. They will follow it to this point, and then it will vanish. Because we are retracing our steps, girl, and then we are going back into the water."

There was a brief, stunned silence as Alin stared up at the big, golden-haired man whose shoulders were block-ing her view of the track ahead. When the silence con-tinued, and Alin did not move, he raised his eyebrows. "Turn around," he said softly. "We are going back."

Alin felt her hands curling into fists at her sides. The dog at the man's heels growled in his throat. Alin spun around and strode away, so angry she scarcely saw the stricken-faced girls who hastily parted their ranks to let her through.

They waded through the freezing stream for another hour before finally they picked up a reindeer track that

ran toward the north. They followed this track until the
sky began to turn dark, the girls growing all the while
progressively colder and hungrier and more depressed,
until finally, in the distance, they saw the light of what
appeared to be several fires. Dogs barked from the encampment.

Hunters! Alin thought, and her heart leaped with hope.
Perhaps they would find help after all.

"It's Mar!" she heard a male voice shout from the
campsite before them. "And he's got the girls!"

The hope in Alin's heart died. More of them, she
thought despairingly.

The dogs she had heard came bursting out of the wood,
barking a greeting to those accompanying the arriving
party. The blue-eyed man, whose name it seemed was
Mar, said to the brown-haired man who had appeared
before them on the track, "We've got them all right, Bror.
And they are weary and hungry, as we are. I hope you
have supper ready."

"That we do, Mar," came the cheerful reply. "The
meat is just about cooked now."

Mar grunted and looked over his shoulder, his eyes
automatically seeking Alin. "There is food ahead," he
said to her. "And fires. We'll have all of you warm and
dry and fed very shortly."

Alin was about to tell him that she would choke on any
food he offered her, but then the succulent smell of roasting boar came floating to her nostrils. Her mouth wa-
tered. None of them had eaten since the evening before.
It would be easier to resist an enemy on a full stomach
than on an empty one, she decided. "Very well," she
said, and walked forward imperiously, gesturing for the
rest of the girls to follow.

The camp looked inviting, and smelled even better.
The new arrivals clustered around the fires, stretching
out their wet and freezing legs and feet to the warmth of
the flames. The men who had evidently been assigned to
hunt and cook their supper handed out chunks of roasted
meat, and silence fell as everyone attended to eating.

"Now," Mar said a little while later, when they were

finishing with the food. He threw the bone he had been stripping into the fire, wiped his mouth with the back of his hand, and rose easily to his feet. His voice was just loud enough to carry to the edge of the farthest fire. ''I will try to explain to you why we have done as we have.''

The silence was intense. Alin looked up from the tips of her drying moccasins to the man they called Mar. He was standing before the biggest fire, his spine straight, his head thrown back, his empty hands relaxed by his sides. The flames danced behind him, gilding his sun-colored hair with a coppery glow. He wore his hair much shorter than did the men of the Red Deer. None of these men had enough hair to braid, Alin thought, glancing around as she waited for Mar to begin speaking. Nor were any of them wearing beards. But then, they all seemed to be very young; many probably had yet to grow a beard at all. But that Mar was not a boy. Her eyes appraised the tall commanding figure in front of the fire. That one surely had a man's beard. It was evidently the custom in their tribe not to wear one.

Alin came to attention as Mar began to speak, looking from face to face as he told his story.

''We come from a tribe you do not know,'' he said. ''Our dwelling place is a long journey from here.'' He paused as a light murmur of dismay ran through the girls seated around the fires. Alin frowned. She was as dismayed as anyone, but they must not betray weakness in front of these men. She shot reproving glances left and right before returning her attention to Mar.

He continued, ''Last year, at the Moon of the Falling Leaves, the men of my tribe attended a nearby Gathering of tribes in order to trade goods and to barter for wives. We left behind all of our women, save those we were looking to wed out to other tribes, with the children and a handful of men to protect them. They were well provisioned and protected, and we would be gone for merely a half cycle of the moon. We thought nothing of it.''

Mar paused. At his sides his hands, once so relaxed, began slowly to close and then to open. He stared straight ahead, as if seeing a picture in his mind. His face was shadowed as the fire was behind him, and Alin could not read his expression. But his hands told her that the picture he was seeing was not pleasant.

"I do not know how it happened," he said. "None of us knows how it happened. But while we were gone, one of the places from which we draw our water went bad. Our people did not realize it, and drank from it."

Alin stared at him now, mesmerized with horror. She had heard of such things happening, but had always thought such stories to be more scare tales than truth. "Twice two handfuls of our women died," came the deep, oddly accented voice through the night. "And almost as many of our children. The future of our tribe died with them." He blinked and the blue eyes seemed to awaken and focus once more on the scene before him. "Men cannot bring forth children," he said to the girls sitting around the fires. "You who worship the Mother know only too well that women are necessary for that."

An animal roared in the distance and the human figures around the fires tensed. A cave lion? An answering roar cave, and then silence. It had been a lion. Then a girl spoke. Alin recognized the voice as Jes's.

"Are you saying that we are to be the replacements for the women you lost?"

"Sa," the man called Mar answered. "That is what I am saying."

Alin felt the breath hiss in her throat. She leaned a little forward. "What of the women you went to the Gathering to fetch as wives?" she demanded. "Are you too niggardly to pay for wives? Must you steal them from the very hand of the Goddess herself?"

She saw his head swing in her direction. His eyes easily picked her out from the figures clustered around her. "It is not possible simply to buy women," he said. "The men of other tribes want wives in exchange for the girls who are too closely bound in blood to wed within their own tribe." He shrugged. "I am sorry, but there is no other way. This is a matter of life and death to my people." He looked away from Alin's blazing eyes to seek the faces of the other girls. "We will be good to you. We do not wish to harm you. We hope you will learn to feel at home with us. But you will live with us, and bear us children, and this is not a matter in which you will be given any choice."

Alin said coldly, "You do not know with whom you meddle. You are right when you say we serve Earth Mother. We are her handmaids and we serve no man save a man we choose for ourselves. You will get no children of us, Outlander. All you will get is the Mother's curse."

She sat in the flaring light of one fire and stared at the man standing in the flaring light of another. The lion's roar came again. This time it seemed farther away. She was astonished at how like her mother she had sounded.

Mar's face was somber as he looked back at her. He said softly but very distinctly, "That is a chance we will have to take since the alternative for my tribe is extinction." Once more he looked away from Alin to the faces of the other girls, raised to him in the flickering firelight. "Get some sleep," he said. "We will be leaving at dawn."

Three

Alin shivered as she stepped out of her deerskin sleeping roll and felt the chill of the morning air. In another moon it would be too cold for such a journey as they were making now. In another moon the Tribe of the Red Deer would hunker down and concentrate on the main imperative of the winter: keeping warm.

Alin blew out of her eyes a strand of hair that had come loose from her braid. She crossed her arms over her chest and looked up at the brightening sky. If their people were unable to trace them quickly, it was unlikely that they would be able to trace them at all before the winter. All the trails and hunting runs would soon be covered with snow. Mar had chosen the right time of the year for his raid. May the Mother curse him, she thought.

"Alin, my blister did not get better overnight."

At the soft voice of one of the youngest of the girls, Alin forced her mind away from her own thoughts and turned to Dara. "Let me see it," she said, and sat on her heels to look at the girl's proffered foot. The heel had developed a nasty blister from being rubbed by Dara's wet moccasin; there was blood pooled under the swollen skin. The small bare foot was also freezing cold.

"I can pad it with some fur," Alin said, and looked up.

Dara's gray eyes looked solemnly back. The girl had been initiated as a woman and so must have begun her menses, but to Alin she was still a child. Dara was dark-haired and small, with slight fragile bones and finely textured baby skin. She was three years behind Alin, and so had never before come very much into the older girl's path. Alin now considered the solemn eyes that betrayed no trace of the pain the child must be feeling.

"All right," Dara said in her soft voice. "Perhaps that will help."

Alin looked once again at the blister and doubted it. She muttered a curse under her breath.

"What is wrong here?" said the arrogant male voice Alin was coming to dislike more intensely with every passing hour.

She continued to look at Dara's blister and answered through her teeth, "This child has a blister on her foot. I shall need something to pad it with."

Before she realized what was happening, Mar was squatting beside her. "Let me see," he said, and picked up the foot in his big hand. Dara put a hand on his shoulder to balance herself, and he looked up at her. "You should not be walking on this," he said.

"She has scarcely been given a choice," Alin told him, still gritting her teeth.

Ignoring her, he continued to look at Dara. The child's big gray eyes looked fearlessly back. "You should have said something to me," he said. His voice was surprisingly gentle.

"I told Alin," Dara replied.

At that he turned to look at Alin, who was still sitting on her heels beside him. "Then Alin should have told me," he said, putting the emphasis on the second syllable of her name, which made it sound strange and unfamiliar to her.

Furious, she stared into a pair of equally angry eyes. He was so close to her that their elbows brushed as she stood up. "Why should I have told you?" she demanded. "You are the cause of the problem."

"Wash that blister well, minnow, and then put your moccasin back on," Mar said to Dara. He stood up, taking away Alin's brief advantage of height. "We'll carry her for a few days," he said. "I do not want that blister to go bad." Those absolutely blue eyes held hers relentlessly. The fact that he was a full head taller than she only exacerbated her temper. "Do not keep such a thing from me again," he said. And turned away.

Alin said under her breath, "May the Mother blast your genitals, son of a hyena."

"Alin!" Dara's eyes were enormous.

Alin glared at her. "You heard him," she said. "Go and wash that foot."

They had been walking for three days and still there was no sign of a rescue. Reluctantly, Alin had come to the conclusion that her tribe had been unable to trace the kidnapped girls. Mar had used other streams and doubled back on trails twice again, and Alin did not think that even Liniut would be able to find their scent by now.

Which meant that their only hope of rescue was for one of them to escape and go for the help that would not otherwise be forthcoming.

Mar had tried to disguise the fact that they had been traveling almost due north the whole time, but Alin's sense of direction was acute. What's more, she had managed to get out of one of the men that the journey would take about two handfuls of days. That pinpointed their destination if she could get a rescue party.

The problem preoccupying her was how the necessary escape might be effected. If it were going to be done successfully, she thought, it had to be done immediately. She could maintain a fast enough pace for three days to outdistance any pursuers. She could live on nuts and berries. The one thing that caused her concern was the memory of those roaring lions.

She did not have a weapon. Nor was there any likelihood of her getting one.

It could not be helped. If she was going to go, she had to go tonight.

The forward pace slackened for a moment as the men up ahead transferred Dara from one back to another. They had been carrying the girl all day, and with the utmost good humor. Alin had heard her laughing at some of the things the men were saying to her.

"Perhaps we should all pretend to sprain our ankles,"

Jes muttered. "If they had to carry all of us, that would slow them down."

Alin turned to look at her closest friend. "I do not think it would make a difference," she said. "I very much fear he has buried our trail."

Jes's blue-gray eyes flickered. She had come to the same conclusion, Alin saw.

Alin lowered her voice until it was barely a breath of sound. "I shall try to get away tonight," she said.

Jes stared back at her. "You cannot," she said. "It is too dangerous. We are three days away from home, Alin. And you will have no weapon. Let me go in your stead."

"Sa," Alin said ironically. "It is too dangerous for me, so I should send you."

"You are the Chosen One," Jes said. "You we cannot afford to lose."

"It is precisely because I am the Chosen One that I must do it," Alin replied. "You know that."

There was a brief pause, and then Jes said resignedly, "Sa, I suppose I do."

They encamped for the night on the bank of a small river. There was venison for dinner, roasted as usual on sticks over the open fires. Alin wondered if the women of this tribe that had captured them knew more about cooking than the men did, for plain roasted meat night after night had quickly become boring. She ate heartily nonetheless. If she were successful in her escape attempt, she would not eat meat again for many days.

She prepared the ground by visiting the pit area a number of times before they lay down for the night.

"I have a pain in my stomach," she told Mar when he asked her what the matter was. "I cannot help myself."

"Don't try to," he recommended. "In such cases it is always better to clean out whatever it is that is making you ill."

"That is what my mother always said," she replied. She allowed a thin line to form between her brows. "I think I had better go again," she muttered, and headed once more toward the latrine area, which was located by the river.

She made three more visits during the course of the

night, and the third time Jes came with her. Then Jes
returned to their sleeping places, whispering to Alin in
the darkness. None of the other girls stirred. The men
on watch paid little attention. Not until the morning did
they discover that Alin was gone.

Mar was in a rage. When he called Jes before him she
found herself intimidated by the fury that glittered in his
eyes. "Where is she?" he asked.

Jes looked down to his buffalo skin vest. "Where do
you think, Outlander?" she said, trying to make herself
sound as cold and insolent as Alin sounded when she
spoke to this man.

"There are lions out there," Mar said. "And she
doesn't even have a spear!"

Jes raised her eyes. "Whose fault is that?" she asked.
And then backed two steps away from the expression on
his face.

Mar turned to the black-haired man they called Tane,
the one who was acting as second in command. "I will
go after her," Mar said. "You take the rest and continue
on."

"Let me go with you," the other man said instantly.

"Na. I'll have Lugh." Mar put a big hand upon the
dog at his side. "And I'll take one of the other dogs,
too," he added. "She'll be going south as fast as she
can. I shall catch up to her,"—he threw a glittering look
at Jes—"if there's anything left of her to catch."

Tane nodded grimly. "We'll wait here a few more
hours," he said. "And wait once again at the next river
crossing."

"All right," Mar said. "If I have not returned in two
days time, take up the usual pace."

Tane paused, and then he nodded. Mar went to get his
spears, his spearthrower, his bow, and his flint knives.

Being weaponless, Alin did not have the time to hide
her trail by evasive maneuvers. Under the circumstances,
her only chance for success was to get there before Mar
could catch up with her.

It still lacked three hours until dawn when Alin set out
from the enemy's camp by the river. As she settled into

the familiar long, smooth hunter's lope, she found her hand continually straying to the small ivory pendant that hung on a leather thong around her neck. Upon the smooth surface of the ivory rectangle was engraved the figure of a woman: narrow-waisted, full-breasted, wearing a bell-shaped skirt that reached to the knees. The face had no features.

Alin had never doubted what the face of the Mother would look like. It would look like Lana's.

The dawn came and even though Alin knew dawn would mean discovery of her absence back at the camp, still she could not help but be glad of the light. The creatures of the day were grazing beasts; if she avoided them they would avoid her. It was the predators of the night, the carnivores, whose unseen presence had caused the skin of her back and her neck to prickle warningly for the last few hours.

Alin thought that the game trail she was following was probably a track forged by the reindeer herds when they migrated into this country during the winter season. It ran almost directly north to south, cutting through the plain on its way toward her own home mountains. There was good grazing for the reindeer here during the winter, when the high mountain pastures had filled up with snow.

Mar must know about this trail, she thought. He was too knowledgeable of the other trails in the area to have missed this one. She thought he hadn't taken it because he did not want his captives to recognize how directly north they were going.

He would take it now, Alin thought grimly as she looked out across a meadow of waving grass where small herds of wild horses and buffalo were grazing. Not all the predators had gone to sleep for the day; the two-legged one, the most dangerous one of all, would be hard on her trail. Of that she was certain.

Alin had halted only briefly: for a drink of water at a stream or to pluck some berries and nuts to eat. She was accustomed to going without food, had been trained to it by her mother, but she knew it was vital to keep up her strength. If she maintained a good pace, she did not think she would be caught. She had always been one of the fastest runners of all the boys and girls in her tribe, and she had had a start of several hours.

The sun rose to its highest point in the sky and began to decline toward the west. Alin ran on and tried not to think of the coming night.

Lugh found the reindeer trail and Alin's scent almost immediately. Mar reckoned he was about four hours behind her, and he knew the girl was fast and strong. He had spent weeks watching the girls of the Tribe of the Red Deer, weeks of plotting the best moment to capture the greatest number of them. He had seen Alin on the hunting trail and he knew she could cover ground as well as most men.

But he had a decisive advantage. The girl would have to sleep. He, on the other hand, knew he could go for two days without sleep if he had to.

He wasn't afraid that he wouldn't catch her before she was able to bring word of their direction to her own people. He was afraid that something would happen to her before he reached her.

Those lions. He had heard them, the night before last, in the country she would be going through right now. A solitary girl, without even a dog at her heels, would make attractive prey for a cave lioness with hungry cubs to feed.

Mar did not want to lose this girl. She had fire in her, and courage. She would make fine children for the Tribe of the Horse. The tribe could make much better use of her than the lions would, Mar thought grimly, and he lengthened his stride a little as the path before him came out of a copse of birch and began to cut across a meadow.

The dark came on. The grazing creatures of the day, the buffalo, aurochs, wild horses, and deer, began to look for a resting place for the night, one different from the place they had rested the night before and as well-protected as possible from their worst enemies: the cave lion, cave panther, and cave hyena and the scavengers that followed them.

An hour before the last light left the sky, Alin stopped. She was exhausted, her legs trembling, her lungs heaving. If she hoped to keep the same pace tomorrow, she knew she would have to sleep tonight.

The first thing she did was gather wood and tinder for a fire. She carried a fire stick in her belt, taken from the gear rolled up in her deerskin sleeping roll. Once she had gathered a sufficient amount of wood and had spread a pile of dead leaves to use as tinder, she set the device beside the leaves, placed the wooden stick in the hole in the small wooden board, and began to rotate it swiftly between her palms.

She was tired, and it seemed forever before she saw the first traces of smoke. Not long after that, the leaves caught, and then the sticks.

The fire would keep away the beasts, Alin thought. And its warmth felt good also. She had not been cold all day long; her exertions in fact had made her sweat. But once she had stopped, the chill began to set in. Nor did she have her deerskin sleeping roll with her; she had to curl up in only the clothes she wore and trust to the fire to keep her warm.

She was extremely weary, but she did not go immediately to sleep. The rustling sounds in the high grass kept her tense with anxiety. Then a lion roared in the distance. She sat up, heart pounding. Something else screeched. An owl hooted, and there came the sound of wings beating close by. Alin's hand closed into a tight fist around her pendant, and sweat once more broke out on her brow and between her shoulder blades.

Never in all her life had she felt so alone.

Finally, out of sheer physical exhaustion, she fell asleep.

She woke to a dog sniffing her face. She stifled a cry and forced herself to lie still.

"Good boy, Lugh. Come here." She knew the voice instantly and closed her eyes again, hard, to blink away the treacherous tears that threatened to disgrace her.

"I hate you," she said through her teeth. Slowly she sat up.

"I'm quite sure you do," came the unperturbed reply. He walked into the small circle of light cast by the dying fire. "You covered more ground than I thought you could," he said admiringly.

She stared up at him as he loomed over her in the firelight. He was carrying a heavy spear in one hand and a lighter, throwing spear set into a spearthrower in the other. Over one shoulder was slung a bow; over the other a pouchful of arrows. Under his buffalo skin vest he wore a belt hung with three bone-handled knives. Another dog had come out of the night to join Lugh, and Alin could hear them sniffing around her small encampment.

She refused to admit, even to herself, the relief that surged into her heart at the sight of all the weaponry and the dogs.

"At least you had the sense to make a fire," he said. "There are lions around here."

As if in answer to his comment, out of the night there came the sound of a mighty roar. Alin could not stop herself from jumping.

It was much closer than it had been earlier in the night.

Mar made a comment that widened Alin's eyes. Then, without another word, he began to build up the fire, which had begun to die while she slept. After a moment, Alin rose and went to help him. A second roar came through the night, this one from a slightly different direction. It sounded close.

"There are two of them," Mar said. And bent to put on another branch.

Once they had the fire burning high again, Mar looked at Alin, hesitated, then shrugged. Next he stunned her by handing her his spearthrower and javelin. "Get over here," he said after she had taken them from him. "Behind me. I will try to take one with the big spear. If I stop him, you should be able to get off a throw with the javelin."

Alin did not reply, but moved to the place he had indicated, between him and the flames. The two dogs came and took up their places on either side of Mar. They sat beside him, still as statues save for the quivering that shook them from their pricked ears to their tense alert tails.

Alin gripped the spearthrower tightly in her fingers and

looked at the broad back that was directly before her. It made an inviting target. One plunge of the javelin, and she would be free to continue her journey home.

Alin's knuckles showed white with tension.

Why had he given her the javelin? How could he stand there in front of her so confidently, knowing what she held in her hand? Did he think so lightly of her, that he did not believe she would dare to use his own weapon against him?

She remembered that moment of hesitation, the shrug before he handed her the spear.

He wasn't sure what she would do, she thought. But he had given her the spear anyway.

Alin frowned angrily. She was not one to put a spear into the back of a man who had trusted her. Besides, they needed each other this night. Once the threat of the lions was gone, then . . . then she would see what use she might make of the spear.

The night advanced. The sound of the lions' roars moved closer and ever closer. Back and forth the mighty roars went, one lion speaking and the other answering, until finally Alin knew that they could not be more than a few hundred yards away from the fire. The pungent meaty smell of lion was heavy in the air. They were in the high grass and scattered trees to the west of the trail, and Alin knew they could be on them before she and Mar even realized they were being attacked.

Alin gripped the spearthrower tightly in her fingers, holding it in such a way that she could use it quickly, and tried to think.

If the two lions charged, and if Mar got the first lion with the big spear, perhaps she would have a chance to get off a throw if the second lion came after. But even if she did, she thought, she would have to make it a killing throw. A wounded cave lion was one of the most dangerous creatures in all of nature.

The roaring went on and on, one lion speaking, the other answering. They were so close that the volume of sound was deafening. They sounded, Alin thought on a bubble of suppressed, nearly hysterical laughter, exactly like a husband and wife having an argument.

An hour passed. The roaring continued, but it was no longer drawing closer. In fact, if anything, it seemed to be receding.

Another half an hour went by. Now it was certain that the lions were moving away. The birds began to talk in the trees. The big man who had been standing between her and the lions for the better part of the last three hours put down his spear. Then he turned, looked down into her face, ran a hand through the bright hair that had fallen over his brow and said, "I am thinking they were having a disagreement."

Even in the pale gray light of earliest dawn, his eyes looked blue. Alin let out her breath. "I was thinking the same thing."

He ran his hand once more through his hair. "I wouldn't want to live through that night again." He shook his head. "Dhu, but they were loud!"

She laughed shakily, grateful to him for confessing his own fright.

"You must be hungry," he said. "You can't have eaten very much yesterday. I'll go see what I can get for us to eat." And he held out his hand for his javelin.

Alin stared at that imperative hand. Caught up as she had been in the danger posed by the lions, she had forgotten for a moment the crucial advantage she held with the javelin. And now it was too late. Her lips tightened and, involuntarily, her hand also tightened around the weapon.

He saw it. His eyes glinted and he quirked one expressive blond eyebrow. "I have a spear too," he said. "And I have the dogs."

Slowly then, with dignity, she placed javelin and spearthrower in his outstretched hand. He looked at the big silver-gray dog who followed everywhere at his heels, and said, "Lugh, stay."

The dog whined and flattened his ears, clearly wishing to accompany his master.

"Take him," Alin said.

He pointed at the ground beside her feet. "Na. He will stay with you."

"You trusted me with the javelin," she protested.

"I had no choice. If the lions had gotten through me, I could not leave you to face them weaponless. But Lugh will stay with you now."

Alin scowled and muttered something under her breath.

His teeth flashed in a good-humored grin. "You'll feel better when you've eaten something." And, whistling to the other dog, he went off into the high grass to kill something for breakfast.

Four

Mar shot a rabbit with his bow, and Alin made no complaints about the boring taste of fire-roasted meat. Then they started back along the reindeer track, retracing the steps of yesterday's journey.

They traveled more slowly this day than both had the day before. Alin had had only a few hours of sleep, and Mar none at all. "No need to hurry," he told her when they stopped at noon for a rest and to spear some fish to eat. "We will catch the others on the morrow. Tane is waiting for me by the next river crossing."

Alin slowly chewed her morsel of fish as she eyed the man seated cross-legged in front of the fire. Then she said, "You were very sure that you would catch me, weren't you, Outlander?"

He gave her a slow, lazy smile. "You are fast, girl, no need to doubt that. But I am faster yet."

Alin's nostrils flared at his confident tone. Arrogant son of a hyena, she thought. She looked away from him to make a brief survey of the small camp he had made for their rest stop. The dogs were curled up in the sun, seemingly asleep, but Alin knew better. If she made a move to run, they would be after her.

Sun and Moon, there *must* be a way she could escape!

"You might as well resign yourself to the fact that you are coming north with me," said the hateful voice from the other side of the small cooking fire. "It will not be so bad. Dhu, you and your friends will be treated like goddesses, we are so desperate for women in my tribe!

You will all be given husbands to shelter and to feed and to care for you. What more could a woman desire?''

"Freedom," Alin said through her teeth.

"Freedom? What do women know of freedom?" came the outrageous reply.

Alin made a sound like an enraged cat. She leaned toward him and spat out the words, "Listen, Outlander. In my tribe we are not 'given' husbands. If a man pleases us, we take him. When he ceases to please us, we put him aside. The women of the Red Deer do not need a man to feed or to shelter us. We are perfectly capable of seeing to such things for ourselves.''

He scooped up the fish bones and threw them into the fire. His big shoulders moved in an easy shrug. "The men of your tribe must be a sorry lot," he said. He dusted off his hands by gently rubbing them together. "I think you will find dwelling with us a pleasant surprise."

"Son of a hyena," Alin said contemptuously. "The touch of your hand would shrivel my flesh."

His head lifted suddenly, in the very gesture Alin had seen stallions make when something unexpected startles them. He looked at her. It was the first time she had ever seen him angry. Her heart began to beat more quickly, but she forced herself to stare back fearlessly into those suddenly icy eyes.

He said, very softly, "Do not call me names."

Her heart thumped once, loudly. Then she shrugged and stood up. "Are you ready to leave?" she asked. "Or do you need to rest further?"

He did not reply, but also came to his feet. She watched him as he silently doused the fire. He was very tall, with great breadth in the chest and shoulders, and yet surprisingly slim of waist and hip, and long of leg. She found him as beautiful and as alien as she would have found the lions they had been listening to the previous night.

"*I* do not need to rest," he said when the fire was finally out. He whistled to the dogs. "Now, let us leave."

They moved fast in the afternoon, loping most of the time instead of walking, and they did not stop to rest at all. Alin was very tired and found it difficult to keep up with the pace he set. She gritted her teeth, however, and

ignored her aching muscles, and forced her legs to keep
moving forward. He was taking revenge, she knew, for
her words at the rest stop, and she would not let him see
how hard she was being pushed.

The sun began to drop in the western sky, and finally
Mar slowed his pace to a walk. In the meadow to the left
of the track Alin saw a family of wild boar setting out on
its evening forage. The big boar must have sensed their
presence, for it stood guard between the track and its
family as the sow and her row of small pinky-brown
shoats went poking and snuffling toward the wooded valley. Mar turned his head to watch them, then said over
his shoulder to Alin, "There's a stream in the wood just
ahead. We'll stop there for the night."

Alin nodded. She did not think she had energy enough
to answer him out loud.

It was dark in the woods when Mar and Alin followed
the track in among the thickly growing pine trees. When
finally they reached the stream the trees fell away and the
sky appeared clearly above them again, pink now with
the light of the declining sun. The rosy evening glow
illuminated a small group of red deer drinking from the
clear stream water: a well-antlered stag and four does.
In a second's time, the does had bounded into the woods.
The stag, which had spun around at the first scent of
humans, was a fraction behind them. Mar's spear flashed,
an arc in the rose-colored light, and the stag fell with the
hard flint point sunk deep under his heart. Mar smiled
with satisfaction. "Supper," he said to Alin as he walked
toward the fallen deer.

He gave her one of the flint knives from his belt, and,
after Mar had made a ritual thanks to Deer God for sharing one of his creatures with them, she helped him skin
the stag. They fed the dogs first, with the intestines and
some chunks of the meat cut off the haunch, and then
Mar built a fire so they could cook their own food.

It was quite dark by the time they had finished eating.
Mar had dragged the stag's carcass some distance away
from the stream so that if it attracted hyenas, they would
not be too close to their camp. Then he had come back
with a huge armful of cut grass, which he dropped in a

pile close to the fire. "A bed for you," he said. "I did not bring your sleeping roll."

Alin, sitting cross-legged by the fire, looked up and found him regarding her with an expression in his eyes that she recognized, even though no man ever dared to look at her in such a way before. A surge of feeling thrilled through her veins. It was a moment before Alin recognized fear.

She had not been at all afraid at the thought of lying with Ban at Winter Fires. That would have been a sacred rite, full of mystery and power. *This* . . . she shivered at the thought . . . this would be profanation. She could not let this man touch her. She was the Chosen One of the Mother. She was sacred. It would have been better for the lions to have taken her last night than him.

Sun and Moon, she thought despairingly, he was so big. And she had no weapons.

Warily, keeping him in her sight every moment, she rose from the ground and stood beside the fire, balancing lightly on the balls of her feet. She glanced away from him once, very quickly, to get her bearings. If she had to run, she would. Better to fall to the dogs than to give in to him without a fight.

"I am not going to hurt you, girl." Oddly enough, she thought he sounded puzzled.

"I do not like the way you looked at me," Alin said, still poised alertly.

A short silence ensued as they regarded each other over the pile of freshly cut grass. "You are good to look at," he said at last. "Many men must have looked at you the way I did just now."

"Na." She shook her head so violently that her long braid swung back and forth. "I am the Chosen One of the Mother," she told him. "No man may look thus at me."

His golden brows drew together. "You are vowed to virginity?" he asked incredulously.

Her eyes widened at the strangeness of the suggestion. "Of course not. I am the life of the tribe. Whom I choose must be . . ." She frowned, trying to find the words to explain. "It must be done correctly, according to the rites of the Mother," she said at last. "Otherwise the herds will not multiply and the tribe will die."

She saw understanding flicker in his eyes. "Ah," he said. "I have heard of such things."

A bit of tension drained from her poised figure. Her breathing slowed slightly.

"That was your mother?" he asked with frank curiosity. "The woman who tried to keep us from taking you?"

"Sa."

"And who is she, your mother?"

"She is the Mistress, the leader of our tribe."

He looked at her for a long moment, clearly trying to understand. Then he asked, "If that is so, why is *she* not the Chosen One?"

"She was. For many years the Mistress made the Sacred Marriage for the life of the tribe. But this year . . ." Alin looked away from him to stare into the briskly burning fire. She spoke softly. "The Mistress has gone beyond her years of bearing children. This year *I* was to make the Sacred Marriage, *I* was to make life for the tribe." Her eyes swung back to his face, and now they were bright with a mixture of anger and grief. "You stole me away before I could do that," she said. "You have left my people bereft, robbed them of their life, Outlander."

"That is the ceremony you were preparing for when we came?" he asked slowly, his eyes fixed on a point somewhere over her shoulder, as if he were seeing a picture in his mind. "This Sacred Marriage? You were to make a ritual mating for the fertility of the tribe?"

"Sa."

He failed to reply. She could not tell what he was thinking from his expression. Then he folded his arms across his chest and looked back at her, his face still impassive, his lids half hiding his eyes. He said, "If what you tell me is indeed true, then I have done well in taking you, Chosen One of the Mother. For my tribe has need of such as you. The life of my tribe died with our women. You will bring that life back to us, you and the other girls."

"You kill my people to give life to your own!" Alin cried passionately.

"Not so." His face was stern in the light of the leaping flames. "There were young mothers belonging to your tribe whom we did not take. Nor did we take any of your girl children. You have many women in your tribe, Chosen One. Believe me when I say that we have a greater need of you than your own people do."

Alin stared steadily into that suddenly hard, merciless face. "Many women," she said, "but only one Chosen One." Though she could not see it, her face was as implacable as his. "Your ways are not our ways," she told him. "What is holy for us is not holy for you. It is not life that I will bring to your people, but death."

He said, "I do not think so."

She tried to think of anything else she could say to convince him. And knew there was nothing. If his tribe's plight was indeed as he had said, then he would take her despite anything she might say. By his own lights, he would have no choice.

"Go to sleep," he said abruptly. "You are weary. I will keep watch over the fire."

At any rate, she thought tiredly, she had prevailed in one way. He no longer seemed inclined to want to share her bed.

She was indeed exhausted, and as soon as he moved off to the far side of the fire she lay down on the bed of grass. She tucked her hand under her cheek, curled on her side, and looked drowsily into the leaping flames.

"No lions tonight," she murmured.

His voice came softly through the night. "I have not heard them. I think we have left their hunting grounds."

Silence fell between them. Alin's eyes began to close. She heard him say something to the dogs. Then she heard her own voice asking, "How did you choose my tribe to rob? You are from far north of us. How did you know of us?"

A hyena whooped from somewhere nearby. "They've found the carcass of the deer," Mar murmured. Then he answered her question: "I went to a new Spring Gathering this year, the one that is held at the fork of the Big

River. I heard about you there. A tribe ruled by women, they said. A tribe that still follows the Old Way, the Way of the Mother. By that time I knew we would not be able to buy enough wives to keep our tribe together. I had to do something. So I came south to see if the stories were true. And I found you.''

"In the spring?''

"In the summer, during the time of Antelope Moon. I was in your hunting grounds for half the length of the moon, watching you, learning about you. Then I went home and gathered the men and dogs that I would need for the task.''

"But why us?'' she asked. "Surely there were other tribes with women you could have raided?''

"Those other tribes had men who would have retaliated,'' he answered simply. "The men of your tribe are subservient creatures, hardly men at all. They will not try to follow you, fight for you.'' He sounded bewildered. "How can such a thing have happened?'' he asked. "Were all men like that, I wonder, before Sky God came to rule the tribes of the Kindred?''

"Our men are not creatures!'' Alin said, incensed. She sat up, and glared at his shadowy figure on the far side of the fire.

"They are not men,'' came the implacable reply. "Men do not let themselves be ruled by women.''

"Men were born to be ruled by women,'' Alin replied, matching his tone. She leaned on her hand, staring at him across the flames. "What is a man, after all?'' she said. "His part in the mystery is soon over. He serves the woman, he gives forth his stream, and he is done. It is the woman who nurtures the child within her womb, the woman who brings forth life, the woman who holds the mystery of Earth Mother in her being. What is a man compared to that?''

There was a long silence. She did not know if her words had angered him or not. He was looking at his knees and all she could see of him was the top of his head. At last he said, "I think that life is going to be very interesting for us all in the coming days.'' And it was not anger that she heard in his voice but amusement.

Arrogant son of a hyena, Alin thought furiously. But this time she did not say it out loud.

One of the dogs began to snore. "Go to sleep, Chosen One," Mar said. "We have a journey to make on the morrow."

Without answering, Alin lay back down on her grass bed. Within five minutes she was asleep.

Alin was awakened once in the night by the sound of a buffalo bellowing. She opened her eyes sleepily and saw Mar heaping more wood on the fire. "Haven't you slept at all?" she asked, her voice thick with drowsiness.

"I shall sleep later today," he answered. "When we have joined the rest of them by the river."

The fire flared up. The night had turned cold and the warmth was welcome. Alin shifted so that she was a little closer to the blaze and once again went to sleep.

They rose at dawn, ate some more deer meat, and set off in a hunter's lope along the forest track. From deep within the trees Alin could hear the sounds of the rutting stags as they bellowed challenges to their rivals. Then would come the clashing of antlers as the battle began.

She remembered the way Mar had looked at her the night before, and her stomach tightened.

By midmorning they had reached Tane's camp by the river. Mar was greeted by his peers with boisterous approval; Alin was met by hers with disappointment and sympathy.

"He must be a shaman," Alin said later to Jes when they were sitting together side by side on a sun-warmed rock. "He does not need to sleep!"

"He's sleeping now," Jes returned. "That's why we're not traveling today—so he can sleep. Dara heard the men talking. We shall stay at this camp until tomorrow morning."

Alin slowly began to unbraid her hair. "I do not think that we will be able to escape from them, Jes," she said bitterly. "The winter is coming on. You know what the tracks are like in the winter; nothing can move through the snow. Perhaps in the spring the tribe will be able to trace us, but by then . . ."

"Sa. But by then . . ."

The two girls sat in somber silence as Alin finished unbraiding her hair. Then, "I will fix it for you," Jes said, and, taking a small comb chiseled from bone out of her belt, she began to smooth the tangles from Alin's long loose hair. "Your hair is so lovely," Jes murmured as she gently worked the comb through a snarl. "So smooth and shiny and bright with little streaks of gold."

"I had it washed in preparation for Winter Fires," Alin replied. She sighed. "It seems such a long time ago."

"I know."

Alin closed her eyes, enjoying the soothing touch of the other girl's hand on her hair. With careful competence Jess began to plait the long brown hair into a single braid as thick as her wrist. When she had finished and was tying the leather thong that held the end in place, Alin said, "We shall have to come to some kind of terms with them. No use in thinking we will be able to escape."

Jes let the braid drop between Alin's shoulders; it reached all the way to her waist. "What kind of terms?"

Alin pulled her legs up and rested her chin on her knees. There was a thin line between her beautifully drawn brows. "I was thinking about it all the morning as we were coming back," she said. "This Mar who is their leader—he is an arrogant, hateful man, but he is not stupid. I think he will see the value of having willing women as opposed to women whom he will never be able to trust."

"What do you mean?" Jes asked. Her own hair, a much paler brown than Alin's, glinted in the sunlight as she tilted her head to look at her friend.

"Perhaps I might convince him to give us some time to learn the way of life of his tribe. They know we are servants of the Mother, that our ways are not their ways. Perhaps I can win us some time. If we can hold out until the spring weather . . . then, perhaps, the Mistress will find us."

Jes chewed her lip. "But how will they track us, Alin? By spring there will be no trace of our going left."

"I am thinking of the story Mar told us, of how the drinking water went bad and so many women of his tribe died. That is an ugly story, Jes."

Jes shivered. "I cannot understand how they did not know the water was bad. Could they not taste it?"

"I have heard of such things . . . that sometimes there is no taste."

Jes said, a little wryly, "I hope they have a new water supply."

"Such a story," Alin said, "is certain to be told at all the Gatherings of the Kindred. And if it comes to the ears of the Tribe of the Red Deer, then surely our people will perceive the connection between the loss of women and our kidnapping."

Jes's lips parted. "Sa," she said on a long drawn-out breath. "I see."

"The Mistress will surely send representatives to the Spring Gatherings," Alin said.

"Still," said Jes, "that means we must wait until the spring weather."

"I am thinking that we must."

"That is a long time to delay . . . things."

"I know that, Jes. I know."

There was a long silence. Then Jes said bitterly, "I do not rejoice at the thought of bearing a child for a man and a tribe that has taken me by force." Her blue-gray eyes turned to Alin. "And it will be worse for the younger girls, those who have yet to lie with a man."

"There must be *some* arrangement I can make for us," Alin said with suppressed violence in her voice. Her fists clenched and her large brown eyes flashed. "I cannot allow this Mar simply to parcel us out, like choice pieces of meat fed to a pack of hounds!"

Jes looked at her. "What was he like when he caught you?" she asked Alin curiously.

"What do you mean, what was he like?"

"Did he try to lie with you?"

"Na."

"He is a beautiful-looking man," Jes said. "I cannot understand why he could not find a wife without having to kidnap one."

"He is the leader," Alin replied curtly. "He must look beyond his own needs to the needs of the tribe. They lost many women he said. Twice two handfuls. A wife for himself would not fulfill the needs of the tribe." She stared moodily at the tips of her moccasins and did not wonder how she came to understand so certainly the mind of her enemy.

Jes also stared at Alin's moccasins. Then she said, "None of them has tried to lie with any of us. Considering the circumstances, and why they have taken us, that is rather extraordinary."

Alin rested her forehead against her knees and closed her eyes. "I do not know," she said. "I do not know the way of life of their tribe. I do not know how men like these live with women."

After a minute, Jes said sourly, "I am thinking we will find out soon enough."

"Sa," said Alin. "I suppose we will."

It was late in the afternoon, and the cookfires were being lit, when Alin made her seemingly casual way to the place where Mar was sleeping. The big silver-gray dog that followed him everywhere was beside him as usual, guarding his sleep. The dog's tail wagged faintly, however, as Alin came up.

"Greetings, Lugh," she said softly, calling him by name. The tail wagged a little more vigorously, though the dog did not move from his post.

Alin looked from the dog to the man who was lying within the buffalo skin sleeping roll. Mar was profoundly asleep, lying on his stomach like a babe, with his cheek pillowed on a roll of hide and his big hand loosely curled into a fist beside his tousled blond head. The golden threads under his skin testified to the fact that he did indeed possess a beard, but even so, Alin was surprised by how young his sleeping face looked. Why, she thought in surprise, he is not more than a few years older than I am.

He didn't stir at all as she stood over him. His long, dark blond lashes lay perfectly still above the hard line of his cheekbone. The clean outline of his profile was clearly silhouetted against the dark brown buffalo skin that lay beneath his face, and the firm, straight mouth looked gentler, if not softer, in sleep.

Her gaze slowly moved from his face down the long length of him under the buffalo skin. The tie that held together the front of his deerskin shirt had loosened, and the shirt had come open at the neck. Alin looked at the strong column of throat encircled by a necklace of pierced deer's teeth, looked at the line of muscle that ran smoothly down the side of his neck and into his shoulder.

He probably could have taken that lion on his spear, she thought.

He is a beautiful-looking man, Jes had said.

He had not stirred at all under her scrutiny. He evidently had the gift of holding off sleep when he did not want it, and calling it up when he did.

Lugh yawned and settled his chin on a fold of the sleeping roll. Alin grimaced wryly. Apparently even the dog had realized that she posed no threat here.

What manner of a man was this Mar? she thought, her eyes on that surprisingly youthful face. What gods did he worship? What ways did he revere? How could she appeal to him, make him agree to leave her and the rest of her girls untouched until the spring?

She could not persuade him to send them back. That fact she accepted. But she *must* be able to persuade him to give them time.

They did not revere the Mother as they ought, but they must revere her in some manner. All men gave some sort of reverence to Earth Mother. If they did not, then the beasts would not propagate, the tribe would not multiply. . . .

The idea struck her with the blinding suddenness of a lightning bolt.

That might do it, she thought. That was where this tribe was most vulnerable. And Mar had said that the idea of a Sacred Marriage was known to him.

It was worth trying, she thought. After a moment's more reflection, she smiled at Lugh, turned, and went on her way.

Five

Mar awoke with the dawn. He lay quietly for a moment, listening to the birds beginning to call in the trees, breathing deeply the cold damp air of morning. It smelled as if it might rain, he thought. Or perhaps even snow. It was getting to be that time of the year. They would be getting the girls home just in time.

They should not delay in moving this morning, he thought, and sat up, running his fingers through the hair that had fallen across his forehead. They had lost all day yesterday and part of the day before because of Alin's escape attempt. He did not want to waste any more time.

Mar got to his feet in a single fluid movement, and, rising on his toes, stretched upward. His muscles felt stiff from such a long sleep. He had been very tired when they arrived back in camp yesterday, but the sleep and the fresh morning air were imparting vigor. Lugh rose also, stretched first his back legs and then his front, then padded over to lean his head against Mar's knee. The man caressed the dog's ears, and then he called in his deep yet clear voice, "Everyone wake up! We are leaving shortly!" He waited a moment until heads began to pop up out of sleeping rolls, and then he strode toward the river to complete his wake-up by splashing cold water on his face.

This day he chose a game trail that ran directly north. No point in trying to disguise matters any longer, he told the others. The girl knew in which direction he was taking them.

He thought, as he walked at the front of the group of men and girls later that morning, that the best plan for him now was to cover as much ground as possible. He did not think there would be any more escape attempts once they had put two more days between themselves and the girl's tribe. But he had given orders that she was to be watched closely. He did not want to lose her again.

Dhu! Those lions! He had never heard anything to equal the noise they had made that night. He had to admire her bravery. In all the time that they had stood there by the fire, she had not once whimpered or made a single sound. Nor had she tried to turn her spear on him. He had not been sure of that, when he had given it to her. If there had been only one lion, he would not have.

Alin. Her name was Alin. The Chosen One of the Mother. She would be chosen by more than Earth Mother, Mar thought, when the time came for giving out the women.

The face of Altan, the chief of the Tribe of the Horse, came into Mar's mind. His mouth set into a bitter line.

Someone came up beside him. "The day's rest helped the little one's blister," said a voice Mar recognized as his foster brother's.

"That is good," he replied.

"Mar . . ." Tane said. "What are you going to do about Altan?"

Mar shifted his grip on his spear. "I made a bargain with Altan," he said. "You know that. Half the girls are to go to him for his disposal, and half are to go to me."

"Altan never expected this raid to be successful," Tane said. "If he had expected success, he would have sent a party of nirum to do the kidnapping. You led him to think there was danger involved in this raid. You know you did."

Mar shrugged. "Nevertheless, he made a bargain with me."

"It is in my heart that Altan is not a one for holding to bargains he does not like."

There was a short silence.

"He hates you," Tane said. "He hates you and he fears you."

Mar said grimly, "I am not overfond of Altan, either."

"If he tries to take these girls away from the boys, there will be great anger," Tane said. "We may well lose them to other tribes, and you have said yourself that this hunting group is too good to lose."

"The initiates cannot expect to have all the girls," Mar said reasonably. "The nirum must have their share."

"Their share," said Tane. "Not all."

Mar frowned, and then he raised his head and sniffed the air, like a stallion. "I think it is going to snow."

Tane grunted, but took the hint and forbore to pursue the topic of the girls. Silence fell as the two men strode along, side by side. They were a study in contrasts, the foster brothers: Mar, fair-haired and blue-eyed, with his great height and big frame; Tane, dark of hair and green of eye, so slim he was almost fragile in build. They had been inseparable almost since infancy, when Mar's mother had died and his father, the chief, had given him to Tane's mother to suckle and to rear along with her own son.

Tane changed the subject. "You got back to us in good time," he said. "The girl did not get far?"

"She got quite far," Mar replied. "I pushed her hard on the return to make up the time."

"She is their leader," Tane said.

"Sa. Her mother is the chief of their tribe. She is the 'chosen one' she tells me, the one who is to succeed her mother." Mar looked up at the gray sky. Then he said softly, "Remember that ceremony we interrupted?"

"Sa. I remember."

Mar narrowed his eyes. "It was the preparation for their ritual of fertility. She was the one who was to mate with the god."

Mar lowered his eyes and looked ahead once more. There was a thoughtful silence. Both Mar and Tane had been reared by Tane's father, the tribe's shaman. They had a reverence for religious ritual, even if that ritual was not their own. Finally Tane said, "I hope that does not prove to be ill luck."

Mar shrugged. "No help for it, I fear."

"I suppose not."

"These girls . . ." Mar said.

Tane looked at him.

"They are very different from the women of our tribe, Tane."

"How so?" Tane asked, quirking one thin black eyebrow.

Mar said affectionately, "You are the only man I know I could have made that remark to without getting a salacious reply."

Tane grinned. "My father does not believe in salacious replies."

"How well I know," Mar replied with feeling, and both young men laughed.

"Well," Mar began, "these are women who are accustomed to ruling, not to being ruled. From what the girl, Alin, told me, it seems that in her tribe it is the women and not the men who choose their mates."

"Dhu," said Tane incredulously.

"Sa. And they are tough, Tane. Look at how they have kept going all these days. With never a complaint. Even the little one with the blister . . . she said nothing to us, only to her own leader."

"All these things are good," Tane said. "These girls will bring good strong blood to the tribe."

"That is true. But they are not going to be easily ruled. Nor are they going to be easily trusted. They have hunted together. They have a different kind of fellowship from the women of our tribe."

Another thoughtful silence. Then Tane said, "I wish we had interrupted any other religious ceremony but that one."

"I know," Mar replied. "I have been feeling the same way." He glanced once over his shoulder, at the young men who were walking a few paces behind him. "Do not tell the others," he said. "No point in raising fears that may be unwarranted."

"We'll tell my father," Tane said.

"Sa. It is in my heart that that is what we should do. He will know if there is some kind of reparation that should be made to the Mother."

"And Altan?"

"We will talk to your father first. Once Huth decides what should be done, Altan will not be able to gainsay him."

"That is so," Tane said. He frowned thoughtfully.

Mar looked up once more at the sky. "It *is* going to snow." As if in answer to his comment, a single flake floated in the air between the two young men.

"I think you had better begin to carry the little one," Mar said to Tane. "I am going to increase the pace."

A fine dust of snow fell steadily for several hours, and then, abruptly, it turned to rain. It was the rain that drove Mar to seek shelter. The snow had fallen lightly, with little wind, and walking had not been onerous. The rain was a graver matter; it would not bead lightly on fur but soak through and chill them to the bone. Mar found an overhanging cliff that afforded decent shelter, and stopped the march.

The girls gathered together near the rock wall of the cliff, as far under the overhang as they could get. The men and dogs came next, those on the outer fringes growing chill and damp from the rain.

There was nothing to do but wait the weather out, and some of the men pulled knucklebones from their gear and began to dig out shallow holes in the ground to play Hunt the Buffalo.

"What are you doing?" a soft voice asked, and Mar turned to see small Dara standing beside him watching the bones being thrown.

"It's a game, minnow," he said. "Don't you have games in your tribe?"

"Not games like that." He moved aside to let her come closer, and she did so, pushing fearlessly up to the edge of the circle drawn in the dirt. The men were aware of her grave, watching eyes and began to grow more animated. After a few minutes Bror, one of the men playing, offered to teach her the game. Dara went readily to sit on her heels beside him and listen to his instructions.

"There is one who has no fear of us," Mar said to Tane, who had come up next to him.

"She reminds me of Tosa," Tane said.

"Hmm." Mar regarded the girl in front of him with interest. Tosa was a young red deer he and Tane had found abandoned when she was a fawn and they were but young boys. They had taken home the poor starving creature, and Tane's mother had fed it with gruel made out of grain, and it had lived. Tosa had grown into a beautiful young deer, so dainty and feminine that it had been a joy just to look at her.

Mar looked now at Dara and smiled. "Sa," he said. "There is a likeness."

After a few more minutes, Mar turned away from the game and made his way to the back of the rock shelter, where the rest of the girls were sitting on their sleeping rolls. Alin was in the dead center of the group, leaning against the cliff, her long deerskin-clad legs stretched out in front of her.

That is no shy little deer, Mar thought, his eyes on Alin's oblivious face. The girls around her were talking and gesturing, but she was very still. He had noted that about her in the brief time they had spent together: how still she could be.

She was a force to be reckoned with, this girl. He recognized that kind of power. Like usually recognizes like.

And she was a beauty. The color of her hair, brown mixed with gold, was inexpressibly lovely. Her face was oval and clear, with a straight narrow nose and finely drawn brows. But it was the eyes that he noticed most: great liquid brown eyes; extraordinary, expressive eyes, with long long lashes.

"I do not like the way you look at me," she had said to him.

Looked at her! Dhu. She was lucky that was all that he had done.

He had not had a woman for . . . how long? Too long. He missed having a wife. It was good to have a woman at hand when you needed one.

Alin suddenly raised her head and met his gaze. He saw her narrow, delicately molded nostrils flare as she realized he had been staring at her. There was no fear in her face, however, only anger. She gave him a flashing look and turned away, pretending to listen to what the girl beside her was saying.

Mar watched the proud swing of that young head as she turned away from him.

What a waste, he thought, to give a girl like that to Altan.

"Mar." Melior had to repeat his name three times before he captured Mar's attention. "What shall we do about food?" Melior asked when finally Mar was looking at him.

"Food." Mar's thoughts focused on the problem. "Give out the smoked buffalo meat," he said then. "There's enough left for a meal for everyone. We'll hunt tomorrow."

"Sa," Melior said. "I will tell the others."

Two days later they saw the reindeer.

"The first reindeer of the season," Jes said as they watched the small herd drinking from a stream. They had stopped for the night and the food was roasting on the fires. Jes and Alin had moved apart from the others, close to the water, and were talking together in low voices.

As they stood there in delighted silence, watching the reindeer, Tane came toward them. Alin and Jes stiffened with hostility at his approach, but the man scarcely seemed to notice them, so intent was he upon the reindeer. He gave them a preoccupied nod and then, when he was a little beyond them, he dropped to the ground, propped a smooth flat stone against his updrawn knee, and began to scratch upon it carefully with an angle graver.

Silence fell; the reindeer were drinking calmly from the stream; the only noise was the sound of sharp flint scratching against stone. Alin was about to turn away when Jes moved first, her steps taking her toward Tane, not away from him. As Alin watched in surprise, her friend walked slowly over to stand behind the man. Jes stared down at the stone propped against Tane's knee.

"What are you doing?" she asked in a strangely hushed voice.

"Drawing the reindeer," came the preoccupied reply.

Very slowly Jes bent closer. Her breath caught audibly. "You are," she said in wonder. "You are drawing the reindeer."

Something in her voice captured Tane's attention. He looked up into her face. Then he took the stone and lifted it toward Jes. "Would you like to look more closely?"

She took it from him and stared at the lines he had drawn.

"But how did you do it?" she asked in amazement. "So few lines, and yet . . . the reindeer are there."

"I am an artist," Tane replied simply. "I draw the pictures for the hunting magic in our tribe."

Jes looked from the stone to the man. "An artist," she said softly. "That is . . . wonderful."

"Sa," he replied gravely. "I think so."

"I have tried to draw sometimes," Jes said awkwardly, and she looked down once again at the stone in her hands. "But I do not draw like this."

Alin stared at her friend in astonishment. She had never known Jes cared about drawing.

"At home," Jes was going on, "in the sacred cave, there are pictures . . ."

"Our sacred cave has pictures too," Tane said. His voice warmed with enthusiasm. "Paintings. Great paintings," he said, "horses and buffalo and aurochs and deer and ibex . . . all the animals that we hunt."

"Do you paint these pictures?" Jes asked.

"Sa, I paint them. There are a handful of us who paint. My father teaches us. He is our shaman."

"A teacher for drawing." Jes drew in a long audible breath.

Tane frowned in bewilderment at her tone. "But don't you have a teacher in your tribe?"

Jes shook her head. "We don't draw any longer in our tribe," she said. "The pictures in our cave were done many years ago. We have lost the skill of it."

There was a moment of silence. Then Tane handed her the graver. "Here," he said. "Draw the reindeer."

"I cannot," Jes said. But she sat down beside him,

and when he offered her the flat stone, she took it from his hand.

Alin walked quietly away.

The dark came quickly this time of the year, and by the time supper was finished and the sleeping rolls were spread, the moon had risen. Alin was about to crawl into her skins when she saw a distinctively tall figure detach itself from the group of men at the fire and walk toward the stream. After a moment's hesitation, she rose from her knees and followed.

Mar was half sitting, half leaning against a rock, looking at the moon's reflected light in the stream, when Alin approached. The white light of the half moon made his hair seem paler than normal, and for some reason his indolent, relaxed posture only served to emphasize his power. So did a lion look, Alin thought, when it lazed upon a rock thinking of its prey.

"I want to talk to you," she said, and crossed her arms over her chest.

"Certainly," he returned. His eyes turned to her indifferently. "Talk."

"What is going to happen when we get to your dwelling place?" she asked.

He raised those expressive eyebrows. "What usually happens? We will eat and rest and . . ."

"That is not what I mean," Alin said a little breathlessly. "I mean what is going to happen to us?"

"Ah." He smiled at her, a sweet, lazy smile such as she had never seen upon his face before. He did not answer.

Alin's heart began to thud. The moonlit night, the strange place, the man . . . it all seemed suddenly unreal to her. This cannot be happening, she thought.

She managed to say, "So it is to be rape then."

The big shoulders moved under the buffalo vest in a shrug. "That is up to you," he answered. "It doesn't have to be." His blue eyes glittered faintly in the moonlight. "We want wives. Babes. We will provide for you, hunt for you, shelter you, fight for you. It is none so bad a life for a woman."

She said, "It is not a life for us."

Once more the shrug. "It will have to be."

Alin swallowed. This conversation was not going the way she had intended. She spoke with difficulty. "I want to know how you will do it. How will you . . . give us out?"

She sensed there was a change in him. She watched him closely as he replied, "That will be up to the chief."

His words shocked her. "I thought you were the chief," she said sharply.

"Na." His voice was curt. "I am the leader of this . . . expedition. But I am not the chief of the tribe."

She did not know why his words should dismay her so, but they did. She said, her voice a little shrill, "Well, you must have made some arrangements."

"We did." The moon reflected off white teeth, bared in a smile that was distinctly nasty. "Altan and I were to share the women, half to him for his companions and half to me for mine."

The words thundered in her brain. Share the women. Half for him, half for me. Alin thought of the girls sleeping back at the camp. Of twelve-year-old Fali, of Dara. A lump rose in the back of her throat. I will not cry in front of this man, she thought desperately. I will not cry!

She said instead the words she had come to say, "The women of my tribe are servants of the Mother. We cannot take a man until it is the proper time, and it is done with the proper ceremony. It is taboo for us to lie with a man whom we have not taken in the proper way. If you force us against our sacred vows, the Mother will revenge herself. We will not bear. And all your trouble will have been for naught."

The moon rode high in the night sky. The stars were out as well. Mar inclined his fair head toward her, and a small, enigmatic smile touched the corners of his mouth. His eyes were hooded by half-closed lids. "And when is this proper time?" he asked.

"It would have been at the first of Stag-Fighting Moon, but now that time has passed. Now we cannot take a man for husband until Spring Fires, which is the first of Ibex Moon."

He shifted a little against his rock. His hooded eyes still watched her face. "Interesting," he said.

Alin had never wanted to hit anyone as much as she wanted to hit him now. All her fear was gone, washed away in a rush of pure anger.

"What do you mean, interesting?" she snapped, furious that he was skeptical of her tale, forgetting that she had in fact invented the whole thing.

"I mean what I said. It is interesting." Again that smile in the corner of his mouth. "And useful."

There was a tense pause. Then Alin said, "Your ways are not our ways . . ."

"Sa," he cut in. "So you are always telling me. Now tell me this, Chosen One of the Mother. If we give you the time you want, the time until this Spring Fires, will your girls marry with us then, and be content to live as part of our tribe?"

Wild hope leaped in Alin's heart. "Sa," she said eagerly. "We will."

He nodded. "We would rather have you willing," he said. "It would be . . . more pleasant . . . for everyone."

Son of a hyena, Alin thought. I would kill myself before I would lie willingly with you.

She smiled. "Sa," she said. "That is my thought also."

"I cannot make any promises," he said. "I will have to consult with the chief."

"I am certain, Mar," Alin said sweetly, giving him his name for the first time, "that your word will hold sway with your chief."

An expression she could not decipher came and went upon his face. He did not answer but pushed himself away from the rock and crossed the small space that separated them. Before she could stop herself, Alin backed up a step.

He reached out, put a hand upon the thick braid that fell down between her shoulders, and tilted her head back so she had to look at him. She gazed, wide-eyed and furious, up into his face. "It is a good story, girl," he said. "I will relate it to Altan."

For a heartbeat's time, their gazes locked. Then he let go of her braid and she shot backward, regardless of pride.

He smiled. Not mockingly, as she would have expected, but with that odd sweetness that had so surprised her before.

"You are a good leader, Chosen One," he said. "Now go back to the camp."

Six

Tane looked at the drawing Jes had done. The outline of a horse's head was deliberately broken and even where the lines of the contour were solid they were nervously executed. The underside of the head was merely indicated—just a few strokes made with obviously rapid movements. The eye was but a point. The erect mane was engraved with a few quick but sure lines.

It was merely a sketch, but it was filled with an appreciation of movement, with a vivid impression of the life of the animal.

Tane said slowly, his eyes still on the small smooth rock that fit in the palm of his hand, "This is beautiful."

Jes felt herself flush with pleasure. "I do not have your skill," she said gruffly.

"You do not have my training," Tane corrected her, his gaze still on the lines of the drawing. "You have the eye of an artist, though. My father always says that the eye is one of the most important things."

Jes's color deepened. She could not say anything.

Tane closed his hand around the rock and turned to look at her. They were sitting together on a rise of dry ground, at a little distance from the others who were getting ready the evening meal. The sun was going down in a blaze of pinks and reds. Tane asked, "Who makes the hunting magic in your tribe?"

Jes looked at him in confusion. "Hunting magic?"

"Sa. Hunting magic. The calling-up of the spirits of the beasts. In my tribe we do it with pictures."

Jes said, "We do not have hunting magic in my tribe."
Tane looked profoundly shocked.

"We have songs," Jes said, a little defensively.

"Songs." Tane's shrug expressed his disdain. "All hunters have songs. But what of other ceremonies? You have no hunting dance?"

Jes shook her head.

"And no pictures?"

She shook her head again, her long braid swaying gently with the motion of her head. "The only pictures we have are in the sacred cave, and no one pays them much mind. They are very old," she said. "I have copied them . . ." She stopped. Twin flags of color flew in her cheeks. She bit her lip and said nervously, "I have never told that to anyone before."

He frowned, his black eyebrows almost meeting over the arched bridge of his nose. "Is drawing taboo in your tribe, then?"

"No. Of course not. It is just . . . no one does it. And . . . and I had to go to the cave when it was not the proper time. . . ." All the beautiful color in her face drained away, leaving it white and frightened. She could not believe that she was telling him this. She had never told anyone, not even Alin, of those secret visits to the sacred cave. She stared at the dry grass beside her, and clamped her lips shut.

He asked, his voice oddly gentle, "It is that important, then?"

Both the words and the tone surprised her. After a minute she answered honestly, "Sa."

Silence fell. At last she got up the courage to turn to look at him. As she met those dark-lashed green eyes, she thought in some wonder: He understands.

He said, still in that oddly gentle voice, "You are very good, Jes." He looked once again at the stone in his hand. "Very good."

She drew a deep, shaky breath. Then she asked, "What kind of drawings do you make in your sacred cave?"

"They are the paintings that make the hunting magic for us," he replied. "They must capture the life of the beast. If they do not, then the spirit of the animal is not there, and the hunting magic will not work. That is why it is so important to draw well. To make each picture real. It is the drawing that brings the spirit.''

"I want to see them," Jes said with stark intensity.

"The cave is sacred. Like your cave, it is not a place you can go except at the appointed times.''

"The artists," Jes said. "They must go there more often. To do the paintings.''

"Sa.''

She stared at him, mute with her need. He sighed. "I will talk to my father," he said. "The women in my tribe do not draw. But you . . .'' For the third time he said, "You are very good.''

"Your father is the shaman?" Jes asked. "The teacher of drawing?''

"Sa. He is the one who makes the hunting magic.''

"Is your father the chief, then? Alin tells me that Mar is not the chief of the tribe as we thought, that someone else is.''

A grim look came over the thin dark face before her. "My father is the shaman, not the chief. The shaman directs the tribal rituals. The chief is the leader of all else.''

"And who is the chief of your tribe?''

"His name is Altan." Tane said the name as if it left a bad taste in his mouth. "Mar's father, Tardith, was chief before Altan, but when Tardith died Mar was too young to become chief himself. So the tribe chose Altan.''

"You do not care for this Altan?" Jes asked.

He had opened his hand and was looking once more at her picture, but at her words his eyes flew upward. He looked startled. After a moment he said, "For a girl, you ask a lot of questions.''

Her chin rose. She gave him a haughty look. "I do not know what kind of women you are accustomed to, Outlander, but in my tribe the women always ask questions.''

He grinned. "So we are coming to learn.''

His obvious good humor left her feeling uncertain. She

snapped, "If you go around kidnapping women, you will have to put up with what you get."

At that he laughed. He took the small round stone that contained her drawing of the horse's head and put it in his belt. Then he took out three more stones and gave them to her. "Draw on these," he said. "Then, when we get home, I will show your drawings to my father."

She reached out to take the stones, and their hands touched. His hand, she noticed, was thin and muscular and long of finger. An artist's hand. She looked up from the stones to his dark face. He was handsome, she thought. Extremely handsome.

"Your name is Jes?" he asked softly.

She nodded.

"And you are the friend of your leader?"

"Sa."

He nodded, then rose to his feet. "Come," he said. "It is time to eat."

On the ninth day of their journey they came to a river the men called the Snake Water.

"Are there so many snakes, then?" Fali asked, wide-eyed, when first she heard the name.

"Na," had come the laughing reply. "It is just that the river coils and coils, in the way of a snake."

Reassured, Fali's eyes returned to their normal size. She did not at all like snakes.

The girls had their first view of the river from the top of a great rocky crag. As Alin stood a little apart from the others staring down into the river valley below, Mar came up beside her. "In two days, we shall be home," he said.

She did not look at him but continued to stare at the river, which was flanked on both sides by flat valley land. "Your home is on this river?"

"This river joins with another river, over there," and he pointed due west toward the rolling hills. "That is the river we dwell upon. There are many caves and cliff dwellings along the sides of Wand River. There have been men there since the beginning of time, nor are we the only tribe to dwell there now.'' He glanced down at her. "But we are the strongest.''

She always felt so small when she stood beside him. It was not a feeling she liked. "What is the name of your tribe?'' she asked. "You have never told us.''

"The horse is our totem,'' he replied.

There was a chill wind blowing off the river, and Alin slipped her cold hands under her reindeer fur vest for warmth. She shot him a swift sideways look. "We did not bring our winter clothing and already there has been snow.''

"We have furs enough to keep you warm,'' Mar replied. He had not seen her look; he was looking up the river and squinting a little in the wind.

Alin regarded his profile with annoyance. His thick bright hair was blowing across one hard cheekbone, screening it. He seemed scarcely to be aware that she was there. She said, "How delightful it will be to wear dead women's clothes.''

That got his attention. He looked down at her. "It is better to wear dead women's clothes than to freeze,'' he said pleasantly.

"That is your opinion, Outlander.''

"It is the only sensible opinion.''

Her nostrils quivered. For about the hundredth time Alin wondered how her mother would deal with this man. Alin herself found him utterly infuriating. And when she lost her temper, she lost her advantage. She could see that. She just didn't know what to do about it.

"Hear me, Alin,'' he was saying now, giving her name that odd stress on the second syllable. "When we reach our tribal dwelling I will tell our shaman, Huth, about your taboo. He will want to speak to you to learn the reasons for such a rule. I tell you this now so that you may be prepared.'' A pause. "Huth is a very great shaman. It is not easy to lie to him.''

"I am not lying,'' Alin said immediately.

"So you say. I am just giving you fair warning.''

They continued to eye each other. Alin thought: He does not believe me, but he wants me to convince this

Huth. She said, "Why should you want to wait until Spring Fires before claiming a wife?"

The blue eyes glinted and a lazy smile touched his mouth. His voice was soft as he answered, "There are yet some women left to the Tribe of the Horse. I am not necessarily doomed to sleep alone until Spring Fires."

Her large brown eyes showed surprise. "You are already married?"

His smile faded and he looked back toward the river. "I was. My wife was one of those who fell to the poisoned water."

"Oh." Under her vest Alin's hand opened and closed. Then she said softly, "I am sorry."

"Sa." His expression was unreadable.

He did not deserve her sympathy, Alin told herself firmly. She forced herself to think of other things. There was a great deal of information she needed to learn, and now was the opportunity to ask for it. She hardened her voice and asked, "How many women remain in your tribe?"

He answered without looking at her. "Three handfuls."

"And are they married?"

"All except the young ones who have not yet come to womanhood. And one other." Still staring at the river, he snorted through his nose. "It has not been a healthy situation, the disproportion of men to women in my tribe. There was murder done in the summer. That's what decided me to come south for more women."

"Murder?" Alin asked, her eyes enormous.

"Sa." The line of his mouth was grim. At last he looked down at her. "When men need a woman, they can become dangerous."

Alin was not accustomed to thinking of men as dangerous. She frowned. "But what happened?"

"Two men wanted the same woman. One man put his spear through the heart of the other," Mar said.

Alin's mouth opened in astonishment. She said, "My mother would never allow such a situation to develop. What is wrong with your chief that he did not prevent such stupidity?"

A muscle jumped in the corner of Mar's jaw. "It was the woman who pressed them on," he said. "She made each man think it was he that she wanted."

"Well, if she wanted them both she should have taken them both," Alin said impatiently. "If she wanted only one she should have taken only one. Your chief should have left the choice up to her, and none of this would have happened."

He looked down at her from his great height. "A woman cannot have two men!"

Alin's lip curled and she said sardonically, "Can she not, Outlander?"

For the briefest moment she could have sworn that he was shocked. Then his eyelids lowered, masking the expression in his eyes, and he said coldly, "I thought it was taboo for the girls of your tribe to take even a single man until Spring Fires, O Chosen One of the Mother."

There was a tense pause. Then, "For the first time," Alin said.

"Oh. I see." The lids lifted and now skepticism was vivid in both face and voice. "For the first time." He studied her for a moment in silence, with a look that provoked her temper again. Then he asked, "And how many husbands have *you* had, Alin?"

Alin could feel the pink color washing into her cheeks, and was furious with herself for betraying the fact that his words had stung her. In her tribe they all understood why she was yet a virgin, but this arrogant outlander . . . "I told you before," she said icily. "I was to make the Sacred Marriage for the first time when you bandits came and carried us off."

At her words, the look in his eyes began to change. He asked, "You have never yet lain with a man?"

The hateful color flushed stronger in her cheeks and she did not answer.

Suddenly he looked alert. "Tell that to Huth," he said. "Tell Huth that you will make this Sacred Marriage of yours at Spring Fires, to bring fertility to the Tribe of the Horse. If you do that, then I think he will give you the time that you crave."

She stared at him, her brain in a ferment. Think, Alin.

Is this a trap? She said slowly, "You have not yet told me why you are so anxious to give us the time until Spring Fires."

He flashed an utterly beguiling smile, one that made him look boyish and young. "It is as you said to me before, if we give you the time, then you will choose to live with us willingly. And I have pity in my heart for the young ones, like Fali and Dara. They need some time to learn to know us."

Alin did not believe a word he said. She gave him a scornful look, swung around on her heel, and walked away.

While Alin was standing upon the cliff over the Snake Water speaking to Mar, the last of the hunters from the Tribe of the Red Deer returned to report their failure to Lana.

Tor had led the group that stayed out the longest. "There is no trail," he said to the Mistress as he stood before her seat in the Women's Cave. "Whoever took them knew well how to cover their scent. The dogs could not pick up anything, nor could we discover any other way of their going."

Lana looked up at him from the pile of reindeer skins that softened and warmed her sitting place. Her face was ragged with grief, and yet it was stern. "Tor," she said, and her voice spoke only of command and nothing of grief, "we must get her back."

"I know."

Lana said, "They spoke with a strange accent, but they spoke the language of the Kindred. They *must* dwell somewhere within our reach."

"They cannot have come from too far," Tor agreed. "If they came from any great distance, they would have done the deed earlier in the year. They would want to have the girls safely home before winter strikes." His jaw tightened. "No point in going to the trouble of kidnapping a group of girls unless you have a use for them besides freezing them to death."

"The use is quite obvious," Lana snapped. "They must not have enough women of their own to propagate their tribe. Why else would they resort to such despicable means as kidnapping?''

"I can think of no other reason," Tor agreed.

Lana's fine brows were drawn together. She looked up at the man who was standing before her. "What chance have we of finding them before the spring weather?"

Slowly he shook his head. "No chance, Mistress. We have sent out searchers in every direction within our immediate vicinity, and none of the tribes nearby knows aught of this. To find them we will have to go farther afield. There are many tribes dwelling to the west of us, in the mountains by the Great Sea. I believe that that is the direction we must go first." His brown eyes, so achingly familiar, regarded Lana soberly. "But we must wait until the spring weather."

"We cannot wait. The tribe needs Alin." Lana's eyes were gray smoke in the white mask of her face. "Who is to make the Sacred Marriage now?"

His head thrust forward a little, his eyes were very dark. He said firmly, "You, Mistress. You have made the Sacred Marriage for us for twice two handfuls of years now, and always our women have borne their babes and the beasts have multiplied. You must do it again."

"I cannot," Lana said bitterly. "Do you not understand, Tor? I can no longer bear a child."

"That does not matter." His dark eyes were so strangely compelling. *He* was so compelling. "You are the one closest to Earth Mother, Lana," he said. "Her power runs in your blood. All who do come near you can feel that. That power is not gone. It is there still, Lana, curled within you." His voice was deep, inexorable. "Call it out of the darkness, Mistress. Take a mate and make the Sacred Marriage for the tribe. There is no one better fit to do it now that Alin is gone."

She stared up into his dark eyes. The look in them roused her blood. He was right, she thought. She felt the power burning in her womb, felt it running like a flame all through her loins and her abdomen. She looked at the man. She would take him, she thought. Once they had made a daughter for the tribe. It was time now for them to come together again. They would make the Sacred

Marriage, and the power that could no longer bring forth a new child would go instead toward keeping strong the life of the living.

And then in the spring, they would search out Alin, and bring her home.

Seven

It was almost nightfall when Mar led his hungry, weary followers along the final track that would take them at last to the dwelling place of the Tribe of the Horse. They had forded the Snake Water early in the morning, and since then they had been once again traveling north. For the last hour they had been steadily going up and down hills.

"I shall be almost glad to reach this tribe's caves," Alin said sourly to Jes. "I am that sick of being forever on the march."

"Sa," Jes replied. "We are all footsore and weary."

"And hungry." Alin made a face. "He did not even let us stop for a berry today!"

Jes opened her mouth to reply, when all of a sudden there came a shout from the men in front of them. Alin and Jes raised their heads and squinted into the setting sun.

"Are we there?" Jes said.

"We must be." Alin shaded her eyes with her hand. "I can see water. It must be the river that Mar told me about."

They were following a well-beaten track now, one that was taking them between two high limestone crags. The glitter of water was coming closer, and in less than a minute Alin and Jes walked out between the huge rocks and onto a gravel beach.

The river lay before them, narrow, winding, and deeply hued with the colors of the sunset. On the far side, the river was edged with gently sloping hills, their trees almost bare of color this late in the season. On their side of the river, towering spectacularly above the shimmering water, was an overhanging cliff. Alin stared upward in amazement. Set within the massive face of the cliff, on at least five different levels, were more than a dozen caves, and at least an equal number of rock shelters. From the skins hanging in the cave openings, Alin deduced that many were inhabited.

The skin covering the entrance of one of the caves in the middle of the cliff was suddenly pushed aside, and a man came out onto the ledge in front of it. He looked down at the beach, then began to walk along the ledge, following the downward slope. Suddenly he turned and started to climb down the face of the cliff. Alin gasped in horror, and then she realized that he was using a ladder.

By now the rest of the girls had come out onto the beach. All were staring upward. It was a moment before Alin realized that Mar had come to stand beside her.

"This is your home?" she asked. "This . . . eagle's aerie?"

"Sa." He smiled faintly. "You are a mountain girl. You will grow accustomed to it. The caves and shelters catch the winter sun for most of the day and are warm and dry. Men have lived here for a long long time. It is a good place to make a home."

He looked away from her toward the man who had almost finished climbing down the ladder. "That is our chief," he said in an expressionless voice. "Altan."

Silence fell between them as they watched the man who was the chief take the last step off the ladder, set his feet onto the gravel, and begin to cross the beach toward them. Alin felt her stomach muscles tighten as she watched the stranger come. She wished, suddenly and desperately, that Mar was the chief here. Mar she knew. This man was the unknown.

She saw that this chief was a big, broad-shouldered man, although he was not as tall as Mar. His hair was the color of wet earth, very dark but not black, and about his forehead he wore a leather headband decorated with oval bone discs. He was older than Mar by perhaps two handfuls of years. He thrust his head forward on his neck as he strode across the beach, like a buffalo charging, Alin thought as she stood her ground and watched him come. This impression remained as he came to a halt before them and lowered his head, the way a buffalo will lower its horns at the last minute to deliver its killing blow.

"So," he said to Mar, "you are back." He did not sound pleased.

"As you see, Altan," Mar replied in the same expressionless voice he had used earlier to Alin. "And we have brought the women."

The buffalo head swung as he took in the numbers assembled on the beach. "They are young," he said. He looked at Alin. "And pretty."

His odd, head-lowered stance put his eyes almost on a level with Alin's. She looked into them and asked coldly, "You are the chief of this tribe?"

He gave her a startled look. His eyes were brown, but lighter than Alin's, and small and almond-shaped. "Sa," he said. "I am the chief."

"We are tired and hungry," Alin said. "We require food and shelter. Then I must talk to your shaman."

Altan's head shot upright in surprise. Now he was looking down at her. "Who is this girl?" he asked Mar.

"She is their leader," Mar replied. "These girls are not like our women, Altan. They are servants of Earth Mother. I think it would be wise to allow her to speak to Huth. We must be careful not to offend the Mother."

Altan's eyes went past Alin to take in the rest of the girls. "They are all servants of the Mother?"

"Sa. As I told you, it is the way of their tribe."

Altan raised his left hand to his shoulder to scratch it and Alin saw that he was missing the thumb. The chief's eyes were passing over the girls. "How many did you bring us?" he asked Mar.

"Three handfuls plus one," Mar answered.

The chief's eyes continued to dart around the beach. "Did you lose any men?" To Alin's amazement, he sounded hopeful.

"Na." Mar's reply was short and hard.

The chief looked at him. "It seems the raid was not as difficult as you had thought," he said. His voice sounded as hard as Mar's.

"We were fortunate to take the girls when they were separated from their men," Mar replied. "They were at a religious ritual. That is why we need Huth."

Altan grunted. "Put them in the cave of the fish," he said. Alin noticed that he was wearing a small leather bag around his neck. The chief's medicine bag? she wondered. Altan continued, "I will give orders that they are to be fed. She can talk to Huth tomorrow."

Mar nodded. "Come with me," he said to Alin. "I will show you where to go."

Alin finished eating the smoked buffalo meat she had been given, and looked around the cave at the rest of the girls. Most of them were still eating hungrily. A fire burned close to the cave entrance, giving off equal amounts of heat and smoke. The buffalo hides hanging over the cave entrance had been parted to let some of the smoke escape out into the night air.

It had grown dark while they were eating. Alin visualized the sheer drop outside the opening of the cave and shivered. She thought with a flash of humor that she might be a mountain girl, as Mar had said, but she was not an ibex! She doubted she would ever grow accustomed to living on the edge of a cliff.

A rustle drew Alin's attention, and she turned her head and saw Jes getting up. Alin watched without surprise as her friend went over to a wall carving of a salmon near the cave entrance. They had all noticed it earlier when they first came in. It evidently had given the cave its name.

Alin got to her feet and went to stand beside Jes. "Do you like it?" she asked after a moment.

Jes gave her a preoccupied nod. "I think it is very old," she said. "Older even than the drawings in our sacred cave."

"Mar said that people have lived in this place for ages," Alin said.

Again Jes gave that preoccupied nod. "Look." She pointed her finger. "There is the faintest tracing of another picture."

Alin squinted at the wall. "It is hard to see in this light."

Jes ran her finger along the wall. "Sa," she said regretfully. "I shall have to wait until the morrow."

The morrow. Alin shivered at the thought. She turned away from the fish engraving and once more surveyed the scene within the cave.

The girls and their gear occupied almost every inch of floor space. Mar had asked if they wished to spread into another cave, but they had said they preferred to stay together. Now that they had finished eating, they were very quiet. Alin understood perfectly that they were afraid.

They had not been afraid while they were on the trail. For whatever reason, the men who followed Mar had let them be. In fact, an odd kind of camaraderie between the girls of the Red Deer and the young men of the Horse had begun to develop. Alin had seen it happening, had not liked it, but had not tried to prevent it either.

Lana would have prevented it. Lana would have held the girls together, would have kept hot their hostility and their anger. Alin knew she should not allow the girls to talk and joke with the men. But the days were so long, the journey so wearying. It had seemed heartless to keep them from what small comforts they could find. And the men, after all, had shown themselves to be harmless.

But now that they were here, the rules would change. They all understood that. They all knew why they had been kidnapped. The pleasant, joking young men of the journey had ceased to exist. Now it was just the women of the Red Deer and the enemy.

Alin walked over to the fire. She waited until she had everyone's attention, then she said, "Listen, my sisters. On the morrow I am to talk to the shaman of this tribe. I shall tell him that it is taboo for us to lie with a new man until such a union is blessed by the Mother at Spring Fires. I shall tell him that if these men do not honor our laws, then the Mother will not smile on us, and we will not bear children for them."

There was absolute silence in the cave. Alin looked from one young face to the next. "I am trying to win us some time," she said. "Come the spring weather, the Mistress will once again search for us." She paused and looked around again. "Do you understand?"

"Sa." The reply came softly from every throat. "We understand, Alin."

"Do not worry, Alin," said Sana. "If we are asked, we shall remember. It is taboo to lie with a new man until Spring Fires."

Elen laughed and tossed her pretty red head. "It is a good story, Alin. Let these men learn to fear the Mother. It will do them good."

Alin did not smile. "I do not know if I will be successful," she said. "I must first convince this shaman. It will be well for all of you to make petition to the Mother for my success."

The faint smiles that had appeared on the girls' faces vanished at her words.

"Let us sing the Praise Song," Dara said, and throwing back her head, she lifted her pure young voice in the most ancient of all the Mother's hymns. After the briefest moment, the rest of the girls joined in, and the cave was filled with the sounds of reverent singing.

A much smaller group was gathered that night in the chief's cave on the third terrace. The nirum's cave was not private enough for this particular meeting of Altan's, as it was inhabited by a large number of the tribe's unmarried men, not all of whom were Altan's admirers.

In the Tribe of the Horse, a boy was initiated at the age of thirteen. Then, for five years, he lived with the rest of the boys his age in the initiates' cave and perfected his skills as a hunter. At the end of the five years, if he had passed all of his tests, he was made a full-fledged hunter of the tribe: a nirum. If he had not already married, the young nirum then moved into the nirum's cave, where he lived until he took a wife.

Only a nirum could be the tribe's chief, which was why

Mar had not been called to follow his father when Tardith had died shortly after the time of Mar's initiation.

Altan, the man who had been called to succeed Tardith, sat this night around his fire with four of his closest companions, discussing this new situation. They were alone; Altan had banished his pregnant young wife to a neighbor's hearth for the evening.

"Mar lied." Sauk, the man who was always seated at the chief's right hand, spoke into the smoky gloom. "He knew it would be easy to take the girls. He lied to keep the nirum out of it."

The rest of the men grunted in agreement.

"Now he is a hero," said Tod, the man seated on Altan's other side. "Even the younger nirum think he is wonderful. The three women we got at the Autumn Gathering are forgotten when set next to this windfall that Mar has brought in."

"The younger nirum did not get any of the three women," one of the other men pointed out. "But they have great hopes of Mar's catch."

Altan slapped his hand upon his thigh sharply. "The initiates have great hopes of these girls also," he said, and bared his strong, crooked teeth in a grimace that was not a smile.

Sauk said bitterly, "He did not lose even one man on this raid. Not one." He turned to Altan. "He played us for fools."

The fourth man, whose name was Heno, said, "He has brought us three handfuls plus one of women. Let us not forget that."

"That is true," said Eoto, the man sitting across from Sauk. He grinned. "The boys did all the work. What is there to complain about in that?"

"The boys will expect to reap the rewards of their work," Tod said calmly. "*That* is the complaint."

"An initiated boy cannot expect to be given a woman before a nirum," said Sauk. He was one of the tribe's most famous hunters, a man of Altan's years, with a large nose, heavy jowls, and coarse black hair. "Is that not so, Altan?"

"I promised half of the girls to Mar," the chief said

sourly. "Before he undertook this raid, we made an agreement. Half to him for the initiates, and half to me."

Sauk said, "You never told me that!"

Altan shrugged impatiently. "I did not think the raid would be successful. A group of boys, who are not yet full-fledged tribal hunters, going against an entire tribe?" Altan threw a bone into the fire. "None of us thought he would be successful."

"He lied," Sauk said again.

"Sa. He did." Tod looked thoughtfully at Altan's profile. "Did you make this promise to Mar in front of witnesses?"

Altan's great head swung in Tod's direction. "Na," he said. "I did not."

"Mar is not the only one who can lie," Tod pointed out, and smiled. There was a moment's silence.

"It is his word against yours," Heno said.

"That is so," agreed Eoto. "He lied to you. He deserves a like treatment."

"Deny that you promised him the women," Sauk said firmly. "There will be nothing he can do about it."

"Sa," Tod agreed. "And Mar will lose favor with the initiates if he is unable to give them any of the women they brought here with such care."

"I might even give a woman to some of the boys myself," Altan said slowly. "I do not like the bond that holds the initiates to Mar. It is . . . dangerous."

"Do not give them too many of the women!" Sauk said.

"You cannot have another woman for yourself, Sauk." It was Tod speaking now, leaning a little forward to look across the brawny figure of the chief. "There was great anger in the tribe when Altan gave you one of the three girls we got at the Autumn Gathering. Now you have two wives, and most of the men have none."

"My wife was old!" Sauk said angrily. "I am the tribe's leading hunter. It was right for me to have a new young wife."

"Sa, but that is all you will get," Altan said. He raised his maimed hand and fingered the leather pouch he wore around his neck. "Tod is right. We all of us have new young wives, and we must be satisfied with them. I cannot give any man a second wife until the other men have at least got one.''

Three of the men nodded in agreement. Sauk scowled into the fire.

''I will speak to Mar tomorrow,'' Altan said. ''I will remind him that he undertook this raid for the good of the whole tribe. And I will not remember any bargain we two may have made.'' His lips drew back to show his crooked teeth, and the rest of the men smiled back through the smoke.

It was a strange feeling, Alin thought, to step out the door of one's cave and find oneself perched on the edge of a cliff. Directly below her was the beach and the ribbon of river shining in the early-morning sun. And the fish cave was only midway up the face of the cliff; there were caves and shelters even higher! Alin looked slowly around her, taking in carefully what she had noticed only in passing yesterday in the fading light.

Most levels of the cliff had a terrace or walkway, which seemed a natural part of the configuration of the rock. Most of the caves and shelters opened off these terraces. The man-made additions to the cliff face were the rope ladders made from animal sinew that connected the various levels, and the hides and branches that made up the fronts and sides of the shelters and that covered the entrances to the caves. The terrace Alin was standing upon was decidedly narrow, and Alin would have felt considerably more comfortable if there had been some kind of a barrier between her and the straight plunge to the gravel beach below.

As she stood there in the early-morning sun, looking around, the skins on a cave to the left parted, and a woman came out. She was young, with a heart-shaped face and wide-set greenish eyes. Alin looked with discreet curiosity at this woman of the Tribe of the Horse. The girl's hair was a pale yellow in color and she wore it wound around her head in several tiers of braids. She was dressed in a long-sleeved shirt and a long buckskin skirt, and around her neck hung an elaborate double necklace of shells and horse teeth. She stopped when she saw Alin and stared with open curiosity.

"Greetings," Alin said pleasantly, looking up the length of the terrace to her neighbor.

The girl's eyes widened with surprise. "You speak our language!" she said. Her voice had the same accent as had the men's, and was oddly husky.

"Sa. We are of the Kindred."

"Mar told us that you were like men." The girl's light eyes looked Alin up and down. "But you are pretty." She did not sound pleased.

"You are a woman of the Tribe of the Horse?" Alin asked, her voice not so pleasant as it had been.

"Sa." The girl took a few steps down the terrace in Alin's direction. "We saw you come in with Mar yesterday. Did he really kidnap you?"

"Sa."

"How exciting," the girl said. She sounded envious.

Alin stared at her in amazement. Was the girl possessed by an evil spirit? Exciting? "I would not say so," Alin replied coldly.

The girl sighed. "I would love to be kidnapped by Mar."

Now Alin was certain there was something wrong with this girl. She formed a kindly smile. There had been a boy in the Tribe of the Red Deer who was like this. There had been no harm in him; he just did not understand the way others did. She said gently, "Does your mother know you are out of your cave?"

The girl stared at Alin as if she were the one possessed by the evil spirit. "Why should my mother need to know such a thing?" she asked. Then she added flatly, "My mother is dead. She drank the poisoned water and died with the rest. Surely you have heard that story. It is the reason you were kidnapped."

Alan was appalled at her own clumsiness. "I am sorry," she managed after a moment. "Sa, I have heard the story. It is . . . terrible."

"I was very sick," the girl said. "But I was one of the few who got better."

Perhaps that accounted for it, Alin thought. The poor girl's mind had been damaged by the poison.

The girl's eyes slid beyond Alin's shoulder, and her pretty heart-shaped face lit with a smile. "Greetings, Mar," she said, her voice slightly huskier than it had been when she spoke to Alin. "We have missed you."

"Greetings, Lian," came Mar's voice from behind Alin. "I see you two have met."

Alin turned a little and then pressed her back against the cliff in order to be able to see the two who stood on either side of her. The girl, whose name apparently was Lian, had come down the terrace to Alin's side; she was still smiling at Mar. He gave her a brief nod, then said to Alin, "I have come to take you to Huth."

Alin's lips parted. "Now?"

"Now. You have eaten?"

"Sa. Bror and Melior brought us a broth made out of sage, and some nuts and apples."

"Huth has said he will see you. It would be well not to keep him waiting."

"All right," Alin said. She straightened away from the cliff. "Where is he?"

"Follow me," Mar said, and turned to go back the way he had come.

"But Mar!" came Lian's voice from behind. "I have not had a chance to speak to you."

"Later, Lian," he said over his shoulder. Then to Alin, "Are you coming?"

"Sa." And without further discussion she followed him to the ladder. From behind, she heard Lian give an exclamation of annoyance, which Mar ignored. Alin thought it was unkind of him to be so curt to an idiot girl.

They climbed down to the level below. There was a wide porch at the bottom of the ladder, with plenty of room for a dozen people to stand comfortably. Mar stopped on the porch and turned to Alin. "It would be well to show reverence to the shaman," he said. "He is a great man in this tribe."

Alin was insulted. "I know how to behave to a shaman," she snapped.

He bent his head and looked at her. Alin stared fear-lessly back. He had changed his clothes, and somehow he looked different to her. It was a moment before Alin realized that Lugh was missing from his side. That was the difference.

"Where is Lugh?" she asked. "It seems strange to see you without him."

"I left him in my shelter," Mar said. "He cannot make it up the cliff to this level."

"Ah," said Alin, enlightened. He continued to study her and she thought, irrelevantly: his eyes are bluer than the morning sky. At last he said, "I did not mean to make you angry. I do not want you angry when you talk to Huth. When you are angry you become insolent."

Alin felt her mouth open in astonishment. Insolent! The man was clearly possessed. Which reminded her: "Is that girl, Lian, simpleminded?" she asked.

Now it was Mar's turn to gape. "Simpleminded? What ever made you think that?"

"Well." Alin bit her lip, feeling ridiculous. He looked so amazed. "She said the most foolish things to me."

"What did she say?"

Alin's long braid had fallen forward during the climb down and now she flipped it back over her shoulder. "She said she thought it was exciting to be kidnapped." Her brown eyes mirrored her incomprehension. "Surely one would have to be simpleminded to say such a thing!"

Mar was both exasperated and amused. "Lian may be simpleminded, but not in the way you are thinking. She is . . ." He hesitated, clearly searching for how to phrase his thought. Then he said, "She is the girl over whom murder was committed this summer."

Alin's lips parted slightly as she took this in. "The one you told me about?"

"Sa."

So that was the girl whom two men had fought over. Alin frowned thoughtfully as she asked, "What happened to the man who put the spear into the other's heart? Is he Lian's husband?"

"Lian has no husband," he replied curtly. "One year must pass before she will be purified enough to wed."

"But she did not do the murder," Alin pointed out reasonably.

"She instigated it."

There was a pause, then Alin shrugged. "I do not know the whole tale, so I cannot say. But you did not tell me what happened to the man who put the spear into the other's heart."

"He is dead," Mar said, irritably, warning her not to inquire further.

Alin thought of Lian's words, "I would love to be kidnapped by Mar." She looked speculatively at the golden lion of a man standing beside her. Somehow, she did not think Mar was a man to be driven to murder for the sake of a woman.

"Alin," he commanded, "remember what you are to say to Huth. If you want to persuade him, tell him you will make the Sacred Marriage for the Tribe of the Horse if we will respect your taboo and wait until Spring Fires to take your girls to wife."

Alin stared back into that much-too-arrogant male face. She said slowly, "But why would such a promise persuade Huth? The Sacred Marriage is not one of the rituals of Sky God. Why should a shaman of Sky God have such reverence for a rite of the Mother?"

"True it is not one of our rituals, but it is a powerful fertility rite, is it not?"

"Sa."

"Well." The big shoulders moved in an easy shrug. "Fertility is the thing we have most need of in this tribe. And Huth is a man who has reverence for all the gods. He is a great shaman, Alin; a man to whom the gods will speak."

"My mother is such a one also," Alin said. "I understand how to speak to such a man."

Mar looked doubtful, but held his tongue.

Alin said abruptly, as Mar was turning to move off, "What of your chief? Will it be necessary for me to persuade him as well?"

"Huth is the one who will have the final word on such a matter. If he says we must wait, there will be nothing Altan can do about it." On the surface Mar's voice was merely informative, but Alin could hear the note of satisfaction that lay beneath.

So, she thought. It has something to do with Altan.

"What happened to Altan's thumb?" she asked curiously. "That is an ugly scar he carries."

"He lost it to a cave bear," Mar returned. He did not seem inclined to continue, but she raised her eyebrows, and after a pause he went on with the story. "Altan first wounded it with his large spear, and when the bear turned on him, he had to finish killing it with a hand-held javelin. The thumb was the price of the encounter, and he wears it around his neck lest anyone forget for a moment what a great hunter they have for a chief."

"You mean his *thumb* is what he carries in that pouch around his neck?"

"Sa."

Alin looked at Mar's sour expression, and then shrugged.

After all, she thought. What did it matter to her if Mar were trying to undermine Altan's authority by delaying the marriages until Spring Fires? What mattered was that she should gain her own ends.

"All right," she said. "I will tell Huth that I will make the Sacred Marriage for your tribe if he will give us the time until Spring Fires."

Mar bestowed on her his most beguiling smile. "Good girl," he said. And Alin was annoyed to find that his praise pleased her.

The shaman's cave was one of those opening off the lowest terrace of the cliff. A small fire danced near the cave's entrance, with a bone cup full of some kind of liquid keeping hot on the hearth stones. As Alin and Mar came in, the young fair-haired boy who had been tending the fire rose and went out. Alin blinked as her eyes adjusted to the dimness inside.

"Huth, my father," she heard Mar saying beside her. "I have brought you the leader of the women who have come to dwell with us. Her name is Alin, and she wishes to speak with you."

A man moved out of the shadows at the side of the

cave. Before Alin turned to him she shot Mar a look out of the side of her eyes. The women who have come to dwell with us? she thought cynically. The women you kidnapped, you mean.

A gentle yet unmistakably authoritative voice said, "I am pleased you are safely returned, my son."

Alin assumed the titles of father and son were courtesy merely. It was impossible, she thought, that the dark-skinned man who stood before her could be Mar's actual father. Huth was no taller than she, and he was slim to the point of fragility. He was not wearing a shaman's costume, but a simple shirt and trousers like Mar. He said, "Come, my child, and sit beside the fire with me."

Alin bowed her head and turned toward the flames flickering brightly near the cave's entrance. Huth gestured her to a buffalo robe heaped on the stone floor, and she folded herself gracefully to sit, cross-legged, upon the skin. There was a very pleasant fragrance coming from the bone cup upon the hearth stones. Alin sniffed and recognized the hot drink made out of sage that the girls had been given for breakfast earlier.

Before Mar could seat himself, Huth said, "I will speak to Alin alone, Mar. You may come back later."

"Very well, Huth." Mar took a step toward the cave's entrance. "Have you spoken to Tane?"

"I spoke to him last night." There was nothing in the shaman's voice to give away his thought, and Alin was delighted to see a shadow of concern pass over Mar's face. He gave her a quick, worried look. She stared right through him. His mouth tightened, but he did not say another word. With one more look at Huth, Mar left. The buffalo skins in front of the entrance swung back into place behind him.

Huth sat beside Alin at the fire. In the light from the flickering flames, she was at last able clearly to see his face.

He was a man a little beyond the middle years. His straight black hair, worn longer than that of the younger men, was streaked with gray, and there were fine wrinkles along the sides of his eyes and his mouth. His eyes were the most remarkable thing about him, a surprising light gray under dark brows and lashes. They were looking at her now with great steadiness and calm, and Alin drew a long faintly uneven breath before she began to speak.

"Mar has made a pretty picture with his words, Shaman. 'The women who have come to dwell with us,' he called us. In fact, we are the women he kidnapped."

The steady gray eyes did not flicker. "Sa," Huth said. "I know."

"Do you know what sort of women we are?" Alin asked. She strove to keep her own voice level and quiet. There was something about this shaman that conveyed the impression that this was indeed a man who knew the gods. She must treat him with honor. In this tribe he was the counterpart of the Mistress.

"Tell me, my daughter," Huth said.

She said, as she had said so many times to Mar: "We are servants of the Mother. Our tribe follows the old way, Shaman. Yours are the new ways, the ways of Sky God, but ours are other." Her braid had fallen forward over her left breast when she had sat down, and now she absently tossed it back to hang between her shoulder blades. "We were preparing for one of our most sacred rituals when your men burst upon us and took us away," she said.

At that, Huth frowned. "They took you during a sacred ritual?"

"Sa."

"That was not well done."

Alin bit back a retort that Mar would surely have considered insolent. She said instead, "It was our ritual for fertility."

The shaman's head lifted. He looked at her, but said nothing.

"In our tribe, at the rituals of Spring and Winter Fires, the Mother mates with the god," Alin said. "That is what brings children to the tribe and fawns to the deer."

She paused. The shaman's clear steady gaze suddenly reminded her of Lana. Mother, Alin thought, and even in her thoughts she was not quite clear as to which mother she was addressing, lend me your power.

Alin closed her eyes, blocking out that all-seeing gray gaze, drew in a deep long breath, and felt the power rush into her blood, felt the strength, the clarity, the authority of it. She could bend this man to her will. She knew it. She sat, straight-backed before his fire, opened her eyes, and let the power speak.

"It was sacrilege to interrupt our rites. It was sacrilege to take the Mother's servants against their will. The Mother is angry, Huth. I can feel it. Here," and she put her hand to her breast. "I am the Chosen One of the Mother. I am her voice. And I tell you now that she is angry."

The shaman did not move, nor did his gaze waver. Then he said, "I cannot send you home, Alin. I do not say that Mar was right to take you as he did. He is a young man and he was brought up in the ways of Sky God. He knows little of the ways of the Mother. But you must know the reason why you were taken. It is for that reason that I cannot send you home."

"You will have no good of this kidnapping," Alin said coldly. "The Mother will take her revenge. We will bear no children for the Tribe of the Horse, Huth. That I swear."

In the ensuing silence, Alin had no trouble meeting the shaman's gaze. Her mother was with her. She felt the power running strong in her blood.

"What can we do to make amends?" Huth asked at last.

"You will not send us home?"

"I cannot," Huth said, and Alin saw that he meant it.

"Then, if we stay here, you must honor our ways."

"What ways are those, my daughter?"

"The women of the Red Deer are not like your women," Alin said proudly. "We are the instruments of the Mother. We choose our mates, Huth, we are not chosen. And we do not lie with a new mate until the Mother lies with the God at the ceremony of the Fires."

For the first time Huth's gaze wavered. He rubbed his nose. "You are saying you wish to choose your own men?" he said mildly.

"We always choose our men." Alin's voice was fierce.

Huth gestured with one slim, graceful hand. "We are followers of Sky God, my daughter. Our men are hunters. Our ways are different."

"I know that. I know your ways are not our ways. But you have brought us here, Shaman. And you have angered the Mother. Even Sky God is careful not to anger the Mother, I think." She paused to let that sink in. "The way to make amends to the Mother is to honor the ways of her servants. I do not care how you treat the women of your own tribe," a shrug indicated the depths of her disdain for those pitiful creatures, "but we are different."

He did not answer. He was looking into the fire and Alin could see he was still not convinced. She thought of what Mar had told her. She said, "I am the daughter of the Mistress of my tribe, Huth. I am the Chosen One. I was preparing to make the Sacred Marriage for my people when your men interrupted our ceremony." She stared at him, willing him to believe her. "It is a very powerful ritual, Huth. Through me, the Mother mates with the God and makes the life of the tribe. The Tribe of the Horse needs a ritual such as that, I think."

He looked up from the fire. "The life of the tribe," he said slowly. "Sa. That is what this kidnapping is all about, Alin."

She bowed her head in acknowledgment.

"If you are the goddess in this ceremony," he asked, "who is the god?"

She answered truthfully, "The leader of the men."

There was a thoughtful silence.

Huth said, "Sky God is the husband of the Mother. It is the two of them together who made the life of the world. And it was Horse God and the Mother who made the first people of the tribe of the Horse."

Alin nodded agreement. "Let Horse God and the Mother Goddess lie together at Spring Fires, Huth," she urged. "Let them make the life of the tribe. And the life of the herds as well, Huth. The Sacred Marriage is for that also."

He looked at her reflectively. "You will do this for us,

Chosen One of the Mother? You will make the Sacred
Marriage for the life of our people?''

"I will," Alin replied, "if you will honor our ways.
If we must live among you, let us do it in a way that is
honorable to us.''

He looked away from her large bright eyes and into
the fire. "Let me understand you, then. You wish to wait
until this ceremony of the Fires to wed, and you wish to
choose your own mates?''

"Sa."

"When will the ceremony of the Fires be?''

"It is too late now for Winter Fires," Alin said firmly.
"It cannot be until the spring weather.''

"When in spring?''

"At the first moon of the spring. It is called Ibex Moon
in my tribe. It is the moon when the ibex come down
from the mountains, the salmon begin to run in the rivers, and the deer begin to drop their fawns.''

He nodded his head slowly. "That would be Salmon
Moon in this tribe. That is the moon after the Ceremony
of the Great Horse. A good time." He looked up from
the fire. He said, "I am not a young man like Mar. I
know how powerful is the Mother, and I respect her
ways. But I must listen to the gods before I decide about
this, Alin. I must listen and I must think.''

"When will you do this?'' she asked tensely.

"I will do it in a little while," he said, rising to his
feet. He went to the door of the cave and, pushing aside
the skin, called "Arn." The young silver-haired boy who
had been sitting by the fire before came in. "Find Tane
and tell him to come for Alin," Huth said. "Then you
and I have work to do.''

With a quick nod, the boy was gone. He was back very
shortly with Tane, who took Alin with him, leaving the
shaman and his assistant behind to begin their ceremony
of consulting with their gods.

Eight

It was a number of hours before Huth came to his decision, and then he emerged from his cave to speak to Altan. By late in the afternoon, the news of what Huth had decided was making its way around the rest of the tribe.

The young men who had gone on the raid with Mar were delighted when they learned of the agreement Huth had made with Alin. When Bror came into the initiates' cave late in the day with the news, there was much laughter and punching of shoulders.

"She actually got Huth to agree to allow the girls to choose their own mates?" Melior asked incredulously as Bror joined the rest of the men around the fire.

"Sa. That is what Tane just told me. They are to have until the spring, and then they are to choose their own mates." A white grin split Bror's brown-skinned face. "Altan was livid. He knows he was outmaneuvered by Mar."

"I can believe that the chief was angry," said Dale. His light blue eyes were sparkling like crystal. "The girls are young like us. A man of Altan's age will seem as old as their fathers to them."

Cort hooted softly in agreement.

"Many of the nirum are young too," Bror pointed out. "The girls may choose some of them over us."

"Still, Altan would have given all the girls to the nirum," Melior said. "We would have gotten none. That is why they want him as chief." Melior's voice was hard and bitter. "He gives them whatever they demand, regardless of the needs of the rest of the tribe."

A little silence fell. They all knew the reason for Melior's hard voice. His own promised wife had been one of the girls to survive the poison, and Altan had taken her from Melior and given her to one of the older nirum.

"What Melior says is true," Dale said after a moment. "Look at these three women Altan got at the Autumn Gathering. He gave them out while we were gone, did not even give us a chance to ask for them." He reached forward to push a stick more firmly into the fire.

"He gave one to Sauk!" said Melior. "And Sauk already has a wife."

"Sauk devours women the way a hungry dog devours fresh meat," Cort said disgustedly.

"Sauk and Altan," Melior said, equally revolted. "What a pair we have as leaders for the Tribe of the Horse."

Bror said quietly, "It may not be for long. At the Ceremony of the Great Horse this year, Mar will be made nirum."

The silence in the cave reverberated.

"It is certain, then, that Mar will make the challenge?" Dale asked. "When he is made nirum, he will challenge Altan for the chieftainship?"

The rest of the boys looked at each other.

"He has never spoken of it," Bror said at last. "But, knowing Mar, I am thinking that he will."

"It is a fearful thing," Dale said, "the making of such a challenge."

"It is not impossible," Melior said quickly. "The challenge would not be there if it was impossible."

"Mar would be a chief to all the tribe," Cort said soberly. "It is not in Mar to be unjust."

Nods of agreement ran around the fire.

"Mar knows that if he needs us, we will be there for him," Bror said at last. "In our hearts, he has always been our chief."

"Sa, sa, sa," came the response.

A brooding silence fell.

Finally, someone sighed and said wistfully, "It would

be nice to have a girl to share my sleeping roll this coming winter season.''

The mood in the cave changed palpably. ''Well, there will be no girl, so don't even think about it,'' Bror said. ''There is a good chance that you will have a girl come spring, though; which is more than we could have hoped for last year at this time.''

This time the silence was grim. All of the young men in the shelter remembered vividly the gruesome sight that had met their eyes when they had returned from last year's Autumn Gathering to find their mothers and sisters and promised brides either dying or already lying dead.

Dale said in a muffled voice, ''Dhu. Sometimes I have such dreams about it. . . .''

Bror put an arm around the younger boy's shoulder. ''We all do,'' he said gruffly. He gave Dale a brief hug, then dropped his arm and turned to the rest, rotating his shoulder so that the boy's face was shielded from the view of the others. ''I'll wager the girls of the Red Deer are going to have a pleasant winter,'' Bror commented, forcing a note of amusement into his voice. ''I can just see us now, all trying to outdo each other to woo them.''

''Dhu,'' said Melior blankly. ''I had not thought of that.''

''Perhaps we should choose now among ourselves which one we each want,'' said Cort.

''The numbers are not even,'' someone pointed out.

''They are in our favor,'' said Cort, looking around the fire. ''There are one more than three handfuls of girls, and there are only two handfuls plus three of us.''

''You have forgotten the younger nirum,'' Bror said. ''They do not have wives, either.''

''And Mar,'' said Dale. He sat forward, having recovered himself. ''Do not forget Mar.''

''Even if we did, it is not likely that the women will,'' said Melior dryly. Everyone laughed.

''If you do the counting, you will find that there are yet far more of us than there are of them,'' Bror said. ''And what is more, *they* are the ones who are supposed to do the choosing. Remember?''

The boys hooted softly. That was the story, but they

all knew the truth of the matter. It would be up to the men to decide which girl they wanted to woo. They cast speculative looks at each other, deciding who was likely to be a rival and who not.

"It will be fine, so long as we don't let it get too serious, the way it did with Davin and Bard," someone said abruptly.

"Never!" they all promised each other solemnly. "We are hunting companions. No woman can ever be more important than that."

"That is so," said Bror. He grinned. "Besides, Mar would kill us first if ever we let matters come to such a point."

The young men laughed, and yipped their favorite hunting call, and from the cave on the beach where they were housed, the dogs howled back.

The girls of the Red Deer were equally delighted when Jes told them of Alin's bargain, though for different reasons than the young men of the Horse.

"The Mistress will have until the spring to find us then," said Elen.

"And even if worse should come to worst, and we should be forced to stay here, at least we will have the choosing of which man we want," said Sana.

"They are not so bad, really," said Iva demurely. "And now that we have the choosing power . . ."

The girls all smiled with satisfaction.

Jes said in a hard voice, "Alin had to promise this shaman that she would make the Sacred Marriage at Spring Fires for the sake of their tribe."

There was a stirring as the girls leaned forward, the better to see Jes's face.

"She promised to make the Sacred Marriage?" Iva said. "But with whom?"

"Their chief. Who else?" said Jes. In the dim light of the cave the girls could see that her face was grim.

"Oh . . ." The general long drawn-out breath was expressive of dismay.

"Sa. Alin said there was no other way to get the shaman to agree to her terms." Jes viciously poked the fire.

"Lana will find us." It was Elen's voice. "Earth Mother will show her the way."

"I hope so," said Jes. "I do not like to think of Alin, our Chosen One, giving life to this tribe of kidnappers."

"Nor do I like the looks of that chief," said Iva, curling her lip in disgust. "He reminds me of a buffalo."

There were general exclamations of surprised agreement.

"The chief already has a wife," said Dara.

A moment of silence. Then someone demanded, "How do you know?"

"I was talking to one of their women before," Dara said. "She told me. There are three handfuls plus three of women in this tribe, and four of the girls are unmarried. One is the girl I was talking to today. Her name is Lian."

The rest of the girls smiled with amused resignation. Leave it to Dara, they thought, to find a friend.

"Why is this Lian not married?" Elen demanded. "If she is the girl in the braids I saw you talking to earlier, she is certainly pretty enough."

"She told me she is to marry Mar."

Silence.

"He was married before," Dara said into the strangely glum quiet. "His wife was one of those who died from the poisoned water."

Jes spoke for the first time in a while. "What of Tane?" she asked. "Is he married?"

Dara shook her head. "I do not know."

Iva propped her chin on her knees and stared dreamily into the fire. "It is so strange," she said. "Less than one moon ago, we were all gathered in the women's cave at home, talking of whom we would go with at Winter Fires. And now . . . here we are in a strange dwelling place, with a strange tribe, talking of wedding with strange men." She shook her head. "I keep expecting to wake up and find this is all a dream."

"I am thinking it is a nightmare, rather," said Jes.

"I do not know." Iva blinked. "It is just so . . . odd."

"The winter is coming," said Sana. "With so few

women to do the gathering, I hope this tribe has been able to store up enough food to feed us.''

Jes looked suddenly alert. ''Perhaps there will be a hunt.''

The hunters among the girls straightened. ''Sa. It would be good to go out once more on the hunting trail.''

Elen grinned and flipped back her braid, as brilliant a red-gold as the fire. ''It would be good to show these men of the Horse how to throw a spear properly.''

There was laughter from all around the fire.

Then Dara asked Jes. ''But where is Alin?''

''She will be back shortly,'' said Jes. ''I think she needed to be alone for a while.''

They all nodded solemnly.

''She is our Mistress now,'' Dara said at last.

''Sa,'' the girls said softly. ''That is so.''

''She will be the Mother to us,'' said Sana. ''We will never be abandoned so long as we have Alin.''

Altan had indeed been livid at Huth's decision about the girls. He had tried to get Huth to change his mind, but the shaman was adamant.

''I have drummed my drum,'' he said. ''The god has spoken and I have heard. The Mother must be placated. We must allow her servants to have their way.''

''We make our reverence to Sky God,'' Altan protested angrily. ''We are hunters in this tribe, the sons of fathers. The Mother has naught to do with us.''

''Close your mouth, foolish man!'' Huth was as angry now as Altan. ''We have great need of the Mother's goodwill in this tribe. The gods do know that even if the chief does not.'' The shaman's gray eyes were narrow as they surveyed the fuming Altan from his thrusting head to his big feet. Huth added with deceptive softness, ''Perhaps it is this lack of reverence in our chief that caused the tribe's tragedy in the first place. The Mother does not like to be disregarded.''

Altan's heavy head swung up. His dark eyes glared at Huth. ''It was not my fault!''

''Then cease your foolish blabbering,'' Huth snapped. ''These girls are servants of the Mother. Their leader is willing to make a powerful fertility rite for us. We will do as they ask, Altan. We will wait until the time of this rite to take them to wife, and we will let them choose their own husbands.''

Altan ran a finger under the leather headband that held his dark hair off his brow. He said, "It is convenient for Mar to have the shaman as his foster father."

Huth's nostrils narrowed. "What are you saying, Altan?" His voice again was soft.

"I have said what I have said."

"Then listen, Altan, to what I say," Huth returned. "I say that the chief should be a chief to all of the tribe, not just to his own companions. I say that if the chief forgets that, then it is not impossible for the tribe to cast him out. And I say too that at the Ceremony of the Great Horse this year, Mar, son of Tardith, will be made a nirum."

Huth stared into Altan's furious face. "Think you on that for a while," the shaman said. And left.

Nine

Two days went by. The girls decided that it was in fact a little crowded with them all packed into one cave, and some of them moved into another, slightly smaller cave that opened off the same terrace. The oldest and youngest girls remained together, as the two youngest in particular, Fali and Dara, had become extremely attached to Alin and refused to be parted from her.

At Huth's suggestion, Altan arranged a general meeting between the girls of the Red Deer and the women of the Tribe of the Horse. But first Alin wanted to meet with Altan's wife, Nel, in the privacy of the chief's cave.

It was Huth himself who brought Alin to Altan's cave entrance, pushed back the skins that hung over the door, and announced her arrival into the faintly flickering lamplit gloom of within. Alin paused and then, after feeling a gentle push from Huth upon her shoulder, she walked in. The girl who was waiting for her walked forward. They met in the middle of the cave's big entrance chamber and stiffly exchanged greetings. Huth left.

Nel was about Alin's age, and obviously gravid. She had dark blond hair, blue eyes, a sulky mouth, and would be very pretty once the puffiness of pregnancy had left her face. Huth had told Alin that Nel was one of the first of the women brought into the tribe after the tragedy of the previous autumn. Alin looked at the other woman's stomach and calculated that she must have become pregnant almost as soon as she was wed.

Nel began immediately by asking questions about the

agreement Alin had won from the men of the tribe. Alin wasn't sure if Nel was scandalized by the fact that the Red Deer girls would get to choose their own husbands, or if she was envious. Alin thought perhaps it was a little of both.

When she got a chance to ask a few questions of her own, Alin's concerns were more practical.

"We shall need furs for the winter," she told the chief's wife. "We brought nothing with us save our ceremonial costumes and the clothes we wear."

"There are furs enough for all of you," Nel said, obviously uninterested in the topic of the Red Deer girls' clothes. She added carelessly, "There is other clothing as well. Mada has stored everything safely away. I shall ask her to give the extra things to you. It is indeed growing cold."

Alin nodded gravely. "We can make our own clothes once we go out on the hunting trail, but it would be impossible to prepare skins for all of us in time for the winter. We will be grateful for your furs."

"Mar told us that the women in your tribe hunted," the other girl said. "Is it true?"

"Certainly it is true," Alin replied. "Now . . . I am concerned about the food supply of this tribe. Men are rarely interested in gathering any foods but meat, and with so few women here I am thinking that perhaps you are not prepared to feed three handfuls more people over the winter."

Nel shook her head. "There are enough of us to do the gathering, and since *we* do not hunt," the faint emphasis on the "we" was not lost on Alin, "we have kept busy collecting grain and drying greens and roots in preparation for the winter." The girl's voice was growing more, not less stiff as the conversation progressed. "The men will get us reindeer when they can, and when they cannot we will eat meat that has been smoked and stored."

There was a faint line between Alin's brows, but after a minute she merely nodded again. The line smoothed out, and she smiled with conscious friendliness. "You

are to bear a child, I see. The Mother has blessed you.
You are the wife of the chief of this tribe?''

"Sa." The girl's round chin lifted a little. Her blue
eyes looked pointedly at Alin's reed-slim waist. "Did
you leave a husband behind you, woman of the Red
Deer?''

Alin gently shook her head.

Nel widened her blue eyes in simulated surprise. "You
are old enough to have a husband, surely."

"I am the daughter of the Mistress of the Tribe," Alin
said matter-of-factly. "I belong to Earth Mother. No man
may call me wife."

This time Nel's astonishment was genuine. "Do you
mean you may never marry at all?"

"Have you no priestess of the Mother in this tribe?"
Alin returned with equal astonishment. "Are her ways
indeed so strange to the women of the Horse?"

"I was born to the Buffalo Tribe," the girl said, "but
our ways and the ways of the Horse Tribe are the same.
Our men are hunters," she looked up at Alin, who was
considerably taller, and continued proudly, "hunters and
worshipers of Sky God. We are people of the sun. The
ways of the dark are not for us."

"The dark? I do not understand you, woman of the
Horse. Earth Mother is the goddess of all of life, the light
as well as the dark, life as well as death. When a child
is made, Earth Mother is there. When a hyena rips the
life from a deer, Earth Mother is there as well. She has
power over all of life. She has as husband both the god
of the sky and the god of the underworld. The god of the
light and the god of the dark, both of them lie in the
embrace of the Mother." Alin shrugged in disdain.
"People of the sun!" she said. "The sun covers but the
half of life, girl. It would be well for you to remember
that."

Nel was staring at Alin as if she were a creature from
another species altogether. "What kind of men do you
have in your tribe?" she asked.

Alin's brown eyes flashed. "Fine hunters are the men
of the Red Deer. But they have proper reverence for the

Mother, who is the source of life both to the tribe and the herds.''

"It does not seem natural, somehow,'' said Nel, "for men to follow a woman.''

"It was a woman who gave them life. They do not forget that, as some men seem to. After all,'' said Alin coldly, "it was not the men of the Red Deer who so angered the Mother that she punished them by poisoning their water and killing their women.''

Nel's blue eyes stretched wide. She put a protective hand upon her stomach. "Do you really think the poisoned water was Earth Mother's doing?''

"I cannot think that she is pleased with a tribe such as this one, where so little reverence is shown to her ways.''

Nel blinked, obviously trying to assimilate this new idea.

Alin said, "I will go and gather the women of the Red Deer and bring them to the women's cave.''

"Sa,'' said Nel hastily. "Our women await you there. I will go and say that you are coming.''

Alin nodded majestically, and left.

There were eighteen women of the Tribe of the Horse waiting to meet the Red Deer girls in the women's cave on the first level of the cliff. Eleven of those present had survived the poisoning; seven had been bought from other tribes since the poisoning to be replacement wives. Of all the women of the Tribe of the Horse present in the cave this day, only four were unmarried. Three were girls who had not yet begun to menstruate and the other was Lian.

The titular leader of the women of the Red Deer was Nel, the wife of the chief, but it was soon clear that the true leader, the woman everyone listened to, was the oldest member of the group, Mada.

All of the women had gathered before Alin and Nel arrived, and they had seated themselves according to tribe, the Red Deer girls along one wall, the women of the Horse along the other. Between the two groups, close to the entrance, a fire was going. Suspended over it by hangers of sinew were several cauldrons made of animal skulls. The cauldrons were filled with a liquid that was giving forth a mouth-watering odor.

Mada came forward when Alin and Nel walked in, and introduced herself to Alin as the wife of the tribe's master toolmaker, Rom, and the mother of Bror. Then she gestured Alin to a seat and began to bustle about with reassuring motherly gestures, handing out bone cups filled with the hot drink, which had been made from apples. It tasted just as delicious as it smelled.

Alin's heart was considerably lightened by the sight of Mada. It was lightened as well by the sight of many bunches of drying herbs hanging from a pole fixed near the front of the cave. The fragrance from the herbs underlay the smell of the apple drink.

Alin sipped her drink and looked at the herbs. She thought she recognized dill and sage and thyme.

Mada said something, and Alin turned to her and smiled. Such a woman, she thought as she made a polite reply, was not likely to let the tribe get low on the necessities of life. Mada would have made certain that the stores were stocked with the necessary fruits and grains and dried plants and herbs that would see the tribe through the winter. Mada had faced a good eight handfuls of winters, Alin judged looking at the round, weathered face of the older woman. Mada would know what needed to be done.

"I am very glad to see your herbs," Alin said now to Bror's mother. "It is too late in the year for us to gather many herbs ourselves, and I must tell you that we were growing very weary of the roasted meat your men kept feeding us on the trail."

A breath of soft laughter ran around the cave.

"Men know only one way to cook meat," Mada said in a good-humored reply.

"Sa," Nel agreed. "I am thinking that if it were not for the women, all men would likely suffer from the wasting sickness. They would eat nothing but roasted meat!"

Murmurs of amused agreement came from all the women of the Horse, and some of the tension in the cave was eased. Alin took another sip of her drink and looked around.

Mada was the only older woman present. The rest of the women of the Horse were considerably younger. Four of them looked to be carrying about a moon's-span of years. They were not yet beyond the bearing of children, though women of that age conceived less frequently than those who were younger. Of the remaining married women, half were in their twenties and half in their teens. Five were gravid; two had babes at the breast.

There were other children of the tribe who were not present in the cave this morning. Alin had seen them, a few toddlers, a few small boys and girls, playing in the mouths of caves and down on the beach. Not nearly the number of children one would expect to find in a tribe of as many men as the Tribe of the Horse. The thought of what had happened to the rest of the tribe's children brought an unwilling pang to Alin's heart.

"But how is it that you are not married, Lian?"

The voice was Jes's, silvery cool and edged with scorn. The question was dropped into a momentary pool of silence, and all the women turned to look at the girl with the heart-shaped face and pale braids.

Lian did not reply, but looked a little apprehensively toward the red-haired woman who was nursing her babe in the corner.

Dara said helpfully, "But she is to be married, Jes. I told you. Do you not remember? To Mar."

There was silence as the women of the Horse exchanged enigmatic glances.

"Oh," said a girl far gone in pregnancy, "did Mar ask for you then, Lian? That is news."

Lian shot an angry look at the speaker. "He has not asked for me yet, Elexa. No one can ask for me yet, as well you know."

"But you told Dara you were to marry him." The speaker now was Sana, one of the Red Deer girls.

"She would like to marry him," one of the Tribe of the Horse women informed the newcomers scornfully. "She has been trying to get him ever since Eva died. But I have not noticed that Mar has ever looked her way."

As the girls of both tribes exchanged satisfied glances, Alin thought with rueful amusement: There is nothing like a common foe for drawing people together.

"Whoever takes that one takes poison into his cave." The speaker was the young red-haired mother in the corner, and the nastiness in her voice sobered everyone.

"Now, that is enough of baiting Lian." Mada's warm, comfortable voice broke the sudden tension. "There is good reason why she is not yet married, as the women of the Horse well know. Blood was shed over her. In the spring, when she is purified of her blood guilt, she will marry. And there will be many men of the Horse eager to take her into their cave."

The older woman turned purposefully to Alin. "If you and a few of your friends will come with me, I will give you the extra clothing I have stored away. It is in a passage in the back of the cave," and she gestured to the tunnel that led off from the big entrance chamber in which they were all seated.

"Thank you, Mada." Alin got to her feet, as anxious as the older woman to divert thoughts to other, safer, channels. "Jes," she said. "Elen and Sana. Come with me."

The other girls rose immediately and followed Mada and Alin into the back passage of the cave.

When they got back to their own caves, the Red Deer girls sorted through the piles of clothing.

"They are good craftswomen, these women of the Horse," Alin acknowledged a little reluctantly as she held up a heavy winter tunic made of reindeer fur. The cut of the coat was similar to the ones they made in the Tribe of the Red Deer, a simple pattern of one panel for the back and two panels for the front, with sleeves attached at the shoulders. It was the careful addition of cave-bear fur for a hood and trim at the wrists and the neck, the ornamentation of ivory and bone set into the reindeer skin in designs showing the clan's totem symbol, that made the tunic more than a simple garment. Alin turned the tunic inside out and examined the stitching. The bone needle had been wielded with exceptional skill, she thought as she felt the run of sinew stitches that held the front panel of the tunic to the back.

"Sa." It was Elen's voice. "I am surprised they gave these furs to us. They are the finest tunics I have ever seen."

"The buckskin of the shirts and skirts is not so soft as the skins we cure," said Sana.

"That is so."

"But the decoration is nicer," said Fali.

Silence fell.

"There are no boots," said Alin briskly. "That will be the first thing we must make for ourselves. These moccasins we are wearing will not do for the snow and ice."

"I wonder why there are no boots?" Dara asked. "Surely these women wore boots with the fur tunics?"

"I imagine the boots were given out to the remaining women of the tribe," Alin said. "It is only necessary to have one fur tunic, but an extra pair of boots is very useful."

Dara nodded solemnly. "That is so."

"We will need furs to make boots," said Iva. "And hides for leather for the soles."

"We will need to go hunting," said Alin with satisfaction. "I shall talk to Mar."

Initially, Mar had not been completely pleased with Huth's decision. He was relieved, of course, that Huth had agreed to the delay. But the shaman had gone even further, had taken the future of the girls completely out of the hands of the chief. And since, come the spring weather, Mar planned to be the chief, that meant Huth had taken the giving of the girls away from him.

Nothing had been said about giving the girls their own choice, Mar had thought in annoyance when first Tane brought him the news. Alin was to have requested a delay, that was all.

However, the longer he thought about it, the more Mar came to the conclusion that Huth's decision had been a wise one. Like the rest of the young men, he realized that the girls were more likely to choose mates their own age than they were to choose Altan's contemporaries.

In fact, giving the choice to the girls might actually make for a happier feeling in the tribe, Mar decided as he thought Huth's decision through carefully. No man would feel he had been neglected or slighted by his chief. The girls would do their own choosing, and there would be an end to it. This was only possible in the case of the Red Deer girls, of course, because there were no fathers involved whose property rights would be violated.

Mar had been gone from the cliff dwellings all day, checking the deep game traps the tribe had laid to the east. He was just finishing laying the fire in his shelter, when he looked up and saw Alin at the open flap that formed his doorway. He had not spoken to her since he had left her with Huth two mornings since, and now he smiled in greeting and gestured her to join him inside.

Mar had moved out of the initiates' shelter when he had married two years before, and he had not returned to his boyhood companions when Eva died. He had found he liked living alone, and since the shelter that had been his marital gift was on the first level of the cliff, able to be gained by the steep cliff path, he had been able to keep Lugh with him. In fact, Mar liked living in a shelter better than a cave. The smoke from the fire dispersed quickly out through the sticks and branches and hides that formed three of the shelter's sides, and within it stayed warm enough through even the worst of the winter. He had never been one to overmuch feel the cold.

The sun had not yet completely gone down and the shelter was still lit by the ebbing daylight coming in the open flap at the door. As Alin advanced tentatively into the single small room that formed his home, Mar gave her his most genial smile.

Lugh, recognizing the girl's scent, raised his head from his accustomed place in the corner and gave a little whine.

"Greetings, Lugh," Alin said. Then, in a noticeably cooler voice she said to Mar, "I want to talk to you."

"Sit," Mar said, and gestured to a buffalo robe heaped on the floor. "I was just about to light the fire."

"Thank you." Alin crossed her legs and sank to the ground, as supple and athletic as any of the young boys of his tribe. Mar took a hot coal from an antler container wedged in the stones that surrounded the laid wood, and held it to the tinder. After a moment, the dead leaves caught. Mar watched the fire until the flames began to snake through the wood, and then he fetched another buffalo robe from his bedplace, dropped it to the floor beside Alin, and sat down himself.

He noticed immediately that she had changed her clothes. He could recognize the workmanship of his tribe in the buckskin shirt decorated with a fringe of thongs along the line of the shoulders. She had put on a long skirt also, the kind the women of the Horse often wore.

One moccasin protruded a little from under the edge of the skirt as she sat, cross-legged, before the fire. He could see the perfect arch of her bare foot before it disappeared into the worn leather of the moccasin.

"I see you have new clothes," he said.

She had been staring into the now blazing fire, but at his words her head swung around, and she looked at him. Her hair was different too, he noticed. It was drawn back as usual, and tied at the nape of her neck, but today she wore it unbraided. He looked at the smooth shining fall of brown-gold hair as it cascaded down her back. Some strands of brown were still dark with damp. "You washed your hair," he added, and felt a sudden desire to reach out and run his fingers through the shining, silky mass.

She ignored his comments. "My sisters and I shall need boots for the winter," she said briskly. "We can make them, but to do so we will need furs. And to go hunting, we need weapons."

He drew up his long legs, propped his chin on his knees, and contemplated her in silence. Her brown eyes, fringed by the longest lashes he had ever seen, began to sparkle a little with temper. She did not like him looking at her. She was, he decided, the loveliest girl he had ever known.

He continued to rest his chin on his knees and look at her and he thought of the pile of skins near the rear rock wall of the shelter that served as his bed. He wanted very badly to take this girl back there with him . . . to lay her down.

"Mar." There was irritation and impatience in her voice. "Did you hear me? We want to go hunting. We need weapons."

He let out his breath and came out of his reverie. "Sa," he said. "I heard you." What would she do, he wondered, if he got up now and closed the flap of skin in the front of the shelter?

"I should think you must need to add to your meat supply also," she was saying. "There are now three handfuls more mouths to feed than you had a moon ago."

"That is so."

He would close the flap, and take her two shoulders between his hands. Then he would put his mouth on her mouth. His eyes narrowed a little as they concentrated on the tender line of that mouth. How soft it would feel under his, he thought. And her breasts . . .

"Very well," she snapped. "I shall go talk to Altan."

Dhu. He forced his eyes to leave her mouth. Her brown eyes were flashing in the light of the fire. "You are as simple as that Lian," she said.

He started at the aptness of her comparison. She was right, he thought. He was mooning over her in the same way Lian mooned over him. He grinned with rueful self-knowledge and ran his fingers through the loose hair that spangled his brow.

"My mind was on something else," he apologized. "So. You wish to go hunting. That is good. We must go hunting as well. You are right when you say that we are in need of meat. The traps I checked today were empty, so we must go hunting instead with our spears."

The irritation left her face, replaced by eagerness. "We will go with you if you can provide us with weapons."

He averted his eyes from her distractingly lovely face and stared into the fire. After he had thought a moment he said, "Every man of the Horse has an extra heavy spear as well as several light spears, but there are not many extra spearthrowers." He considered some more. "We will be able to provide you with one heavy spear and one light spear each, but I can provide only a few of

you with spearthrowers. Nor are there enough bows to
go around. My tribe hunts mainly bigger game." He
looked at her in faint apology. He had seen her hunt, and
he knew she was experienced. "We will make you your
own weapons. But for now you will have to make do with
what we can spare."

Alin nodded. "I understand." She leaned a little forward. "What kind of game will we hunt?"

"It is still the season for hunting buffalo. It will not
be reindeer season until the next moon."

Alin nodded again. "There must be many buffalo in
this area," she said. "I have noticed that your tribe
makes much use of buffalo hides."

"Sa. There is grassland to the east of us where we can
usually find buffalo herds."

"We did not have so many buffalo in my home hunting
grounds."

"It is too hilly and too full of trees in your homeland.
The buffalo likes open space. There are many horse herds
on the grassland as well, and deer and antelope too.
Horses are our totem, of course, and we do not usually
hunt them. This is the time of year we go for buffalo.
They are wearing their full winter coats by now, and their
hides are good for the making of clothing and robes
and," he smiled at her, "boots."

Alin leaned a little more forward. "What else do you
hunt?"

"Aurochs," came the immediate reply. "They make
the best eating of all, but they are not so plentiful as deer
or buffalo." He frowned as if he had just had a particularly unpleasant thought.

"No ibex?" Alin asked.

"Not on the grassland. We get some ibex in the hills
around the river valley here."

"Do you get mammoth?"

"Occasionally. When winter is at its coldest, mammoth will sometimes come to the upland lake that is part
of our hunting grounds."

"Have you ever hunted mammoth, Mar?"

"Sa. Once." He grinned. "It is not an experience to
forget."

Alin's great brown eyes sparkled. "I have never seen a mammoth," she confessed.

"They no longer come so far south as your hunting grounds. Often they do not even come so far south as ours." He looked at her eager face. "I will take you mammoth hunting one day if you like."

"Oh Mar," Alin said. "I would like that very much."

He half closed his lids to conceal his eyes and continued to look at her. She was lovely even when she was angry and irritated, but when she was like this . . .

She got to her feet. "I shall go and tell the others," she said. "When will we go?"

He did not get up. "I must speak to Altan," he said. "But we will need a day to make the hunting magic before we can begin a great hunt."

She looked a little puzzled. "A whole day?"

"Sa."

She searched his face with those luminous eyes, and then she nodded. "I will tell the others," she said again, whirled around so that her skirt fanned out around her legs in a circle, and then she was gone.

Mar looked around the suddenly empty shelter. He remembered how nice it had been to come in through the door flap and find a wife waiting here for him. The actual woman's face had begun to blur in his memory. She had been a good girl though, Eva, and pretty. He remembered that she had been pretty. And she had been soft between his hands, and warm and wet and yielding to his driving need.

Dhu! This was torture, to sit here like this, thinking of things that could not be.

Until the spring weather. Then, things would change for them all.

Ten

It had grown fully dark by the time Mar left his shelter to seek out Altan. He took a torch to light his way, and, with Lugh at his heels, scrambled up the cliff path to the second-level terrace, where the nirum's cave was situated. There was a rumble of voices from within, and Mar leaned his torch against the cliff face, pushed aside the deer hide that hung across the cave opening, and went in. Lugh followed.

There were well over a dozen men sitting around the smoky fire, and they all looked up when Mar came in. Five dogs were fighting over a bone in the corner and Lugh eagerly trotted over to join in the fray.

"Lugh," Mar said sharply, and, reluctant but obedient, the dog returned to his side.

Altan squinted through the smoke and stiffened visibly when he saw who it was at the door. For the briefest of moments the two men stared at each other across the fire; if they had been stallions their ears would have been laid flat back. Then Altan said, "What brings you to the cave of the nirum, Mar?" His voice was abrupt, making it clear that this was not a place where Mar belonged.

Mar had come only two steps into the cave: he made no move toward coming farther. Instead he replied briefly, "The traps were empty. We will need to make a big hunt."

"So." Altan's maimed hand fingered the leather pouch he wore around his neck. "I was just saying much the same thing. Even if there had been game in the traps, we will need more meat if we are to feed these new women.''

A murmur of agreement ran around the circle. Mar flicked his eyes from face to face, taking quick note of who was there. A number of the older men sat around the fire this night, not just the younger ones who made the cave their home. An inimical silence had fallen and the seated men were all staring narrow-eyed at Mar through the smoke.

Then the oldest of the nirum, a man who had been friends with Mar's father, cleared his throat and said, ''Will you join us at the fire, Mar?''

Tension, silent but palpable reverberated in the air. It was an honor for a young man who had not yet been made nirum to be invited to take a seat in the men's cave. Mar looked once more around the hostile faces of those at the fire, and shook his head. He smiled at the man who had issued the invitation. ''I told Huth I would visit him tonight. But I thank you, Rom.''

''Huth,'' said Tod, the man sitting on Altan's left. ''That is a strange decision the shaman has made, to allow these girls to choose their own mates. Did you and your following invent that idea?''

Mar looked at him consideringly. ''Why should we do that, Tod?'' His own voice was merely curious.

''You had all that time with the girls on the trail home.'' Sauk's harsh, gravelly tones filled the quiet cave. ''Plenty of time to seduce them to your ways.''

Mar slowly turned his head in the direction of the new speaker. ''You already have two wives, Sauk,'' he said, his voice still soft. ''Were you thinking of taking another while so many men are still without?''

The younger nirum snapped to attention.

''Sauk will take no more wives.'' It was Altan's deep voice, reassuring his own following. The chief stared at Mar. ''What he means is that you and your companions had all those days on the trail to . . . influence . . . these girls. It will not be well for the tribe if they choose the boys, and leave the tribe's men unsatisfied.''

''That is so.'' It was Zel, one of the younger nirum

speaking now. The rest of the younger men rumbled agreement.

"You lied to Altan to keep the nirum out of the raid," Zel accused Mar.

Mar raised his brows. "How did I lie?" he asked Zel.

"You said there would be great danger involved!" It was Sauk, answering loudly.

Mar smiled. "The danger did not stop the boys from coming."

A furious silence fell.

"There was no danger!" Sauk shouted at last. "You lied."

"I did not lie." Mar's voice was cold. "I said we would have to take these girls from under the eyes of the men of their tribe. This we did. I did not know we would be able to come up on them while they were performing a woman's ritual."

Lugh had been standing beside Mar, with ears pricked, listening to the sounds of the men's voices. Now he advanced toward the fire, growling softly.

"Look you," Mar said. "The dog senses that I am among unfriends."

There was a rustle of movement as the men looked at each other. Then Rom said, with genuine emotion, "No one in the Tribe of the Horse could be an unfriend to your father's son, my boy."

Mar was staring at Altan. "I am thinking there are some here who would like to forget that I am my father's son, Rom."

"We are all our father's sons," Altan said. His head was lowered and he shook it, as a buffalo does when it is bedeviled by flies.

Mar smiled grimly. Then he looked at the younger men, and said with a tinge of humor, "The girls of the Red Deer would say we are our mother's sons."

The tension eased, and a ripple of amusement ran around the fire.

Tod said, with no amusement at all, "These girls have strange ways."

"They are different from our women," Mar agreed. "And one way that they differ is that they are hunters."

He hooked his thumbs in the armholes of his vest. "They wish to go with us to get buffalo, so they can make themselves boots." He looked at Altan. "I think we should let them come."

Pandemonium erupted around the fire.

When he could once more make himself heard, Mar said, "I have seen them hunt. They are good. They will be a help to us, not a hindrance. And if they join us on the hunting trail, they will be able to see for themselves what kind of hunters are the men of the Horse."

Quiet fell in the cave.

"That is so," said Sauk, who was one of the tribe's foremost spearsmen.

"I do not like the idea of taking women on the hunting trail," said Tod. "It is not lucky."

Mar shrugged. "In their tribe, the women hunt as well as the men. I am thinking that it will be wise to keep these girls busy until the spring. After that . . ." He shrugged again.

At that, laughter ran around the fire.

"After that, they will be kept busy with other things, eh?" someone said.

Mar grinned.

Altan was staring at Mar, his big head thrust forward. The expression on his face was not pleasant.

"Let the girls come, Altan," said Zel. "Mar would not be fool enough to risk them if they were not capable of looking out for themselves."

Altan grunted. "Very well," he said. "The women of the Red Deer may come hunting with us. But if something happens to any one of them," here Altan showed his teeth, "then it is you, Mar, who will have forfeited a wife."

Some of the tension went out of Altan when the skins had fallen back into place behind Mar. He picked up the cup of sage tea he had been drinking and finished it.

"I cannot imagine women on the hunting trail," Zel was saying, shaking his head in amazement. "Yet if Mar says they can hunt, it must be so."

Altan felt a familiar flash of fury at the words. Mar,

Mar, Mar, he thought. I am sick unto death of hearing about Mar.

It had been thus ever since Tardith's death. The tribe had named Altan chief, but all had known that if Mar had carried a few more years, then would things have fallen out differently.

It was a good thing for Altan that Tardith had died while his son was yet a young initiate.

Altan had always wondered if Mar suspected aught about Tardith's death. The look on Mar's face sometimes, when he looked at Altan . . . well, there was no love lost between the two of them. All the tribe knew that.

Every day it became clearer that there was a division in the Tribe of the Horse. The boys of the initiates' cave followed Mar, as did the younger nirum who had spent a year or two under Mar's leadership before graduating to the nirum's cave. Even some of the older men, like Rom, respected Mar for his father's sake.

The older men, the ones to whom Altan had given wives, followed the chief. But every day it seemed to Altan as if more and more of his leadership was slipping away.

It was infuriating. Mar was too clever to oppose the chief directly. He just . . . constantly undermined Altan's authority.

Tonight was a good example of what was continually occurring these days, Altan thought. Mar had come into a group of Altan's own men, a group that should have been hostile to Altan's acknowledged rival, and Mar had persuaded them all to do exactly what he wanted them to.

As was happening far too often, Altan had found himself in the position of having to agree to things he did not want. But he could not afford to alienate his supporters, and the nirum had wanted the girls to come hunting with them.

"This hunting trip is a good idea," Iver was saying now, in ironic counterpoint to the chief's bitter thoughts. "If we are indeed forced to abide by this mad decision of Huth's to allow the Red Deer girls to make their own

choice of husband, it will be well to give the nirum a
chance to make an impression on the new women."

"Sa," said another. "The boys had all that time with
them on the trail home. We must have our chance too."

Sauk's loud voice sounded next to Altan's ear. "The
shaman has overstepped himself in making this decision.
No one in the Kindred has ever heard of women being
allowed to choose their own husbands."

Everyone looked at Altan.

The chief was furious. He did not wish to have to take
a stand upon this matter; he did not wish to be put in the
position of overruling Huth. The shaman carried too
much power with the older men, whose support Altan
needed.

The chief lowered his head. "Huth has said it would
be ill luck for us to take these girls to bed before the
proper time. The shaman is the one who has knowledge
of such things. If he says we must wait, then we must
wait." Altan shot a quick look to his left and then to his
right. "I am thinking that it will not be difficult for a
nirum to outmatch a boy in the eyes of these girls. Is that
not so?"

Dutifully, the men around the fire agreed. What else
could they do? Altan thought with bitter understanding.
Admit that fully grown men could be outshone by a pack
of cubs?

There were too many men in the tribe, the chief
thought as his eyes went from face to face around the
fire. Even with these girls that Mar had brought back, it
would be impossible to satisfy all the men who needed a
woman.

Altan's mind settled on the latest grudge he bore
against Mar. Mar had not lost one single man on that
cursed raid. Altan had sent him off with hopes of lessening the number of womanless men, and Mar had
brought them all back.

That was a dangerous bunch, the chief thought next,
his mind following a too-familiar path. There was a bond
among the boys of the initiates' cave that Altan feared.
They were almost a small tribe within the tribe; no other
group of initiates within Altan's memory had ever bonded

like that. Always before there had been rivalries . . . petty jealousies . . . but not in this group. This group hung together. And they followed Mar.

Altan would have been delighted to lose some of them. He would have been even more delighted if the tribe had lost Mar.

At the Ceremony of the Great Horse this year, Mar would be made a nirum. He would be made a nirum and he desired the chieftainship. Altan knew that, and he also knew to what extremes that particular desire could drive a man.

Altan did not think Mar would formally challenge him. The rules of the challenge too heavily favored the incumbent chief for it to be a feasible way for Mar to gain what he wanted.

Altan very much feared that Mar might take the path he himself had taken in regard to Tardith.

It would be better, Altan thought, to dispose of Mar, before Mar had a chance to dispose of him.

Once he was outside the nirum's cave, Mar picked up his burning torch and walked farther up the terrace until he came to the last cave in the cliffside. With the easy familiarity of a beloved son, Mar pushed aside the hide at the door and stepped inside. Just as naturally, Lugh followed.

Huth was sitting in front of the fire, his head bent over his drum, tightening the skin. Tane was there as well, drawing intently with his ubiquitous graver on a large horse bone. Sitting in Mar's old place and staring dreamily into the fire was the young, fair-haired boy named Arn who was Huth's apprentice.

Mar looked at the boy, and for the briefest of moments he felt the pain of the outsider. Then Tane looked up and saw him. "Mar," he said, and smiled. "Brother of my heart. Come and make our circle complete." And the pain fled.

Mar sat down between Tane and Huth and the two slim dark men looked at him with pleasure. "There was nothing of worth in the traps, I gather," Tane said.

Mar shook his head. "Bror and I checked every one. We shall have to make a great hunt."

"I was thinking that we would have to do that anyway," said Tane. He snapped his fingers and Lugh came over to have his ears fondled.

"Sa," agreed Huth. "There was one hunt while you were gone. Altan burned the trees beyond the river, but we did not get as many deer as he thought we would."

Mar's thick golden brows snapped together at Huth's words. "He made a fire hunt?"

"Sa." Huth looked at him. "Burning has ever been the easiest way to get meat, Mar. You know that."

"Burning is also the easiest way to destroy your hunting grounds," Mar returned grimly. He picked up a piece of leather thong that Huth had discarded and threw it forcefully into the fire. "You know how I feel about burning, Huth."

"I know. Altan knows also. That is why he waited for you to be gone to do it."

"You may have convinced most of the younger men that burning is foolish, but few of the nirum would agree." Tane looked up from Lugh's ears to tell his foster brother, "It is such a simple way to drive animals into your traps. And men have been hunting that way since time out of mind. They do not understand why you should object to it so." Tane's green eyes were sober. "This is going to be a thing that will keep the nirum from accepting you, Mar, if you challenge Altan for the chieftainship."

The fire danced across Mar's fair-skinned face, illuminating the straight, grim set of his mouth. "If we continue to burn down the trees and the plants that feed the herds, then the herds will no longer come," he said. "It is happening already. It will continue to happen so long as men are foolish enough to make such a use of fire. If ever I become chief, I will never allow a fire hunt. I swear this by the four corners of the wind, Tane."

A short silence fell in which Lugh left Tane and curled up beside Mar. Then Huth said, "I have come to think that you are right about this, my son. Fire is one of the greatest of Sky God's gifts, and we must not misuse it.

But Tane is right also, Mar. If you forbid the fire hunt, you will lose the support of many of the nirum.''

A small quiet voice from across the fire asked, "Is Mar going to challenge Altan for the chieftainship? I did not know that could be done."

The three startled men looked at the slim, fair-haired boy sitting on the other side of the fire.

"Arn," said Tane. "We forgot you were here."

"But I am here," the boy pointed out. He spoke gravely, with a solemn dignity that seemed odd in one of but fourteen years.

"Sa, you are here," Tane agreed with rueful amusement. "But you are so quiet that I fear we forget that sometimes."

"It is good for a shaman to be quiet," said Huth. "It is only thus that he can listen for the voices of the spirits."

"Sa," said Arn. "That is so."

Huth's eyes moved away from Arn and came to rest on the figure of his other foster son, Mar. Two boys had he fostered, he thought, and both of them sat this night before his fire. He loved the young lion who sat beside him, had loved him since first Mar had come into the shaman's cave when his mother had so untimely died. Even when he was but a babe, Huth remembered, holding Mar had been like holding a lion cub on your lap. Those blue eyes of his had always seen the world straight on—clearly, fearlessly. And he had the gift of calling men to him. His father, Tardith, had had that gift also, but Huth thought that it was even stronger in Mar. It was a thousand pities that Mar had been so young when Tardith had died. But it simply had not been possible to name a newly initiated boy chief.

Huth had always known that he would not find his successor as shaman in Mar. It had taken him longer to recognize that he would not find his successor in his own son either. Huth had recognized Tane's genius for drawing early, and had been glad of it. The great cave paintings that were so important a part of his tribe's ritual life needed the hand of a born artist, and it was right that the tribal shaman participate in drawing the pictures for the hunting magic. It had been a while before Huth had realized that the passion for drawing in Tane was too strong to allow room for any of the other talents of the shaman to grow. His son's vision was relentlessly outward, to the world of nature he was driven to capture so brilliantly in paint; not inward, as it must be with a shaman.

Huth had found his successor at last in this slim, silver-haired boy who sat across the fire from him in Mar's old place and waited gravely for his question to be answered. Nor had the question been improper. If Arn was to be the future shaman for the Tribe of the Horse, it was important that he know all the tribal laws and traditions.

The shaman looked through the drifting smoke into the crystal gray eyes of his chosen successor. Two boys, he thought. Two sons of the heart. One the color of the sun, the other of the moon.

He answered Arn, "It is not a common practice in the tribe to change chiefs. But it is possible."

"How is this done, my father?" Arn asked.

Huth looked at Mar, and it was Mar who answered. "A man of the tribe can challenge the chief at the time of the Great Horse Festival," he said. "If the chief wishes to keep his position, he must accept the challenge."

The crystal clear eyes asked a silent question.

Mar smiled a little crookedly, and described the challenge.

There was silence when he had finished.

"Not a thing that is easily done," Arn said.

"Nor is it a thing lightly done," Huth said. "When two stallions fight for the leadership of the herd, there can be only one victor. So it is with the challenge. One man wins and that man is the chief. The other man is like the defeated stallion. If he lives, he is driven out of the tribe and can never return."

The words seemed to drop portentously into the silence of the night.

"So," said Arn, a bare breath of sound. He looked at Mar. "You will make this challenge, Mar?"

"Sa." The answer was given calmly and firmly, and Huth felt a sudden pang. "But the challenge can only be

made by a nirum," Mar explained further. "That is why
I have waited so long. This is the year when, at long last,
I am old enough."

"You will not speak of this." It was Tane talking now,
but his tone made the words more a comment than a
command.

Arn shook his head and his soft, moon-colored hair
lifted and swung with the motion. "Na. I will not speak
of it."

Huth put down the drum that he had ceased to work
upon and changed the subject. "We shall be making the
hunting magic, then," he said. "What beast shall you
hunt? Buffalo?"

"Sa, I told Alin that we would go for buffalo. They
need to make boots for the winter, and buffalo hide will
make good boots."

"Not so good as reindeer fur," said Tane.

"We cannot afford to wait for Reindeer Moon."

"Buffalo does not taste as good as aurochs," said a
dreamy voice from the other side of the fire.

Huth and Tane laughed.

"There are not so many aurochs as there used to be,"
Mar said, and the grim look had returned to his face.
"The sacred cave is filled with pictures of bulls and cows,
but we rarely see such herds hereabouts anymore. The
burning has driven them away."

"Mar, when it comes to the fire hunt you are like a
bird with one note," said Tane with affectionate exasperation.

Mar looked at his foster brother, and the grim look left
his face. He rubbed his head, and then he laughed. "All
right," he said.

"When were you talking to Alin?" Tane asked.

"At sunset." Mar squinted a little against the smoke
that had puffed into his face, and turned to Huth. "My
father," he said, "I have a problem to put before you."

Huth tried to look exasperated. "What problem now?
It must have to do with these girls."

Mar grinned. "It does. They are coming hunting with
us, and I do not know if they should make the hunting
magic with us or not."

Now Huth did not have to pretend to be exasperated. "Make the hunting magic! Women?" He glared, not at Mar but at Tane. "First Tane wants me to take one of them into my drawing classes, and now you want to take them to the sacred cave."

Mar and Tane exchanged a glance.

"Do not look at each other like that," Huth said irritably.

"I am not saying that I want to take the girls to the sacred cave," Mar said patiently. "I do not know what it is proper to do. We have never gone hunting with women before. I do not know if it will bring bad hunting if they do not make the hunting magic with the rest of the hunters, or if it will bring bad hunting if they do."

At the moment, Huth did not know either. He stared at Mar. "Have you spoken to Altan about this?"

"Sa."

"He agreed that the girls could join the hunt?"

"Sa."

Huth snorted.

Mar said, "The rest of the nirum want to show off their prowess."

This time Tane snorted.

"Are these girls able to hunt?" It was Arn's soft voice, drifting with the smoke across the fire.

"Tane and I stalked them for half a moon last summer," Mar said. "We saw them take red deer and fallow deer and giant deer and great boar. They can hunt."

"We never saw them take buffalo," Tane commented.

Mar shook his head. "They do not have the open grass game in their own hunting grounds."

"Buffalo are far more dangerous than deer or boar, Mar," Tane said. "There are some that say buffalo are more dangerous than any of the other animals, even mammoth or lion. Why don't we wait and go for reindeer?"

"Because they need to make boots."

"They will need boots within the space of a moon," Huth agreed.

"And we will need a greater supply of smoked meat,"

Mar said. "There is not enough stored for the winter, not with the extra mouths that we have to feed."

"What shall you do about the hunting magic, Huth?" Arn asked.

Huth sighed. "I shall make a seance and ask Buffalo God," he said. "You shall help me, Arn."

The boy nodded, his eyes suddenly luminous.

"When shall you make the seance, my father?" Mar asked.

"I must fast for all the day tomorrow. Then, tomorrow night, I shall make the seance." Huth picked up the drum he would need for the ritual and bent his head once more to the task of tightening the skin that covered it. Mar rose to his feet and whistled softly to Lugh.

"I shall come and see you when my father has decided," Tane said quietly to his foster brother.

Mar nodded, bade a general good-night to the three left around the fire, and went out through the hides into the night, his dog at his heels.

Eleven

Huth fasted for all the following day, and as the night began to fall he ate three mushrooms and drummed upon his drum until the ecstasy came upon him. When he awoke it was dark. It was acceptable for the girls to enter the sacred cave to watch the hunting magic, he told Arn. They could not participate, but they should watch. Then Huth fell into a profound sleep.

The following morning Tane sought out Jes to tell her of Huth's decision. He found her at last in one of his own favorite spots, a fissure in the rocks a half mile up the river from the cliff dwellings. She had a graver in one hand and a stone in the other. Tane smiled when he saw her. How many hours had he sat thus, he thought, protected from both the chill wind and human interruption by the hidden fissure.

"I feel as if I am seeing the ghost of my younger self," he said as he came in through the narrow crevice to join her in the more open space within.

She looked up in surprise. "Oh," she said. "It's you."

"It is I," he agreed. And he told her of Huth's decision.

"The older men are scandalized," he said. "But I have a feeling that at one time in the past women were part of the ceremonies at the sacred cave." He was sitting on his heels, his back leaned against the face of the rock opposite to her. "Women did not make the hunting magic, perhaps," he continued, "but there are symbols in the cave that I think are signs of the Mother. Perhaps

at one time the Tribe of the Horse had a ceremony somewhat like this Sacred Marriage of your tribe.''

"I think that is likely so,'' Jes agreed. She put down
her tools and, drawing up her knees, linked her arms
around them. "The Mistress says that at one time all the
tribes followed the Way of the Mother. But your tribe has
lost its reverence for Earth Mother, Tane. Alin says that
is why she punished you by taking your women.''

Tane's chin came up in surprise. "That does not make
sense,'' he said. "If Earth Mother was angry at the men
of the Horse for neglecting her, why would she punish
the women?''

"I did not say that the Mother was more angry at the
men. It was the women who gave over their power.'' Jes
picked up a stick from the ground and began to scratch
in the dirt, drawing something Tane could not make out.
She said, more bewildered than accusing, "From what I
can discover, there are virtually no women's rites in this
tribe.''

Tane looked uncomfortable. "There are some. There
is an initiation rite.''

Jes flashed him a scornful look. "And immediately
after, the girl is given in marriage to some man. That is
not an initiation rite!''

"You have been busy gossiping, I see,'' Tane said
acidly. "Soon we will find our own women wanting to
go out on the hunting trail with you.''

Jes put down her stick. "And what is wrong with
that?''

Tane opened his mouth to answer, then closed it without saying anything. He looked at Jes's suddenly blazing
face, and then he started to laugh. "Nothing,'' he said
placatingly. "Nothing at all.''

She gave him a suspicious look, then looked away from
him, toward the gleam of the river visible through the
fissure. He said, "I showed your drawings to my father.''

Her eyes swung back. "What did he say?''

"He was . . . surprised.'' Tane raised one black eyebrow. "He asked me if I had actually seen you draw
them.''

"He did not think a woman could draw?''

"He did not think a woman could draw like that."

"Yet the women of your tribe have great skill with their fingers," Jes pointed out. "The winter tunics they make are beautiful."

"Our tribe is well known for the workmanship of our women," Tane said proudly.

Jes made a sound deep in her throat.

Tane stared at her. When he spoke again he sounded faintly defensive. "Perhaps it is true that my father never looked to see if there was a girl who could draw, Jes. But drawing and painting are an important part of our tribal life. If you had grown up in such a tribe, would you have been content to sew garments?"

Jes picked up the stick again and began to stab it into the ground. After a moment she shook her head.

Tane sat quietly, watching the bent head of the girl. Then he asked, "Would you like me to tell you about what you will see in the cave, or do you want it to be a surprise?"

Her head jerked up. Her lips parted. "Tell me," she said.

"That is what I thought you would say," he replied with satisfaction. He settled himself more comfortably on his heels. "Well, the first thing you will notice when you come in are the bulls . . ."

The next morning, the male hunters from the Tribe of the Horse, together with the girl hunters from the Tribe of the Red Deer, left the cliff caverns where they made their home for a short journey upriver to the sacred cave of the Horse Tribe.

They went north on foot along the river's morning side, and their traveling formation resembled that of the recent kidnapping journey: half the men went before, then came the girls, and then the rest of the men. The mood of today's party was very different from what it had been on that previous journey, however. Today the girls followed curiously, expectantly, eagerly.

The land rose higher as they walked, and when they left the river path the girls found themselves going along a track that led through a forest of pine and chestnut and juniper. Alin looked off to the east, where Mar had told her were the grasslands where herds of horse and buffalo and aurochs ran.

The thought of Mar caused Alin, who was following behind several of the nirum, to look beyond them to the front of the line, to where Mar's head rose above the heads of the smaller men. She watched him for a moment, but the ground was becoming rougher and she had to look down to mark her footing. A short time later, the men in front of her came to a halt.

Alin could not see what was happening at the head of the line, but suddenly, through the forest stillness came the sound of a great *thump*, as if a huge rock had been dropped onto the earth of the forest floor.

They keep the entrance to the sacred cave sealed off, Alin thought. They must be taking the rock away now.

The man in front of her turned and said, ''You must climb down a narrow shaft in order to reach the main chamber of the cave. There is a rope ladder.''

Alin nodded gravely.

They waited. The men who had been carrying stone lamps took them out of their packs, and one of the younger boys went from one man to the next with a live coal, lighting the wicks. When all the lamps had been lighted, the men in front of Alin began to move forward.

When first she saw it, the entrance to the cave looked like a mere hole in the ground. It was indeed narrow, and Alin thought with a flash of humor that Mar's shoulders must be a tight squeeze. Then the man who had been posted at the entrance gestured her forward, and she set her feet upon the rope ladder, and climbed swiftly down. Jes came after her.

The white, crystalline walls of the cave were illuminated by the flickering light of the lamps the men were carrying. Alin halted, looked around curiously. She saw the animals.

The paintings covered the walls and the ceilings, brilliantly colored in black and red and yellow and brown. It was the bulls she noticed first: four huge aurochs dramatically outlined in black, seeming almost to leap out at her from the walls of the chamber. Alin's eyes enlarged

and her lips parted as she stared in astonished wonder at
the painted bulls. And there were horses too . . . horses
all over the place, horses with stiff, bushy manes and
flaring nostrils, galloping all over the walls. And deer.
Alin's head swiveled around as she tried to take in the
entirety of the chamber. By the door there seemed to be
a strange unknown animal. Alin tried to see it clearly,
but the men were crowding in now and blocking her view.

Alin turned to Jes to say something, and was brought
up short by the expression on her friend's face. After a
startled moment, Alin closed her mouth and looked away.
It was not right to intrude on that kind of feeling.

The chamber they were in was large, perhaps a hundred feet long and thirty feet across. At the far end of
the room Alin could see what appeared to be a narrow
passage going off in the same direction as the main chamber. A number of the men were filing into this axial passage, and Alin found herself checking to see if Mar was
among them. He was.

Her gaze traveled away from the passage, back along
the walls of the entrance chamber. There was a second
passage, she saw, opening off of the right wall shortly
before it narrowed into the axial passage at the back. No
one seemed to be going into that passage.

Most of the men remaining in the large chamber were
pressed back against the walls, leaving the center of the
floor open. There was no sign that anyone planned to
make a fire.

"I don't see any hearthplace," Elen murmured on
Alin's other side.

"Smoke from a large fire would harm the pictures,"
Jes snapped, not even taking her eyes from the wall long
enough to give Elen a scathing look. Elen looked hurt,
and Alin laid a hand briefly and understandingly upon
her arm.

"Look," she murmured in a low voice. "There will
be music." Elen followed her look and both girls watched
the men and boys lining the right wall taking out small
bone pipes from their packs. Then all the men's heads
turned as one toward the rear of the cave, and Alin and
Elen swung around with them. Coming out of the axial

chamber was a man Alin supposed to be Huth. It was difficult to name his identity with any certainty because, upon his shoulders, where his head ought to be, was instead the head of a great black-maned horse. The horseman was dressed in a long woven grass cloak and carried a shaman's carved stick in his right hand. As they all watched in silent awe, the shaman went to sit upon a high ledge, in a place that was clearly the position of honor in the cave. He was followed by a young fair-haired boy, carrying the shaman's drum. The boy sat at his master's feet. Slowly and reverently, the rest of the men also began to take seats along the wall. After the briefest of pauses, the girls of the Red Deer did likewise.

It was intensely quiet in the cave. Alin could not even hear the sound of breathing. As they waited in the breathless, anticipatory silence, Alin looked around once more at the paintings on the white walls.

Only a hunter could have done these paintings, she thought. Only a hunter would know an animal as well as the painters of these pictures obviously did. The beasts on the wall *lived*. Never had Alin seen such an intensity of life portrayed on a flat surface. The deer in the sanctuary of her own sacred cave had the same look as these pictures, but the deer were statues. None of the pictures in the sacred cave of the Tribe of the Red Deer could match them.

Alin understood in her bones what the purpose of these pictures was. They were the spirits of the beasts, caught and held under the power of the hunters of the Tribe of the Horse.

There was movement on the other side of the cave, and Alin turned once more to Huth, the man-horse. Slowly, with a stately and impressive majesty, the shaman was raising his baton. In obedience to what was clearly a signal, the men with the pipes made out of small marrow bones raised the instruments to their mouths, and the clear high sound of music filled the cave. Then the shaman gave his baton into the hands of the fair-haired boy who sat before him, and took up his drum.

With the first sound of the drumbeat, a man leaped from the axial passage into the flickering light of the great

painted chamber. He wore buffalo horns upon his head,
buffalo paws upon his hands and feet, and a loincloth
upon which was sewn a buffalo tail around his waist.
Otherwise he was naked.

The dancer's face was painted with ochre, but Alin had
little difficulty in recognizing Altan, the tribal chief.

The drum increased its rhythm, and now other naked
men, all carrying spears and javelins, leaped forward into
the light. Alin recognized Mar immediately. No amount
of ochre could hide the size of him.

The small marrowbone pipes trilled their high clear
notes into the sacred air of the cave. Then another, deeper
sound, blown upon the thighbone of a large bird, joined
with the flutes. Under all, steady and deep, beat the pulsing rhythm of the drum. On the floor the hunters closed
in a circle about the man-buffalo, and began to crouch
and stamp in a hunting dance.

Altan mimed the buffalo brilliantly, charging, retreating, stamping, and goring with his horns. The hunters
stalked him, feet stamping in time with the drum, feint-
ing throws with their spears, forward and back, forward
and back, across the whole length and width of the chamber floor. The flutes soared higher. The horn boomed
louder. The rhythm of the drum grew faster and more
urgent, until the whole chamber was awash in a frenzy
of sound.

Now, even above the feverish music, it was possible
to hear the panting of the dancers as they passed close
by the feet of the spectators. The drum pounded; the
pipes went higher. Alin could feel the wild throbbing of
the beat of the music in her blood. Closer and closer the
hunters came to the frantically charging buffalo, still
driving him, but in an ever-decreasing amount of space.
The hunting magic filled the cave, resonated off the
watching animals on the walls, until, finally, the drum
began to beat for the kill.

The hunters closed in a circle about their prey. The
buffalo was surrounded. His bellow of outrage and defiance resonated through the cave. The first spear fell. Then
another. Then a third. The buffalo was down on the
ground, hidden from view by the circle of ochre-painted

hunters. Spear after spear fell in the flickering lamplight of the cave. A triumphant roar went up from the hunters. The drum and the flutes ceased.

The hunters in the center of the floor looked up from the dead buffalo, laughing and panting at the same time.

"A good dance." Huth's voice sounded strange and muffled from beneath the horse's-head mask. "The hunting magic is made."

"Sa. A good dance." The words were repeated around the cave. Out on the floor, Mar reached a hand down to the dead buffalo and pulled Altan to his feet. Mar's teeth gleamed white in the red-brown paint of his face as he smiled and said something to the chief. Altan shook his head as if to clear it.

"We will have a good hunt tomorrow," Altan said. "The spirit of the buffalo is ours."

The men built a great fire near the cave entrance and roasted the deer meat that they had carried with them. There was a mood almost of exaltation upon the men of the Horse Tribe. They were not exuberant—in fact, they were rather quiet as they sat around the fire eating their meat—yet a feeling of intense emotion crackled in the air.

After the food had been consumed and the fire extinguished, the hunters began to retrace their journey of the morning. Their mood was different from what it had been earlier. For one thing, the women of the Red Deer were no longer isolated from the rest of the hunters. The girls' presence at the cave ceremony had somehow brought them within the circle of fellowship all hunters who hunted together regularly knew.

Jes walked beside Tane for the entire way home, both of them absorbed in what they were saying to each other. They were talking about the pictures, Alin thought with a mixture of amusement and exasperation, as she looked at the two people walking side by side in front of her.

Alin looked away from Jes's familiar back and glanced around the rest of the group, curious to see who was pairing up with whom.

The sight of Elen's red head next to Dale's fair one did

not surprise Alin, nor did the sight of Sana walking with
Melior. Those four had become noticeably friendly on
the journey north. What did surprise her a little was the
sight of Iva walking comfortably with one of the younger
nirum. A few of the other girls had paired off with nirum
also, Alin saw. And some walked together in an all-
female group, as they had walked earlier in the morning
on the way out. But a pack of the young men walked just
behind the group of girls, and there was good-natured
banter going back and forth between the two parties.

Next, Alin looked around for Mar. Then, when she
realized what she was doing, she frowned in annoyance.
Resolutely she turned her face forward again, lengthened
her stride, and walked on alone.

In a little while a step sounded behind Alin as someone
caught up to her. Mar, Alin thought instantly, and forbore to turn her head.

"Alin," said a voice that was not Mar's, and she
turned, in surprise and dissatisfaction, to see Bror walking beside her. He gave her his attractive, friendly smile.
"What did you think of our ceremony?" he asked.

Alin made a polite answer, and smoothed the line that
had mysteriously appeared between her brows. She returned his smile. "I am looking forward to the hunt tomorrow, Bror," she said. And hardly noticed how his
face lighted at her response.

It was not until they were back at the cliff caves that
Mar finally appeared. "If you and the rest of the girls
will follow me," he said as he came up beside Alin on
the beach, "I shall give you your weapons."

Alin nodded and gestured to the girls. They followed
Mar to one of the large storage caves located high up in
the cliffside. The sun had not yet gone down and they
left the hides at the entrance rolled up so that the daylight
could come into the cave. A handful of the young men
had come in with Mar and were sorting through the pile
of weapons laid in readiness against one of the walls.

"We'll give out the spears first," Mar said to the assembled girls. "There is one for each of you."

It was Tane who handed Alin her spear. She took it

with a nod of thanks, and hefted it in her hand, testing its weight and balance. Then she rested it on the ground and examined it closely.

The shaft of the spear was very like the ones Alin was accustomed to handling at home; it was made of yew and was approximately eight feet in length. The point was different, however. It was made of bone, not of the flint they used in the Tribe of the Red Deer. Alin looked closer. The bone point was exquisitely carved, and certainly sharp and strong enough to accomplish its deadly purpose.

Next, Alin lifted the spear. The wooden shaft had finger notches carved into it, but when she tried to use them, she found that they had been made for a bigger hand than hers. The notches spread her fingers too wide for her to get a comfortable grip, and she had to turn the shaft a little so she wouldn't use them at all.

The rest of the girls were examining their weapons as well, and murmuring with pleasure. It was a good spear, Alin thought. Strong and straight. Well made.

When the girls were once again looking expectantly toward Mar, he said ruefully, "I regret that I have only five spearthrowers to give to you."

A murmur of combined disappointment and protest ran around the group of girls.

Mar shrugged and said, "I am sorry."

Tane said, "You must realize that though each man has an extra large spear, it is not really necessary to have an extra spearthrower."

"But how are we to hunt without small spears?" Jes asked. She spoke to Tane, and her voice was surprisingly mild.

Tane said, "We have javelins for each of you, but only five spearthrowers. You cannot get as good a throw without the thrower, I grant you, but if you can handle the large spear, you can surely throw a javelin also."

"Of course we can," Alin said briskly. She looked around the faces of her followers. "Now, who is to get the spearthrowers?"

"The best of the hunters, of course," said Dara immediately.

"Sa, Sa," came the sounds of agreement.

Alin nodded. "Then I would say that the throwers should go to Jes, Sana, Elen, Iva, and me."

Nods of approval all around.

Mar said, "I am impressed. If this were my tribe, there would be great outcries from those who had not been named as best."

"Why?" Dara's great gray eyes looked a genuine question. "Do you not know who are the best hunters in your tribe?"

"I am thinking that every man thinks he is among the best," Mar said with amusement.

"Truly?" Dara asked. "Or do they just make a show of thinking that?"

Now Mar grinned. "I cannot answer that question, minnow. I do not know."

"Men who follow Sky God do not learn to be humble," Alin said calmly. "I have noticed that."

Mar's grin faded. He looked at Alin, and even in the dimness of indoors his eyes got noticeably bluer. "I have not noticed overmuch humility among the women of the Red Deer."

Alin allowed her own eyes to open wide. "But you just complimented us on our humility."

"Perhaps I should have said that I have not noticed overmuch humility in the *leader* of the women of the Red Deer."

"Alin is our Mistress," Jes said, and now all the mildness was gone from her voice. "The only one she need be humble before is Earth Mother herself."

Tane made a small gesture to distract Jes's attention. But Mar and Alin stood, with eyes interlocked, and it was as if they had not heard Jes at all.

"Shall we give out the spearthrowers, Mar?" Bror asked after a moment of uncomfortable silence.

The two pairs of eyes broke apart. "Sa," Mar said. "Give them out."

The spearthrower was one of the most useful of all the implements in a hunter's arsenal, as it served to greatly increase the distance and accuracy of the javelin throw. The end of the javelin was fitted onto a peg at one end of the yard-long thrower, and when the hunter advanced the thrower up and forward, the javelin was released and flew forward to find its prey.

The spearthrower Bror gave to Alin was made out of a reindeer's antler, and on the broad tine that was the handle someone had carved a sly sculpture of a slinking hyena.

"They even decorate their weapons," said Jes in an odd, low voice. Alin looked over and saw that the holder Jes had been given was also made of antler and had carved on its handle the sculpture of a mammoth.

"I have some extra bows also," came Mar's voice, and both Jes and Alin looked up from their absorbed inspection of the spearthrowers. He continued, "We use our bows on smaller game than buffalo, but a spray of arrows will sometimes help to turn a herd."

"We will take them," said Alin. And she named the girls who were to have the bows and arrows.

"Your arrows are very straight," said Bina, as she examined the weapon Bror had given her.

"My father knows just how much to heat the wood before he passes it through the shaft straightener," Bror said with pride.

"Your father is a fine craftsman, Bror," Alin said. "We will make a good hunt with these weapons." She smiled at the young man, and, delighted, Bror smiled back.

Mar frowned.

Tane said, "That is all the weapons, I believe."

"Sa. That is all the weapons," Bror agreed.

Alin turned away from Bror to look at Mar, and her expression became noticeably less pleasant. "When do we leave?" she asked shortly.

"At dawn. Have your girls bring their sleeping rolls as well as their weapons. We will have tents in case the weather turns bad."

Alin nodded. "We will be ready."

"Good." Mar gestured toward the entrance of the cave. "That is all, then. You may take your weapons and go. Be on the beach tomorrow at dawn."

The girls smiled with pleased anticipation and began

to move toward the cave entrance. Alin stayed where she
was for a moment, staring at Mar through narrowed eyes.
She did not like what she had heard in his voice. She was
not his dog, to come when he said come and go when he
said go. He was not even the chief of this tribe!

"Alin?" It was Jes's voice and Alin turned to see her
friend standing under the rolled-up hides and regarding
her with a puzzled frown.

Without a word, Alin spun on her heel and stalked,
long-legged and graceful, to the cave's door. Behind her
she thought she heard Mar saying something, his voice
tinged with amusement. Her temper was not soothed.

Twelve

By the morning Alin had put aside her anger. She had not forgotten it, but she had put it aside, and her face was bright with anticipation as she gathered with the rest of the Red Deer girls on the beach as the dawn came up behind the cliff.

The morning air was cold, and a keen wind was blowing down the river. The girls wore their second-hand winter tunics. In addition, they had stuffed their fur vests into their sleeping rolls, in case the day should grow too warm for the heavier garments. The combination of wind and excitement had brought pink to each girl's cheeks, and Fali and Dara were playing with the dogs that had come down to join them on the rough gravel of the beach.

A few at a time, the men of the Horse Tribe came to join the girls and the dogs by the river's edge. When finally the entire hunting party was assembled they numbered some forty men, twenty dogs, and sixteen girls. Both men and girls carried large and small spears, and all the men had spearthrowers, bows, and a collection of javelins and arrows. The men also carried packs, which Alin presumed contained their sleeping rolls, tents, the means of making fire, and the tools they would need to skin and butcher the buffalo they hoped to kill. A number of the men also carried long wooden poles, from which swung a large assortment of baskets. The baskets, Bror told Alin, were for carrying home the meat, which they would smoke first to make transporting it easier.

The hunters headed east, for the grasslands where Mar

had told Alin buffalo herds could often be found. Burdened as they were with heavy winter clothing, they did not use the hunter's lope, but strode forward instead in a long, ground-covering walk.

It took them a day to get out of the trees. They slept the first night in their sleeping rolls around five leaping fires. The air was cold but still, and the men did not bother to put up the tents.

Halfway through the second morning, they reached the grasslands. There was no immediate sign of buffalo, and Altan gave orders for a tactic that the Horse Tribe hunters apparently used often. They would split into two parties, he said, and explore the plains down toward the Snake Water on parallel lines. As soon as one group spotted a buffalo herd, it was to send a messenger to let the other group know.

The men broke into the two groups very easily. Alin, shrewdly observing, saw that there was a clear division among the tribe's hunters as to which leader they preferred. There had been no question of who the two leaders were to be. Mar was younger than most of the men, but he was clearly the one everyone assumed would lead the group not led by Altan.

Not surprisingly, all the young men chose to go with Mar. But there were a number of older men, Alin saw, who joined Mar's group as well.

Then it was time to assign the girls to a group. All the girls wanted to go with Mar and the young men. Alin could see that this did not please Altan's group at all. For a moment it looked as if an argument would ensue.

"I will go with the chief," Alin said, stepping forward with her spears grasped firmly in her hands. She looked at Jes.

"I will go with Alin," she said in instant response, and came forward to stand beside her friend. Alin gave her a quick, grateful smile. Then little Dara said, "I also will go with Alin."

At this point, all the girls started to protest that they would go with Alin. Alin began to laugh. "Na, na," she said. "If everyone changes it will be all to do again. Jes will come with me, and Dara, and . . ." Her eyes swung over the group. "Fali," she said, "and Iva and Mora and Bina."

The groups were formed, the plan was understood, and the hunters moved off across the open plain.

There had been frost for several weeks, and the grass was not the thick lush green it was in the summer. Even so, it made for hard walking. After half an hour, Alin could feel the sweat starting to form under her arms and between her breasts. She stopped to change out of her fur tunic and into her vest; the rest of the girls immediately followed her example.

The hunting party continued to walk on for another hour, but though they saw several large herds of horses, and an occasional small herd of deer and antelope, there was no sign of buffalo.

It was an odd feeling to be walking so companionably with these strange men, Alin thought. These were not the familiar beardless faces of the boys they knew, but the older, more mature faces of men whose obvious interest in the girls was less lighthearted and more intent.

One of the men Alin had seen usually accompanying the chief had walked beside her for the first part of the day. Tod, he had told her he was called. He was very pleasant, and did not appear to understand that she found his uninvited hunting advice both condescending and insulting. Finally, Alin had given him a short word and a haughty stare, and he had backed away, to be replaced by a younger man whose diffidence was more to her taste.

The plain they were crossing was not like anyplace Alin had ever seen. Though it was open, it was not flat; it undulated and rippled in the sun, a sea of low grass-covered hills. There were trees on the plain, but they grew in scattered clumps, small dots on the rolling grassy landscape. Never before had Alin seen such a vast open expanse of grass. In the summer, she thought, when the grass was thick and high, it must be almost impossible for a man to walk through it.

At last the scouts in front returned to report fresh buffalo spoor, and the man walking beside Alin assured her that they were certain to sight a herd soon. Still they walked on. Alin was beginning to wonder if the scouts had been mistaken, when they came over the top of one of the higher hills and found themselves right at the edge of a great shifting herd of enormous buffalo.

The hunters stopped short, as surprised as were the animals by the suddenness of the contact. The closest beasts were but a hundred yards away from them. There was a moment of stillness, as men and animals confronted each other. Then the great beasts all swung around in the direction of the men and drew closer together. They began to stretch out their necks.

Alin thought in stunned astonishment, They are going to charge!

Then, bellowing through the strangely still air, came a fearful roar of sound. At almost the same moment, a rain of javelins came flying from the ranks of the hunters, hitting one of the big bulls in the shoulders and flanks.

The effect of the action was instantaneous. The herd turned in almost a single motion and poured down the hill and off across the valley, flowing like a ribbon of black over the grass in the direction of the deep blue horizon.

It was not until the herd was no longer in sight that Alin realized that the sound that had produced such an effect had come from the throat of Altan.

They all looked at the empty place where the buffalo had just been. "Now we have lost them again," Dara said.

"They will stop shortly, and graze until the sun begins to go down," the nirum who had been walking with Alin told Dara. "Altan will send a messenger to Mar, and we will wait here until he and his men come up to us. Then we will go after the buffalo."

It happened exactly as the nirum, whose name was Iver, had described to Dara. Two messengers did indeed run off in search of Mar, and by the time the sun had passed its highest point in the sky, Mar and the rest of the hunters had joined Altan's group. The combined hunting party promptly set off in search of the stampeded buffalo.

After two more hours of walking, they once again found the herd, this time grazing peacefully in a hollow between two of the rolling hills. The hunters managed to stop at a great enough distance to avoid spooking the animals again. Alin stood with the rest of the girls and watched the buffalo with fascination while Altan and some of the nirum conferred.

None of the girls had ever gone after such big game. Alin remembered what Iver had said to her as they walked together earlier: "A buffalo has the eyesight of a hyena, the hearing of a mammoth, the speed of a lion, and the smelling ability of a dog. Don't ever underestimate him. He is very dangerous."

As she looked at the great powerful horned beasts grazing at a little distance from the group of hunters, Alin believed what she had been told. Indeed, she was watching the herd so intently that she did not hear Mar coming up until his voice sounded almost in her ear. "Buffalo are very dangerous," he said, eerily echoing her thoughts. "They are generally ill-tempered, and you can never be quite sure of what they will do next."

Alin turned her head slowly and looked up at him. "So Iver was telling me," she said. She frowned, "But if they are so dangerous, then surely it isn't safe to get too close to them." She turned back to regard the placement of the buffalo. "Where will we throw our spears from? If we try to throw from here, the herd will only stampede again, and we will be lucky to kill any of them."

"That is why we will not throw from here," Mar replied with good humor.

Alin continued to survey the landscape before her. One of the ways the Tribe of the Red Deer made a large kill was to build a corral with trees and branches and drive the game into it. But this plateau was too open for that tactic to be successful. There was only a single thin stand of trees to the south and east of the grazing herd. To the west of the hollow was a small river. The rest was open grass.

"Where then?" Alin asked, her brow still wrinkled in puzzlement.

"The trees," came the prompt reply.

Alin looked up into his face again. "The buffalo are not anywhere near the trees," she pointed out.

He gave her that oddly boyish smile that was disarmingly attractive. "Most of us will take up positions just within the wood," he explained. "Then some of us will drive the buffalo toward the trees. As the herd gallops by, the hunters will have a good opportunity to throw their spears." He narrowed his eyes until they were mere slits of blue, and looked also at the peacefully grazing herd. "The trick," he said, "is to get the buffalo to stampede past the trees."

Alin looked away from his face and went back to regarding the buffalo. She said, "If this morning is any indication, buffalo are easily stampeded."

He grunted. "Easily stampeded, perhaps. But not so easily driven in the direction the hunter desires. As I told you before, buffalo are unpredictable."

She folded her arms across her chest. "Give me an example."

"Well . . ." He was carrying his long spear and now he braced the wooden shaft against the ground and leaned his weight on it. "I am thinking of one time when I was among those chosen to drive the herd." She saw out of the side of her eyes that he was still regarding the peacefully grazing animals, and so she watched his profile as he spoke. "It was a situation much like the one today," he continued. "There were three of us who were to do the driving, and we came charging down a hill, waving our weapons and shouting, expecting the herd to flee in the opposite direction."

He paused, turned toward her, and cocked one golden eyebrow.

Alin found herself smiling at his dramatics. "Well?" she prompted dutifully.

"They charged us," he said. "The whole mass of them packed into close formation, turned, and came straight for us. And I am telling you, buffalo run fast!"

Alin looked once again at the buffalo, and pictured the scene in her mind. She looked again at Mar, her eyes wide. "What did you do?"

"We ran," he said. "There was a clump of trees at a little distance behind us, and I ran for those trees as fast as ever I ran in my life. But even so, when I looked overd my shoulder, the herd was almost upon us.'' He gave her a look of comical horror. ''I was sweating, I am telling you that. By the time those buffalo trampled us there wouldn't be anything left even to bury.''

Alin's eyes became even larger. Her cheeks were lightly flushed, her lips parted. ''What did you do?'' she asked again.

His eyes on her face, he shrugged. ''I did not much like the idea of being killed from behind, so I shouted to the other two men to halt. Then I picked out the biggest bull that was coming directly at me—and he was close!—and I threw my spear.''

He paused again, still watching her. This time Alin didn't smile. ''Sa?''

''I thought I had got him, it looked like I had hit the right spot, but he kept on coming. Buffalo are hard to kill. You have to get them right between the neck and the shoulder to drop them with one throw.'' Mar pursed his lips slightly, remembering. ''Then—just as he had almost reached us—he collapsed. Landed right at my feet.'' Mar shook his head in rueful wonder. ''To say true, I hadn't thought much about anything except killing that one buffalo, a sort of final gesture, I suppose, but what happened was that when that big bull went down, the animals that were running behind him jumped to the side to get out of his way. Then the ones coming behind *them* parted to avoid crashing into the carcass. And the three of us stood there, in front of the fallen bull, and watched the herd gallop by on either side of us.'' He grinned at her. ''I've come close to death one or two times in my life, but I was never closer than I was that day. I still start to sweat whenever I think of it.''

Alin smiled back. Her large brown eyes were sparkling with pleasure from the tale. ''I believe you,'' she said. And laughed.

''Sa.'' His voice was soft. ''So when you say that buffalo are easily stampeded, I will agree. But they are not so easily driven.''

''Alin, I am sorry to interrupt, but we are making ready to begin the hunt.'' Alin turned to see Elen standing nearby, looking curiously from Alin to Mar and then

back again to Alin. Alin was suddenly conscious of how
they must have looked, talking together and laughing,
and the sparkle in her eyes was quenched. She did not
wish to be paired off in people's minds with Mar.

"I am coming," she said to Elen, and without a word
to Mar she swung past him and went to rejoin the rest of
the hunting party.

The plan Mar had outlined to Alin was in fact the one
decided upon by Altan and his companions. The great
majority of the hunters, including all the girls, were instructed to make a flanking move to the left that would
bring them up at the line of trees to the south and east of
the buffalo. A smaller group of men and dogs remained
behind, to drive the buffalo in the direction of the trees.
Alin looked to see if Mar and Lugh were in the party
that would drive the buffalo, and they were. Then she
was annoyed with herself for looking. Consequently, she
was in an ill temper when finally she set off with the rest
in the direction of the small wood.

Iver, the nirum who had walked beside Alin all the
morning, came to accompany her again, but he was un-
ceremoniously pushed out of his place by the older man
who usually walked beside the chief. Sauk, Alin thought,
and remembered hearing bitterness in the boys' voices
when they had said his name.

Sauk smiled at her through his heavy, dark beard. He
was a powerfully built man, with huge shoulders and
long arms, though he was not as tall as she. He smelled
strongly of sweat. He looked at her the way Mar had once
looked, and Alin was glad she was not alone with him.

He began to tell her, in great and gory detail, about
his hunting exploits. Alin listened, a distant but polite
expression fixed upon her face. It was not until he announced: "Now you girls of the Red Deer will have a
chance to see how real men hunt," that her back went
up like an angry cat's.

"The men of my tribe are fine hunters," she informed
Altan's obnoxious friend in the same haughty voice that
had banished his other friend earlier. "I can assure you,
man of the Horse, that the girls of the Red Deer are quite
familiar with how real men hunt."

His mouth fell a little open, more at her tone than at her words. Alin then deliberately slowed her steps to fall in once again with Iver, who had been walking directly behind them.

"That man is offensive," she informed the young ni-rum, unaware of how her eyes were glittering.

"His name is Sauk," Iver said, lowering his voice. "He is an important man, Alin."

"I do not like him," Alin said, glaring at the powerful, outraged back stalking before them.

"He is Altan's closest companion," the nirum told her. "He is the most famous hunter in our tribe." Iver also looked at Sauk's back. "Once," Iver said with real awe, "once he came upon two leopards fighting in the grass. As soon as the cats scented Sauk, however, they decided to forgo their own differences and go for him instead." Iver drew in a long breath. "Sauk choked them to death at the same time. One in each hand!"

There was a moment of silence as Alin took in this truly remarkable feat. Then she said, "I still do not like him."

Iver looked once again at Sauk. He lowered his voice further. "You are not alone," he said.

The flanking movement took a while, as the hunters swung very wide of the herd to keep the buffalo from catching their scent. Finally, however, they reached the small stand of trees and took up their positions.

Thus far everything seemed to be going as it ought, Alin thought, as she stood by the edge of the trees with spear and javelin balanced in her hands. The buffalo had not yet seen the men, or if they had, they had not yet been alarmed. The herd was still grazing peacefully; a number of beasts were even lying down in the grass, resting.

Then the men and dogs came racing down the hill, shouting and waving their weapons. Alin picked out Mar immediately. His story had been on her mind, and she was considerably relieved when the great herd swung away from the advancing men and set off at a gallop toward the trees. The waiting hunters lifted their spears into the ready position.

Alin watched the buffalo herd thunder toward her, her heart racing with excitement. She narrowed her eyes against the sun and the dust, and sighted a big bull running near the outside of the herd. His horns looked enormous. The pounding hooves sounded very loud in the clear afternoon air. They were coming very fast. The whole herd was heading directly toward the trees, the hounds driving them, yipping at their heels.

Dhu! What if they didn't turn? What if they came crashing right into the trees? If that happened, Alin thought, the only thing the humans could do to avoid being trampled would be to climb. She glanced quickly upward, to check the sturdiness of the tree branches directly above her.

The buffalo bulls in the front of the herd saw the small wood that was in their path and veered to avoid crashing into it, galloping instead directly alongside the clump of trees.

A deadly rain of javelins and spears began to fly through the air. Buffalo fell, slowing up the herd and giving the hunters a chance to make more throws. Alin smiled with satisfaction as she saw the bull she had sighted go down with her javelin in its neck. The thundering hooves, the crashing bodies, were so close! Alin's smile changed to a frown of frustration as she realized she did not have another javelin to fit to her spearthrower.

Then the herd was by, leaving both the dead and the dying stretched on the grass before the trees. The hunters ran out from the trees to finish the job on those animals who were yet alive.

Then the real work of the hunt began, the work of butchering and smoking the meat. While most of the hunters immediately began the job of butchering the carcasses, a smaller number went into the trees and, using sharp-edged flint tools, cut down branches of green wood to use as racks for smoking the newly butchered meat.

Alin and the girls helped with the skins, carrying them to the river and washing them clean of blood and of lumps of flesh before packing them up in baskets for the journey home. By the time the last light of the sun was gone, some of the carcasses had been fully butchered and the fires to smoke the meat had been built.

Alin stood with a few of the other girls and watched as the meat-laden racks were lifted onto the heavy Y-shaped posts that the tribe had cut. Slow fires had been made between the posts, and, carefully tended, these fires would keep the meat enveloped in smoke for at least one full day, until the thick steaks were shrunk down to black curled twists of leather. Well-smoked meat would keep for several months and was a tribe's insurance against the winter days when it would be too cold or too inclement to hunt.

Once all the racks had been filled, the men began to leave off the dirty, exhausting work of butchering. It was completely dark by this time, though the encampment was bright enough with the flames from the big fires that had been lit in a circle around its edges. The fires were to keep off the predators, as the fresh meat would be tempting bait for any cats or hyenas that might be lurking in the vicinity.

In groups of ten and fifteen, the hunters began to go down to the river to wash. Alin took some soapwort from her sleeping roll and joined a group of young men and girls who were heading for the river. The young men carried torches, to light their way and to keep off lurking predators. A few dogs ran at their heels.

After the sun had gone down, the air had turned very cold, and the river water was freezing. But Alin had been working with the hides for hours, and blood was caked on her arms right up past her elbows. Resolutely ignoring the fact that she was shivering, Alin took the soapwort and scrubbed her hands and her arms and her face and her neck. All around her people were doing the same as she, and the sound of splashing water alternated with the sound of muffled exclamations of discomfort and chattering teeth. In the flare of the torches, Alin looked at her buckskin shirt and saw that it was splattered and stiff with blood. She had a clean shirt in her roll and she thought that she would change into that when she got back to camp, and wash this one in the morning.

"Is everyone finished?" a male voice asked.

"Sa."

"Sa."

"Ready."

The replies came from all around the group.

"I am starving," the original voice said then. "Let us head back to camp."

There were no dissenters, and everyone picked up their things and fell in behind the young men who were carrying the torches.

When they were halfway back to the campfires they smelled the roasting meat. It was discernible even over the odors of offal and smoke and dead carcasses that permeated the air of the encampment.

"Come and eat!" a voice called. Alin and the others moved with alacrity toward the biggest fire, and saw that most of the other hunters were sitting around it, already eating. Someone handed Alin a hunk of buffalo steak, and she bit into it hungrily and then closed her eyes and let the juice run down her throat. It tasted absolutely delicious. She finished chewing and took another bite.

"There is nothing so good as meat after a long day's hunt," said a male voice, and Alin looked up to see Bror.

"Sa." She smiled, her teeth white in the firelight. She took another bite from her hunk of buffalo meat.

Bror sat down beside her. "The girls of the Red Deer are fine hunters," he said. "There were many of your spears in the dead buffalo."

Alin felt a thrill of pride, though outwardly she looked perfectly noncommittal. "Of course. We have never hunted buffalo before, but throwing a spear is throwing a spear." She shot him a sideways look. "The men of the Horse are none so bad as hunters either," she said.

He gave her a radiant grin.

There was a little whine, and Alin looked around to see Lugh sitting before her, his eyes on the meat.

"Doesn't Mar feed you?" she asked the dog severely.

He looked at her sadly, and whined again.

"Pay no heed to him." It was Mar's deep voice and Alin followed the sound of it and looked to the right of the fire to find Lugh's master. "I thought I had cured

him of begging." Mar sounded distinctly annoyed. "Do
not give him anything, Alin. He has been well fed, I
assure you."

Alin looked to either side of Mar and noted that he
was sitting with Tane and Jes and Dara and Elen and
Dale. They appeared to be enjoying themselves; Jes's face
still held the distinct trace of laughter. Alin felt an un-
accustomed flash of anger. I must be tired, she thought,
surprised by the emotion and trying to rationalize it. It
had been a long day.

"No food," she said to Lugh, and there was that in
her voice that caused the dog to get up immediately and
return to Mar. The dog's desertion made Alin feel suddenly and absurdly rejected. She finished her meat, said
an abrupt good-night to Bror, went off to crawl into her
sleeping roll, and fell instantly and deeply into sleep.

Thirteen

The following day the hunters finished butchering the buffalo, packed away the meat that had been sufficiently smoked, and began to smoke the rest of it. It would be at least another day before they would be able to begin the return trip, laden down with meat for the winter.

The smoking was the easiest part of the job. Once the carcasses had been stripped, the hides washed, the fat melted, and the meat readied for the smoking fires, there was nothing to do but watch and relax. By afternoon the sun had warmed the air to a comfortable temperature, and Alin and Jes and Elen took their blood-splattered clothes down to the river to wash them. A group of initiates and nirum was already there, several of them stripped to the waist in the cold air, washing off the evidence of the day's work as best they could.

"Elen!" Dale called. He was one of those stripped to the waist, and his slimly muscled young body shone like ivory in the afternoon sun. He had rolled up his trousers and was standing in the shallow water at the river's edge. Now he laughed at the girls and flung back his hair. "Join us?" he said teasingly.

"I have come to wash my shirt," Elen called back.

"Wash both shirts," Dale suggested. "The one on your back as well as the one in your hands."

Elen put her hands on her hips, tossed her red-gold braid, and said, "I am thinking perhaps I will wash your mouth for you, Dale."

Dale yelped in mock terror and Elen began to laugh.

"I'll punish him for you, Elen," Zel said, and stepping forward into the river, he pushed Dale on his bare chest. The fair-haired boy yelped in earnest this time as he lost his balance and fell backward to sit in the water.

"Zel!" Elen said in reproach, and ran forward to watch as Dale regained his feet, silvery hair sparkling with drops of river water, murder in his eyes.

The rest of the men, seeing a fight ready to begin, gathered around and started to call encouragement to the participants.

"Go for him, Zel!" the nirum cried. "Show these boys how a real man of the Horse should fight!"

"Throw him over your back, Dale!" the boys shouted. "You know how to do it!"

"Dale's but a babe," one of the nirum said scornfully to Cort. "He has scarcely grown a muscle yet." And the man flexed his own well-developed bicep in demonstration.

Cort bared his teeth. "Big words, nirum," he said. "Big words out of a big mouth."

Scarcely had the words passed Cort's lips, when Dale gracefully eluded a blow aimed by the heavier, larger Zel and came up under his shoulder to knock him off his balance and onto his knees.

Cort shot the nirum beside him a look of triumph and hooted loudly. "That's the way, Dale!" he shouted. "That's the way!"

"Zel!!" screamed all the on-looking nirum, fearful now for the honor of their cave.

"Punch him in that pretty face of his," the man beside Cort yelled. "Let's see some blood."

Out in the river the two men were fighting now in earnest, thigh-deep in the icy water, both of them ignoring Elen's pleas for them to stop. Zel redoubled his efforts and rushed at Dale, trying to take advantage of his superior height and weight.

The bottom of the river here dropped off steeply after the first few feet, and Zel's rush carried both men beyond the shallow part to topple into the deeper water beyond. They came up breathless with the shock of the cold.

The men on the shore yelled for the battle to continue as both combatants struggled to regain their footing. While this was going on, Alin pushed her way through the men until she was standing beside Elen, at the forefront of the little group of spectators. She watched as Dale and Zel came plunging out of the deeper water to stand in the shallows, dripping and shivering. Then, as Dale reached out a foot to hook Zel's leg out from under him, Alin said in a dead imitation of her mother's voice, *"Enough!"*

Dale and Zel froze into surprised stillness. The voices of the men died away as they looked at Alin. Then Lugh came cantering out of the woods, followed by Mar and Tane. Mar looked at the scene before him, taking it in. "Get dry shirts on you," he said authoritatively to the two young men in the river. "It is too cold to stand there soaking wet."

The silence was absolute as Zel and Dale waded out of the river, still dripping and shivering, and went to find dry shirts.

"What is happening here?" Mar asked the rest of the silent men, and his mild voice was in direct contrast to the look on his face.

"Dale and Zel were trying to impress Elen," Melior answered after a moment.

Mar looked at Elen and his face grew even grimmer. "Do not play men off against each other, girl," he said. "That is a game that can have consequences other than a trifling dip in the river on a cold day."

Elen was furious. "I did nothing! It is not my fault if they act like children!"

"They are not children, however," Mar said. "They are men. We had a murder done in this tribe last summer over a woman." He looked around the faces of the men who were watching him. "I am thinking that rivalry over a woman can all too easily get out of hand," he said to them.

"Murder?" said Elen, aghast.

"Sa," said Iver. "But it was only a game between Dale and Zel, Mar." The nirum's voice was faintly aggrieved. The nirum were beginning to feel that they had lost face by allowing Mar to dictate to them. "There was no need for you to stop it."

"It did not sound like a game," Mar said. "And even if it was, games can quickly turn into something else."

There was silence as all the nirum looked back at him resentfully. Mar turned to Alin. "I am thinking the women of the Red Deer will have plenty of skins to make boots for the winter," he said. "It was a good kill." His voice was genial and he came forward to stand beside her at the river's edge.

"Sa," Alin replied. Like Mar, she sensed the resentment in the air and felt it was time to lighten the atmosphere. So even though she was annoyed with him for his chastisement of the innocent Elen, she backed him up by smiling generally around the group and saying lightly, "The men of the Horse are fine hunters. We are impressed with the kill."

The young men, their pride restored, grinned cockily at her praise, and Mar looked down at her, his blue eyes glinting.

For the first time, Alin noticed how filthy he was. Earlier she had seen him engaged in some of the heaviest of the butchering work. Even his hair was matted with dried blood; he must have run his hands through it, Alin thought, with a mixture of disgust and amusement.

"I hope you have a good supply of soapwort," she said expressionlessly.

"Sa," he replied, grinned, and held up a filthy hand to show her the plant clutched in his fist. His teeth were the only clean thing about him, Alin thought. She turned away and bent to remove her moccasins and roll up her trousers so she could wade into the water to wash her shirt.

There were splashing sounds behind her and Alin heard Mar say something in a muffled voice. She finished with her trousers, picked up her bloodstained shirt, and turned to carry it to the river.

She halted as she saw that Mar was there before her. He had waded hip deep into the freezing water, and was making suds with the soapwort and scrubbing his hands and his arms. Like the boys, he had taken off his shirt and was naked to the drawstrings of his trousers. His skin was as fair as Dale's, but there the resemblance between the two ended. There was nothing boyish about Mar's body. Those wide shoulders and strong upper arms, the muscles flexing smoothly as he squeezed the soapwort and scrubbed his skin, belonged to a grown man. Even the slim waist and narrow, supple hips did not look boyish.

Alin realized she was staring at him, and flushed. She stepped quickly into the water herself, and yelped involuntarily at the shock of the cold. Mar heard her and turned to look.

"You've only got your feet wet," he said. "You should feel it out here."

"No, thank you," Alin replied firmly. "There is quite enough water to wash my shirt right here."

He peered down at his chest and dabbed at a streak of blood that had evidently leaked through his clothes. The hair on his head was thick, but his wide muscular chest was only lightly dusted with gold. He looked up. "Be a good girl and wash mine too," he suggested.

Alin stared at him in stupefaction. "Wash your shirt?"

He began to scrub his arms near his elbows. The water around him was staining red. "I butchered your meat for you," he pointed out.

"I will wash your shirt for you, Mar," Elen said graciously.

"The man can wash his own shirt," Alin snapped.

"I don't mind, Alin," Elen assured her. "It would not be proper for you to do it, but I can easily scrub it along with my own."

"Thank you, Elen," Mar said.

Jes said to Tane, in a voice so sweet that anyone who knew her would instantly take warning, "Would you like me to wash your shirt, Tane?"

"Not at all," Tane said hastily. He had yet to go into the water, but he was much cleaner than Mar. Tane had been tending the fires, not doing the butchering. "My shirt is not that dirty," he assured Jes.

"Elen will do it," said Alin. "And, since she is in

such a generous mood, she can do mine and Jes's as well.''

Elen stared at her leader, her hazel eyes wide with astonishment. ''But Alin . . .''

''Sa?''

Alin and Elen looked at each other. It was Elen's gaze that fell first. Then, ''All right,'' she said. Her voice was expressionless. ''I will wash the shirts.''

Dale and Zel had put on dry shirts as ordered, and now they came up to the girls just in time to hear the last part of the conversation.

''I will help you wash the shirts, Elen,'' Dale offered gallantly.

''So will I,'' said Zel instantly.

''Me too,'' said Cort from behind Zel.

Out in the water, Mar began to laugh. Alin gave him a furious look. He grinned at her, then ducked his head under the water and began to suds his hair. Alin said to Elen, ''When you are finished I shall be at the camp.'' Then she and Jes strolled away, leaving Elen washing shirts with the help of every young man in the vicinity who could get his hands on one.

''What ever possessed Elen to volunteer to wash Mar's shirt?'' Alin asked irritably when she and Jes were out of earshot.

''The sight of Mar without the shirt, I imagine,'' Jes answered drily. After a moment she gave her rare chuckle. ''I am thinking I would love to draw Elen and her followers washing our shirts.''

Alin grinned. ''I don't think Elen will end up washing any shirts at all.''

''We must send her to do all the laundry from now on,'' Jes suggested. And both girls broke into peals of laughter.

Under Mar's watchful eye, the shirts were washed in forced amity and spread out on some rocks to dry. Then Elen returned to the camp, escorted by six eager young men.

''She is a very pretty girl,'' Tane said to Mar as the

two stood by the river's edge and watched Elen and her followers depart. "But she's not like Lian, Mar."

"I know that." Mar had pulled on a clean buckskin shirt and was slowly tying the leather strings at his throat. Next, he looked around for the clean trousers he had brought, and, stripping off the soaking wet ones he had worn into the river and washed while they were still on him, he began to put on the dry. "None of these girls of the Red Deer are like Lian. But that doesn't mean there can't be trouble over them, Tane."

"I suppose that is so."

"They are accustomed to being the equals of men." Mar tied the trouser drawstring at his waist, looked at Tane and grinned. "Did you see the look on Alin's face when I asked her to wash my shirt?"

Tane shook his head. "I was behind her."

"I am thinking she could not have looked more astonished if I had asked her to mate with me right there on the shore in front of everyone."

There was a startled silence. Then Tane said, "That remark is not like you, Mar."

Mar ran his fingers through his wet hair, then shook it, as a dog will shake himself when he comes out of the water. Drops flew, and Tane backed away. "I'm freezing," Mar said. "Let's go back to the camp."

Tane obligingly fell into step beside his foster brother. They walked for a short while without talking, Mar whistling softly between his teeth. Finally Mar said, "I suppose I said that because it is on my mind." He ran his fingers through his hair once more. It had begun to dry to its usual sunny color, feathering at the edges into wisps of curl.

Tane sighed. "It is on all our minds. You are right when you say the situation is fraught with danger. My father's decision has . . . complicated things."

"Sa. At first I thought it would prevent ill feeling among the tribe to have the girls choose their own mates. And, if the situation were a normal one, that may be true. But not when the numbers are so uneven."

"I do not know what we can do about it," Tane said.

"The girls have until the spring weather to make their choices. We must just wait until then."

"Sa," Mar said grimly. They walked in silence for a while. Then Mar said forcefully, "I did not like the sound of that fight, Tane. Initiates against nirum. I did not like it at all."

Tane grunted.

"Perhaps I will talk to Alin," Mar said. "If she can be made to understand how . . . volatile . . . the situation is, if she would explain matters to the girls. . . ."

Tane nodded. "She has them firmly under her rule. They will do what she says, that is certain."

Mar said, "Things will grow much worse with the winter weather, when we are confined within the caves and there is little hunting."

Tane puffed out his cheeks and blew. "It could grow ugly," he agreed. "And I am thinking there is little hope our own chief will do aught to help the situation. In fact, he would probably be delighted if the nirum killed some of the boys. He hates the initiates. He knows they follow you."

"Altan." Mar said that name as if it were a curse.

"He has grown worse of late," Tane said. "More openly hostile. He and that creature of his, Sauk."

"He is afraid," Mar said with some satisfaction. "He knows the time is drawing near when I will be made a nirum."

Tane rubbed his nose. "He also knows what the challenge is, Mar. It is nigh on impossible. I doubt that he thinks you can do it."

"I can do it." Mar was grim.

"You think you can, but I doubt that Altan does."

"Altan may be thinking I mean to take the chieftainship by foul means if I cannot win it by fair." Mar's voice was deeply bitter. "It is a thought that would come to the mind of a man like that."

Tane turned to stare at Mar's profile. "You think he killed your father, don't you?" Tane asked at last. "I have always wondered . . ."

Mar was looking at Lugh trotting in front of them. Then, "Sa," he said. "I think he killed my father. I have always felt it . . . here," and he pointed to his heart. "But I cannot prove it."

Tane nodded slowly. After a moment he said, "If it is so, Mar, then you will need to watch your back."

"Lugh will watch my back for me," Mar said with confidence.

"Lugh," said Tane soberly. "And me."

The smoking fires went on all the afternoon. The hunters had dragged most of the buffalo carcasses into the woods and, with appropriate words of thanksgiving to Buffalo God, had left what remained on them for the scavengers. But the stench in camp from the smoke and the carcasses was far from pleasant. When Mar told Alin he wanted to talk to her, and asked her to take a walk with him, she agreed with alacrity.

"I will come too," said Iver, the nirum who had been sitting with Alin and Jes and a small group of others before one of the tents that had been pitched for the night.

Mar looked at Alin and, very slightly, shook his head. Alin said to Iver, pleasantly, but in the unmistakable voice of one who expects to be obeyed, "Another time."

Mar saw with amusement the man's shock at that confident dismissal. Alin seemed not to notice, but rose with lithe grace to her feet and came to fall into step beside Mar. They walked in silence until they were beyond the camp, and then he said, "You are the only woman I have ever walked with whom I do not have to shorten my stride to accommodate."

Her long lashes lifted for a moment as she glanced up at him. "You may be bigger than I am," there was a definite trace of bitterness as she said that, "but I have long legs."

"Sa," he agreed. "You do."

"What did you want to talk to me about?" she asked abruptly.

"This morning," he answered, his tone as abrupt as hers had been. "I did not like what I saw happening at the river."

"It was not Elen's fault!"

"I am not saying that it was Elen's fault. And if we

had not had that trouble last summer, perhaps I would not say anything at all. But there was the smell of something in the air that I did not like, Alin." He reached out a hand to stop her. "Nor did you. You would have halted that fight if I had not come. You know it."

She looked up at him for a moment in silence. The day was drawing on toward sunset and the wind had picked up. The cold had brought a faint pink color to Alin's cheeks and to the tip of her straight delicate nose. The wind stirred the smooth brown-gold hair at her temples. Her large luminous eyes looked thoughtful. "Sa," she said at last, with palpable reluctance. "There was something in the air I did not like."

He grunted. "Two stallions fighting over a mare. It can be dangerous."

Alin said coldly, "That is the stallions' problem, not the mare's." And she turned and walked on.

They were coming up to the river, and from within the short scrubby trees that grew alongside it came the sound of animals growling. As Alin and Mar approached they could see five wild dogs engaged in killing a pig. To Alin's surprise, Mar immediately fell to his knees and threw his arms around Lugh's neck.

"Stay, Lugh!" he commanded.

The dog whined and pulled against the man's iron grip, but let himself be held. The wild dogs yanked and tore at the dying animal, and the whole picture was bathed in red from the light of the setting sun. Lugh quivered and shook, but he stayed within Mar's hard embrace. Within a few minutes the pig was dead and eaten and the dogs had run off to find new prey. Mar released Lugh.

"He hates pigs," Mar explained to Alin. "I do not know why, but when a pig in involved, Lugh loses all reason."

"He is usually so obedient," Alin said with amazement.

"Not when a pig is around," Mar returned.

At the river they saw a family of red deer drinking. "Soon the reindeer will be here," Mar said. The two stood for a moment, watching the deer sip daintily at the river's edge. Then Mar added, "It will be a long winter for the men of the Horse, I am thinking."

Alin said nothing. He noticed again how utterly still she could be.

"Alin?" he said softly. "Would it not be possible for the Red Deer girls to make their choices before the winter?"

At last she looked at him. The sunset was a red glare over the river, pouring through an opening in two high-piled clouds. The reddish glow illuminated her face, glistened off the exquisite cheekbones and fragile-skinned temples, and made a mystery out of the darkness of her great eyes.

"I think you are forgetting how we came here, Outlander," she said. "We had a home in the Tribe of the Red Deer. We had families. Dara and Fali still cry at night because they miss their mothers. Mora cries because she misses the boy she was to wed. We are all missing our parents, our brothers, our sisters." Mar's eyes had narrowed a little as she spoke, and he was watching her face intently. "Na, man of the Horse," said Alin bitterly, "we cannot make our choices before the winter. And if your men fall to imitating fighting stallions, that will be for you to deal with. Not me."

"I see," said Mar.

"Good. Perhaps we ought to go back." She turned her shoulder to him, but he reached out and caught hold of her, wrenching her around to face him again.

"I see," he repeated. "All of this delay is just a ploy, isn't it? You have no intention of wedding with us. You are only trying to gain time for yourselves. Are you thinking that the men of your tribe will find you, after all?"

Alin did not attempt to pull away from his grip. She must have known she could not. She put up her chin, stared back at him, and said nothing.

"If I tell this to Altan," he said, "he will give you out to the men now."

"He cannot go against Huth," Alin said a trifle breathlessly. "You said that yourself."

"Huth will agree also," Mar said. "The tribe cannot

afford to lose you.'' His face was as hard as his hands and his voice. ''If you go, there will be no women for the young men and the boys. They will leave. The tribe will die. Altan cannot allow that to happen. Huth cannot allow that to happen. I will not allow that to happen.'' His fingers had tightened on her upper arm and he felt the muscle under them quiver. He realized he must be hurting her, and relaxed his grip without letting go completely.

Alin said, ''The only way you can be sure to hold us is to tie us down. Make us live with a man we do not like for all the winter, and we will be gone with the reindeer in the spring. That is something you can be very sure of, Mar.''

He looked into those steady brown eyes and realized she spoke the truth.

''I thought it was so clever of me to find a tribe like yours,'' he said slowly, still looking into her eyes. ''I thought you would be easy because your men would not fight for you. I had not thought about you fighting for yourselves.''

''You would have done better with women like your own,'' Alin agreed.

He rubbed his forefinger lightly on her right arm. ''I do not know,'' he said. A bright blue light came into his eyes. ''The men of the Horse have always liked a challenge.''

Alin looked skeptically at his suddenly boyish face. ''You think you can hold us?'' she asked. ''How?''

He smiled. ''You do not know this, of course, because your tribe does not go to the Kindred Gatherings. But the men of my tribe are known to be great lovers.'' He began to exert more pressure on her right arm, forcing her to take a step toward him. ''I am thinking that your girls may find they will not want to leave us in the spring.''

He put his other hand on her left shoulder and drew her closer. He saw the surprise in her eyes, and then the disbelief. ''Alin,'' he said. ''You are so beautiful.'' And, bending his head, he put his mouth on hers.

He could feel the shock that ran all through her at the touch of his mouth. She stiffened and pulled back, hard, against his hands. "Na," he murmured. "Do not do that." He took one hand away from her shoulders and brought it up to cup the back of her head. Fierce, hot passion rocked him. He wanted her. He wanted to hold her hard between his hands, to capture her and hold her down, to drive into her . . . again . . . and again . . . He shuddered with the effort it took to get himself under control. More than anything else, he did not want to disgust her . . . to frighten her.

Her head fit into his hand so perfectly. Her mouth under his was so sweet. So very sweet. He bent to it, bent over her so that the whole length of her body was pressed against his. She had stopped pulling away. He felt her softening, felt her slender body relaxing, fitting into his. He wished fiercely that she was not wearing a fur tunic. He moved his mouth on hers a little: asking, seeking.

A flock of birds glided over their heads, coming in to land on the shore to drink from the edge of the river. Alin pulled back again, and this time Mar released her. They stood for a moment, face to face, separated by scarcely a hand's breadth of space. Mar made a heroic effort to control his breathing; he did not want her to see how affected he had been by her touch.

Her huge eyes were unreadable. There was a faint flush of color along the lines of her cheekbones. The more he looked at her, the more he realized how utterly beautiful she was. He had absolutely no idea what she was going to say.

She said nothing. Instead she turned and began to walk back toward the camp. Mar hesitated, and then caught up to her. He stared down at her as she walked beside him, her head bent a little forward, her long braid hidden under her fur tunic. She looked thoughtful.

"Alin?" he said at last, feeling absurdly tentative. He had never felt tentative with a woman in his life.

"What will you say to Altan?" she asked.

His own expression became thoughtful as he realized that she was not going to mention the kiss at all. He said, "What do you think I should say to him?"

"Nothing."

"I do not know if I can do that."

At that she stopped. "If you say nothing to Altan," she said, "I will do what I can to help keep the peace for the winter."

"You will help to keep the stallions quiet?"

"Sa." She shrugged. "We must stay here for the winter. There is no help for that. Come the spring weather . . ."

"You cannot get away from us," Mar said. "Your girls are good hunters, and they are fast, but you cannot get away."

Alin said, "The men of my tribe will come for us. My mother and the men of my tribe."

He looked at her searchingly. "Is it so?"

"The men of the Red Deer revere the Mother. But they are men, Mar. In every way but that, they are the same as you. They will come."

"I buried the trail."

She shrugged.

He rubbed his head. "It is more complicated than I thought it would be," he admitted, "this kidnapping of women."

"It is because you want wives, not captives, that you are having all this trouble," Alin said. Her voice was kind. "I understand you better now, too. I understand the necessity that drove you to take such an action. It was a terrible thing that happened to your tribe."

"Sa," he said somberly. "We are missing our wives and our mothers and our sisters, too."

"I am starting to think that, even if our tribe comes for us, some of the Red Deer girls may choose to marry with your men," Alin said. "There are some fine men among the Tribe of the Horse." And she began to walk on again slowly, her hands thrust within the sleeves of her fur tunic.

He followed. "What of this Sacred Marriage you promised Huth you would make for us?" he asked. "Was that tale a lie also?"

"It was your idea that I tell Huth I would make the Sacred Marriage," Alin pointed out. "Perhaps you have forgotten that. I have not."

"I doubt you ever forget anything you can hold against a man," Mar said bitterly.

"Don't sulk." Her voice was softly amused.

He ran an impatient hand through his hair. This discussion had not gone as he had planned at all.

"From what you are saying, you will give the Tribe of the Horse the trouble of feeding you over the winter, and then come spring you will be gone, leaving us worse off than we were before!" He did sound sulky. He could hear it himself. He frowned in annoyance.

She opened her mouth. Before she could speak, however, he warned, "Alin, do not dare tell me we have brought it on ourselves."

She met his eyes. She closed her mouth. Quite evidently, that was what she had been about to say. He supposed he couldn't blame her. He whistled to Lugh, who had ventured off too far.

He said, "What of the Sacred Marriage? Is it true what you told me, that it is a powerful fertility rite?"

"Sa." Alin kicked a dried piece of dung out of her path. "That is true. It is made between the Mistress and the man of her choice, at Spring and Winter Fires." Seeing him about to interrupt, she added, "It is very powerful."

He was frowning. "I thought you told Huth the marriage was made between the Mistress and the chief of the men."

"That is true. But the chief of the men in my tribe is whoever the Mistress chooses."

There was a pause. A small animal rustled in the grass in front of them and Lugh took off in chase. Mar asked, "And that is the life you were to have?"

"Sa. I am to be Mistress after Lana."

He walked beside her in silence, struggling with unfamiliar emotions. At last he said, in a voice that he did not recognize, "Will you make this Sacred Marriage for my tribe, Alin?"

Her head jerked around toward him. Her eyes were wide. "If I say I will not, will you tell Altan?"

He looked into her eyes. Responding purely on instinct, he slowly shook his head.

The large brown eyes remained fixed on his face, but all of a sudden they seemed to turn inward. He saw them go out of focus and he reached out to grasp her arm, to keep her from stumbling. They halted once more.

Ten feet to their left, a bevy of birds rose from the grass and ascended noisily into the sky. Alin's lips parted, and her eyes focused to follow the birds.

"Sa," she said, when the birds were but specks in the sky. Her voice was filled with an odd note of wonder. "I will do that for your people, Mar. It is very strong magic, the Sacred Marriage. And this time will be particularly powerful, for it will be my first. It will bring you fertility: children for the tribe, foals for the herds." Her voice was very soft, very compelling. Her enormous brown eyes were luminous. "It is in my heart that it is the Mother's wish that I do this for the Tribe of the Horse."

He pursed his lips in thought. "And this Sacred Marriage takes place at the first of Salmon Moon?"

"Sa. In your tribe it is called Salmon Moon. It must be done then, when the ibex come down from the mountains and the deer fawns are beginning to drop."

The faintest of smiles touched his mouth. Salmon Moon, he thought, was the moon *after* the Great Horse Ceremony. If things went as he planned, Mar himself would be chief at the time of Salmon Moon.

Alin was still talking. "I will do this for you, Mar, because it is in my heart that the Mother has called me to bring the people of the Horse back to her worship. You have forgotten her in this tribe. You have forgotten the Goddess, who is the giver of life."

He shook his head. "My father and my father's father and his father before him, all have been followers of Sky God. That is the way of the Tribe of the Horse, Alin. Our chiefs are chosen by the men of the tribe; they are not the mate of the sacred woman." His newly washed hair was blowing in the chill evening breeze, and he pushed a feathery, sun-colored strand away from his cheek. "Do not think to change us."

She did not answer. She smiled.

Many miles to the south, the Tribe of the Red Deer had also held an early-winter hunt. The snow fell sooner in the mountains, and it was snowing when Tor and the men returned to the Greatfish River, their deer kill slung across their shoulders.

Lana was reclining by the fire in her hut, and she looked up slowly when the door flap opened and the figure of Tor stood between her and the snow-filled sky. His furs were thickly frosted with white.

"Come in," Lana said. The man obeyed, coming into the warm dim light of the hut. "You had better get the snow off your furs before it begins to melt," the Mistress said, gesturing to a piece of wood that was propped in the corner. Tor nodded, fetched the wood that was curved like a saber, went back to the doorway and energetically began to beat the snow crystals out of his skin coat, to keep it from getting wet.

"So," Lana said when he was finished. "You had a successful hunt?"

"Sa." The man's voice was quiet, but it was a quiet that sounded forced. "In more ways than one."

Lana sat up, more in response to his tone than his words. "What do you mean?"

Tor sat on his heels across the fire from her. "On the first night out, as we made camp, three strangers came to join our fire. We fed them, of course, and then they told me a strange story."

Lana's face had sharpened. She leaned a little forward.

"They told me of a tribe that had lost all of its women and children to a poisoned water hole," Tor said.

The two looked at each other.

"*That* is the tribe that took Alin," Lana said at last.

Tor nodded gravely. "It seems likely."

"What could they tell you of this tribe?" Lana said, her voice urgent.

"Very little, unfortunately. It was called the Tribe of the Horse, but there are several tribes that have the horse for a totem. These men heard the story in the west, however, so I am thinking that this Tribe of the Horse must dwell somewhere to the west of us."

"Sa," said Lana slowly. "I would think that too." Her eyes went beyond Tor, to the closed flap of the hut. "The snows have started," she said bleakly. "There is nothing we can do until the spring."

"The girls will be all right, Mistress," Tor said. "If it is indeed this Tribe of the Horse that has taken them, the men will be very tender of their welfare."

"That is so." Lana let out her breath in a long, careful sigh. "This is good news, Tor. The first news we have learned that might prove useful."

The man nodded, then rose to his feet, reaching for his fur tunic.

"Where are you going?" Lana asked.

Very faintly, the man's brows lifted. "Home."

"Don't," said Lana softly. "Stay the night here."

After an infinitesimal pause, the man dropped the fur tunic once more, then walked around to her side of the fire.

PART TWO

The Winter

Prologue

Alin sat on the terrace outside the girls' cave, keeping a steady watch on the sunset. It had rained earlier in the day, a cold driving rain, and Alin had feared her lunar watch would be ruined. But the rain had lifted suddenly, and the sun was triumphantly going down over the river in a blaze of orange and red.

Most of the tribe were still at supper, eating and talking behind the snugly drawn hides that protected their caves from the wind that was blowing down the valley. Only Alin was out of doors, dressed for the chill in her fur tunic and hood, sitting on her heels with her back pressed against the limestone rock of the cliff face. Arranged neatly beside her on the ground were the long leg bone of a deer, a stone burin, and a round hammer stone. Tane had found her the necessary tools earlier in the week.

Alin blew on her fingers, then thrust them once again inside the sleeves of her tunic. Her breath hung white in the chill air. At last, just as she had taken out her hands to blow on them once more, the sight that she had been watching for appeared: a small sliver of a moon floating in the western sky over the sunset. Alin stared hard to make certain that it was not merely a wisp of a cloud.

It was the new moon.

"Welcome, First Moon," Alin said out loud in the lilting tone of voice that her people always used for ritual. "May your face in the sky bring good fortune to the tribe."

Alin felt a thrill of awe as she said the prescribed words. Never before had she been the one designated to keep the sacred moon calendar of the tribe. That had always been the duty of the Mistress. But Lana had instructed her chosen successor in the ritual, and now that the task had fallen upon Alin, she was profoundly grateful she knew what must be done. She picked up the leg bone and wedged it between her feet to hold it steady. Next she took up the burin and hammer stone, and with a swift, expert blow she notched the correct mark onto the surface of the bone. Then she looked up at the pale splinter of moon, and chanted the remainder of the ritual words.

When she had finished she paused. She looked from the moon down to the mark she had chipped into the bone. Every day after this one she would chip another mark, until this moon had disappeared under the rim of the morning side of the sky. Then, when the new moon appeared over the afternoon sunset, she would begin the count again, using a different-shaped mark.

She looked at the single mark set into the smooth, polished bone. "This is the first moon of our captivity in this tribe," she said, and her voice no longer held the ceremonial lilt. It sounded rather as if she were making a promise. "This is the first moon of the winter, Reindeer Moon. When the time comes for the moons of the spring weather, the women of the Red Deer will once again be free."

Fourteen

The new moon marked the opening of reindeer hunting season for the Tribe of the Horse, and the day after the new moon was officially noted by Huth upon his own calendar, Altan made the ritual kill of the first reindeer.

The killing of reindeer was always easy. The herds migrated along the same tracks year after year, and the hunters had only to post themselves at a river ford and spear the reindeer as the herd swam and waded across. The first reindeer of the season, however, was always slain by the chief. It was not eaten. As a sacrifice to Reindeer God, it was ritually carved and buried. Then its antlers were hung in the nirum's cave for the whole of the year until they were replaced by the first reindeer antlers of the succeeding winter.

The girls of the Red Deer were finding that winter in the valley of the Wand River was considerably milder than the weather they had been accustomed to in the mountains. Though the valley was windy there was little snow, and the cliffside caverns were well positioned for the winter weather: the sun of Reindeer Moon hung very low in the sky, and the way the caves and shelters of the Horse Tribe were situated, the low sun shone deep into them for the greater part of the day, warming the stone and the people who dwelled within.

The girls occupied themselves during the growing part of Reindeer Moon with working the skins they had taken on the buffalo hunt. The women of both tribes had come to an amicable agreement about their areas of expertise.

The girls of the Red Deer were superior in preparing the skins; all could see that the buckskin of their garments was softer and more pliable than the buckskin produced by the women of the Horse. And the women of the Horse were superior in sewing and decoration. So the girls of the Red Deer volunteered to prepare the skins, and then to turn them over to the women of the Horse to be worked into clothing.

The problem of boots for the new women had been quickly solved. Mada had collected a few extra pairs from the Tribe of the Horse, and then all the women joined together to make the rest of the boots that the Red Deer girls so sorely needed. The work went quickly, as there were so many hands involved. And the women of each tribe watched curiously to learn the secrets of the other.

Thrown into such close proximity, Alin could not help but be appalled at the true poverty of the life the women of the Horse led. Not only did these women lack any religious rites of their own, but they also lacked the close fellowship that the girls of the Red Deer shared. Part of the reason for this was the lack of ritual, Alin thought. And part of it was that in the Tribe of the Horse, a woman's first allegiance was to her man.

"That is so also among the married folk of our own tribe," Sana said when Alin commented on this fact one afternoon while the two of them were rubbing skins in a corner of one of the big caves out of the hearing range of the others. "I remember well how my mother would spend much time cutting up fish and wrapping it in a packet of leaves to cook over hot stones, because that was how my father liked it." A little reminiscent smile curved Sana's lips.

Alin was silent. "I suppose that is so," she said at last. "I am thinking that perhaps I find the women of the Horse so strange because I have never lived in such a family."

"You are the Chosen One," Sana said. "Your life has been different."

"Sa," said Alin slowly.

"I think *we* are different, though," Sana said unexpectedly. She put down the bone tool she was using to

rub the skins, rocked back on her heels and looked at
Alin. "The women of the Red Deer have always learned
to hunt, true, but it was your idea, Alin, to make a girls'
hunting companionship. And I think because of that,
there is a stronger feeling among us than there is among
the rest of the women of our tribe."

"The boys always had a hunting companionship," Alin
said.

"Sa." Sana smiled at her. "It was a good idea to do
the same for the girls. We were missing the best of the
fun."

Alin grinned and flipped her braid back over her shoulder. "Sa," she said. "We were."

"Alin," said a clear, imperious voice, and Alin looked
up from her work to see a sturdy little boy standing beside the skin she was working. "What are you doing?"
the child asked.

"We are rubbing the buffalo hides, Ware," Alin answered gravely. "It is a thing you must do when you are
making them into buckskin."

"Why?"

"It makes them soft."

The child nodded his curly brown head and squatted
to peer more closely at the skin that was pegged out along
the ground.

Five-year-old Ware had lost his mother in the tragedy
of the poisoned water hole. He had been one of three
tribal children left motherless, and Altan had given the
fathers of these children first choice at the new women
the tribe was able to acquire at Kindred Gatherings. The
rest of the tribe had not been as impressed by Altan's
selflessness as they might have been had not Altan himself been one of the fathers in need of a wife. Ware,
however, had no father, having lost his the previous year
to an enraged woolly rhinoceros at a river crossing, and
Mada and Rom had taken in the child to rear.

For a reason Alin could not fathom, Ware had become
very interested in her. He followed her around and
watched her constantly out of large, solemn, dark gray
eyes. Alin wondered if she reminded him of his mother,

but when she asked this question of Mada, the older woman had said there was no physical resemblance.

For her part, Alin found the little boy intriguing. For a girl who had grown up in a tribe with many children, Alin was strangely unfamiliar with them, and Ware was almost the first child with whom she had had any ongoing relationship. She had always been kept separated from her half brothers. Lana had never nursed her sons, had given them over to the care of a nurse almost immediately after they were born. They were only boys. They were not worth the attention of the Mistress.

Alin didn't question the way her mother chose to conduct her affairs, but she was conscious of finding a pleasure in the company of children that she had not been allowed to enjoy in her own tribe. And this motherless little boy, with his curly hair and big gray eyes, pulled at her heartstrings in a way she found unsettling yet oddly sweet.

Ware looked up at her now from his intent study of the buffalo skin and demanded, "Show me."

Alin smiled. "This is the tool we are using," she said softly, holding up the bone skin burnisher for him to see. "You can hold it," she said and offered it to him.

Ware took the tool from her and regarded it seriously. The burnisher, from Rom's workshop, had been made from the rib bone of a deer, and was exquisitely fitted for its job. The curved deer rib had been carefully split in two along its length, and the tool was actually made out of half of the bone. The burnisher was thus slightly bowed, with the spongy side forming the outer part of the bend. The actual working end, the end rubbed against the skin, was slightly ground down from use.

Ware looked up again at Alin. "How do you work it?" he asked.

"I'll show you." Alin took back the tool and bent over the skin on her knees. "You do it with both hands," she said. "See. You place your right hand thus on the base of the burnisher. That is the hand that controls the angle made to the skin. Then you take the fingers of your left hand and press from above, back and forth." She demonstrated the use of the burnisher for a minute, and then she looked up. "You try it," she said to the child.

Ware accepted the tool from her eagerly and knelt in front of the skin next to her. At first he tried to rub the tool with too open an angle. "No," Alin said, "you will break the bone if you do that. Here. Like this." And she lowered the burnisher until it was closer to the hide. This time the child was successful in rubbing the tool back and forth across the skin.

"All skins must be rubbed thus if they are to be made into buckskin," Alin said. "The rubbing presses down the skin and makes it shiny. Next we will rub animal fat into the skin. The fat will make the skin more flexible, and help to keep the water out."

Ware nodded. "Can I rub some more?" he asked eagerly.

"Certainly," Alin replied.

"I wish I had a helper like you," Sana said.

Ware's eyes shone. "I will help you next," he promised Sana with a happy grin.

The eyes of the two girls met in a look of maternal amusement. "Thank you, Ware," Sana said. "That is very kind of you."

There was a sudden icy draft in the cave, and the lights in the stone saucer lamps flickered. Someone had lifted the hides at the door. Alin looked over her shoulder and saw one of the women of the Horse coming into the cave.

"Where is Mada?" The urgency in the woman's voice caught the attention of everyone present.

"Here," said Mada's voice from the corner opposite to Alin's, and then the older woman was on her feet.

"It is Elexa. The waters of life have broken. The babe is ready to be born."

"I will come," Mada said calmly, and began to walk toward the cave's entrance.

Alin watched as Mada ducked under the hides, which were held up for her by the woman who had come to fetch her. The hides dropped behind the two, and the lamplight steadied. The voices in the cave started up again, but they were noticeably quieter than they had been earlier.

Ware went back to rubbing the skin. Alin said to Sana, "Do you think the women of this tribe have a birthing statue?"

"Perhaps Mada does," Sana replied.

They looked at each other doubtfully.

"What's a birthing statue?" Ware asked, raising his head.

"Birthing statue?" Ona echoed. Ona was young. She had been one of the first women traded for after the tragedy, and she was obviously near term with a child.

"It is a statue of the Mother," Alin said quietly. "It shows her giving birth. We bring it to every woman who is laboring in childbirth, and there are special songs to sing as well, to ask the Mother's blessing on both woman and child."

Ona was nodding. "We had such a statue in my tribe. It was used only when the birth was difficult."

Alin raised her eyebrows. "There would be fewer difficult births if proper recognition was paid to the Mother in the first place."

Ona's eyes, which seemed very large in her pale, tired face, remained on Alin. "Do you really think so, Alin?"

"Sa," Alin replied shortly.

"We have never used a birthing statue in this tribe." It was Thora, one of the women of the Horse, speaking.

"Whom do you ask to protect you in childbirth, then?" Alin asked. "Sky God?"

"Well . . . no."

Alin looked at the faces of the women in the cave. She shook her head in disbelief. "I am constantly amazed by how the women of this tribe neglect Earth Mother," she said. "The men do not surprise me so much. Men are men. They play only a small part in the mystery that is life. But a woman . . . a woman *is* life. Her womb, her blood, her waters . . . that is life. And to make that life and bring it into the world, a woman travels very close to death. Life and death. Both of these belong to the Mother." She shook her head once more, this time in bewilderment. "I do not understand you," she said.

"We had statues of the Mother in my tribe." It was the voice of Nel, Altan's wife. "The women kept them.

They were used at a girl's initiation, and at childbirth, also. And there were special prayers.''

Thora said doubtfully, "Perhaps Huth has a statue of the Mother for our tribe."

"Huth!" said Alin. Her eyes flashed. "Huth is a man. A man should not be entrusted with the sacred things of the Mother!"

"We of the Horse have not worshipped the Mother in many years, Alin," explained one of the older women of the tribe. "We have long followed Sky God."

"Sky God is a god for the men," Sana said.

"That is not so," came the softly spoken reply. "Sky God is a god for all the people. Do you not know in your tribe that he is the earth namer?" Zena, the woman who was speaking, looked from Sana's face to Alin. "It was Sky God's mating with Mother Earth that created all the world," the Horse woman said earnestly. "Humans and animals and trees and grasses—all these were made and named by Sky God. I am thinking that makes him a god for all the people, not just a god for the men."

"You say true when you say it was a mating of Sky God and Earth Mother that made the world," Alin responded. Her eyes moved from Zena's face to circle the entire cave, taking in all the feminine faces illuminated by the flickering stone lamps. "We are all women here," she said. "We know how small a part it is that a man plays in the bringing forth of life." Her eyes stopped at Ona's weary young face. "Is that not so, Ona?"

"That is so," said Ona, immediately and emphatically.

There was laughter.

"They get all of the pleasure and none of the pain," another woman said, and her voice held a distinct trace of bitterness.

More laughter with less amusement.

Alin said, "It is the Mother who bore the first man as well as the first woman, the Mother who bore the deer and the horse and the buffalo and all the other animals. It is the Mother who brings forth the plants from her own body in order to feed the herds. Sky God is only the Mother's mate." She shrugged. "Any woman should be able to tell you that. I cannot understand how the women of this tribe have so lost their understanding of who they are."

"I never thought of it that way," said Ina, one of the young girls of the Horse who had not yet reached womanhood.

"I think you are being foolish with all this talk of the Mother." It was Lian's deep husky voice, and every head snapped around to look to where the girl sat near the fire. "A woman without a man is nothing," Lian said defiantly. She looked at Alin. "We worship Sky God because he is all-powerful." Her full mouth wore a stubborn look. "He is the husband of the Mother, and the Mother must do as he says."

"You have a very strange idea of marriage in this tribe." It was Jes's voice at its most ironic.

"Sa," said Elen. Her voice was not ironic but amused. "A very strange idea."

The hides that covered the cave began to sway. Then they lifted and the same woman who had come to fetch Mada earlier was there again. "Thora," she said into the cave. "Mada wants you to come."

"There is trouble?" Thora asked, rising to her feet.

"Perhaps." The woman sighed. "It is more that Elexa is so frightened, I think. Her sister died in childbirth two years since, and that is preying on her mind."

Thora had not yet started toward the door. She turned to look at Alin. "Do you have one of these birthing statues in your possession?" she asked the girl.

"Na." Alin shook her head regretfully. "We had no chance to gather our religious things when we were taken."

Thora was disappointed. "That is too bad. I wonder if such a thing as this statue might help Elexa."

"I will draw a birthing picture of the Mother for her if you like," said Jes diffidently.

"Sa!" Alin looked across the cave at her friend. Jes had come in after the rubbing work on the skins had begun, and she had chosen to help with the sewing. Consequently she was sitting by the fire with the women of the Horse. "That is a fine idea. If you will draw the

picture, I will bring it to Elexa." She turned to Thora.
"And I will say the prayers over her and enact the rituals.
I have watched my mother many times, and I know the
ceremony well." Her brown eyes commanded Thora's
blue ones. "The Mother will help your friend," she said
with absolute certitude. "I promise that in her name."

Thora looked toward the fire at the women of her own
tribe. "There can be no harm in trying," she said tentatively.

"Na. There can be no harm in letting the girl look at
a picture."

"It is true that Elexa lost a sister to childbirth. We do
not need to lose another woman of this tribe."

The responses were all affirmative. Only Lian looked
as if she did not agree, but she held her tongue. Jes got
up and went to get her drawing things.

Jes drew on a smooth stone a picture of a great-bellied
woman, with her knees spread wide in the birthing posture. The head of a baby could be seen just beginning to
descend. As in all renderings of the Mother, the face was
left blank.

Alin took the picture and showed it to the laboring
woman. Since her initiation, Alin had watched her mother
each time Lana had presided at a childbirth, and so she
knew exactly what to do. Elexa was indeed extremely
frightened, but Alin's firm assurances that her prayers to
the Mother would bring about a safe delivery had a mark-
edly soothing effect on the girl.

It was a first labor, and a long one. Mada was obviously an experienced midwife, and Alin made no attempt
to interfere with the older woman's handling of Elexa.
But Elexa expressed an almost frantic wish that Alin remain with her, and so the Red Deer leader did remain,
all through the night, assisting Mada where she could,
encouraging Elexa when the weary pain-racked girl began to flag.

At last, just as the dawn was breaking, Elexa's babe
was born.

"It's a girl!" said Mada in triumph, as she cut the cord
with an ivory dagger and held the child up in her hands.

All of the tired faces in the cave broke into radiant smiles. "A girl!" they said. "Praise be to the Mother. She has given us a girl!"

Soon the news was running all around the cliffside caverns:

Elexa has had a girl!

A girl has been born to us!

Another girl for the Tribe of the Horse!

All the tribe had been waiting for weeks for this birth, the first since the tragedy of the water hole. They had all fiercely wished for a girl. They had all feared to lose Elexa. The happy fulfillment of their desires seemed to be a sign that the bad luck of the Tribe of the Horse had finally turned.

"That is excellent news," Mar said, when a sleepy-eyed Tane came in the door of his shelter to bring him the word. Mar sat up in his skins, stretched, yawned, then rubbed his head. He grinned at Tane. *"Very* good news. And how is Elexa?"

"Very well, the women say."

"Wonderful news." Mar rubbed his head again. His grin broadened. "A girl."

"Sa." Tane began to build up the barely smoking fire. "It begins to seem as if there is a future after all for the Tribe of the Horse."

"Of course there is a future for the Tribe of the Horse!" Mar said, glaring fiercely at his friend.

Tane was too busy with the fire to notice. "Think of it," he said. "The four women we acquired at the Spring Gathering are with child: Nel and Lina and Ona and Rena." He poked the stick he had picked up into the center of the slumbering fire. "The three new women Altan got while we were away are certain to be gravid soon, if they are not so already. If we are lucky enough to have many girls and few boys . . ." Tane looked up from the fire. "In less than three handfuls of years, we will actually have women in hand to trade to other tribes in exchange for wives for ourselves."

"Sa," said Mar. "And that does not even count the Red Deer girls."

Tane heaved a sigh. "Last year at this time, things

looked so bleak. I do not ever want to pass a winter such as the one we passed in this tribe last year.''

"It was not pleasant," Mar agreed.

Tane looked around the small shelter that Mar had once shared with Eva. "I am thinking that it was harder for those who lost a wife than it was for those who had yet to wed," he said soberly.

"This winter looks to be a long one also," Mar said. He grimaced. "When I think that I was the one who encouraged Alin to ask Huth to give her until Spring Fires!" he shook his head. "I must have been possessed of an evil spirit."

"Do not say such a thing." Tane's voice was sharp. The son of a shaman, he was never comfortable jesting about evil spirits. He added more softly, "You were trying to save the girls for the younger men. And you were right. Without your interference, Altan would surely have given them to the nirum."

Mar grunted and pushed his tousled hair out of his eyes. He said, "I am glad that Elexa is safe. I was worried about her."

"So were we all. Cort was pacing the floor all night. He has already lost one sister to childbirth and one to the poisoned water. He did not want to lose another."

Mar said neutrally, "Tod must be pleased."

"Tod is preening himself," Tane replied, his voice faintly bitter. "He is one of the few men in the tribe with a wife, and now he can also claim a daughter. He has done well out of being Altan's friend."

Mar cocked an eyebrow, then got to his feet and stretched once more. "I am starving," he said.

"There is food in my father's cave," Tane said. "Come and share it."

Fifteen

Four days after the birth of Elexa's daughter, Zel came crawling home with a great wound in his thigh, and another even more vicious wound in his side. Alin was not quite sure what he had been doing so far away from home with only a dog for companion, but he had evidently paid dearly for his adventurous spirit. The first news that came to the girls' cave was that he had been injured miles down the river, and had walked home, fainting many times from pain and loss of blood along the way.

Huth was immediately summoned.

The atmosphere hanging over the cliffside caverns that winter afternoon was hushed and subdued. From within the cave where the hurt man lay, the tribe could hear the rhythmic beating of Huth's drum as he summoned his guardian spirit for assistance in treating the injuries. Alin was watching Ware for Mada that afternoon, and after an hour of so of trying to keep the little boy quiet, she decided to dress him in his furs and take him for a walk along the frozen river.

As soon as they rounded the first curve in the river and were out of sight of the cliffside caverns, Alin saw Mar ahead of her, giving Lugh a run.

"Mar!" Ware called before she could stop him, and the big, fur-clad figure in front of them looked around. When Mar saw the girl and the child, he stopped to wait for them. Alin frowned in annoyance. She had been trying to avoid Mar ever since the occasion when he had put his mouth upon hers. She didn't trust him not to do it again. She didn't trust herself not to let him.

Mar smiled at her as she came up to him. He was wearing his fur tunic, but the hood had slipped back and the front of his thick bright hair was blowing in the cold winter wind. His right hand was pushed into the front of his tunic; in his left hand he carried a medium-size spear.

Ware and Lugh began to race each other down the beach, the little boy laughing, the dog panting with almost equal glee. Alin and Mar followed more slowly, walking side by side.

"You are growing a beard," Alin heard herself say.

"It is warmer in the winter to wear a beard," he returned. "In the warmer weather it is too hot, and I shave it off."

"That is a useful ability men have," she said, "to be able to grow a coat of hair when the weather is cold. Women do not have such a choice."

He looked amused. "You would not look half so beautiful in a beard." He cocked his head a little to one side, narrowed his eyes, and considered her face.

Alin felt herself flush a little, and was glad that the cold wind would account for the color in her cheeks. She said crisply, to cover her lack of ease, "I am watching Ware for Mada, and he was growing weary of keeping within the girls' cave. That is why we came out."

He nodded, and his eyes returned to the boy and the dog, running so joyfully down the beach before them. "You should not come out alone, though," he said. "Look what has befallen Zel because he went off by himself."

"What did happen to Zel?" Alin asked, both because she wanted to know and because she did not want to listen to Mar's advice.

"He was gored by a buffalo."

"Oh." Alin called to Ware who was getting too far ahead of them. Then, "How did it happen?" she asked.

"It is not a pretty story." He gave her a sideways look. "It seems that Zel was hungry and tried to spear a buffalo. He misfired his throw, wounding but not killing the bull."

"Why would one man want to kill a buffalo?" Alin asked.

"He should not have. Buffalo God is angered when his children are killed for such a small reason as one man's dinner. Zel could have taken a boar, or a hare, or even a fish. The ice is not yet too thick to break." Mar's face was very serious. "I think Zel was punished for his ill deed."

"What happened?" Alin asked again.

He removed his hand from under his tunic to pull his hood a little more forward. Then he replied, "As you can imagine, the buffalo was furious at being wounded, and, being a buffalo, of course he charged. Zel ran for the nearest tree. He made it to the tree before the buffalo, but Zel's foot slipped as he started to climb, and the buffalo got him in the thigh with one of his horns. The buffalo gored again, and this time he got Zel in the side. He also threw him up in the air, high enough for a tree branch to poke through the neck of his shirt."

Alin pictured the scene in her mind. Her lips thinned.

Mar continued, "Poor Zel tried to get free of the branch, but he was caught by his shirt and hanging upside down. Luckily, his dog managed to distract the buffalo, and the bull went charging off, leaving Zel still hanging from the tree. At last the ties of his shirt gave way, and he came crashing to the ground. Fearing the return of the buffalo, he crawled immediately into some undergrowth and hid.

"Sure enough, the buffalo got tired of chasing Zel's dog and came back for his original prey. Zel said he seemed to spend forever searching the area for Zel, but luckily couldn't find him. Finally the bull went away, and Zel crawled out of his hiding place."

Mar looked at Alin. "He had a huge hole in his thigh, and his guts were hanging out through the hole in his side."

"Dhu!" said Alin. "It is a miracle he made it back to the cliff."

Mar nodded. "Sa. He is tough, Zel. He shoved his guts back into his stomach, and tied himself up with his belt. Next he tied some leather from his sleeping roll around his thigh, to stop the bleeding. Then he walked home.''

There was a little silence. Ware and Lugh turned and began to race back in the direction of Mar and Alin. Alin said, "But what was Zel doing, to be so far from home and alone like that? No one in my tribe would ever go such a distance without a companion.''

"It is not our practice, either," Mar said.

"Then why was Zel alone?''

Mar stabbed his javelin into the gravel of the beach and did not reply.

Alin began to feel suspicious. Why wouldn't he tell her? "Mar?" she said quietly.

He shrugged. The reindeer fur tunic he wore made him seem even larger than he actually was. He looked like a great bear, Alin thought. A great golden bear. She narrowed her eyes at his averted face. "Very well," she said. "I shall ask someone else.''

He set his jaw. She could see the twitch of a muscle in the corner of it. He said, "You are a nuisance.''

She imitated his shrug and did not reply.

"He was going to the salmon cave," Mar said at last, almost sullenly.

"And what is the salmon cave?''

"It is a cave that lies two days' journey down the Wand. In the direction of Snake Water.''

"That is nice. And why was he going to the salmon cave?''

This time Mar jabbed his javelin into the gravel with a vicious thrust. "There are women there," he said at last. "Women who have been expelled from their tribes. You can lie with them, if you are willing to pay.''

Alin wasn't sure she had heard correctly.

"Lie with them?" She looked at his profile. "You mean they will mate with any man for a payment?''

"That is what I said.''

"I don't believe you.''

The sideways look he shot her was ironic. "That is your choice.''

Lugh arrived at Mar's feet, panting. He looked up at his master and gave one short, sharp bark. Mar laughed and pulled a bone from beneath his tunic. "Go and get it!" he said to the dog, and threw the bone. Lugh streaked off. Ware shrieked with delight.

"Why were these women expelled from their tribes?" Alin demanded.

"Their husbands found them lying with another man."

"And for that reason they were expelled?" Alin was incredulous.

"In the Kindred we do not like our women to be unfaithful," Mar said.

"And is a married man also expelled if he is found to have been unfaithful?" Alin asked.

"Na." He still was not looking at her. "He is punished, of course. It is wrong to take another man's woman. But he is not expelled."

"I see."

At that he looked at her. "Na," he said. "You do not see."

"You are right," she agreed instantly. "I do not."

"Is it true that in your tribe, married women are free to take whatever man they will?" His voice was hard, abrupt.

Lugh was racing back across the gravel, the deer bone in his teeth. "Me!" Ware cried. "I want to throw the bone for Lugh!"

Mar took the bone from his dog and gave it to the boy. "Go ahead," he said. His voice had gentled when he spoke to the child. "Throw it."

Ware threw the bone. It did not go very far, but Lugh skidded off anyway.

Alin said angrily, "Married women in my tribe do not lie with other men. Before marriage, a girl may do as she wishes. But once she chooses a man, she must be faithful. As he must be faithful to her. That is one of the ways the tribe is held together."

Mar looked a little relieved. "That is not unlike the ways of my tribe, then."

"But no woman of my tribe would ever be expelled for lying with another man!" Alin cried passionately.

He raised his eyebrows. "But you say that such a thing is a wrongdoing in your tribe also. What would the people of the Red Deer do, then, if such a thing should happen?''

At a little distance from them, Ware was throwing the bone for Lugh to retrieve.

"It doesn't happen," Alin replied. "If a husband and wife agree so ill that the wife should desire to take another man, then she has only to declare her intention of doing so to the Mistress, and the marriage is dissolved."

"And is it so for a man as well?"

"Sa. It is so for a man as well."

He blew out through his nose. "That is not our way. If a man grows tired of his wife, he may take another wife. But in doing so, he does not put aside the first wife."

"And may a woman take a second husband as well?"

His mouth tightened. "Na."

Her lips curled in a smile that did not indicate amusement. She said, "You are not inclining me to desire to become a woman of your tribe, Mar."

"It does not happen very often that a man takes a second wife," Mar said a little defensively.

"That is because there are too few women," Alin replied.

As this was indisputably true, he found himself without a reply. He too often found himself on the defensive and without a reply when he talked to this girl. It was not a situation to sweeten the temper. His jaw tightened even more.

They had moved within the windbreak of a protruding rock, and now the two young adults stood silently and watched the child throwing the bone for the hound on the beach. Ware managed to make a particularly good throw, and Mar murmured under his breath, "Good boy." Alin glanced up at the man beside her as he watched his dog take the bone in his teeth to return to Ware.

Had Mar ever gone to see one of those women?

And why was that thought so violently distasteful to her?

Alin frowned and stared down at the new boots on her feet. His voice came as a welcome distraction. "One thing has always puzzled me about your tribe," he said.

"I am thinking that it is more than one thing that has puzzled you about my tribe," she answered with genuine amusement.

He caught the humor and shot her a startled look. Their eyes met, then suddenly he grinned. Alin found herself smiling back. She felt a sudden breathlessness, a tightness in her stomach.

Danger, she thought, and took a step back from him. "What is it that is puzzling you, Mar?" she asked.

He noticed her withdrawal, raised an eyebrow, but otherwise ignored it. He answered, "In the Tribe of the Horse, it is taboo to mate within a certain degree of kinship. That is why we go to the Gatherings, to find husbands in other tribes for our girls, and to find wives for ourselves. There are only a certain number of men and women who can mate within the tribe; the others are all within the forbidden degree of kinship." It was comfortable within the shelter of the rock, and he pushed his hood carelessly back off his head. "This is the rule within all the Kindred," he said seriously. "It has been that way since the beginning of time. But the women of your tribe do not leave the tribe. Is it acceptable, then, for you to marry within your kinship?"

"Na," Alin answered immediately. "Like the rest of the Kindred, we have a degree of kinship within which it is taboo to mate." She gave him a long cool look. "The answer to your question is very simple, Mar, as you would have realized if you had stopped to think about it. The Tribe of the Horse trades its women into other tribes in order to get new women for themselves. In the Tribe of the Red Deer, it is the men who marry out, and the women who bring in new husbands."

His mouth dropped open.

"*Men* leave their own tribes and marry into yours?"

"Sa."

"That is . . . astonishing."

She gave him a mysterious smile. "The women of the Red Deer are much desired as mates by the Kindred tribes in our area," she said. "We are known, you see, to be great lovers."

There was a startled silence. Then he began to laugh.

When he had got his breath back, he said, "We should deal well, then, the men of my tribe and the women of yours."

Alin looked slowly up at him, up at the great height of him, up into laughing eyes that were as dazzlingly, as brilliantly blue as the sweeping arc of cobalt winter sky above them. Those eyes, she realized for the first time, were the mark of Sky God. This was a man whom Sky God had taken for himself, an utter and complete male; there was no touch of the Mother about him at all.

It was comfortably warm within the windbreak of the rock, but Alin found herself shivering. "I am thinking it is time to return," she said. "Mada will be looking for Ware." And she moved out of the shelter of the rock into the wind.

As soon as they stepped back onto the beach, Lugh left the child he had been playing with and came tearing over to Mar. Ware followed, his cheeks whipped a right red color from the game and the wind.

"Would you like a ride home?" Mar asked the child.

"Sa! Sa!" came Ware's instant reply, and he raised his arms to the big man who was smiling down at him so genially. As Alin watched, Mar swung the little boy up onto his shoulders.

"My father used to do this with me. I remember how I loved it," Mar said to her with a laugh, and he began to jog back along the beach, the child riding high upon his shoulders. Ware's small hands clutched at the man's bright hair, and the child's shrieks of delight were carried by the wind all the way back down the beach.

A smile curved Alin's lips as she watched the joyous trio in front of her: man, child, and dog.

"Alin!" Ware craned his head around and called to her. "You come too!"

"All right!" she called back, and broke into an easy lope to catch up to the three in front.

Huth tended Zel for the rest of the afternoon, binding his wounds and dosing him in accordance with the instructions of the spirit the shaman had summoned. The

boy, Arn, remained with his master all the while, but at
supper time Huth sent him away.

"Zel is sleeping well," he said to the boy. "I will
watch with him for a while longer. Go and get yourself
something to eat."

Arn knew that Huth himself would not break his fast
until the morning, so he did not offer to bring back food
to the shaman. "I may come back?" he asked.

"Certainly. But I want you to eat. You have fasted long
enough this day."

Arn had obeyed, going to the initiates' cave for some
food, as no one was cooking in the shaman's cave this
night. Arn had been initiated the previous year, two years
behind his brother Dale, but he had never become a
member of the close-knit circle of the initiates' cave. He
was the shaman's apprentice, and as such he was regarded with some uneasiness, and a great deal of awe,
by the rest of the tribe's initiated boys.

In the initiates' cave, Arn ate buffalo stew, which Mada
had slow-cooked for the boys all the afternoon with hot
rocks in a pit lined with hide. Mada always slow-cooked
with bay leaves, parsley, and marjoram, and it gave the
meat and broth a taste that Arn particularly loved.

Like the rest of the boys, Arn ate his meal out of a
deer frontal bone that, with the antler removed, was cup-
shaped and held food neatly. The edges of the cups had
been retouched and polished so that there were no sharp
edges to cut the mouth. Arn chewed his stewed meat,
which he scooped up with a spoon carved out of mammoth ivory, and drank the broth, and realized that he had
been starving. Zel had crawled home just after dawn, and
neither Huth nor Arn had eaten any breakfast.

The talk around the fire in the initiates' cave centered
on the usual two topics: hunting and girls. Arn listened
with half an ear. When he had finished every bite of his
stew, he said to his brother, who was sitting beside him,
"Where is Tane? When he was not in Huth's cave I
thought for certain he would be here. I have not seen him
all the day. I do not even think he knows about Zel."

"I have not seen him all the day, either," Dale replied. "He has been working in the sacred cave this moon. Perhaps he has not yet returned."

"But it is growing dark," Arn said.

"Perhaps he is with Mar, then," Dale suggested.

"Sa." Arn's silvery head, which was even fairer than his brother's, nodded. "Perhaps he is with Mar."

It was Cort's and Melior's turn to gather up the eating utensils, and some of the other boys pulled out the knucklebones for a game of Hunt the Buffalo. Bror took out a piece of bone he had been working on and continued engraving a picture. Two other boys produced wooden sticks and began to whittle with razor-sharp flint knives. There were no dogs to fight over any leftover scraps of food, as the initiates' cave was too high on the cliff for the dogs to reach. The atmosphere in the cave was companionable and peaceful. The air was comfortably warm, from body heat and from the fire.

Arn got to his feet a little reluctantly.

"Stay for a while," Dale said. "There will be a cold fire in Huth's cave this night."

Arn smiled at his brother. "I will come back," he said. "I am going first to see if Huth needs me."

Dale looked as if he would object, then he shrugged and nodded. He turned to the boy on his other side and began to tell him about something Elen had said to him that day. Arn slipped silently out under the hides at the door.

The sun had almost set and darkness was spreading over the valley of the Wand. Arn set his foot upon the rope ladder and descended swiftly to the next terrace level. At the bottom he almost bumped into a girl who was beginning to ascend.

"Oh!" Dara said. "I did not see you. It is getting so dark."

"I am sorry," Arn said in concern. "I almost stepped on your head!"

They stood side by side at the bottom of the ladder, and looked at each other. They had seen each other before, of course, but neither had yet spoken to the other. "You are the boy who helps Huth," Dara said.

"Sa. I am Arn."

"I am Dara."

They looked at each other some more. Arn was particularly pleased to note that the top of her head only came to the level of his eyes.

Dara thought that this boy had the most beautiful hair she had ever seen.

"What are you doing out by yourself, Dara?" Arn asked at last. "It is growing dark, and in the dark it is all too easy to miss your step on these ladders."

Dara's dark gray eyes were solemn. "I was looking for Jes. She is not back yet."

"Back from where?"

"She went to the cave with Tane," Dara said. "To watch him paint."

There was a startled silence. Then, "Does Huth know this?" Arn asked.

"Oh." Dara's eyes flickered with alarm. "I do not know. Perhaps I should not have told you . . ."

"It is all right," Arn assured her. "I won't say anything. And Huth is otherwise occupied this night."

Dara remembered how Huth was occupied. "How is Zel?" she asked.

"He is still alive. That is something."

"Sa." Her voice was very soft. He thought he had never heard so soft a voice. "They said he was badly hurt."

"He was."

"Well," Dara said hesitantly. She looked at the ladder and then back to him. "I had better be getting back to the girls' cave."

"I will go with you," Arn said. He looked down at the small fragile figure before him. It was not often that he could look down, even to a woman. Though this girl scarcely looked old enough to be a woman. "How many winters do you have, Dara?" he asked, following this train of thought.

"Two handfuls and three," she replied.

He smiled with pleasure. "I am one winter ahead of you."

"Oh." She gazed up at him out of eyes that, even in the poor light, he could see were gray like his, only much

much darker. She said, with honest admiration, "You are important, Arn, for one so young."

He was a modest boy, but that pleased him. Still, "Na," he assured her. "I am not important. One day, perhaps, I will be. When I am a shaman."

"And when will that be?"

"When Huth says I am ready." His crystalline eyes took on an inward focus. "It is very hard, Dara, becoming a shaman," he said. "There is so much you have to learn. So many journeys for your spirit to take."

She gazed at him in wonder. "We do not have a shaman like you in our tribe," she said. "In our tribe we have the Mistress, who is the voice of the Mother."

"If your Mistress speaks for the Mother, then she is a kind of shaman, too," he said.

Dara nodded thoughtfully. "Sa. I suppose that is so."

"Are you going back to the girls' cave now?"

"Sa."

"Come," said Arn. "I will go with you and see you safe."

Sixteen

At the full of Reindeer Moon, Huth had allowed Jes to join the two uninitiated boys he was teaching to paint. As the weather grew ever colder, Jes would go each afternoon into the warmth of Huth's cave and listen avidly while he taught his three young pupils how to make the different colors for paints, how to add the mineral he called the "stretcher" to the pigment to make a larger quantity, and how to add water to the whole so that it would stick to the rock of a cave wall and not crack.

"Each tribe has its own secret for making paint," Huth said, as he ground up the earth pitch with which he made one of the blacks the tribe used for outlining. "Earth pitch and charcoal for black, ochre for brown and yellow and red. It is also possible to make white from clay, but yellow is a better color to use than white."

Huth had many lumps of the necessary minerals stored in the back of his living cave. The raw materials came from deposits situated at a place conveniently near to the sacred cave itself. With these lumps of raw minerals, Huth taught the boys and Jes how to grind the minerals into powder in naturally hollowed stones; how to heat the pigment to produce a variation of colors; and how to mix the pigments to produce still more shades of color.

The main business of the lesson, however, was not painting but drawing. For this exercise, Huth provided smooth stones and gravers. "Now," he would say, to start off a lesson, "let me see you each draw three horses, and let you show each one closer to me than the next."

No matter what the exercise, the consistently superior student was Jes.

The time of Reindeer Moon was the time the full-fledged artists of the tribe worked in the sacred cave. It nearly broke Jes's heart to see Tane and Bror and Finn and Cal leaving each morning, packs of food slung over their shoulders, to spend the day painting in the place where Jes longed with all her heart to be. But she had not yet been fully accepted by Huth; she knew that. She knew she must tread carefully with the shaman, not seem to ask for more than he felt was seemly, lest he take away from her the little that she had.

But she ached for a chance to look more closely at the magnificent paintings she had seen all too briefly during the ceremony of the hunting magic, and when Tane had offered to take her one day, she jumped at the chance.

"The others are not coming today," he said, in explanation of the invitation and in warning that she was to keep it quiet. "It will be just you and me."

"Good," Jes said, and had not noticed the half-rueful smile he gave to her obviously preoccupied face. "There will be no one around to get in the way of my looking at the paintings, then."

"That is so," he answered, still with that rueful look. "I have said I am going in order to finish up something I have been working on, so I will indeed have to work. You may look your fill. I won't get in your way."

They spent the day underground, hidden away from the cold bleak sky in the magnificently painted warmth of the underground cave. Jes spent hours prowling around the chambers, gazing with hungry intensity at the great bulls, the horses, the little foals frolicking along after their mothers, and the magnificent antlered stags.

"My father painted these," Tane said, gesturing to the four huge black bulls in the main chamber.

"Huth did these?" Jes said, staring with wide-eyed awe.

"Sa. He is a fine painter, my father."

"He does not paint any longer in the cave?"

"Cave painting is hard on the back," Tane explained.

Jes nodded. "Were all these pictures done by the men of your tribe, Tane?"

"So the shamans say. In truth, there are some pictures that have been here almost since the beginning of time."

"And every generation paints more pictures in the cave?"

Tane shook his head. "There are not always the artists. My father was the first real artist to work in here since beyond memory. But he is training more to follow him, so the cave is waking to life once again."

Truly, Jes thought, the sacred cave of the Tribe of the Horse did seem to be filled with artistic energy these days. She saw the signs of it everywhere as she walked through the chambers. Lying on the floor in front of the walls she saw hollow bird bones, filled with the remnants of paint; an assortment of flint gravers and burins and backed bladelets; a flat stone that was obviously being used as a palette was in front of one of the cows in the main chamber; animal hair brushes and small bones for the blowing of paint rested on rocks.

In front of one of the horses in the axial chamber, there was a wooden scaffold that Tane said Bror had been using to work on one of the horses. The scaffolding was cleverly erected; twenty sockets had been cut into the rock on both sides of the wall. The artists had fitted branches into the sockets and cemented them into place with clay. This series of solid joists then supported a platform of cut oak, which provided easy access to the upper walls of the chamber as well as to the ceiling.

Jes spent the latter part of the day watching Tane work. He was painting in a cavern that opened off the lateral passage that led away from the right wall of the main chamber. The place he had chosen was on the left wall, immediately visible to any visitor as he left the lateral passage. There had been an older painting of a small light brown horse on the wall, and over it Tane was painting a frieze of stag heads.

It was one of the most marvelous pictures in all the cave. Tane had drawn a herd of red deer, one behind the other, stretching across the wall for a length of perhaps sixteen feet, each deer about three feet high. The deer were drawn as silhouettes, outlined in black, with only the head, neck, shoulders, and antlers shown, but they were drawn so elegantly that, encountering them, the eye was shocked by the sheer beauty of the picture they made. Having only shown these five magnificent heads, Tane had somehow also managed to suggest that the deer were just beginning to rise out of the water as they reached a riverbank. The whole picture had so perfectly captured the life and feeling of the moment that Jes found it impossible to find the words to express her feelings about it.

"Red deer?" was all she had managed to say. But the look on her face had said a great deal more than her words.

He had smiled at that look. "I was inspired by the idea of red deer," he said. "I don't know why."

When they had finally climbed out of the cave and seen the sunset, they had both been startled.

"Dhu," Jes said, looking with some apprehension at the man who accompanied her. "Now they will be wanting to know where we have been."

Tane said something under his breath. "I did not realize it had grown so late." He shrugged. "Well, there is nothing we can do about it now. Come. If they ask, we shall just have to tell them."

"They" and "them." The two scarcely noticed the way they had taken to consigning all the world that was not Jes or Tane into the category of "others."

They began to walk through the woods, along the track that would take them to the river. "It is wonderful the way just leaving that small white space between the horse's far leg and the chest gives such an impression of depth," Jes said after a minute, thinking of something she had observed earlier in the morning. She pictured the painting she was thinking of in her mind: the horse's small stretched head, the reaching legs that captured all the energy of flight. "I would never have thought of that by myself."

"The ability to suggest depth and motion is one of the greatest tricks of the painter," Tane said.

"Sa. Your father has been making us work on that,"

she said. "But it is hard to have to figure it out by your-self."

He nodded. "But once you have tried to figure it out by yourself, you will be quick to notice how others have done it. If you had not tried to draw a horse in depth yourself, would you have noticed that trick with the space of white?"

She thought for a moment, her head tilted a little to one side. "Probably not."

"There is a reason in what my father does. By the time I was finally allowed to see the pictures in the sacred cave, I was ready to see with the eyes of a painter."

They had begun now to walk along the southerly track that would take them back to their home caves. They were unencumbered, as all the painting material was kept stored in the cave and they had eaten the food they had brought with them.

Jes's stride matched with Tane's very well, and she walked beside him as easily and naturally as she walked beside Alin.

He was a magnificent artist, she thought with reverence, picturing once again in her mind the frieze of red deer he had been working on. She thought she could be happy watching him paint forever, watching those thin clever hands as they created such living, vibrant beauty on the sparkling white walls of his tribe's wonderful cave. Half of her was wild with joy that such brilliance could actually exist in the world, and half of her despaired, because never, for as many winters as she might live, would she be the artist that he was.

"But your father did not actually forbid you to bring me to the cave?" she asked now, as he held aside a branch that had swung out to block the track in front of them.

"Na." She went past the branch and he let it swing back behind them. "But, then, I did not ask him, Jes. He said it was all right for the girls to go into the cave for the hunting magic, and so I just . . . assumed . . . that he would say it was all right for me to take you to watch me paint." He shot her a quick look. "Do you see?"

"Sa. I see." Her voice was very quiet.

"If he asks where we have been when we return today, then I will have to tell him."

"And if he says I may not go to the cave anymore?"

He looked unhappy. "Then you will not be able to go."

She did not answer. He looked at her. He said, "Jes! Do not look like that!" He stopped.

She stopped as well. "I do not think I could bear that, Tane," she said desperately. She was making no attempt to conceal her feelings; she, Jes, who never exposed herself to anyone. But it did not matter if he saw her pain, she thought. He would understand.

Yet . . . even though he understood . . . he might take it away from her. Her throat ached. "I could not bear it," she said again.

"But you are working with the new students," he said. "It is not as if you are not painting at all."

"It is not enough," she said. Her voice was desolate. "Don't you see, Tane? It is not enough."

He let out his breath in a long gust and frowned. Then, with a movement that completely surprised her, he reached out and drew her into his arms.

Jes felt the fur of his tunic silky and cold under her cheek. They had not needed fur tunics within the cave, where the temperature scarcely varied from one season to the next, but outdoors it was cold. It was warm in his arms, though, she thought, warm and strangely comforting. She did not try to pull away.

All her life Jes had suffered from a driving desire to draw things. It had isolated her from her fellows in the Tribe of the Red Deer. Even Alin did not know about her secret trips to their own sacred cave, her solitary struggles to learn to draw correctly. Jes had wondered sometimes if she had got this strange passion from the man who had fathered her. He had been a man from outside the tribe, a man whom her mother had met at a small local Gathering when she was yet very young. They had mated but not married, and Jes had been born.

"Jes," Tane was saying now. He was only slightly taller and slimly built, but his arms around her felt so safe and strong. He put his cold cheek against hers. "We will think of something," he said. "If my father forbids you to visit the cave, then we will have to change his mind. Or we will work in another cave. You will paint. Do not doubt that. I will swear it to you, if you like."

Her breath caught painfully in her throat, and she drew away from him, just far enough to be able to see his face. "You would swear such a thing to me?"

"Sa," he said. His eyes were very green from so close a perspective. "I know you have been starved," he said. "I know it is hard to wait. But . . . you will paint. Great paintings, Jes. Horses and bulls and stags." His eyes glittered. "I swear it. I won't let anything stop you ever again. But . . . you must have patience."

A faint smile touched her lips. "Sa," she whispered. And then his mouth came down on hers.

No one had ever done such a thing to her before. Jes was fifteen winters old. She had taken her first boy at Spring Fires two years before, and she knew very well what transpired between a man and a woman when they lay down together to mate.

But no man had ever put his mouth on hers before. Her initial surprise caused her to stiffen, but then, as Tane drew her even closer, she began to realize how nice such a touch was. She linked her arms about his waist, so bulky now with the furs he was wearing. She could not feel him through all the clothing, and regretted that. She felt his tongue lightly darting against her closed mouth and she opened it since it seemed that was what he wanted. To her astonishment, his tongue slid in.

The penetration of that tongue did amazing things to Jes's insides. It was not long until she realized that the mock play of tongues they were doing was only a prelude to a much greater enactment. And she wanted it. She wanted Tane. Wanted those thin, talented hands touching her; wanted that slim, strong body naked next to hers; wanted his phallus inside her the way his tongue was inside her mouth.

Dhu! What would Alin say? She was betraying her tribe by this kind of behavior with Tane. Jes stiffened her back, exerted all her considerable willpower, and pulled away from him.

"It is wrong for me to do this with you," she said abruptly. "I am betraying my companions," and she swung around and began to walk swiftly along the river track.

Tane caught up to her almost immediately. "It is not wrong, Jes," he said. His voice sounded breathless, and she did not think it was because he had hurried to catch her. "At the first of Salmon Moon, the women of the Red Deer must choose a mate," he reminded her. "How are you to know which man to choose unless you learn something about us first?"

Jes shot him an oblique look, and did not reply. She continued to stride forward briskly.

Tane put a firm hand upon her arm to halt her. "Answer me," he said, his voice not breathless now but hard.

Jes tore her arm away, but she halted. "I will answer you nothing, man of the Horse."

"So." They were facing each other upon the path, and Tane narrowed his eyes. "Mar was right, then. You are still hoping for a rescue."

Only the flicker of her lashes betrayed a reaction.

Tane's mouth set. "Have you ever thought what would happen, Jes, should the men of your tribe come here seeking you?" he asked. "Do you think it is likely that the men of the Horse will relinquish lightly the only hope for our tribe's survival?"

Jes stared into his face. "What are you saying?"

"I am saying there will be fighting," he answered bluntly. "Killing, likely. Men against men. That is what I am saying."

Jes's eyes widened. "I thought it was taboo in this tribe to kill another man," she said. She added with faint sarcasm, "There is horror enough every time the incident of last summer is mentioned, that is for certain."

His face was grim. "It is taboo for one member of the tribe to kill another member, that is true. But the men of another tribe are a different matter. There has been killing between us and other tribes before. Do you think we would allow another tribe to poach on our hunting grounds? Well, no more would we allow another tribe to poach our women.''

Jes's chin went up in a gesture of defiance. "We are not your women!"

Tane said, "You are."

Seventeen

So concerned was the tribe with Zel's injury and subsequent sickness that scarcely anyone realized that Jes and Tane had even been gone. As the night went on, Zel seemed to grow worse instead of better. His skin was hot as fire, and he mumbled and tossed and cried out strange things that had no meaning.

"His spirit has left his body," Huth said to Arn as they stood together watching over the restless man. "I have called it and called it, but it does not respond. It is wandering in the land of the dead. If we do not bring it back soon, he will die."

Arn swallowed. "Shall you go seeking him, Huth?"

"Sa," said Huth gravely. His thin dark face was drawn, but his voice was resolute. "There is nothing else to be done."

And so they made preparations for the journey of Huth's spirit. In order to release Huth's soul from his own body so that it could cross the threshold to the invisible spirit world and establish contact with the departing soul of the sick man, Huth would have to put himself into a deep trance. To do this he required his drum, his shaman costume, and seven sacred mushrooms. All of these Arn fetched for him, while Huth readied his mind for the long and exhausting ritual of the journey to the land of the dead.

The hides of Zel's cave were rolled up when Arn returned. This was done, he knew, so that Zel's spirit could easily find its way back home. Zel's two brothers had

come to sit beside his bedplace of buffalo robes, along
with Huth and Arn. Everyone was silent as Huth dressed
in his shaman's costume of long grass robe and horse-
head mask.

The moon had just risen in the morning side of the
sky, bringing a glimmer of light to the frozen river below. By the time the moon went down, Arn thought,
Huth's journey would be over. Then would they know if
Zel was to live or to die.

Huth called to him and Arn went to take his place by
the shaman's side. Huth began by drumming lightly and
invoking Zel's soul by name: "Your father is Durin," he
chanted, "your mother is Ela. Your own name is Zel.
Where are you lingering, Zel? Whither have you gone?
We sit sadly in this cave, waiting for your return. Come
back to us, O Zel! Come back to us!"

The sick man tossed restlessly, and mumbled indistinguishable words. The two brothers wailed their distress,
adding their own pleading tones to those of the shaman.

The fire by the door flickered in the wind that was
coming into the cave because of the open hides. Huth ate
his seven sacred mushrooms. Now Arn also picked up a
drum, and, beating in rhythm with Huth, he listened as
the shaman began the prescribed words of the ritual:

> The horse of the grasslands,
> The strong bull of the earth,
> The great stag of the forest.
> I summon you to my aid.
> The stallion is screaming,
> The strong bull bellows,
> The stag is braying.
> Hear me, O hear.
> God of the Sky
> Lord of the Earth
> Prepare my way
> To the Land of the Dead.
> Horse of the grasslands,
> Strong bull of the earth,
> Stag of the forest,
> Fly before me and show me my way!

The drumming grew louder, faster, as the song went on:

> The drum is my horse!
> The drum is my bull!
> The drum is my stag!
> I am a man!
> Shaman of the tribe
> The Tribe of the Horse
> Spirits I call you
> Show me the way!

The drumming now was intense. It was cold in the cave, but Huth's forehead was beaded with sweat. His gray eyes were glazed, looking beyond the cave and its occupants for the spirits in the land of the dead.

The drumming stopped. Huth gestured, and Arn leaped to his feet. The boy took the shaman's arm and helped him to the door of the cave. Huth inhaled deeply, breathing in not only the cold air of the night, but also the guardian spirits he had summoned to assist him on his journey.

"The soul of Zel has traveled the road to the land of the dead," Huth said in a voice that was not his own. Then he sagged. Arn braced the shaman with his shoulder. Huth was a slim man, but his dead weight was heavy for the even slimmer Arn. The boy bore him up, however, and half carried him to the buffalo robe that had been spread earlier beside the patient. Huth dropped to the floor, facedown, and lay still.

For a very long time he did not stir. The Reindeer Moon continued on its journey down the sky. Arn and Zel's two brothers sat patiently in the flickering light of the fire, waiting for the shaman to wake.

The night passed. The first streaks of dawn were lighting the sky when Huth finally stirred. Arn was on his feet in a flash, moving to help the shaman rise shakily to his feet. Huth stood over Zel and made a magic sign upon his breast.

"I have made the journey," Huth said hoarsely. "I have found the soul and called it back."

Murmurs of joy and hope came from the brothers of
Zel. "Now we must wait and see if it has followed,"
Huth said.

"It will, it will," the eldest brother murmured. "You
are a great shaman, Huth. Rarely does a spirit refuse to
follow you."

"I do not know," Huth said. "Zel's spirit was with
his wife."

There was silence.

"She will not let him go," one of the brothers said at
last.

"She does not want to," Huth acknowledged. "There
was a battle between us. I am not sure which one of us
has won."

Upon the bedplace robes, the body of the man over
whose soul war was being waged slept on. As the watch-
ers waited for Zel to return from the land of the dead,
the sun began to rise above the rim of the world, returned
once again from the land of darkness to bring light and
life to the world of men.

"I have done all that I can," said Huth. "I can do no
more. Now we must wait and see."

To the wonder and admiration of all, in the following
days Zel began to recover from his wounds. The wonder
was for Zel and his tough constitution; the admiration
was for Huth, whose shamanizing had saved the hunter
from the consequences of his own folly.

Reindeer Moon disappeared, and after two days of in-
visibility, the first pale crescent of Snow Moon rose in
the afternoon side of the sky. Alin duly made the proper
mark on her deer bone for the first day of Snow Moon,
and on the very same night a daughter was born to Altan's wife, Nel.

At this birthing, Alin had been sent for as a matter of
course, and her prayers to the Mother for a safe delivery
were heard by the women of the Horse with noticeable
reverence.

"I wish we had a proper birthing statue," Alin said
the following afternoon, after she had slept for several

hours to recuperate from being up all the night with the laboring Nel.

"Bror could carve one for you," Mada offered. The older woman had taken the same midafternoon rest as Alin, and now the two of them were seated by the fire in the women's cave drinking hot sage tea and discussing the delivery. "He is a fine carver," Bror's mother said. "He could easily work from Jes's picture."

Alin's head lifted, like a dog who has caught a particularly welcome scent. "Could he, Mada? That would be wonderful."

"I will ask him," Mada promised.

Bror's response was that he would be delighted to carve a birthing statue for the tribe's women. The question then arose about what material the statue would be made of. Bror had been thinking of wood.

"Ivory," Alin said. All of the birthing statues in the tribe of the Red Deer were made of ivory. Some of the other women mentioned that the statues of the Mother in their tribes had been made of stone, but Alin was adamant. If ivory was not available, then they might as well just keep using Jes's picture. Bror finally brought the problem to Mar, who had a solution. "If Alin needs ivory," he said with a grin, "then we shall just have to go mammoth hunting."

This suggestion met with a mixed reaction among the boys. The Tribe of the Horse rarely hunted mammoth. Reindeer provided more than sufficient meat during the winter; and reindeer, besides being more plentiful than mammoth, were far easier to kill. However, it was true that upon occasion, when the Horse Tribe needed more ivory than they could easily trade for, they would attempt a mammoth hunt.

"A mammoth hunt?" Tane said to Mar when he heard of the proposal. "You know how slender are the chances of finding mammoth in our own hunting grounds. Or do you intend to make a great trek to the east?"

Mar shook his head. "Na. I am thinking we will try the upriver rapids. Some winters the mammoth herds come that far south."

"Some winters. Not all. And if there are no mammoths, we will have made the trip for naught."

Mar cocked an eyebrow. "Not for naught, Tane. It is three days going to the rapids, and three days coming, as well as the time that is spent searching for mammoth once we get there. That is easily a half moon of time we could spend mammoth hunting. If we do find mammoth, that will be all to the good. But even if we do not, still we will have kept the men busy for a half moon of the winter season."

Tane said, "I do not think you will get many volunteers to go mammoth hunting, Mar. The unmarried men will not want to leave the girls."

They were alone together in Mar's shelter, seated around the hearth, and now Mar rested a big, fur-booted foot on one of the stones that ringed his fire. "I will take some of the girls, too," he said.

Tane stared at him. "Are you serious? The weather is bitter."

"Alin will want to go mammoth hunting," Mar returned positively. "And if Alin goes, the rest of the girls will follow."

"If all the girls go, then all the unmarried men will go," Tane said. "I am thinking that will breed even more trouble than keeping them at home!"

"I will take half of the girls," Mar amended, and stretched a second foot out to the fire.

There was a small silence as Tane considered the figure of his foster brother, lounging so comfortably on a buffalo robe on the other side of the fire. Slowly, he shook his head. "I cannot see Alin leaving half her girls behind, even if she does decide to go mammoth hunting herself."

Mar shrugged. "I'll think of some way to persuade Alin," he said.

Tane looked again at that big, lazy, confident figure, and then he laughed. "If you do," he said, "I am going to name you to be our next shaman."

Mar looked at his foster brother. "It is not Alin I need to shamanize about," he said. The line of his mouth grew hard. "It is Altan."

* * *

Altan was furious when he heard that Mar had proposed a mammoth hunt.

"Actually, it might not be a bad idea," Tod said to the chief. He had been the first of the older nirum to hear the rumor, and he had brought it immediately to Altan's cave. "Things are beginning to grow tense among the men," Tod went on. "Getting a number of them out of the way for a while would help. It is yet more than two moons until the Spring Fires."

Altan slammed his right fist onto his thigh. It was not the idea of the mammoth hunt he objected to so much as the fact that, once again, Mar had taken the initiative away from him.

"And the girls desire to go?" Sauk said to Tod, with less astonishment than he would have evinced a month ago. The girls' ability on the buffalo hunt had impressed the men of the Horse.

"Huth told me that half of the girls are to go," Tod said. "Half to go and half to stay."

"Who does Mar think he is?" Altan roared suddenly. The two nirum fell silent as the chief glared at them, the veins popping in his temples. "He arranged this hunt, and never once did he ask my permission!" Altan shouted. "Who is the chief of this tribe? Mar? Or me?"

The two nirum looked at each other. Then, "You are the chief, Altan," Tod said quietly.

"If that is so, then why has no one come to me about this hunt!"

"They will come," Tod said, still pacifically. "Mar cannot take the men and the girls out of camp without your permission. He knows that."

"Well, he will not get my permission," Altan said, and glared furiously into the fire.

Once again Tod and Sauk looked at each other. Then Sauk said, "I have a better idea, Altan. Let me go with them. Everyone in the tribe knows that I have hunted mammoth in the east. Mar knows nothing about mammoth compared to me." He rubbed a hairy hand along his black jowls. "Name me to go on this hunt as the leader. Mar will not like that at all." He smiled, showing surprisingly small teeth.

"I am sick unto death of being manipulated by Mar," Altan said bitterly. He threw a stone into the fire.

Sauk continued to rub his jowls. "Many things can happen on a mammoth hunt," he said. "Accidents. Deaths." Still he rubbed his hairy jowls. "Mammoth hunting is very dangerous, Altan."

Both Altan and Tod turned their heads to stare at Sauk. Sauk continued to smile at the chief. "Send Eoto and Heno with me," he said. "And let Mar take the boys."

The wind blew hard outside, causing the buffalo skins at the door of the cave to ripple inward. After a moment, "All right," Altan said. He returned Sauk's smile. "I will."

When Mar finally approached Altan to request permission to take a group mammoth hunting, he found the chief surprisingly agreeable.

"A good idea," Altan said pleasantly. "I have been thinking myself that it would be wise to busy the men this time of the year. The winter is long and cold when there is no woman to warm your sleeping skins."

"Sa," Mar agreed warily. He looked from Altan to the thickly built man who sat beside the chief. Sauk stared unwinkingly back.

Altan said, "You are in luck, Mar. Sauk is the only man of the Tribe of the Horse who has actually hunted with the mammoth hunters in the east, and he has agreed to lead your party."

Altan smiled at the look he saw on Mar's face.

"Sauk is coming?" Mar asked, his narrowed eyes holding the nirum's own coal black gaze.

Sauk grinned.

"I am surprised that you are willing to leave your new wife's sleeping skins to lie alone and cold on the hunting trail," Mar said to him slowly.

Sauk's grin broadened.

"Have you chosen the rest of the party?" Mar asked Altan, his eyes still on Sauk.

"Eoto and Heno wish to go," Altan said. "The rest of the choices I leave up to you."

"Eoto and Heno and Sauk," Mar said, his voice expressionless. "I see."

"All experienced hunters," Altan said. "I must protect the girls, Mar. We cannot afford to endanger them due to your own inexperience. After all, you have never hunted mammoth, have you?"

"Once," Mar said flatly. "With my father."

"I spent a whole season with the mammoth hunters," Sauk said. "I will know what to do."

"Sa," said Mar, still in that same flat tone. "I am sure that you will."

"Good," said Altan. "I will tell Huth to prepare to make the hunting magic."

On the morning of departure for the mammoth hunt, Alin and the eight other girls she had chosen assembled on the beach. Awaiting them there were Mar, Tane, Cort, Dale, Bror, Melior, and the three nirum named by Altan. Alin thought it was an odd assembly of men, but she made no comment.

Once they had tied the gear they were to carry on their backs, the mammoth hunters left the beach to begin their journey to the north. They had no problem in finding a track, they simply walked along the solidly frozen river. The walking, however, was far more toilsome than it had been when the tribe had gone buffalo hunting during Stag-Fighting Moon. At the Snow Moon time of winter it was necessary to wear a heavy fur tunic, with the hood pulled up and tightly closed. Buffalo skin boots kept the feet warm, but were much heavier to walk in than soft leather moccasins. Reindeer fur mittens limited use of the hands, but were absolutely necessary to avoid frostbite, as were the buffalo hide masks that could be drawn up over the mouth and nose as protection from the biting wind.

As yet there had been only a few dustings of snow during this moon of the snows, and the ice underfoot was slippery. There was a north wind blowing down the river valley, and walking into it was not pleasant. The backpacks, full of necessary survival gear, were heavy. In

fact, the only members of the hunting party who appeared to be enjoying the day were the unencumbered
dogs, who frisked along beside the humans, their breath
hanging white in the freezing air. There was little talk
until midday, when Sauk decreed they should stop for
some food.

Alin and Jes and Mar and Tane foraged in the woods
that fringed the river to find some fallen branches, and
Sauk got the flames started with the wooden fire stick he
was carrying in his backpack. They all huddled close
around the fire's welcome warmth and chewed on smoked
buffalo meat.

The dogs ate also, then fought each other over a stick
that had not been piled onto the fire.

After the food had been consumed, the hunters put out
the fire, shouldered their packs, and began to walk once
again.

It grew colder as the afternoon advanced, and the wind
grew stronger. Alin, walking directly behind Mar, was
glad to have the shelter of that big body in front of her.
At last, as the sun was hanging low in the sky, the river
made a sharp bend to the east, and the hills on the western shore that had been making a tunnel for the wind
were suddenly to their north, forming a windbreak. "We
will stop here," Sauk said.

Sauk climbed up the riverbank to the shore, the party
of hunters close behind him. The shore was relatively flat
and lined with trees, and the men seemed to know exactly where they wanted to make camp. Mar and Tane
went into the woods to cut down some saplings to support the buffalo hide for the tents. Alin left the rest of
the men spreading out the hides and took the girls to go
and gather wood to build the fires.

When the girls got back to the campsite, their arms
full of small branches, they found two good-sized buffalo
hide tents standing in the center of the small clearing.

"Dhu, but they look welcome!" Elen said.

"Sa," Sana agreed. "I am cold and hungry, and if a
whole herd of mammoths crossed my path just now, I
would look the other way."

"Bring the wood along," Alin said, "and we will get some fires going."

When they opened the flaps of the shelters, they found that a small hearth of stones had been laid beneath the smoke holes in both tents, and in the larger tent, Mar was twirling the fire stick over a kindling nest of dried leaves. Within a very short time both fires were going, the tent flaps were closed, and the hopeful mammoth hunters were chewing on smoked buffalo meat and melting the water they had carried with them in containers made of animal bladders.

The larger tent held five women and five men, the smaller tent four of each. As Alin looked around the larger tent, to which she had been assigned, she saw the three nirum, Mar, and Tane, as well as Jes, Mora, Bina, and Iva.

Alin had almost protested spreading the girls between the two tents. She had expected the girls to be placed together, as they had been on the buffalo hunt. But there was a tension in the air between the nirum and the initiates that she did not like, and she had decided that perhaps it would be better if all the men were not cooped up together after all.

It was warm within the buffalo hide tent, and from the woods around them they could hear the hungry calling of the wolves. Mar and Tane built another, larger fire outside the two tents to keep off predators, and the hunters sat together within, shoulder to shoulder, and Iva said to Sauk, "Is it true that mammoths are as big as a tree?" Her eyes shone in the firelight. "There is a picture of one in our sacred cave, but it is an old picture and hard to see clearly. How big are their tusks? We have traded for ivory ourselves, of course, but the tusks are already split when we get them."

Sauk smiled with pleasure at the chance to show off his knowledge. "Mammoth are very big," he announced importantly.

"Amazing," Alin heard Mar mutter under his breath. He was seated at her right shoulder and she shot him a look from under her lashes. He was scratching Lugh's ears and looking unconcerned.

"Very big," Sauk was going on. "Enormous. The biggest animal you will ever see. They have immense, curved tusks of ivory. They have a peaked head and a humped, sloping back." He made a gesture, as if sketching the slope of the back. "They have long reddish brown outer hair, and a thick undercoat of wool. They used to come south in large herds along with the reindeer, but that was when the weather was colder than it is now. Now they stay to the north for most of the year, only migrating to the river valleys around here in the deepest part of the winter."

Sauk leaned forward a little, looking to make sure he had everyone's attention. "They are not easy to kill, because they are so big. You need a hunting party to bring down a mammoth. It is not a job for one man." He frowned at Mar, who appeared to be absorbed in scratching Lugh's ears.

Alin was fascinated and forgot for the moment that she disliked Sauk. "Are they dangerous to drive?" she asked eagerly.

Sauk grinned at her. "Mammoth are very dangerous to drive." He looked around the fire once more, reveling in the girls' attention. "For one thing, they cover an enormous amount of ground with every step, so to chase them any distance is exhausting. And they can force their way through any kind of territory. If a tree is in a mammoth's way—bang!—down comes the tree!"

The girls' eyes were enormous. Mar snorted. Alin ignored him. "Will they charge, Sauk?" she asked.

The nirum nodded. "They can be very aggressive. A bull mammoth who catches the scent of a man is just as likely to attack as he is to flee."

Jes said, "I do not think I would like to feel the points of those tusks."

Sauk laughed scornfully. "A mammoth wouldn't waste his tusks upon a human. His trunk and his feet are his weapons. He saves his tusks for pushing the snow off his grazing areas." Once more he grinned at the attentive girls. "One advantage we have over mammoth is that their eyesight is very bad," he went on. "That helps when you are trying to creep up on them. On the other hand, their hearing is very sharp. A mammoth can hear even the slightest sound at a great distance. And he can judge where it comes from, because his smell is so good. When he sticks that big trunk of his up into the air, he can scent better than a dog.''

The two nirum had been listening closely also, and now Eoto asked, ''What do they eat, Sauk?''

''Grass, herbs, twigs, leaves, berries, fruits, bark. They eat enormously. They wander great distances in search of food, and sometimes, during Snow Moon, when the food is scarce to the north, the herds will even come as far south as the hunting grounds of the Tribe of the Horse.''

''Have you gotten a mammoth recently at these upland rapids?'' Alin asked.

''The last time the Tribe of the Horse went mammoth hunting was the year that Tardith died,'' Mar said. He had not spoken for so long that he startled Alin. There was a note in his voice that was distinctly odd, she thought, and she turned to look at him. He was staring at Sauk, a very grim look around his mouth.

''I have never heard how Tardith died,'' Alin heard her own voice saying.

There was a deadly silence. Finally, Tane answered her. ''It was a stupid accident. One of the small children got hold of a javelin and was playing out on the highest terrace. Children are not supposed to play on the terraces, but whoever was watching this one had turned her back. The child dropped the javelin. It fell straight and true, point down.'' Tane was looking at Sauk, not at Alin. ''Tardith was standing on the beach just below,'' he said.

Mar did not move a muscle, but Alin was close enough to feel the tension vibrating in him. She felt a sudden and surprising desire to reach out and put a comforting hand on his shoulder.

Heno said, ''It was a pity. Tardith was yet a young man.''

Sauk said, ''The tribe was fortunate Altan was there to take his place.''

Alin saw the hands lying on Lugh's fur slowly begin

to open and close. Mar said deliberately, "At the Ceremony of the Great Horse this year, I will be made a nirum, Sauk. Altan may not remain our chief for very much longer."

The hostility between the two men crackled as hot as the fire. Then Jes asked, "Are you saying that you may replace Altan as chief, Mar?"

Mar's "Sa," clashed with Sauk's jeering laugh.

"It is hardly likely, Jes," Sauk said. "The challenge for the chieftainship is well nigh impossible."

"Nothing is impossible," Mar said flatly.

Jes's lips opened again, but Tane reached out and put a bare, long-fingered hand over hers where it rested on her knee. Jes fell silent; neither did she make any attempt to throw off that possessive hand.

Alin looked at Mar's hands, which were buried now in the thick fur of Lugh's neck.

He would challenge Altan for the chieftainship, she thought in astonishment. The chieftainship. Mar.

She had promised to make the Sacred Marriage with the chief of the Tribe of the Horse, but she had never once thought that the chief would be Mar. Alin did not like Altan, but he would have served her purpose. And when the drums of the Fires beat in your blood, what did it matter who the man was?

But Mar.

That frightened her. The thought of lying with Mar frightened her. That could be . . . dangerous.

Tension lay heavy in the air as the hunters arranged their sleeping skins. Alin was dismayed to discover that the only place left for her to spread out her things was beside Mar's pile of skins. On the far side of the fire, Sauk was spreading his skins between Mora and Iva. By mutual agreement, it seemed as if the two men were keeping as much space between them as possible.

There was a blast of cold air from the tent flap as it lifted, and Mar came in from seeing to the fire outside. Lugh followed him, and he began to pick his way across the crowded floor to his own sleeping roll. Alin could feel the cold from his furs as he sat on his heels to spread out the skins. Lugh came and sat on his haunches at the edge of the tent, waiting for Mar to finish so he could pick a warm spot to nest in.

Without a word, Alin took off her reindeer furs, crawled into her sleeping roll in her buckskin shirt and trousers, and began to spread the furs on top.

"I'll do it for you," Mar said. "Lie down."

His face was looking grim, and without a word she curled up inside her familiar deerskins. He spread the reindeer fur coat over the outside of the sleeping roll to add to her warmth.

"Good night, Alin," he said, his voice softer than it had been all evening.

"Good night," she replied. She shut her eyes and listened to him taking off his furs and getting into his own skins. He called quietly to Lugh, and she could hear the padding of the dog's feet, and then the satisfied grunt as Lugh snuggled into his place for the night. Everyone else had settled down, and the only noise within the tent was the sound of the small fire's occasional crackling. Outside the wolves continued to howl.

Alin cuddled under her covers, feeling much warmer and much more comfortable than she had dreamed would be possible during that long cold afternoon walk.

She was young and tired from a long day, and in a very short time she fell asleep.

She awoke once, disturbed by movement next to her. She opened her eyes to see Mar sitting on his heels and tending to the fire in the tent's small hearth. The fire flared up a little as he fed it, illuminating his face. After a minute he rose, went to the door flap, and disappeared outside. He was back shortly. Alin heard Tane's voice from the other side of the fire, asking a question.

"The fire is all right," Mar replied softly. "I built it up a little. There is no sign of animals nearby."

Then he was back beside her, getting in under the layers of buffalo skin that composed his own sleeping roll. Alin saw that he had not bothered to put on his furs to go outside.

Lugh whimpered.

Mar said, with a faint laugh in his voice, "Na, you cannot have the middle of the roll, Lugh. Move."

There was a shifting of skins, a soft grunt that could have been either Mar or the dog, and then silence.

A wolf howled in the distance.

Alin moved a little closer to the warm bulk of Mar, closed her eyes, and drifted comfortably back to sleep.

Eighteen

They walked all the next day, again following the frozen river, and saw nothing but the ice and the cliffs and the barren trees and an occasional herd of reindeer. Alin was disappointed; she had expected to see some other inhabited caves in the limestone hills that rose above the banks of the river. She said as much to the others later that night after supper, when the hunting party was sitting about the hearth fire in the large tent.

Mar answered, "All of the tribes of the Kindred who dwell in the Valley of the Wand live to the south of the Tribe of the Horse. This land we have been walking through is all our hunting grounds." Iva made a murmur of wonder, and he smiled at her fleetingly. "There is fine deer hunting here in the spring," he said, "and antelope and aurochs hunting in the summer. There are ibex too, that come down from the mountains far to the morning side of the river."

"Sa." Eoto too smiled at Iva. "We have one of the largest hunting grounds of any of the tribes of the Kindred. In the good weather, we make summer camps along the river here. It is better not to hunt in all seasons near our home caves, lest we drive the herds away."

"No one else hunts along these shores?" Jes asked in amazement.

"Not if they have a care for their lives," Sauk said.

The girls looked at him. Alin said, "What do you mean, Sauk, 'not if they care for their lives'?"

Sauk's small teeth showed. "I mean that the men of

the Horse know how to protect their own. What else should I mean, girl?''

Alin turned her head toward Mar and asked incredulously, "You would kill a man who took game from your hunting grounds?"

Mar answered almost impatiently, "Of course we would not kill 'a man.' " He was scratching Lugh's ears as he spoke, and the dog was almost humming with the bliss of it. "If a man, or a party of men, are making a journey through our hunting grounds, then they are welcome to take what they need in order to live. But if a hunting party from another tribe comes into our area only to make a big kill, and particularly if they do it more than once, then there is likely to be some killing that does not involve only animals."

"I have never heard of such a thing," Alin told him.

"That is because your men are cowards," came Sauk's contemptuous voice.

"They are not!" The angry reply came from five feminine throats.

"It is that such a thing has never happened in our tribe," Alin explained, still looking at Mar. "Our hunting grounds are our hunting grounds. All the tribes in the area know them, and none try to transgress our boundaries."

"You are fortunate," Mar said ironically, stopped scratching Lugh's ears, and looked at her.

"They are all afraid of the Mistress." It was Iva's voice this time. "They are afraid she will cast a spell upon them if they try to come into her hunting runs."

Sauk made a rude, sneering noise. "Only a coward is afraid of a woman," he said.

The girls glared at him.

"You say your men are not cowards?" the nirum continued, looking from one firelit face to the next. "Why, your men did not even fight for you when you were kidnapped by a group of mere boys." Here his black eyes flicked dismissively over Mar and Tane.

"Our men did not know where we had been taken!" It was Mora, almost hissing in her fury. "Mar stole us away and left no trace of our going. But our men will find us, Outlanders." Her flashing eyes went from one male face to the next. "And then you will see how real men can fight!"

"Mora." It was Alin's voice, quietly warning.

"I would like to fight your men," Sauk said. He flexed his strong, hairy hands and grinned. "I would like that very much."

Mar said, his voice as quiet as Alin's, "It is growing late and we have a long cold journey to make on the morrow. I am thinking it is time we went to sleep."

"Sa," said Alin. "I agree."

Alin lay on her back, looking wide-eyed up at the smoke hole over the fire, with no thought of sleep.

It had never once occurred to her that this kidnapping could end in violence. There had never been any fighting in the Tribe of the Red Deer. The Mistress would not allow it. Neither, for the reason Iva had mentioned, was there ever any fighting between the people of the Red Deer and the tribes that surrounded them. Alin had lived her whole life in the peace and security of a serene and ordered world.

And then the men of the Horse had come into her life.

The world of the Red Deer still existed, she thought. In the caves on the shore of the Greatfish River, there yet dwelled a people who lived in peace and harmony, led by the unquestioned rule of Mistress and Mother.

But for how long?

Lana would come looking for her daughter.

And Tor would come also, along with the other men of the Red Deer. Lana would call upon the best and the strongest of the men for this, for upon the outcome of this quest rested the future of all the tribe.

I am the Chosen One, Alin thought. I am the one to be Mistress after Lana. They cannot let me go.

I cannot wait for the spring weather, Alin decided, lying there with her wide eyes on the tent's smoke hole. I cannot wait for my mother to search me out. I must get home on my own. If I do not, if I wait, then . . . then there may be bloodshed. She shivered, though she was not cold. There may even be killing.

All of a sudden she could lie still no longer. Quietly, careful not to wake any of the others, Alin crept out of her sleeping roll and pulled on her boots. She picked up her fur tunic, made her way to the door flap of the tent, ducked, and went outside into the freezing night air.

The fire Mar had built to keep away animals was still burning. Alin pulled her fur coat closely around her and looked up at the sky.

The stars were far above. They were so beautiful, Alin thought, the stars of winter. Her eyes fixed themselves upon the moon. It was almost at its fullest now, almost at its time of power.

She could not travel alone during Snow Moon. It would be too cold; she would not be able to carry all she needed in order to survive. After Snow Moon came Shadow Moon . . . still too cold, Alin thought. After Shadow Moon came the moon when the men of the Horse tribe held their great annual ceremony, when the young boys were initiated and the fully initiated boys were made nirum; when the chief was consecrated and the horse was sacrificed for the blessing of the whole people.

Alin had heard about this ceremony from Bror. It was a ceremony only for the men; the women did not participate at all. It went on for three full days. She decided now that it would be the perfect time for her to escape.

"Alin." The voice behind her made her jump.

"When you did not come right back, I thought I had better see if you were all right," Mar said.

"I am fine. I could not sleep, so I came out here for a little. That is all."

He nodded and went to lay some more wood on the fire.

"Mar . . ." she heard herself asking, "are you going to challenge Altan for the chieftainship?"

His back was to her. He had not bothered to put on his furs, and the buckskin of his shirt could not disguise how he stiffened at her question.

He put another big branch on the fire, then stepped back, away from the flames. They flared up, illuminating his figure, his bright hair, his short golden beard. Still with his back to her, he said, "Sa."

She thought for a little, her eyes on that massive back. "Did you have to wait until you were old enough to be made nirum? Was that it?" she guessed.

He turned slowly to face her. He nodded.

"And you will be made nirum at the Moon of the Great Horse?"

He nodded again.

"Is it permitted to tell me what the challenge is?"

"Better not to," he said. "Not yet."

She bowed her head. Alin perfectly understood the need to keep sacred things secret.

She had not put up her hood when she came out of the tent, and now she snuggled her chin down into the fur around her throat and hugged her coat around her. She changed the subject, said, "You must be freezing out here without your furs."

"I do not feel the cold much."

There was a whine behind her and then a whirl of black-tipped silver as Lugh went racing by to come to a skidding halt at Mar's feet. Everything about the dog said so clearly, so indignantly, *You left me!* that Alin began to laugh.

"It was your own fault," Mar said to his dog severely. "You were sleeping."

The dog whimpered and flattened himself at Mar's feet, tail thumping in abject abasement.

"Enough," Mar said, not severe now, merely cross. "There is no need to fawn all over me." Then, as Lugh continued to lie at his feet, *"Up!"*

Lugh got up, looked adoringly into Mar's face, and pricked his ears. His tail began to wag briskly.

Alin said, her voice full of mirth, "That dog is more like a person than a dog."

"I have had him since he was weaned," Mar said. "We have been friends for many years, Lugh and I."

The sound of a wolf howling came through the cold night air. Lugh's tail stopped wagging and he froze.

Mar said pleasantly, "And what was it that was keeping you awake this night, Alin?"

"I am thinking that you know the answer to that question, man of the Horse," she replied.

"You are worried about what may happen if the men of your tribe should come to find you?"

"I am worried about what may happen *when* the men of my tribe come to find me," she corrected.

He did not answer her. The wolf howled again. Lugh began to quiver.

Unwillingly, Alin asked, "Do you think there is likely to be fighting?"

"There might be," he said.

She looked away from his unrevealing face and stared broodingly at the quivering dog.

"Alin . . ." His voice was suddenly soft. A-*lin* was how he pronounced her name. No one else said it that way, not even the others of his tribe. Only Mar.

"A-*lin*. Even if your men do find you, have you ever thought that perhaps you might choose to stay with us?"

She burrowed her chin deeper into her coat. She shook her head.

"Why not?" She was not looking at him, was watching Lugh, but his voice sounded as if he had moved closer.

She answered, still without looking away from the dog, "I am the Chosen One of my tribe. I cannot desert it."

"Why must you be the one to follow your mother?" he asked. He sounded very close to her now. "When Huth realized that Tane was not the one to follow him as shaman, he sought another, more suitable successor. And so it is with all the shamans of the Kindred. Why can it not be thus with the Tribe of the Red Deer?"

"Because it cannot."

"What would your mother have done if she had not had any daughters? She would have been forced to find someone else."

"But she *has* a daughter, man of the Horse," Alin said, and at last she looked up.

That was her mistake. He was right in front of her, and before she could realize what he was about, he had reached out and put his hands on her. Then, as had happened once before, his mouth came down to cover hers.

All around them the deep darkness of the camp and

the surrounding forest was breathing with the life of the world. And with the touch of Mar's mouth, it seemed to Alin as if that breathing darkness entered deep into her very soul. The stars were a part of it, so keen and bright and pure in the dark breathing night. The man whose body she was held against was like the stars in the darkness, a shaft of light, cold and pure, yet at the same time hot and burning, like a flame. She wanted to be part of it all, part of the night, part of the stars, part of him.

His mouth moved on her mouth, his tongue on her tongue. He held her close against him. Her untied fur coat had opened, and they were pressed together, body to body. She could feel the power of him, feel the power in him, the power that was life itself. And she wanted it.

"Alin," he breathed, his head bending lower, his mouth moving from her mouth to touch her cheek, her jaw, and then the hollow of her throat. His hands slid under her coat, to touch her through the thinner buckskin of her shirt. One of those hands cupped her breast and began to caress it.

Alin quivered and quivered, like Lugh when he had heard the wolf. Mar's mouth came back to hers. His hand on her breast closed harder. She felt the opening to her womb shiver, begin to moisten and open. She leaned against him, leaned into him. Her head was bent back, her mouth fully given up to his.

"Alin." His voice came to her through the breathing passionate darkness. It sounded harsh. Raw. "Dhu," he almost groaned. "Where can we go?"

Nowhere. The answer formed in her mind, clear, distinct, final. Nowhere. Not for we two. Not now. Not tomorrow. Not ever.

She brought her hands up until they rested on his chest, and then she pushed. She had surprised him. He released her and she stepped back. One step. Two steps. Three.

"There is nowhere for us to go, Mar," she said. Her voice was husky. She drew a long, shaky breath. "Do not touch me so again," she said. "It is wrong."

He shook his head, as if to clear it. His hair had fallen forward over his forehead almost to his eyes. Even in the darkness she could see how his eyes glittered. She could see also the hurried movement of his chest, could almost still feel the strong pounding of the heart within. "Na," he said. "What is between us is right. Can you not feel it, Alin? Can you not feel the call of the Mother when we touch?"

For a moment, she wavered. Could it be so? She wanted to lie with him. That she could not disguise, not from him, not from herself. Perhaps Mar was right, perhaps the Mother was calling her to her proper mate.

Then the words of Lana came into her mind:

Never choose a man you cannot control . . . Most men are safe, are properly respectful, spill their sap and worship the Mother who will bring forth life out of it. But every once in a while there is a man who challenges that . . .

Alin knew that this was such a man.

From somewhere she found the right words to say. "I must save my maidenhood for the Sacred Marriage. It makes for a powerful fertility ritual, when the goddess's maidenhood is broken. It is not for you, Mar, to take what I have promised to the Mother."

He flung up his head in what she had come to think of as his stallion gesture. His nostrils flared a little. "And you have promised to make that Sacred Marriage for the Tribe of the Horse?"

Breathe in, she thought. Breathe out. Look him in the eyes. "Sa," she said. "I have promised."

"And you will make it with the tribe's chief?"

In, she thought. Out. In. Out. "Sa," she said again. "With the chief."

His face in the firelight looked arrogant and proud; his eyes were bright and faintly narrowed. He flung back his head again and said, "I tell you now, Alin, that I will be that chief."

Part of her wanted him to be. Part of her was aching to step forward once again, into his arms.

Part of her feared him. This was a dangerous man. Dangerous to her, dangerous to all that she held most sacred. This was not a man in whose arms she could ever lie with safety.

"We shall see," she said, "at the first of Salmon

Moon." She pulled her fur around her, turned, and walked steadily back to the tent.

He did not come in for quite a while. She worried about him, outside in the bitter cold without his furs. But she made no move to go after him, and after what seemed a very long time he came in. She lay perfectly still, feigning sleep, making herself breathe evenly and slowly as he got into his sleeping roll beside her.

She thought, I will never be able to sleep with him lying so close.

She heard him mutter something under his breath as he turned so that his back was to her. He sounded distinctly ill-tempered.

I will not sleep for the whole of this hunting trip, Alin thought dismally. Not with Mar beside me like this.

The thought was scarcely formed in her mind, when she fell deeply and dreamlessly asleep.

Nineteen

As the hunters advanced further north the following day, the ice covering the river began to thin, and then to break up. They were approaching the upland rapids.

"The river's current is so strong here that, no matter how cold it may get, the water never freezes," Bror told Alin. "It is the water that attracts the game, of course. You can get deer, giant deer, and roebuck at these rapids, as well as reindeer and elk and boar."

The hunters had moved completely off of the river and onto the shore. Alin could see the many game tracks that led away from the river and into the surrounding hills.

"Time to choose a spot and pitch the tents," Sauk ordered.

It was well after midafternoon by the time camp was set up. Then the hunters set out to search the shore for mammoth spoor.

They found it.

"We're in luck!" Mar crowed. "When I came last year to the rapids to check for mammoth, there wasn't a sign of them anywhere."

All of the men stared at him.

"You came here last year?" Heno said. "Alone?"

Mar didn't answer.

"What were you, a boy not yet a nirum, doing alone at the upland rapids?" Sauk demanded, eyes narrowed, chin jutted forward dangerously.

"Looking for mammoth," Mar said. He looked down from his great height into Sauk's belligerent face.

Heno laughed nastily. "And what were you planning to do, Mar, if you had found mammoth? Kill one with your spear?"

Eoto laughed with him. The faces of the initiates were sober.

Mar said to Heno slowly, "If I had found traces of mammoth, I would have gone back to get a hunting party." His eyes moved to Tane. "It occurred to me that we could make use of ivory to trade for women at the Spring Gathering," he explained. "But I did not want to raise anyone's hopes if there were no mammoth for us to hunt. The tribe did not need any more disappointments last winter. So I came by myself. When there was no sign of any mammoth, I went home." He shrugged. "It was really very simple."

"You did not think to ask me to accompany you?" Tane asked expressionlessly.

"You are always so occupied in the sacred cave during Snow Moon," Mar said, his voice apologetic.

"You might have been killed," Sauk snapped. "You are as vulnerable as the next man, Mar." These words were accompanied by a particularly nasty smile, and the nirum added as he looked around the group, "It is never wise to hunt alone. Look at what happened to Zel," he said.

"I was not hunting," Mar said impatiently.

"Neither was Zel," said Sauk with a leer. "Or at least, he was not hunting meat."

The other nirum laughed knowingly.

Bror asked Mar, "How did you manage to get away by yourself without anyone knowing?"

Mar frowned and, very slightly, shook his head.

"I know!" Dale said brightly. "It was when you said you were going downriver to the tribeless women, wasn't it? You came here instead."

"What tribeless women?" Elen asked.

Dale looked suddenly flustered.

"What women?" Elen repeated, looking from Dale to Mar and then back again to Dale.

"What about the mammoth spoor?" Alin put it, taking pity on Dale's confusion. She said to Sauk, "Shall we follow it today?"

"Na." Sauk looked up at the late-afternoon sky. "It is too late today." His voice changed, became almost insolent. "Mar," he said, "you and Dale and Bror go and get us some hares to cook for supper."

Alin was standing next to Mar, and she could feel how he tensed at the order. It was not that he minded getting the supper; of that she was certain. It was taking orders from Sauk that was galling him so.

Over supper in the big tent, Sauk regaled them with stories of his mammoth hunting days in the east. Alin, growing tired of listening to the nirum's harsh, never-ending voice, finally said to Tane, "Have you ever been on a mammoth hunt, Tane?"

"Sa," he replied, smiling at her. "I was on the hunt led by Tardith the year Mar and I were initiated. We got a fine bull that year, do you remember, Mar?"

Mar nodded. He was staring broodingly into the fire. Alin wondered if he had heard any of Sauk's stories at all.

"Was it exciting?" she asked Tane.

Tane made a face. "Actually, it wasn't."

"It was always exciting among the mammoth hunt-ers," Sauk began importantly.

Tane cut in. "Mar and I did have some excitement on that hunt, though it did not have to do with the mammoth that we killed." He grinned at his foster brother's bent head.

Mar looked up, frowning slightly. "Do you have to bring up that escapade?"

"Alin wants to hear an exciting mammoth story."

"Sa," Alin said immediately. "Sauk's stories have been very exciting, but it would be nice to hear a story about a mammoth from our own hunting grounds."

Mar looked at her.

"Go on, Tane," Alin said. "What happened?"

Tane settled down. "Well," he began, "Mar felt the same way about the mammoth hunt as I did. He thought it had been very dull. Of course, since Mar's father was the chief and the hunt leader, Mar could not very well

say this out loud, but he decided that while the rest of
the men were butchering the mammoth, we would go off
by ourselves to try to observe a live mammoth close up.
We had got our mammoth so quickly, you see, that we
had had scarcely any chance to watch the beasts. We
were curious.''

"We were very young," Mar murmured.

Tane smiled. He looked at Jes. "I wanted to draw
one.''

She nodded with perfect comprehension.

"What happened?" Alin asked.

Sauk shifted around, obviously irritated that the attention was no longer on him. Seeing this, Mar began to
take a little more interest in the story and took up the
tale: "Tane and I slipped away from our camp very early
in the morning, and went looking for mammoth spoor.
We were lucky, or unlucky, depending upon how you
look at things, and found a trail very quickly. We followed it, grasping our spears importantly, even though
we had no intention of having to use them.''

A faint, reminiscent smile touched Mar's lips. "After
a short while,'' he continued, "we heard the sound of
crashing in the wood ahead. The mammoths were eating
breakfast! we thought. We crept along, very quietly, very
proud of ourselves. The only two initiates who would be
able to say they had spied on a mammoth herd.'' His
smiling eyes rested on Tane.

Tane began to laugh. "It wasn't a herd at all," he said,
clasping his thin, long-fingered hands about his updrawn
knees. "It was one old bull, very like the one we had
killed the day before. He was making all that noise stripping bark off a tree for his breakfast.'' Tane looked across
at Mar, nodding that he should continue.

"We were disappointed, of course," Mar said, "and
we began to retreat. We thought quietly.''

"We *were* quiet," Tane put in. "It wasn't our sound
he got hold of. It was our scent.''

"True.''

"Mammoths have a very keen sense of smell," Sauk
said officiously.

"What happened next?" Jes asked Tane.

He answered, "Well, first the bull raised his head; then he raised his trunk and extended it toward us; next, he spread his ears, let out a shrill trumpeting call that turned my blood to ice, and came for us."

Even Sauk was paying close attention now.

"We ran, of course," said Mar prosaically. "But you would be amazed at how fast an animal of that size can move. He was much faster than we were. Then I remembered my father saying that mammoths have very poor eyesight. So I called to Tane to jump off the path to the side and hide. I jumped one way, Tane jumped the other." Mar rubbed his head, mussing his hair, and gave Alin a rueful smile. "I tripped," he said. "On a root. I tripped and fell headlong, beside a big tree. I was so petrified I just lay there, my spear on the ground a little distance away. I lay like one already dead, except my heart was hammering as loudly as Huth's drum."

Sauk began to rub his bearded jowl.

Alin's eyes were huge. "It didn't see you?" she asked Mar.

"It didn't actually see me, but it got my scent," Mar answered. "I had brushed against the tree when I fell, you see, and the mammoth got my scent off the tree. I don't know if he thought I was hiding inside the tree, or if he thought I *was* the tree, but I do know he screamed and flung the tree to the ground, right next to my poor shaking body. Then he put his trunk around the felled tree, and lifted it and slammed it down a few times. Finally he fell to his knees and stabbed his tusks into the ground, one on either side of the tree. For good measure, when he got up again, he gave it a kick. Then, with a last nasty glare, he went crashing away, very pleased with himself for disposing of that upstart human creature."

The girls all sighed with pleasure. Even Eoto and Heno smiled. Sauk was frowning.

"I couldn't believe my eyes when I saw Mar crawl out from under that tree," Tane said. "With all the noise that bull had been making, I was certain the mammoth had killed him."

"It was sheer luck that it didn't," Sauk said, "not any skill on your part, Mar."

Everyone stared at the nirum, surprised by the vicious note in his voice.

"I am thinking Mar knows that," Eoto murmured.

"I am going outside to pee," Sauk said, and rising he stalked from the tent. When he came back in, he found the others crawling into their bedrolls preparing to sleep.

The hunters woke as usual with the dawn. Melior, who was particularly skillful at the trick, harpooned some fish for breakfast. Then they lifted their spears and went forth to search for mammoths.

"If we were looking for meat and not for ivory, the hunting of mammoths would be much easier," Mar explained to Alin. "Then it would not matter which particular mammoth we brought down. But the older bulls have better tusks. It will be acceptable for us to take that bull, because of our need. But it would not be acceptable for us to kill many mammoths when we only have need of the one. So we must wait until it is possible for us to take the one that suits our purposes."

It was easy to find mammoth tracks, even on the hard, frozen ground. No other game tracks were as wide, or had as many trees felled beside them as had the mammoth tracks. There were a number of such tracks in the snow-hung woods, and the hunters chose one and followed it, their fur boots going silently and carefully along the frozen ground so as to give no warning of their coming.

Sauk went first, as befitted the leader. Mar said nothing, but Alin could see how he chaffed at having to take a secondary role to the nirum. She herself followed close behind Mar's broad reindeer fur back as the line of hunters moved silently along the mammoth track.

The ability to move soundlessly through the forest is a skill that must be learned in childhood if it is to be learned at all. It is not a skill that can be taught by words, for it is not a skill of the mind but a skill of the body. In the hunters who stalked the mammoth track this day, every nerve and muscle in the body functioned as an eye, aware not only of where it was, but also of where it was going to be. This was not something any of them thought about consciously; it was simply something that they did.

In front of the line, Sauk slowed his pace, and stopped. Silently, he pointed to the frozen earth before his feet. Mar and Alin came to stand beside him.

There, still steaming a little in the cold morning air, was an enormous pile of fresh droppings.

"Mammoth," Sauk said soundlessly, merely moving his lips. He looked at Mar for a moment, a strange speculative look. Then the nirum leader said softly, "Do you want to go ahead and scout?"

Mar looked surprised, then nodded agreement. Sauk turned and signaled to the rest of the party to fall back and let Mar go ahead alone.

Alin said, "I will come too," and moved forward to follow Mar.

His head swung around and for a moment she thought he would send her back. Then he smiled at her faintly, and turned back to the trail. A space opened up between the two and the rest of the pack.

Alin and Mar crept slowly forward along the track. In a little while they heard the sound of trees crashing in the distance.

Alin felt excitement bubbling in her stomach and she gripped her spear tightly. It sounded as Mar had described the mammoth breakfasting on bark, she thought.

In front of her, Mar stopped abruptly. The halt was so sudden and so unexpected that Alin actually bumped into him. He stood like a rock and said nothing. She peered around his shoulder, her nose in the fur of his tunic, and saw, standing before him in a little glade into which the morning sun was shining, a mammoth with a small calf by her side. The huge animal was perfectly motionless, perfectly silent, watching them.

Mar didn't make a sound either. But very slowly, very quietly, very carefully, he began to back up. Alin backed with him.

Her heart was slamming so hard she was certain the mammoth could hear it. She is going to charge, Alin thought. We are much too far into her territory, much too close to her baby. . . . She is going to charge.

The mammoth's ears pricked, but her trunk did not go up. Surely Sauk had said that the trunk went up when they charged? Mar had his arm slightly raised, Alin noticed, and somehow he had managed to pull off his right mitten so that the spear was held more dexterously in his bare hand.

The sun shone brightly into the glade's small open space. Framing the glade, the mother, and the baby, were the great bending trees of the forest, faintly dusted with white from an earlier fall of snow.

Back and back and back they went, retreating into the woods, retreating out of the mammoth's limited range of vision. Except for the ears, the great beast never moved. The sun reflected off the reddish hair of mother and calf and, all at once, Alin knew that she and Mar were safe. The mammoth would not charge.

Just once, before they backed completely out of sight, her ears twitched. Otherwise she remained motionless. Then Mar halted, and Alin did likewise. As they watched, the great beast turned and lumbered off down the mammoth track, her calf at her side.

They stood and listened to the sound of her going. Alin's pulse began to return to normal. Then, when finally there was silence once more, Mar lowered his spear and turned to look at her. "So," he said. His eyes were very blue. "Now you have seen a mammoth."

Unfortunately, they did not see any mammoths again until the very end of the day, when they had turned to go back to their camp on the river. As was usual, the hunters heard the beasts before they actually saw them. This time it was not the sound of eating that attracted their attention, however, but a series of loud clarion calls that rang through the still cold air of the forest. The hunters moved silently in the direction of the noise until they found themselves on the edge of a large open white meadow spread at the foot of a sloping wooded hill.

In the midst of the meadow Alin saw two young bull mammoths moving to and fro around each other, tails and trunks held high in the air. It was their challenging cries that had attracted the hunters.

Alin heard Mar's breath catch audibly. She felt the same way herself. Without anyone giving a direction, the entire party melted back into the trees and concealed themselves to watch.

The two great animals continued to weave around each other for a while, obviously taunting each other with voice and action. Then one mammoth finally left off his posturing, went up to the second, and laid his trunk on the other's forehead.

This was evidently the signal for action. Forehead to forehead, the two young mammoths locked tusks and began to strain together in combat. The earth beneath their huge feet shook. The sound of the ivory tusks clinking together filled the air. Their great bodies quivered with exertion, the long reddish brown hair rippling and shivering in the slanting rays of the late-afternoon sun.

Finally, one of the combatants was pushed back upon his great haunches. The winner stood over him, raised his trunk, and trumpeted his victory to all the world in a deafening fanfare of sound.

Awestruck, Alin watched the scene unfolding before her. She could not believe her luck. How many people, she wondered, had ever beheld such a sight as this?

The defeated mammoth lumbered to his feet. His trunk hung low. His ears drooped. Alin began to smile. The poor thing looked as woebegone as a dog that has been cheated of a bone.

Suddenly a cold blast of wind came whistling through the trees within which the hunters were concealed. As if by magic, the ears and trunk of the defeated mammoth flicked to attention as he caught the scent of man. This time the noise that filled the air was not a trumpet of triumph but a scream of danger. And then the two bulls turned and rushed into the trees on the far side of the meadow. The very forest seemed to tear from its roots at their going. The hunters stood and listened to the cataclysm of crashing trees and made no move to follow.

Elen said, "Even if we never get a mammoth, that sight is worth the whole of the hunting trip."

"Sa."

"Sa."

"That is so."

There was a great sigh, as if the hunters had let out their collectively held breath.

Tane said to Jes, "I am going to draw that."

Sauk said, "Time to be getting back to the tents. Dale and Melior and Elen and Iva—you are in charge of getting us something to eat. The rest of us will see to the fires."

There was reindeer to roast over the cooking fire that night, and after eating, the hunters sat around, talking companionably and sucking melted marrow from the leg bones. The following morning Melior and Dale got them fish for breakfast. They sang a hunting song and set out along yet another of the mammoth trails, hoping to have better hunting luck this day than they had had the day before.

"Not that we have been unlucky," Tane said to Jes. "That sight yesterday was one I would not give up for a handful of mammoth bulls with tusks as big as I am."

"Sa." Her face glowed with remembrance. "That was something to remember."

They had not gone very far along the track before Sauk sighted a promising spoor. As before, he sent Mar and Alin ahead to scout.

This time the sound that alerted Alin to the presence of mammoth was not the familiar cataclysm of crashing trees, but a low rumbling noise, rather like the sound of thunder in the distance. Sauk had once remarked that the bowels of peacefully occupied mammoth rumble continually, and she halted even before Mar put up his hand.

After a brief silent moment, Mar began to creep forward along the track, Alin coming behind him. Abruptly, the huge, hairy, red-brown hindquarters of two big bulls loomed before them.

Once again, the hunters halted. This time Mar held up his hand, waggled his fingers, and pointed east. Alin read his signal. They were going to circle the mammoth downwind so that Mar could get a look at the tusks.

It took them almost an hour to make the relatively small circle, but the result of the slow, unnerving stalk was worth it. Both bulls had just the long curving ivory tusks the Tribe of the Horse was looking for.

Slowly, and with infinite care, Mar and Alin retraced their steps. Then they went for the rest of the party.

"Two of them," Mar reported with satisfaction. "Right on the track."

Sauk grinned. "Good news." He turned to Tane and Bror. "You two can go ahead, then, and set the spear trap." As the initiates began to move off, Sauk added, "Watch the wind."

Tane was insulted. "Of course we will watch the wind," he muttered to Bror.

Bror grunted, and addressed his next remark to Mar. "We will give the wolf call when we have finished," he said.

Mar nodded and the rest of the hunters watched as the two young men set off, carrying an extra spear whose shaft was weighted with a rock.

When they had disappeared up the track, "It is cold work, this waiting," Elen complained, stamping her feet and slapping her hands together.

"If girls wish to hunt, they must learn to endure like the men," Sauk said with satisfaction.

Elen flashed him an angry look.

"I am afraid there is nothing to be done *but* endure," Mar said to her. "We cannot light a fire. The mammoths might catch the scent of smoke."

"Tell us again how you will set the trap," Alin suggested, thinking that talk would help to distract them from the cold. "I want to have a clear picture of it in my mind."

Mar gave her a faint, approving smile. "It is called the trap of the falling spear," he answered agreeably. "That is the trap most used by the tribes of the Kindred for killing mammoths. It is not used by the mammoth hunters to the east because it only gets you one beast, but it has the virtue of never failing so long as you can get the mammoth you want going forward along a single track."

Mar propped his shoulders against a tree and dug the shaft of his spear into the earth. Lounging comfortably, he continued his explanation of the trap. "Tane and Bror will circle around the bulls and then find a treetop that hangs right over the mammoth track further on. They will take the weighted spear, attach a long piece of sinew to it, and fix it in the tree. Then they will stretch the sinew across the track below the tree. When the mammoth rushes along the track he will break the sinew, and the spear will fall."

"I understood all that the first time you explained the trap to us," Alin said. "But what I do not understand is how you can be sure that the spear will fall where it needs to in order to kill the mammoth."

Mar cocked his eyebrows. "A good question. The secret of the success of the falling spear lies in the calculation of exactly where to fix the spear. You have to calculate the mammoth's speed, you have to calculate the distance between the trees, and you have to fix the spear at such a height that when it falls it will enter the mammoth's body at a vital point." Mar's eyes moved from Alin to Jes. "That is why we sent Tane and Bror," he said. "They have a talent for such calculations."

They waited. The thin winter sun filtered down through the bare trees onto the mammoth track, but it held little warmth. Finally, when they were all beginning to feel very cold indeed, the blood-curdling howl of a wolf came keening through the pale winter sunlight.

"They have set the spear," Sauk said with satisfaction. "Now it is up to us to drive the mammoths along the track." And he took his fire stick out of his wide belt and bent to the tinder that he had already made ready. In ten minutes, he had a fire. The rest of the hunters took the long branches they had passed the time cutting, and lit them. Then they all began to move along the mammoth track, torches in their left hands, spears in their right, dogs at their heels. When they were almost on the mammoth, Sauk raised his voice in the eerie yodeling hunting call of the tribe, and began to run forward. The rest followed.

A resonating scream of warning ripped through the air. Then they heard the crashing noise of mammoths leaving in a hurry. Alin could feel the earth under her feet vibrating with their going.

The hunters ran on in pursuit. Suddenly, from up ahead on the track, there came another scream, this one of a different quality from the first. Mar grunted. "The spear got one of them," he said to Alin, and increased his speed.

They almost ran into the fallen animal, they came up on him so quickly. Instinctively, they drew back from the immense thrashing beast, and then a voice called to Mar. Alin looked up to see Tane perched high in a tree, his spear in his hand. As she watched, he launched it. The mammoth shuddered and quieted. Then Bror, who was in a tree on the other side of the track, let go his spear.

From farther down the track came a typhoon of crashing as the second bull fled the death scene of his companion.

"I think that's done it," Mar called to Tane and Bror.

The hunters stood together as Sauk left the group and went over to the fallen beast. There was silence as he plunged his spear into the fallen mammoth's ear.

"That's finished it," Sauk said. He grinned at the rest of them. "We have got a mammoth."

Twenty

The hunters built a fire right on the mammoth track to warm themselves, and then Bror took off the precious tusks. He did it carefully, using the burin and hammer stone he had brought with him for just this purpose. The flint burin he used was a brilliantly simple engineering tool, with one cutting face and one cutting angle. Tapping carefully with the hammer stone, Bror notched a circular groove into the first layer of ivory, close to where the mammoth's tusks came out of his face. Once the groove had been cut, it was relatively easy for Bror to break off the tusks evenly.

Then the rest of the hunters butchered part of the mammoth for that night's supper, first taking care to bury the heart, which was sacred to Sky God. It was starting to snow by the time they returned to camp, tired and cold, but triumphantly laden down with meat and ivory.

While fires were being lit in the tents, some of the men hauled water from the river to wash off the blood of the butchering work. The river in front of the tents ran about six feet below the steep clifflike shoreline, and to get water it was necessary to secure a container with rope and lower it into the tumbling white water. The river was deep right to the shoreline rocks, and the containers submerged and filled immediately.

The water they had fetched was soon stained red, and Mar said, "I had better get some more for drinking."

Sauk grunted agreement, and, after telling Lugh to

stay, Mar put on his furs and went back out into the growing darkness.

The snow was light but steady, and it fell onto Mar's bare head. He pulled up his hood. When he reached the river, he untangled the ropes that were tied to the bladders he was going to lower into the water, and stepped up to the edge of the steep clifflike shore.

It was almost dark by now, and snowing more heavily. Mar looked at the churning white water, and dropped his containers into the river.

He was standing right at the edge of the cliff, looking down. When the blow smashed into the back of his head, he staggered. It was his hood that saved him; had the rock hit his bare head, it would have crushed his skull. As it was, the blow stunned him, and the subsequent shove between his shoulder blades unbalanced him completely. With almost no struggle, Mar dropped off of the cliff and into the river.

The shock of the cold was mind-shattering. The river here was deep, and Mar went right under the freezing water. He kicked to bring himself afloat, but already the cold had begun to do its deadly work and there was scarcely any strength in the muscles of his legs. His fur coat was incredibly heavy, and would get heavier as it became fully saturated. His boots were dead weights on his feet, pulling him downward.

The current was carrying him swiftly downriver.

He yelled. Useless, he thought. Even if someone heard, this cold would kill him in minutes. But he had to do something. He opened his mouth to yell again, and churning, freezing water filled his throat. He choked.

He was barely afloat, still moving his arms and his legs, trying to aim for the shore. But he knew that even if he made the shore, it would be no good. He would never be able to climb out of the river, not with those sheer, slippery rocks in his way.

His arms and legs moved ever more slowly. His brain began to grow fuzzy. The rushing water slapped him in the face, and he choked again.

Why fight? he thought. You're a dead man.

He had no feeling in his arms or his legs. They had

almost ceased to move, and he was beginning to sink. He tipped his head back, to keep his nose and mouth above water, and the snow fell on his face.

"Mar!"

Dimly, as if from a long way away, he heard a voice. "Mar!"

He tried to look toward the shore, but the dark and snow obscured his vision. It sounded like Tane.

"Grab this!"

Can't, Mar thought. Can't move.

A deer bladder hit him in the face.

Tane screamed a curse at him. "Grab it, Mar! Now!"

With the most tremendous effort of will he'd ever made, Mar lifted his arm and closed his fingers around the bladder. The rope holding it began to tow him through the water toward the shore.

No use, he thought. Can't climb out.

"Mar!"

He held to Tane's voice the way he was holding to the bladder. Mindlessly. Tenaciously.

"The shore along here is lower," Tane was saying. "You can climb out. Come on!"

Mar bumped into the rocks. Tane grabbed the sodden coat at the shoulder. He was kneeling only a little way above Mar. "Mar, you son-of-a-hyena!" Tane screamed. "Get *out* of there. You've been in too long! *Get out!*"

Tane heaved on Mar's shoulders. "Help me," he said despairingly. "You're too heavy. I can't move you alone."

Mar put a foot down, and felt rock underneath. The river was shallower here. Tane had put one of Mar's hands around a rock, and now he pushed off with his foot, and dragged himself upward.

"That's it." Tane's voice was breathless.

I can't, Mar thought.

"*Now,*" said Tane, and they both heaved again. Mar landed on the rocks.

"Get out of those clothes," Tane said next, and kneeling over Mar, he began to strip off his fur coat. Mar struggled to sit up so Tane could work more easily. "Shirt too,'' Tane said. "Come on. Hold up your arms so I can get it over your head.''

Mar did as he was told, and Tane ripped off the soaking, freezing buckskin, leaving Mar's bare torso exposed to the falling snow. "Now,'' Tane said, "put this on,'' and he ripped off his own coat and began to stuff Mar into it.

"One more minute and you would have been dead,'' Tane was muttering under his breath as he belted the coat around Mar.

"S-sa,'' Mar said.

"What happened?''

"S-someone p-pushed me.''

Tane's busy fingers stilled. "Sauk,'' he said then, his quiet voice filled with pure hatred.

"I d-don't know. D-didn't see him.''

"Get up,'' Tane said. "I want to get you back to the fire.''

Mar managed to get to his feet. He was shivering uncontrollably, but he was able to move his arms and his legs. Slowly, the two men began to walk away from the deadly river.

"H-how did you f-find me?'' Mar stuttered.

"I thought we needed more water, so I came after you,'' Tane replied. "Sauk had already left the tent, so he couldn't know I was behind you.''

"D-did you s-see him?''

"Na,'' Tane said with great regret. "I did not. I heard you yell, and I ran like the wind down the river, where you were being carried. I saw nothing else.''

Mar halted. "D-don't say anything about my b-being pushed, Tane. Not y-et. It w-will only cause t-trouble.''

"It certainly will cause trouble,'' Tane said grimly. "The boys are like to murder Sauk.''

"T-that is what I mean. W-ait until I can h-handle him.'' Then, when Tane was silent, "I'm not up to it just n-now, Tane. P-please?''

"All right,'' Tane answered. "I don't agree with you, but . . . all right.''

Sauk was sitting before the fire when Tane and Mar came into the big tent. The look of shock on the nirum's face when he looked up and saw who was in the door was enough to convince both of the younger men of his guilt. Then Alin cried, "Mar! What happened?"

"I f-fell in the r-river," Mar replied through chattering teeth, and Tane pushed him forward toward the fire.

"Get his sleeping skins to wrap him in," Tane ordered Jes. "I am going to get the rest of his wet clothes off of him."

Tane worked in silence, wrapping Mar in his buffalo skins and then stripping off his freezing trousers and boots. Mar huddled by the fire and shivered, and Tane piled his own sleeping skins on top of Mar's. Lugh sat next to his master and gazed at him worriedly.

"Food," Tane said next. "Food will help to warm you."

"Sa," said Mar, managing to speak for the first time without a stutter.

The mammoth meat was cooked enough to eat, and Alin gave Mar a big hunk of it. He bit into the meat and chewed it slowly.

The three nirum had been silent all during the time the girls and Tane were fussing over Mar. After Mar had been served, Sauk got food for himself, and the other nirum followed suit. They all sat around the fire, chewing silently. Mar chewed and shivered. Tane and the girls watched him.

Finally, Alin said expressionlessly, "I would very much like to know how you came to fall in the river."

Mar said, "I don't know. Can't remember. I must have hit my head."

Sauk looked up alertly.

Alin frowned. "Hit your head? Where?"

Mar pointed to the spot on the back of his head where Sauk had hit him, and Alin got up and went to look. His hair had almost dried and when Alin's fingers touched his scalp, he winced.

"A strange place to hit yourself," Alin said, still with no expression in her voice. She looked down at her fingers, resting light as air on the distinct lump they had discovered. Wisps of damp golden hair clung to them.

"I don't remember," Mar said. Then, fretfully, "My head hurts all over."

Alin took his chin in her hand and turned his face upward so she could scan it. He was too pale, she thought, and his eyes seemed cloudy.

"You must have hit your head on a rock," Heno said. "The river is full of them. You were very lucky, Mar, that Tane came out after you."

"Sa," said Sauk. "Very lucky."

Mar looked at the nirum, who did not look back.

Alin said to Tane, "Where are Mar's furs? And his shirt?"

"Back at the river." Tane stood up. "I had better go and get them."

"Sa. They will need to be dried before he can travel," Alin replied.

Mar said to Tane, "Take Lugh."

The foster brothers looked at each other, then Tane nodded and whistled to the dog, who went only after a word from Mar.

They spread Mar's clothes on a dryer made of branches. "You won't be going anywhere for a while," Tane said to him with a grin. Mar smiled back a little crookedly. He had stopped shivering, but his eyes looked heavy. He had eaten very little of his meat.

"Lie down," Alin said softly.

He nodded, and while the rest of them shifted their places to accommodate Mar's hanging clothes, he went to sleep.

Mar's fur coat and boots were still wet the following day. His shirt and trousers had dried, and even though they were hard and stiff, the buckskin needing to be re-scraped, he put them on. "You're too big to fit into anyone else's clothes," Tane told him. "You will just have to stay in the tent until your furs are dry."

"I don't mind," Mar replied with a grin. "The girls will keep me company."

The initiates kept him company as well, having decided among themselves that it was not safe to leave Mar alone. None of them believed the story of Mar "falling" into the river.

"Mar never loses his balance," Dale had said scornfully when first he was told the tale. "Something happened that he is not telling us about."

"Sa," Bror had agreed. "I am thinking it would be well if we did not leave Mar alone with the nirum."

And so all day the large tent was crowded with people. It snowed off and on, and the many bodies packed in together made for warmth.

Jes asked Bror to explain how he would go about carving the mammoth tusks into a statue.

"First he must steam the ivory to soften it," Melior answered. "Is that not so, Bror?"

"If this were ivory that we had traded for at a Gathering, then I would have to steam it," Bror agreed. "But ivory or antler or bone from a fresh-killed animal has not had a chance to dry and is still soft." He smiled at Jes. "Actually, for splitting, it is better that the ivory be slightly dried. It is easier to work with thus. But not for work with the burin or whittling work with a knife. Then it is necessary that the ivory be softer. If I make the statue as soon as we get home, I may not have to steam the tusks."

"How do you steam them?" Jes asked next. The rest of the hunters were listening idly, but Jes's interest was intense.

Bror drew in a deep breath, obviously delighted to hold forth upon his craft. Sauk moved restlessly, but said nothing.

"First," Bror said, "you must soak the ivory for a handful of days. Next you take a piece of fresh skin and soak it until it is swollen. You wrap the skin, with the fur turned inward, around the ivory three times. Then you put the whole thing into a low-burning fire and keep it there until the skin is completely charred. When you take it out of the fire, the wrapping falls to pieces and the ivory is so hot it is impossible to hold it in your bare hands. When it cools it can easily be whittled with a flint knife. It can also be bent, if that is necessary."

Dale nodded. Melior made a noise denoting interest.

Jes said, "Is that how an ivory headband is made? The Mistress has one, and I have always wondered how it was done."

"Sa," Bror replied. "You take a knife and flake a long piece off the length of the tusk right after you have steamed it." Bror was now talking only to Jes. "When I make a statue I will use both a whittling knife and a burin, and I will need the ivory to be somewhat soft. I shall have to see how it handles before I decide what I must do."

"May I watch you?" Jes asked.

Bror nodded. "You will be most welcome."

Jes smiled.

Tane frowned.

Mar sneezed.

"Poor Mar," said Elen. "I fear you are going to suffer for yesterday's wetting."

"If a dripping nose is all he gets out of it, he is lucky," Alin said. "Water like that kills very quickly." Her voice was hard, and she was looking at Sauk.

Alin had lain awake for most of the night, listening for Mar's breathing and thinking about his "accident." Her thinking had brought her to the same conclusion the boys had reached, and her stare at Sauk was inimical.

"Sa," said Bror in an equally hard voice. He too directed a hostile stare at the nirum.

Eoto spoke up. "Mar has the constitution of a cave bear." He gave Mar a tentative smile.

Mar looked back at Eoto, his blue eyes enigmatic. Then he said deliberately, "It is true that I am hard to kill. Neither do I turn my back upon my enemies twice."

Sauk spoke into the tense silence. "What enemies?" he asked. "What are you talking about, Mar? You fell in the river."

"Sa. I fell in the river. And Tardith was killed by a falling spear." Mar's voice was quiet, and it took a moment for the meaning of his words to register with his listeners.

Sauk's eyes narrowed.

Bror's breath hissed in his throat.

Eoto looked bewildered. "What do you mean?" he asked.

Mar's eyes moved from his face to Heno's. Heno was frowning in faint puzzlement.

"You are from an unlucky family, Mar," Sauk said.

Melior began to rise.

"Sit." Mar waited until Melior had obeyed, then he said to Sauk, "I am thinking that we shall learn very shortly who is unlucky in the Tribe of the Horse, Sauk."

The nirum bared his little square teeth.

Alin said, "I think that Bror and Melior and Dale should sleep in here tonight. The nirum can sleep in the other tent."

Sauk blustered, "You are not the one giving orders here, girl."

"Where were you last night, Sauk, when Mar went into the water?" Alin asked. "You left this tent right after him. We all saw that. Where did you go?" She turned to Elen. "Did he come to the other tent?"

"Na." Elen shook her head. "He did not come in to us."

"I was using the pit," Sauk said. He stared furiously around the fire. "It is not my fault if Mar slipped and fell into the water!" He glared at Mar. "Are you saying that I pushed you in?"

"Na," said Mar softly. "I am not saying that, Sauk. I did not see who hit me over the head and pushed me. They came up behind me, and it was dark."

Heavy silence fell over the tent.

Eoto said, "I did not know of this."

Mar said, "I do not believe you did."

"You lost your balance, fell, and hit your head on a rock," said Sauk contemptuously. "Do not try to save your face by blaming your clumsiness on me, Mar."

The initiates and the girls were staring at him with hostile eyes.

"But why would Sauk want to do such a thing?" Heno asked, looking from face to face as he spoke. "There is no reason!"

"Mar is to be made a nirum this spring," Tane replied. "He will be eligible to challenge the chief."

Heno laughed with genuine amusement. "The challenge is impossible," he said. "Everyone knows that."

"Do not count on that, Heno," Mar said. His voice was calm. Confident. "Neither do I think that Altan and Sauk are as certain of the impossibility as you are."

Eoto and Heno looked at him, and then looked back to their own leader.

Sauk's unwinking stare was fixed upon Mar. Slowly, with real menace, the nirum rose to his feet. "I will not forget this accusation, Mar," he said.

Mar sneezed.

Sauk gestured to his two followers. "We will go to the other tent," he said. "The air in here stinks."

There was silence as the three nirum made their way through the packed tent to the door flap. After they had gone out, Mar said to those still within, "I cannot accuse him before the tribe. I did not see him."

"We understand," Dale said somberly. "But we know, too, that if someone pushed you, Mar, it was Sauk."

"Sa." The agreement came from a variety of male and female voices.

"When you go anywhere in the future," Alin said, "make certain you take Lugh."

Twenty-one

The nirum found themselves ostracized by the rest of the hunters on the return journey, a state of affairs that enraged Sauk. Heno and Eoto vacillated from being angry with Mar to being angry with Sauk, whose behavior had resulted in their alienation from the girls. Everyone was relieved when the cliffside caverns came into sight, and the enforced proximity of the hunting party was at an end.

Bror, watched intently by Jes, began the delicate work of carving the ivory birthing statue of the Mother. Alin notched the beginning of Shadow Moon on her deer bone calendar, and the days began to grow longer.

During the time of Shadow Moon, both the women of the Horse Tribe and the women of the Red Deer were busily occupied with the making of clothing. This was a skill in which the women of the Horse excelled, and the Red Deer girls had become comfortable enough with the Horse women to be able to express their admiration of that skill, and to learn.

The dearth of women in the tribe meant that there were many men who had no mothers or sisters or wives to make their clothing for them, and Alin and Mada agreed between them that each woman would make one shirt and one pair of trousers for a man who did not belong to her.

Mora was the only Red Deer girl to object when she heard this edict. "We are to make clothing for our kidnappers?" she asked indignantly.

Alin's authority was rarely challenged, and when it

was, her usual response was to become very still. She answered now, softly, "I am thinking that this tribe has had a terrible thing happen to it, and that it will not harm us to help them by making a few extra pieces of clothing."

"Let the men make their own clothes," Mora mumbled.

"The men have no skill in the making of clothes." Alin's voice was still soft. "The men are hunters. You have eaten the meat of their kill all winter long, Mora. I have not heard you complaining about taking their food."

There was mutinous silence from Mora.

"Alin is right," Jes said. "What harm in making a shirt for a man who will otherwise go naked?"

Mora's chin came up. "Sa, you will make a shirt for Tane," she said nastily. "And Sana will make one for Melior, and Dara for Arn. But there is no one *I* wish to make a shirt for, I am telling you that."

"Then you need not do so," Alin returned, her voice very quiet. "If there is so little generosity in your heart, Mora, then I release you from the duty."

As usual, Alin's quietness was effective in a way that bullying would never have been, and Mora burst into bitter tears. In the end, she agreed to make a shirt and a skirt for Elexa, one of the Horse women, while Elexa would make clothing for both her husband, Tod, and for her brother Cort.

A few of the women of the Horse were also working with the reindeer furs that the men had collected since reindeer hunting season had opened two moons since. It took seven whole reindeer skins to make one single fur tunic, and it was hard, painful work to push the bone needle with its thread of sinew through the skin and the thick animal fur.

The atmosphere in the women's cave was dramatically different these days from what it had been when first the two groups of women had met. A camaraderie had grown among them, a sense of shared lives and shared destinies and shared powers.

The Red Deer girls knew that even if they did not marry Horse Tribe men, they would marry other men, and bear children and raise children the way the women of the Horse were doing. And the women of the Horse were coming to learn from the new women that as the bearers of life, they possessed a power that was greater than that of men. As Alin had told them, a man's power was the power of the hunter who took life away from the world, while it was the power of a woman to put life back in.

A watershed moment for the Horse women's growing pride in the power of their own womanhood came when Alin conducted an initiation ceremony for one of their girls. It was held for Ina, Melior's twelve-year-old sister, who had begun her first menstruation during the time of the growing Shadow Moon. It was the first initiation Alin had ever conducted, and it was probably the most satisfying any of the Red Deer girls had ever known.

The women of the Horse were so impressed! It was a revelation to them, that a girl's becoming a woman was an occasion as important to the tribe as was a boy's becoming a man.

The initiation had gone beautifully, even though half of the attendees did not know any of the songs or rituals.

"With beauty before her, she comes, she comes . . ." Alin chanted as the flutes played by Sana and Elen and Iva followed her, and Jes painted the sacred signs on Ina's budding woman's body.

"The secrets of the earth shall open before her, the Way of the Mother shall be her Way . . ." Still chanting, Alin placed a shell headdress upon Ina's long flowing hair.

"She shall walk in beauty always, walk in the harmony of the earth, bringing life to the tribe, life to the herds, life to the world of men."

There was a great feast in the women's cave, and singing and dancing. A girl had become a woman and her sisters in the tribe celebrated with joyful reverence. The women of the Horse were profoundly moved by the entire two-day ceremony, and the feelings it engendered lingered for a long time in their hearts.

* * *

As the growing Shadow Moon became full and then waned, a change came over the men's caves as well.

The Moon of the Great Horse was approaching. This was the time of year when the Sacred Horse was sacrificed, the new fire kindled, the young boys initiated, the five-year initiates made nirum, and the chief dedicated. This ceremony, called the Ceremony of the Great Horse, was held at the time of power, when the moon was at its full.

This was always a time of excitement for the men of the Horse. This year, however, the great annual ceremony promised even more drama than usual. This year there would be a challenge for the chieftainship. This was the ceremony Mar had been awaiting since the day that Altan had first been dedicated, and the young boy who had been Mar had watched with burning blue eyes and a face like a white mask.

The topic came up between Altan and his closest companion as he and Sauk sat together around the smoky fire in Altan's cave one rainy night during the last days of Shadow Moon. "The tribe is edgy," Altan said moodily, after a long silence. "Too many men have been without women for too long, and the coming spring makes it worse."

Sauk grunted. "There was a fight today between Iver and Bror."

Altan's heavy brows drew together. "What about?"

"Supposedly it was about Iver borrowing Bror's spear."

"It was over the girls," Altan said. "Dhu, but I am glad it is coming time to give out the girls! The younger nirum and the initiates are like stags in rut."

"Stags in rut is the way to describe what was happening between Bror and Iver today," Sauk agreed.

"You stopped it, Sauk?" Altan asked with confidence.

Sauk pulled at his lip. "They were on the beach and I was on the first terrace," he replied. "I moved to stop it, but someone was before me."

"Mar," Altan said. Bitterly.

"Not this time. It was the girl. Alin." Sauk began to rub his jowls. "She stopped it with a word. And Bror and Iver were incensed, Altan. I would have sworn it would have taken physical force to separate them." Sauk looked at his chief broodingly. "That one needs some taming, Altan. I do not like the power she has taken to herself. If we are not watchful, the men of the Horse will become like the creatures of her own tribe, subservient to a woman."

Altan showed his crooked teeth. "I will tame her," he said with pleasure. "At this Spring Fires, she has promised to come to my bed. I will teach her what it means to be a woman who is under a man."

Sauk grinned back. Then he sobered. "Before Spring Fires," he said, "we must get rid of Mar."

Altan fingered the bag that hung at his neck. "He will have to make the challenge soon if he is to do it at all." Then, speaking strongly, "He cannot win the challenge, Sauk." A pause. "Can he?"

"He is a tricky dog," Sauk was back to worrying his lip. "I do not trust him."

Altan let out a great oath. "I am sick of him, Sauk! When I got rid of Tardith, I never thought I would be so bedeviled by his cub!"

"He is tricky," Sauk said, "but I am trickier yet." He spoke to the chief but his face was toward the fire. "Mar was lucky on the mammoth hunt. Such luck cannot continue."

"Sa," Altan said slowly. "That is so." He leaned a little forward. "But you must be careful, Sauk. There must be no evidence."

"There won't be," Sauk said with simple confidence. Outside the rain continued to beat against the cave-opening hides. Both men frowned thoughtfully into the gloom.

"No one is talking about anything else except this challenge," Dara said to Arn as they walked hand in hand along the beach one particularly fine afternoon late in the time of the disappearing moon. "But no one has told us what this challenge is, Arn. What must Mar do in order to take the chieftainship from Altan?"

Arn hesitated.

"Do not tell me if you are not supposed to," Dara said quickly. "I should not have asked you. . . ."

Arn's smooth, silvery eyebrows were slightly knit. He shook his head. "It is not that, Dara. It is not really a secret."

Dara looked at him, her gray eyes grave. "I don't want you to tell me if you don't think you should."

He shook his head again and said somberly, "No one talks of it because it is such a fearful thing. But now that it is upon us . . ." His hand tightened on hers. "I will tell you what it is," he said. There was a large smooth-topped rock near the river shore just ahead of them, and the two young people moved to sit upon it with a naturalness that suggested they had come to this place before. In an identical gesture, they raised their winter-pale faces to the warming sun. After a moment Arn began to talk.

"Each year the men of the tribe capture a stallion for the Ceremony of the Great Horse. Usually we build a stockade, drive a herd into it, and then we separate out the stallion." Arn glanced at Dara. "The horse, as you know, is my tribe's totem. It was Horse God many years ago who created the first men of my tribe, and so we owe him special reverence. That is why we do not eat his children, unless it is a matter of dire necessity. And that is why we capture a stallion and make the Sacred Sacrifice to him each year at our great annual ceremony."

Dara nodded solemnly. None of this was strange to her, even though the Tribe of the Red Deer did not have a taboo about eating deer meat. It was one more way in which the Way of the Mother differed from the Way of Sky God.

Arn squinted a little to screen the brightness of the sun. "This year there will be no building of a stockade," he said. "This year it will be up to the men who wish to be chief to capture the stallion."

Dara drew in her breath. "Mar and Altan must bring in a stallion together? A *live* stallion?"

"Na." Arn shook his head so vigorously that his pale hair swung against his cheek. "*Each* must bring in a live stallion, Dara. The first one to come in with the horse is the one Huth will name to be chief."

Dara stared at him. "But it is not possible for one man to capture a stallion," she said.

"Huth says that is the test."

"But what happens if neither of them can bring in a stallion?"

"Then Altan remains the chief."

Dara said childishly, "I do not want Altan to remain the chief. I want Mar."

Arn nodded. "So do I. So do all the initiates, and a number of the nirum, too. But for Mar to become chief, he must win this challenge."

"If more people want Mar to be chief than want Altan, then Mar should be chief," Dara said stubbornly. "Why do you need a challenge?"

"Think, Dara," Arn said gently. "If the men of the tribe were to allow a chief to be overthrown every time they thought they liked someone else better, there would be no order, no authority. There must be a test."

"I suppose so," Dara said doubtfully. "Well, perhaps Mar will be able to bring in a stallion. If anyone can do it, he can." She looked at Arn's somber face. "Is there more, Arn? What you have said thus far is not so terrible."

"Sa. There is one other thing," Arn said. "It is this: the man who fails the test is cast out from the tribe."

Dara sucked in her breath audibly. "Dhu! Are you saying that if neither of them capture a stallion, then Altan is the chief and Mar is cast out?"

"Sa," said Arn gravely. "That is what I am saying."

"But that is not fair!" Dara cried passionately.

"It is necessary. Otherwise we would have men challenging for the chieftainship every year, just to try their luck. That would not be good for the tribe, Dara. If a man knows failure means exile, he will think long and hard before he makes a challenge."

Dara said in a low voice, "I think I was happier before I knew all of this."

Arn sighed and looked at the sky. "Come," he said. "Huth will be looking for me."

The two youngsters slid off the rock and began to walk back toward the caves, hand in hand, keeping close to the limestone cliff. After they had gone a little way, Arn shook his head and said, "Such admiration for Mar. I am beginning to feel jealous."

Dara looked up at him, wide-eyed, a little distressed. "Do not be foolish," she said.

"Dara . . ."

Arn's steps slowed, and he stopped. He let go her fingers and rested both his hands lightly upon her shoulders. He was not a tall boy, but Dara was so small that she had to look up to see into his face. He was bending toward her. "I was joking you," he said. Then softly, very softly, his lips touched the baby-soft skin of her cheek. She felt his warm breath and her lashes fluttered down. She stopped breathing.

They stood thus for a long quiet moment, his lips waiting on her cheek, light and gentle as a butterfly on a flower. Then Dara let out her breath, sighed, and swayed toward him. His hands tightened on her shoulders and he drew her closer, into the curve of his arms. His lips moved, slid across her cheek, touched her mouth.

Dara stood perfectly still, forgetting once again to breathe, her lips under his. He pressed his mouth on hers. Her lips moved, answered, pressed his back. Their bodies, encased in fur vests for the warmer day, leaned together and touched.

It was Arn who broke away first, removing his mouth from her mouth to rest it on the top of her small dark head. He held her close against him. "Dara," he breathed. "Dara. I love you."

She pressed her cheek into his shoulder. A great joy welled up in her soul. She shut her eyes to contain it. "I love you too," she whispered back.

After a moment, they leaned away and looked at each other, two solemn-eyed, fur-clad children dwarfed by the limestone cliff above them.

"There will be trouble if you choose me," Arn said. He touched her cheek, briefly, tenderly, a touch as soft as his mouth had been. "I am too young to be married ahead of a nirum."

"Huth said the choice would belong to the girls," Dara said. "And I choose you."

His light, crystal clear eyes began to glow. "Do you?"
"Sa."

They continued to stare at each other, too exalted even
to smile.

Then, "I shall tell Alin," Dara said.

A faint frown puckered Arn's white brow. "Will that
be wise? Perhaps it would be best to keep this to ourselves. . . ."

"Na." Dara was very sure. "Alin is . . ." she sought
for the word she wanted. "Alin will understand," she
finally said. "And she has the power of the Mother. You
can see that upon her, I think. That power."

"There is a power in her," Arn agreed. "I am enough
of a shaman to see that." He nodded. "Very well, then,
perhaps you should tell her." He thought for a minute.
"If Alin will speak for us, her voice will count with
Mar."

"Sa." Dara looked grave. "We must hope that Mar is
the one to win this challenge, Arn. That Mar will be the
new chief of the Tribe of the Horse. Mar will honor
Huth's decision. Mar will let the girls choose their own
mates. I do not know if Altan will do the same."

"If Mar loses this challenge, I do not know what Altan
will do either," Arn said with unusual grimness. "He
has always ruled with the shadow of Mar looming at his
shoulder. Once that shadow is removed . . ."

Dara shivered.

Arn looked once more at the sky. "Come," he said.
"The sun is journeying toward the river and Huth will
be wondering where I am."

Immediately after his return from the mammoth hunt,
Mar once again sought out a small herd of horses he had
discovered. The stallion was one of the kind most favored by the painters of Mar's tribe: a bay, with big eyes
and a bushy black mane. He was a good leader. He knew
all the places where his mares might still find food, although food was scarce for all the animal herds this time
of year.

It was his usual hour and, even though Mar had been
gone for half a moon, the horses were waiting in their

usual place. When the man appeared, the stallion raised
his head and stood quivering, ears pricked forward. He
snorted. The five mares, heavy with advanced pregnancy, stopped in their attempts to find something to
graze on, and watched the man also. Last year's foals,
two yearling colts and one filly, actually came eagerly
forward before a second snort from the stallion made
them halt.

"So, my beauties," Mar said softly to the listening
herd. "Did you miss me?"

One of the mares blew down her nose, as if in answer.
Mar grinned. Then he walked forward out of the trees,
and for the first time the horses saw clearly the two large
baskets he was carrying.

The stallion squealed and threw up his head. He pawed
the ground restlessly. Mar moved closer, toward the corral that he had built. He climbed between the branches
of the fence.

"Here it is," Mar said, and he lifted the dried grass
out of the basket and arranged it in nine separate mounds
upon the ground, in the exact spots where he always put
them.

As the mares and yearlings pushed forward toward the
open side of the corral, the stallion watched them and
made no noise of warning. After his dependents had begun to feed, the stallion himself advanced into the corral,
went to the remaining pile of dried grass, picked up a
few strands and began to chew, keeping an eye on both
Mar and the mares as he did so.

Mar stood where he was, at arm's length away from
the horses, and watched them eat.

They had been looking for him, he thought. They had
known his scent immediately. They knew the sight of
him. They were cautious of him, but not afraid.

Mar had been cutting dried grass for these horses for
two summers now. And for two winters he had been
feeding them.

He began to move, slowly and deliberately, along the
side of the corral. The horses continued to eat. The stallion raised his head, watched Mar for a moment, and

then lowered his head again to take another mouthful of grass.

Mar continued to walk until he came to the open part of the corral. He stopped then, completely out of view of the horses. The stallion swung his head around occasionally to look, but the man's position did not disturb the rhythm of the horse's eating. When all the grass was gone, the stallion efficiently herded the mares and youngsters out the open side of the corral. The herd went by Mar without noticing him.

Mar had stored the dried grass in a cave downriver from the dwelling caves of his tribe, and each day of Shadow Moon he would bring the cut grass to the small herd, who waited for him faithfully in the same place at the same time each afternoon.

He had told no one, not even Tane, what he was doing. He had thought out this plan carefully, and he was beginning to be optimistic that it might indeed work. But if it did not, he did not want anyone but himself to know of his failure.

I have had plenty of time to think up a plan, Mar thought bitterly as he made his way back to the storage cave by the river, the empty baskets slung over his back.

Five years it had been since Tardith's death and Altan's installation as chief over Mar. But the long wait soon would be ended. Soon Mar would overthrow this usurping murderer and drive him mercilessly out of the tribe, both Altan and his treacherous companion, Sauk.

Very soon now, Mar would make the challenge. And then he would close up the corral behind the horses. And Altan would be finished.

So wrapped was Mar in his thoughts that he did not see the figure watching him from the deep shadows of the overhanging cliff. Sauk waited until Mar had gone up the beach before he came cautiously out of his concealment. The nirum's face was deeply thoughtful.

At the foot of the cliffside path, Mar met Dara and Arn.

That twosome was a problem, Mar thought, even as he smiled genially at the youngsters and made a pleasant comment. The nirum had been complaining bitterly over

Dara's evident preference, and the nirum were right. Arn was much too young to be given a wife over older men.

"It seems so strange to see you without Lugh," Dara was saying.

Mar could not take the dog when he went out to the horses.

"He was sleeping," he told her easily, and left them behind as he climbed up the steep path to the first terrace and his own shelter.

Lugh had not been sleeping at all. He had been told to stay in the shelter, and he had stayed, although not happily. He leaped up the moment he heard Mar's step, and crowded around Mar's legs as he came into the shelter, a quivering silver gray bundle of joy, his tail pumping back and forth so fast it created a breeze.

Mar laughed. "I wish that stallion were as glad to see me as you are, Lugh," he said. "Then would I have no trouble at all in catching him." He bent to scratch the dog's ears.

"He has been looking for you." It was Alin's voice, coming from the entranceway. "And so have I."

Mar looked up slowly. He had left the skins open so the rays of the slowly sinking sun would slant in and warm the shelter, and she was standing framed in the squarish entry, the sun behind her illuminating the gold threads in her brown hair.

"I have been thinking you were avoiding me," he said, and straightened up away from the dog.

She did not move. "Where have you been?" she asked. "And why did you not take Lugh?"

Mar drank in the picture she made, and did not reply.

Alin came forward a few steps so that she was fully inside the shelter. "Tane told me about this challenge," she said. "It's not possible for one man to capture a stallion." Her brown eyes looked him up and down. "You have a plan, don't you?"

"What makes you think that?"

"You always have a plan." Her voice sounded faintly bitter.

"Don't you want me to succeed, Alin?" he asked

softly. He quirked an eyebrow. "Wouldn't you rather make the Sacred Marriage with me than with Altan?"

She looked at him without answering. Then she shrugged. "If you do not want to tell me, that is your right," she said. And turned to leave.

All of a sudden, Mar found that he did want to tell her. He did not know why; he had never wanted to tell anyone else, not even Tane. But now he wanted to tell Alin.

One reason for this was that he did not want her to leave his shelter.

He called her name, sharply. She turned her head, an infinitely graceful gesture, and looked back at him over her shoulder.

"I do have a plan," he said. "I do not know if it will work, but it is a chance." He motioned. "Come in and I will tell you."

She turned around composedly and came back in. He gestured to a buffalo robe, and she sank down with her customary lithe grace. He sat himself and propped his back against the sapling that functioned as the main shelter pole. He had not had time to light a fire, but the shelter was not cold. It had been an unusually warm day.

They looked at each other, and then he told her about the little herd of horses.

When he had finished, she smiled at him, the kind of friendly smile he so rarely had from her. "How clever of you, Mar," she said warmly.

Her words made him feel as if he were chief of all the Kindred.

Alin raised her knees and comfortably linked her arms around them. Like the rest of the tribe on this warm day, she had shed her fur coat for a reindeer vest. She said thoughtfully, "However did such a strange test come to be, Mar?"

He pushed the thick hair off of his forehead and answered by relating the creation story known to all members of the Tribe of the Horse. "At the beginning of time, when the world tree was first grown and the sky and the earth and the land below were first created, Sky God and the Mother mated and made all the beasts of land and sea. The first horse they created was Horse God, and he has never died. He lives in the sky with the rest of the gods and watches over his children here on the earth. It was Horse God who made the herds of horses, and Horse God who made the first man of my tribe and bade him take the horse as his totem.''

Mar paused and Alin nodded gravely. He continued, ''So you see, the people of the Horse are kindred to the horse herds that roam our land, and that is why we never kill them for their meat. But once a year, at the time of the Great Horse Ceremony, we capture a stallion, one of Horse God's most splendid children, and send his spirit back to the god to intercede for the fortunes of the tribe.''

Mar's chin lifted slightly. ''The chief is to the Horse Tribe what the stallion is to the herd,'' he said. ''There is a kinship between them. Huth says that is why the test of chieftainship is the capture of a stallion. It shows that the stallion recognizes his brother by allowing himself to be so taken.''

''Ah,'' said Alin. She rested her chin on her updrawn knees. ''I see.'' Her large brown eyes were fixed on his face. ''Has any man ever done it alone before?'' she asked. ''Captured a stallion?''

Mar shook his head. ''I do not think so.''

They sat in silence for a moment, contemplating that statement. Then Alin got to her feet. ''Well, it seems as if it will be done this time.'' She gave him the brief, brisk nod he was too familiar with, and turned toward the door.

''Alin.'' She halted and swung back again, her brows lifting in inquiry. ''You did not answer me before,'' he said. He gained his feet with the swift grace of a giant cat. ''I asked you if you wouldn't rather make the Sacred Marriage with me than with Altan.''

He watched her face close up. Before she could turn once again to the door, his hand shot out and grasped her left arm.

She did not try to pull away. Alin had never tried to pit her strength against his, Mar thought in the brief seconds that they stood there thus. She relied instead on her tongue, most of the time to very good effect.

Her tongue was silent now, however. He looked down

into her averted face. Every time he looked at her he saw
something else he found exquisitely beautiful, something
else he wanted to touch with his hands and with his
mouth. Just now he was looking at the faint hollow at
her temple. The skin there was so fine and delicate, the
small hollow so infinitely tender.

"I think about you all the time," he said truthfully.
"That has never happened to me before."

At that she turned to him. An expression he could not
decipher, which almost looked like regret, flitted across
her face. Then it was gone, and she answered him, "It
is so with me also."

He put his other hand on her right arm and drew her
toward him. To his surprise, she came willingly into his
embrace.

He held her slim young body in his arms, and was
filled with a kind of wonder at having her there. His legs
felt suddenly weak, and, still holding her, he leaned back
against the sapling that supported his shelter. He felt Alin
slide her arms around his waist and rest her cheek against
his shoulder.

As the blood-red sun pooled on the buffalo robe at his
feet, Mar held her in his arms and an emotion he did not
recognize welled up deep inside of him. It was not lust,
he thought with confusion. He knew what that felt like,
and it was not lust. It was . . . it was like the feeling he
had surprised on Tane's face once during the mammoth
hunt, when he had caught his foster brother gazing at Jes
across the fire.

Against his shoulder, Alin sighed. She loosened her
grasp on his waist, and stepped away.

He said softly, "I do not like it, but you were right.
We must wait for the Sacred Marriage. For the good of
the tribe."

She tipped her face up so she could see into his. His
eyes went to the fragile hollow at her temple, and he bent
to touch it with his mouth. The skin under his lips was
exquisitely delicate. He raised his head reluctantly. "I
will capture the stallion," he told her. "I swear it."

That oddly regretful look crossed her face once again.
But all she said was, "I know." When she was at the

door, she turned. "Take Lugh with you when you go out, Mar," she said.

He gave her a cocky grin. "Sauk can't harm me, Alin. I am watching for him."

"You have only two eyes," she answered somberly. "Take Lugh." And then she left.

Twenty-two

The disappearing Shadow Moon marched ever eastward in the sky, moving on its ineluctable journey toward the place where it would disappear under the earth, only to be resurrected again in a few days' time as the Moon of the Great Horse. Alin notched the moon's progress on her deer bone calendar, each notch signaling to her one less day that she would be awakening in the now-familiar cliffside caverns that towered so high over the winding Wand River.

On the first day of the Ceremony of the Great Horse, Alin was planning to escape.

She had debated long about taking one of the other girls with her. A few moons ago she would not have hesitated to ask Jes. Now she was not sure.

Jes would come if Alin asked. It was not her friend's loyalty that Alin doubted. It was that she thought perhaps such a request would be asking more of Jes than a true friend ought to ask.

There was a quiet yet intense happiness about Jes these days that Alin knew was connected partly to the pictures Jes was learning to draw, and partly to Tane. Alin feared that it would be mean of her to rip apart that happiness by reminding Jes of prior claims.

Alin sat before the fire in the girls' cave, holding her deer bone calendar, listening to the soft breathing of the girls asleep around her and thinking about Jes and Tane.

In all the years since Jes's initiation, she had never once indicated a preference for any one man. At the time

of the Fires, when the drums were pounding and the blood
ran hot, she had taken a man like the rest of the girls. But
that one mating had been the extent of the relationship.
Neither had Jes ever shown any interest in meeting men
from the other tribes at the local Gatherings. She had always appeared to be content with her hunting, and with
her friendship with Alin.

And then Jes had met Tane.

Alin's eyes rested on the sleeping face of her friend,
faintly illuminated by the night fire. In sleep, Jes's face
looked softer. Younger.

Alin sighed. She could not ask Jes to go with her. It
would be unfair to lay upon her friend such a duty. Let
her bide here, where her talent was recognized and val-
ued. Where she was happy. Where she was loved.

The problem Alin found herself facing as she sat before her fire contemplating the prospect of escape was
that most of the Red Deer girls seemed to have settled
into the Horse Tribe almost as happily as Jes.

There were some exceptions, of course. Fali was still
homesick. But Fali was too young to act as a partner on
such a journey as the one Alin was planning to under-
take. She would be more hindrance than help.

Mora? Mora was not happy. Mora had never reconciled herself to the kidnapping, had never forgotten Nial,
the Red Deer boy who had been her promised husband.

The problem with taking Mora was that Alin did not
overly like the girl. Mora was a whiner. Alin herself had
never become reconciled to the kidnapping, but she had
not whined and complained all winter long, the way Mora
had.

Suddenly in the still quiet, it was as if Mar's voice was
sounding in Alin's ear: *I think about you all the time.*

His face seemed to hang in the air between her and the
fire. She could almost feel his presence in the cave.

Perhaps it was not true after all, Alin thought with
painful honesty. Perhaps she was not as unhappy as Mora
was.

I think about you all the time.

But there was no point in thinking about him. Nothing
was there for her but bitterness and regret. She was des-

tined to be the Mistress of her tribe. He was destined to be the chief of his.

And he would be. She had been glad to hear of his plan, glad to know that he would come into his proper place in the world.

Alin ran her finger along the notched length of her deer bone calendar and then, with abrupt decision, she knelt and put it in its proper place at the foot of her sleeping skins.

She would make her escape alone. It would not be as it had been the last time she had tried to escape from Mar. This time she would have weapons. This time she would take one of the dogs. Roc would come with her. Alin had been as busy making friends with Roc all winter as Mar had been busy making friends with the horse herd.

With the burden of that decision off of her mind, Alin crawled into her sleeping skins and went to sleep.

The last of Shadow Moon disappeared into the eastern sunrise and, after two days of no moon, the first sliver of the Moon of the Great Horse rose above the sunset in the west. That night, Mar went to the nirum's cave and made his challenge.

This was a momentous occasion for the tribe, and Altan did it justice. The only emotion to be read on the chief's face was a kind of stern dignity. The other nirum present in the cave were not so enigmatic. Rom looked sorrowful. The younger nirum looked expectant: whatever the outcome, they would have the excitement of the challenge to look forward to. Altan's companions looked triumphant: at last, their faces said, Mar has overreached himself.

Sauk stared unwinkingly at Mar and said nothing.

In the quiet that followed Mar's words, Altan rose. "Come," he said to his youthful challenger. "We will seek out the shaman."

"You have between now and the first quarter of the moon to capture a stallion for the Sacrifice," Huth told Mar and Altan when they appeared before him to receive formally the challenge test. "If neither of you has taken a stallion by then, the tribe can wait no longer. We must have a stallion for the ceremony.''

Altan said, ''And if neither of us takes a stallion, then I remain the chief?''

''That is right,'' Huth said.

Altan's great buffalo head lowered and swung toward Mar. ''And if I am the chief, then Mar must go into exile. That is the law.'' Still with his eyes on Mar, ''Am I not right, shaman?'' Altan demanded.

''Sa,'' said Huth, his voice cold. ''That is the law.''

Mar's blue eyes did not flinch from Altan's hard stare. ''And if I capture a stallion and Altan does not, then it is Altan who must become the exile. Is that not so?'' Mar asked of his foster father.

''Sa,'' said Huth. ''That is so.''

''So then.'' Altan showed his strong crooked teeth in a grimace that was not a smile. ''The challenge is made, the law is stated. In a quarter of a moon's time, we shall know for certain who is the true chief of the Tribe of the Horse.''

When he issued the challenge, Mar had almost completed the corral fence. The horses had not balked at entering through the smaller opening he had left them, and on this particular day, the third after the challenge, Mar stood in the bright sunlight watching the small herd file out of the corral after they had eaten. The sun shone brilliantly on shaggy winter coats of bay and chestnut, and Mar smiled as the horses disappeared into the trees.

Mar had taken care these last few days to make certain that he was not followed when he left his cliffside home. The curious eyes of the tribe were on him, and he did not want anyone accidentally spooking his horses. To have come so far, and then to lose all because of the sudden appearance of a stranger! Mar shuddered at the very thought.

He took care, and he was not followed. What Mar did not anticipate was that someone had already discovered the corral and could come after him at leisure.

I will finish this tomorrow, Mar thought now as the sounds of the horses died away. I will bring Huth and

Arn with me, and when the horses are inside the corral, I will close up the gate.

Joy pumped through him. The stallion will be mine, he thought exultantly. The chieftainship will be mine.

Mar was facing the corral, and the baskets in which he had brought the grass were lying at his feet. He never heard the man coming up behind him. Sauk had won his reputation as a great hunter honestly, and he could move with utter silence when he chose to. In Sauk's hand was a large rock, and the nirum's concentrated black eyes were fixed on the back of Mar's bare head.

Sauk raised his arm and kept coming on those eerily silent feet. Mar stared across the corral, at the place where the horses had disappeared. The rock started its noiseless descent, and Mar bent to pick up his baskets.

The blow landed on Mar's left shoulder instead of his head. Sauk cursed and grabbed Mar's arm to hold him as he raised his weapon again. Mar tried to pull away and the blow struck once more upon his shoulder.

Sauk was a powerful man and the rock was big. Mar felt excruciating pain run from his shoulder down through the whole length of his arm. Sauk was raising the rock again. Now the nirum was at a disadvantage because he was so much shorter than Mar, and his face was contorted with hatred. His merciless fingers still held Mar in place and this time he swung the rock directly at Mar's face.

Fury swept through Mar, and instinctively his fist hooked up and slammed into Sauk's jaw. The rock came down with crushing force on the vulnerable spot between Mar's neck and his left shoulder. Mar cursed and launched himself at Sauk.

Sauk was a strong and powerful man, but in a fair fight he was not the equal of the much bigger Mar. Mar's rush overbalanced the nirum and knocked him to the ground, and Mar dove after him.

The two men rolled in the dirt, first one on top and then the other. In the end, however, Sauk's oxlike physique availed him nothing against the sledgehammer blows of the infuriated Mar. When Sauk scrambled once more for the rock, Mar pounced on him and ground his hand into the dirt. Then, with his knee planted on Sauk's chest, Mar picked up the rock and held it over the nirum's forehead.

"Why shouldn't I do to you what you were going to do to me?" he panted, staring down into Sauk's sweating face. The pulse beating in Sauk's temples was clearly visible and under Mar's knees the nirum's chest was heaving.

Sauk showed his teeth. "Go ahead," he said. "Then try to explain my death to the rest of the tribe."

"How were you going to explain mine?" Mar countered.

Sauk managed a choking laugh.

"You chose a rock," Mar said, still panting heavily. "Not a spear. You wanted my death to look like an accident."

Sauk set his teeth and did not reply.

"You did not follow me today," Mar went on. "Of that I am certain." Sauk squirmed and Mar pressed his knee harder into the nirum's laboring chest. "Which means you must have followed me earlier, when perhaps I was not being so careful. So you had already seen the corral and the horses."

The flicker in Sauk's eyes gave him his answer.

"Was the rock supposed to look like the blow from a horse's hoof, Sauk?" Mar asked. "Was that it?"

Sauk cursed and surged upward. He was very strong and his sudden movement managed to dislodge Mar. The two struggled together again and then Mar had Sauk back under him once more.

"I will not kill you," Mar gasped. His face was bruised and streaming with sweat. "I don't want to start my chieftainship with a death. But I will throw you out of the tribe with Altan, Sauk. Tomorrow I will capture the stallion, and then I will throw you both out."

Sauk's skin went red with rage. "I should have used a spear," he snarled.

Mar's teeth showed white in his filthy face. "Sa," he said. "You should." And he raised his fist and slammed it into Sauk's jaw until the nirum was unconscious.

Mar took the rope that he had used as a holder for the

baskets and tied Sauk's hands and feet together. Then he slung the nirum over his shoulder, and began the long weary trek toward home.

There was an uproar in the tribe when an obviously bruised and battered Mar came in with Sauk tied up on his shoulder, but Mar refused to speak and took the nirum directly to Huth. Heno ran to tell Altan the news, and the chief too disappeared into the shaman's cave.

It was a grim-faced Huth who faced the men in the nirum's cave and told them of Sauk's attack upon Mar. "He saw that Mar had found a way to win the challenge, and he tried to kill him," Huth said.

"That is what Mar says," said Heno. "What of Sauk?"

"Sauk denies it, of course," Huth said.

"Mar has found a way to capture a stallion?" Iver asked with amazement.

"So he says. Arn and I are going to go with him tomorrow, to see him do it."

Rom said, "What of Altan?"

"Altan shall come too," Huth said. "It is his right to be a witness if Mar does indeed capture a stallion." Huth did not add that he wanted to keep Altan safely in his sight, but most of the nirum understood.

"Sa." Agreement ran around the cave.

"I do not think Mar can do it," one of Altan's companions said loyally.

"What of Sauk?" Rom asked.

"Sauk is not feeling very well at the moment," Huth said grimly. "He will remain in my cave until tomorrow afternoon. Then . . . we shall see."

A circle of heads nodded approval.

"How is Mar going to do it, Huth?" Iver asked eagerly.

But Huth shook his head. "Tomorrow," he answered. And left.

Altan was in a state of shock. Sauk was a virtual prisoner within the shaman's cave, and Huth said that Mar was going to capture a stallion.

I do not believe it, Altan thought, as he waited in his cave the following day for the shaman to come and fetch him. It is impossible. No single man can capture a stallion.

Altan clutched that thought to himself as, early in the afternoon, he put on his furs to accompany Mar, Huth, and Arn. It is impossible. It is impossible. The words formed a rhythm for him to lope to. It is impossible.

The rhythm faltered only when Mar stopped to collect the baskets full of dried grass.

"What are they for?" the chief asked suspiciously. But Mar only smiled an infuriating smile and replied, "Wait."

Their pace slowed after the baskets had been collected. "We must be careful of the wind," Mar said to Huth. "If the herd scents you, they will not come. They know my smell, but the smell of strange men will spook them."

Following Mar, the three of them circled until they were downwind of the clearing that Altan knew existed to the east of the thick trees within which they were hidden. They continued to move slowly and carefully until they were at the edge of the clearing, and it was then that Altan saw the corral.

He stopped breathing.

"Ma-ar," came Arn's awed whisper.

Mar looked at Huth. "I am going to put the grass within the corral," he told the shaman. "The horses will go in to eat. But it is essential that they have no suspicion of your presence. You wanted to bring Altan, Huth. I tell you now, it is up to you to keep him quiet and out of sight."

Huth nodded. "The test will be conducted fairly, Mar." Then the shaman turned to the chief. "Hear me, Altan," he said, his voice hard and cold as ice. "If the test is conducted fairly, and Mar fails, I will so report to the tribe. But if you try in any way to hinder this capture, then I will proclaim Mar chief and drive you out of the Tribe of the Horse forever. Do you understand me?"

"Sa," Altan said sullenly, his eyes shifting away from Huth's hard stare. The chief had always been afraid of the shaman, and both of them knew it.

"Go on, Mar," Huth said. "He will be quiet."

Mar nodded, lifted his baskets, and left the shelter of the trees.

Altan stood between Huth and Arn and watched as Mar arranged the grass into separate piles inside the corral.

No stallion would willingly bring his mares within so small an enclosure, Altan told himself. Mar was a fool if he thought otherwise.

Mar did not come back to rejoin them, but stayed instead by the rails of the corral.

"Why isn't he coming back here?" Altan asked uneasily.

"Shh," Arn replied.

Time passed. Suddenly, on the far side of the clearing, Altan saw the face of a horse peering through the trees. There was the sound of hooves and the rustle of branches. Then a small herd of nine horses was filing into the clearing.

To Altan's horror, the horses went directly to the corral opening, entered, and began to eat the grass. There was no fighting over which pile belonged to which horse. Each animal went with the confidence of what looked like long habit to a particular pile, lowered its head, and began to chew.

Last to enter the corral was the stallion.

Mad fury fired Altan's brain. He opened his mouth to shout, to frighten the horses away, but before he could make a sound a hard hand closed ruthlessly about his wrist. The pain cleared his head and, startled, he looked at Huth.

Don't. The shaman's lips formed the word, though no sound came forth. Huth's eyes were merciless.

Altan closed his mouth.

In the clearing, Mar had walked around to the back of the corral and, while the horses grazed peacefully, he lifted a branch and fitted it across the opening. Quickly he bent and lifted a second.

The stallion's head came up. He whirled around, snorting in alarm. By now, Mar had the third rail in place. The stallion screamed and galloped toward the fence.

Mar took one step back and then held his ground. The
stallion reared up on his hind legs, pawing at the man
who was safely on the other side of the strong fence. The
mares, alarmed by their leader's alarm, raised their heads
and also swung around to face Mar.

Arn laughed softly. "Well," he said to no one in particular, "it seems that Mar has captured a stallion."

It was Arn who brought the news to the tribe, Huth
deeming it safer to remain at the corral with Mar and the
stunned Altan. After speaking to the nirum, Arn went to
the women's cave and once more recounted his story.

The Red Deer girls were delighted, as were a number
of the women of the Horse. Then Nel's voice wailed
through the excited exclamations and questions, "But Altan hasn't even tried to capture a stallion. What is he
going to do now?"

Silence fell, then Arn said to her gently, "He has three
days until the quarter moon. If he wishes to remain as
chief, he had better do something."

Nel gave him a blank look, shifted her babe from one
shoulder to the other, and muttered, "I must go to my
own cave."

Another silence fell as Nel passed out.

"If Altan is exiled," Dara asked Arn once the sound
of Nel's footsteps had faded, "what will happen to Nel?
Will she have to go with him?"

"I do not think so," Arn replied. "I do not think Mar
would give up one of our women so easily."

"But what if she wants to go with him?" Dara asked.

At that, all of the women looked at Alin. It was a
measure of the position she had gained over the course
of the winter that the women of the Horse turned to her
as readily as did the girls of the Red Deer.

"If she wishes to go with him, then she shall go with
him," Alin said calmly. "And if she wishes to stay, then
she shall stay."

The women all nodded. "Sa. It should be Nel's choice
whether or no she will go or stay," they agreed.

Arn said nothing.

Alin looked at him. "Where is Mar's corral?" she asked. "Where are these horses he has captured?"

"The corral is downriver from here," Arn answered. He looked from Alin to Dara. "All of the men of the tribe are going out to see them. I do not see why the women cannot go also, if that is what you wish."

Within half an hour, all of the girls of the Red Deer and most of the women of the Horse were going south along the river, following Arn to the corral containing the stallion that would make Mar their chief.

Altan had been standing in grim silence, watching the bay as it trotted, head and tail held high, along the branches that made the fence of its prison. Huth stood watchfully at his side, but in truth Altan was incapable of action. He was numb. He could not believe that this had happened.

Finally, Altan spoke. "He used magic," he muttered. "It is not permitted to use magic."

"There was no magic," Huth replied. His gray eyes were cold as the winter sky as he looked at the beaten chief. "The Horse Sacrifice recognized the chief. That is what it was, Altan. We both saw it. The stallion came in of his own free will."

Altan swung his great head, as a buffalo does when it is bedeviled with flies.

"You are free to try the same method," Huth said with faint scorn.

A healthy spark of anger ran through the chief. "This was planned for many moons, shaman. Both you and I know that. No stallion is going to walk into a corral for me!"

From behind Altan, Mar's voice said coolly, "Then think of some other way yourself. You have three more days."

Blind hatred possessed Altan. He muttered a curse at Mar, turned, and plunged away from the corral. Out of fury-blurred eyes, he saw Alin approaching. Mar's woman, he thought viciously, and with deliberate force, the chief brushed past her, slamming his heavy shoulder into her and knocking her to the ground.

From Alin there came a high sharp cry of pain.

"Watch where you are going," Altan snarled and continued on his headlong way toward the woods.

Mar was on his knees beside the fallen girl. "Where are you hurt, Alin?"

She answered, in an oddly strained and breathless voice, "My ankle."

"Let me see it." Huth had come to sit on his heels beside Mar, but when he put his hand upon the ankle, Alin cried out again. Then she set her teeth in her lower lip.

Mar muttered something under his breath.

Huth said, "Did it turn under you when you fell?"

"Sa," she answered, still in the same strange breathless voice.

Huth looked at Mar. "We must get her home. Then we must bring cold water from the river and have her put the foot into it."

Mar nodded. His face under the bruises was very pale. "I will carry her," he said. He turned again to the girl. "Did you hear, Alin? I am going to carry you home."

She nodded. Her teeth were still set in her lip and her face was white.

"Is she hurt?" It was Jes running up to them, with Elen just behind her.

"She has turned her ankle," Huth replied.

"I saw Altan knock her over." Jes's voice was furious.

"He was . . . upset," said Huth.

Mar was kneeling beside Alin. "Put your arms around my neck," he said to her gently. When she had done as he asked, he slid his arms beneath her, and began to rise to his feet. He wavered slightly as his sore shoulder took her weight, then he finished the upward movement smoothly. Alin gasped as her foot dangled free.

Huth said, "Let me get one of the other men to carry her. That bruised shoulder of yours . . ."

But Mar was shaking his head. "I am fine," he said. "But Alin . . ."

"I am all right," Alin said, gritting her teeth against the pain. "Just get started, Mar."

"I will come with you," Jes said.

"I too," Elen seconded.

Mar began to walk down the hill, toward the animal track that would take him part of the way home. Huth followed, trailed by Alin's two worried friends.

Two days before the full of the moon, Alin sat alone by the fire in the women's cave and stared broodingly at the bone cauldron containing the ubiquitous sage tea. Her ankle had improved considerably in the days since first she had injured it, and she had even begun to walk a little with the stick that Huth had given her.

It was not enough, she thought. In two days' time the Ceremony of the Great Horse would begin, and she was tied here by her ankle as securely as if Mar had tied her with a rope. There was no hope of an escape now, not with her ankle still so sorely injured.

Throughout the whole of the painful, wearisome week she had been trapped in the lower level women's cave by her hurt ankle, Alin had done nothing but drink sage tea and think about how she might resolve the inevitable conflict that would occur over the girls when the men of the Red Deer met the men of the Horse.

It would happen soon, Alin thought, staring intently at the cauldron set so securely on the stones of the hearth circle. The winter was ending. The reindeer had started on their trek back to the mountains. The stags in the forest were dropping their antlers. Soon the salmon would start to appear in the rivers, rushing upstream to their ancient spawning grounds. In the mountains of the Red Deer tribe, the snow would be melting in the high passes. In another moon's time, the tribes of the Kindred would be holding their Spring Gatherings.

Lana would hear the story of the tragedy of the Tribe of the Horse and would come north, seeking her daughter.

Lana and Mar. That was a confrontation Alin had no wish to see.

The decision of where they would bide must be left to the girls themselves. That was the conclusion Alin had come to.

Lana would not like such a solution, but as long as her

daughter was one of those returning, Alin did not think
she would deem the matter worth a fight.

And Mar? His years under Altan had taught Mar how
to compromise. Then, too, Alin thought that Mar was
arrogant enough to believe that most of the girls would
choose to remain with the Tribe of the Horse.

Who would choose to remain? That was the question
that Alin considered next as she reached with her stick
to poke a bone back into the dimming fire.

Jes would stay with Tane.

That thought produced a pain as severe as any pain
from her ankle had ever been. She and Jes had been heart
companions for so long . . . had shared so much. . . .
Life without Jes was not a pleasurable thought to contemplate.

Alin did not contemplate it. Instead she drew a slow
careful breath, and thought of the other girls.

Dara would choose to stay with Arn.

Sana would not leave Melior.

Elen? Alin's mouth curled. Pretty Elen, who had Dale
and Cort wholly and securely within the grasp of her long
slender fingers.

Elen liked to rule. Alin thought Elen would choose to
return with Lana.

Fali and Mora would go home without a second glance.

At the thought of those two, Alin frowned. She had to
speak to Mar about them.

Alin did not want Fali to mate at Spring Fires. Fali's
body was that of a woman, but in every other way Fali
was a child. Lana had brought her to Winter Fires because she had been initiated, but Lana had not planned
to give Fali a mate.

"She is one for whom it is best to wait," Lana had
said. "Her spirit is yet young. She is not ready to bear a
child. Next year will be time enough for Fali to take a
mate."

Alin agreed with her mother's judgment. Fali was not
ready to choose a husband. Nor was Mora, although for
an entirely different reason.

Mora had never ceased to grieve for Nial, her promised
husband. It would be cruel, Alin thought, to force her to

take another man to her bed while she was still so heart-sore for the man she had lost. Alin thought that Mar would understand that.

The fire began to die down, and Alin stirred it with her stick.

Why do I always think that Mar will think as I do? she asked herself, as the red of the fire glowed hotter in response to her stirring.

He has the heart of a chief, she answered herself. Unlike Altan, Mar was not concerned with power for himself. Like Lana, like Alin herself, his concern was for the welfare of those in his charge.

Alin had sometimes manipulated that feeling in Mar to gain her own ends. But she respected it. She respected him. Somehow, over the course of the past few moons, she had begun to regard Mar as a partner in her care for the tribe's women. It had been a very long time since she had thought of him as an enemy.

If she were not who she was . . .

Dangerous thinking.

Alin shook her head, as if to clear it, and braced her stick into the ground so that she could rise. She would practice walking some more. She was sick unto death of sitting here in this cave!

Alin was not the only one counting the days until the ending of winter. Like her daughter, Lana watched the signs accumulate: the departing reindeer, the foxes barking in the mountains, the snow melting in the passes.

After Spring Fires, a party of men would leave for the west, to ferret out this Tribe of the Horse that had lost its women. Lana and Tor had discussed what could happen when they did locate the girls.

"This tribe may not give them over willingly, Mistress," Tor had said. "They are desperate. Nothing else could account for such a kidnapping. I do not think they will relinquish what they have taken without a fight."

"Then we will fight," Lana had said. Tor had smiled faintly and, unconsciously, flexed his fingers into fists. He would like a fight, Lana had realized grimly. The rest of the men probably felt the same way.

At heart, men were destructive creatures. As always, Lana thought as she sat all winter over her fire planning and plotting, it would be up to her to save them from their own natures.

The fire in Lana's hut glowed this night, a small beacon against the dark and cold. Lana stared at it and thought: In a half moon's time, it will be Spring Fires.

For the first time in her life, Lana's blood did not stir at that thought. Her heart and her mind were too concentrated on her absent daughter, plotting endlessly to extricate Alin and the rest of the girls bloodlessly from the clutches of the hated Tribe of the Horse.

Lana meant to get her daughter back, but she also wanted to avoid a fight. The men of the tribe were in her charge; she did not want to waste their lives unless it was absolutely necessary.

And she had formulated a plan. All she needed now, she thought grimly as she sat alone staring into her solitary fire, was to find the girls.

Twenty-three

The stallion searched the wind. They had taken his mares away from him yesterday. Some of the humans had held him pinned in a corner of the corral with spears, while others let his mares and yearlings out through the opening they had made in the fence.

The mares had not wanted to leave him. He had called to them frantically, and they had tried to come to him, galloping back around the fence to the place where he was held, but the humans had driven them away. Now he was alone.

The human scents had all been foreign, except for one. The man with the grass. And it was his scent for which the stallion searched the wind as the light began to rise in the east.

It was not a large corral, and the stallion circled it ceaselessly, swinging his head, lifting it, his nostrils wide and pulsing as he sought for that one scent.

He was not looking for a friend. He was a stallion. He had no friend. Only his band of mares and their yearling colts, his sons of the previous year, whom he would ruthlessly drive away once the new foals the mares were carrying had been dropped.

The stallion suddenly halted in his endless trotting, and reared, slashing the air with his great front hooves.

He was not looking for a friend but for a challenge. They had taken his mares. He would never have surrendered his mares to another stallion, not without a fight to the death.

But there had been too many of them to fight, and he felt the hot, frustrated anger surging through his body. He wanted a fight. He wanted to kill. He wanted his freedom. He wanted his mares.

He wanted the man.

The man who had put him here was his enemy.

Once again he began to trot around the perimeter of his prison, head lifted high, mane blowing, nostrils flared as he sought for . . .

The scent. Coming from the east was the unmistakable scent of the man. The stallion swung around to face the sunrise. He reared, pawing viciously as he brought his hooves back down to the earth. He flattened his ears and bared his teeth. He was ready.

Mar had not slept all night. The custom was for the chief to fast and keep a watchful vigil upon the sky the night before the Horse Sacrifice. For at dawn, the hour when the sun returned once more from its overnight journey to the land of the dead, the first day of the Ceremony of the Great Horse would begin.

On that first day the Horse Sacrifice and the anointing of the chief took place.

On the second day there was the initiation of the young boys, and the making of the new nirum.

On the third day the Sacred Dance was made by all the initiated men of the tribe. The dance, held within the sacred cave, was an offering of thanks to Sky God for the animals and plants he had seen fit to give to his people. It was also a prayer for continued sustenance in the upcoming year.

The night before, as Mar was preparing to begin his vigil, Altan had left the cliffside caves that had been his home since birth, an outcast and an exile, a chief who had been deposed by another.

With Altan had gone Sauk, the would-be killer of a tribal brother, driven out by the tribe in retribution for his breaking one of their most sacred taboos.

Neither man had taken their wives, who had chosen to remain with the Tribe of the Horse.

It was Altan's wife, Nel, who had negotiated the terms

of the women's remaining. "If we stay, will we be allowed to choose our mates?" she had asked the new chief. "If we are allowed to make our own choices, then we will stay. But if we are to be given to some man as a gift, the way one gives a dog, then we will return to our own people, as is our right."

Mar had thought of that conversation with Nel during the long night's vigil. "Given to some man the way one gives a dog." Those were not Nel's words, Mar thought. He knew whose words those were. Alin had got the women of the Horse as securely under her sway as were her own girls of the Red Deer.

If he gave in to Nel and Sauk's two wives on this, then he would find himself in a position where every girl who came to puberty in his tribe would expect to be able to choose her own mate.

And what is so wrong with that?

He held an imaginary conversation with Alin on the subject, while his eyes followed the bright round moon on its progress across the night sky. That is what she would have asked, he knew.

It is wrong, he answered, because it puts a power into a young girl's hands that she has never before had in this tribe. It is the fathers who make the marriages in the Tribe of the Horse. The fathers in consultation with the chief. It is the same with a young man. He takes the wife his father chooses for him. That is the way it has always been.

It is not that way any longer, Alin would answer. It will never be that way again. Not since you lost your women, and the whole of your world turned upside down.

She was right, Mar thought. He could not afford to lose his tribe even one single woman, and certainly not one who suckled a girl-child at her breast. Nor could he keep Nel and the others against their wills. Nel had been correct in saying that it was their right to be returned to their own families. Altan and Sauk were dead to the tribe. Their wives had all the rights of widows.

Mar could not afford to lose three women, and that was why he had told Nel that she and the others would be given the freedom to choose their own mates.

Huth came for the new chief just before the dawn broke, and for the first time the shaman dressed Mar as once before he had dressed Mar's father, Tardith. First Huth put around Mar's neck a necklace of wooden beads, each one beautifully carved with the picture of a horse's head; then on his arms the shaman clasped twin ivory bands, both of these magnificently engraved with the great crested heads of stallions. Next, on Mar's bent golden head, Huth placed the splendid black-maned headdress of the chief, with the proud stallion crest still springing erect, and the thick bushy mane falling down onto his strong broad shoulders. Into Mar's hands Huth then placed the sacred spear, which was used but one time a year, at this particular cere-mony. Engraved on its shaft was the picture of a mus-cular stallion falling to the earth with a spear buried in his breast.

Mar would wear the chief's regalia again on the mor-row, when the boys were initiated, and once more when he made the Sacred Dance with the rest of the men on the last day of the festival. At that time, the headdress and ornaments would be all that he would wear. The dance was done barefoot and naked. But today, in the chill of outdoors, he wore his buckskin shirt and trou-sers, his fur vest, and his soft leather moccasins.

The men of the tribe were waiting for Huth and Mar on the beach. The first streaks of pink had begun to stain the eastern sky when the band of men began their trek downriver, toward the corral where the Horse Sacrifice awaited them.

The stallion saw them coming out of the trees. Hu-mans. Many of them. And at the front . . . his nostrils flared. He tossed his head. The scent was right, though the man looked different.

The many humans halted at a distance from the corral. The man came on alone.

The stallion snorted, and once again sought the scent. Catching it, he rose on his hind legs and screamed his defiance. It was the most ancient of challenges that he gave, that of stallion to stallion before they came to blows over the one thing that mattered most in their lives.

Mares.

The man had taken his mares. The man must die.

Mar came forward steadily. The stallion was in a fury, slashing the air with his forelegs, pawing up the earth with his great hooves. Hate poured out of every powerful bunched muscle under the scarred dark bay coat.

Mar felt a pang of regret. For two long winters he had been the stallion's friend, helping him to feed his little band of mares and colts, helping them to get through the long bitter season of scanty ice-covered grass. And now it had come to this.

But he had no choice. The tribe must send a sacrifice to Horse God. It was expected. And the sacrifice must be a worthy one, a strong, healthy stallion to represent the strength and health of the tribe. A life was called for, one life for the good of the tribe.

Mar knew, beyond question, that if ever the life called for was his own, he would give it. That was what it meant to be the chief. That was why it was by his hand that the sacrificial horse must fall.

The stallion had stopped plunging and was standing in the dead center of the corral, watching him out of white-rimmed eyes. Mar went to the space between the two big branches that had closed the corral upon the horse herd, and ducked through. He straightened up, the sacred spear clasped in his strong right hand, and faced the stallion.

For a long moment there was no movement in the corral. The early morning air was faintly misty, and from within the woods Mar could hear the high-pitched screeching and calling of the birds. The stallion stared at him. Mar could see the murderous hatred in the animal's eyes.

The stallion flattened his ears, bared his teeth, lifted his tail, and came for him.

The bay stallion fought the maned man the way he would have fought another male horse. He stopped before Mar, reared on his hind legs to his full height, and aimed a mighty right hoof directly at the man's hated black-maned head. Had it landed, it would have killed him.

It didn't land. As the stallion began to come down, when that murderous hoof was but inches from his head, Mar thrust with his sacred spear. Once.

Blood gushed from the fatal wound. The stallion's plunge downward faltered, he wobbled as his hind legs gave way beneath him, then he crashed sideways to the ground.

He lay still, his life's blood pouring away into the earth. Mar knelt beside him and rested the hand that had delivered the death blow on the horse's powerful, muscular bay neck. The stallion's lashes lifted, and his brown eyes looked at Mar.

"Go well on your journey," Mar said to him softly.

A deep shuddering sigh came from the stallion, and with it his spirit left his body, to run forever free in the land of his gods.

Huth brought Mar a bone cup, and Mar filled it with the blood of the Sacrifice. Then, raising the cup in both hands, he looked toward the rising sun and chanted in a ringing voice: "Praise Sky God for the blood of the stallion which brings strength to our men and fertility to the wombs of our women."

Mar passed the cup to Huth, who raised it likewise and chanted the same prayer. Then Huth dipped his finger into the cup, and, with the blood, made the sacred signs of anointing on Mar's face and chest, thus transferring the spirit of the stallion into the tribe's chief.

Then the men butchered the stallion, taking care to leave all his bones intact. These they placed on the ground in the same position they had been inside his body, so that where the stallion had once lain, there was now his skeleton.

Mar took the liver and cut it into four equal pieces: for himself, Huth, Arn, and Rom, the tribe's oldest hunter. The liver they ate raw, but the rest of the horse meat they cooked. This was the only time in the year that the men of the Horse would eat the meat of their totem. It was a sacred meal, an important part of the ceremony, eaten out in the open air beside the ritually arranged bones of the sacrifice.

It was nearing the hour of sunset when the men of the Horse returned home. The first person Mar saw as he came along the beach was Alin, walking along the gravel shore without her stick, a look of absolute concentration on her lovely face.

It is done, he thought with fierce satisfaction. I am the chief.

He halted and looked at Alin. He was the chief. And there was his woman.

She raised her head, as if his gaze had touched her, and stared directly back at him. He saw her eyes widen slightly, and realized she had been startled by the blood signs that still marked his face and his bared chest.

The signs of the chief.

The signs of the Horse God, who would make the Sacred Marriage with her in a half moon's time.

They stayed thus, looking at each other for a long silent moment, and then Alin turned away. Mar did not go to speak to her. There was nothing that needed to be said.

He thought of her, however, as he climbed the cliff path to his shelter. Never before had he wanted a woman the way he wanted Alin. Toward her he felt the same singleminded possessiveness that he felt for the chieftainship.

From the moment of his father's death, Mar had felt the chieftainship to be his. He had felt it in his bones and in his blood. The Tribe of the Horse was his.

Alin was his also. In his bones and in his blood.

He had gotten rid of Altan at last, had driven him out ruthlessly, the way a stallion would drive out of the herd any other male who might challenge his right to be the sole mate of his mares.

Mar stopped on the terrace outside of his shelter, turned, and surveyed the scene before him. His head lifted, in the movement Alin always thought of as his stallion gesture, and in his heart there was a fierce burning joy.

His people. His tribe. His to lead, his to care for. His to die for, should that time ever come.

Lugh had been waiting for him within the shelter, and now he felt the dog's head under his hand, the dog's warm body pressing against his legs.

Down on the beach, a man and a girl stood shoulder to shoulder, looking at the sunset. The man's hair was black; the girl's was pale brown.

Tane and Jes.

That was a sure match, Mar thought contentedly. Then his mind moved to the rest of the girls, calculating whom they were most likely to choose.

Dara would choose Arn. That would be a problem with the nirum, but if Arn was Dara's choice they would just have to accept it. Sana would take Melior. That would be all right. Melior was old enough, would in fact be made a nirum along with Mar. Elen? Elen would probably take Dale, which would leave Cort and a number of nirum deeply unhappy.

Dhu, Mar thought. Instead of ending our troubles, the girls' choices seem likely to increase them! He frowned and ran the rest of the girls quickly through his mind, assessing which man each would be most likely to choose. His thoughts stopped when he came to Fali.

Little Fali. Dara had grown up these last few months, but Fali had not.

He would not make Fali choose a mate yet if she did not feel she was ready, Mar decided. The tribe needed women, but they were not so desperate that they could not wait another year if they must for her to grow up.

Perhaps Cort or Dale, whichever one Elen did not choose, would be a good mate for Fali. They were good boys. Kind boys. Either one of them would be a good choice for her. In a year.

The one girl he had held off considering came now into his mind. He could see her face clearly, see the great, expressive eyes, the delicate modeling of cheek and jaw, the firm, exquisite line of the mouth.

Alin's choice had been finalized today, when he had killed the stallion and Huth had anointed him with the blood of the sacrifice. Alin must choose the chief. And the chief of the Tribe of the Horse was now Mar.

Altan shifted his backpack to a more comfortable position, gripped his spear more firmly, and plodded grimly along the river path. Bitter gall filled his heart.

A trick. Mar had won the chieftainship by a trick.

At his side walked Sauk, shoulders hunched, heart fully as bitter as Altan's.

Neither could quite comprehend what had happened.

"Not even Tod spoke up for me," Altan said out loud. "Not Tod, not Heno, not Eoto. And after all I have done for them!"

Sauk grunted.

It was because of Sauk that his companions had deserted him, Altan thought. None of them had wanted to associate themselves with Sauk's transgression of one of the tribe's most powerful taboos.

Yet Sauk was the only one who had tried to help him. If Sauk had been successful, if Mar had not bent to pick up his basket at just the wrong time, then would Altan still be the chief.

Altan could not believe that he was an outcast, dead to his tribe, his friends, his wife.

The desire for revenge burned in his heart.

"If only I could get back at him," Altan said to Sauk. "If only I could ruin him as he has ruined me."

"I have been thinking," Sauk said.

Altan looked at him.

"What if we find the dwelling place of the Tribe of the Red Deer?" Sauk asked slowly. "What if we tell this Mistress the girls are always talking of exactly where to find her followers?" The nirum's black eyes shifted from the ground to Altan and then back again to the ground. "She would come after them," he said. "If she is anything like Alin, she would come after them."

Altan thought, Mar would not like that at all.

"Whatever the result," Sauk was saying, "it will be ill luck for the Tribe of the Horse. And for Mar."

"Sa," said Altan. "It would."

For the first time since Mar had come up the beach

carrying Sauk's bound body over his shoulder, Altan smiled.

"They came from the south," he said. "From the mountains."

"Sa," said Sauk. "We shall find them."

"The Tribe of the Red Deer," Altan said. And his smile increased.

Twenty-four

There was only one boy to be initiated on the second day of the Great Horse Ceremony. There should have been more, but most of the uninitiated boys had been with the women and other children on that fatal day when the poisoned water had done its work. And so there was just skinny, long-legged Pol, whose voice was only now beginning to deepen into the register of a man, to make the long lonely trek up the narrow dark hallway of the sacred cave to the place where the final passage of initiation was accomplished: the Sacred Well.

Earlier, Pol had passed all of the tests put to him by Huth in order to prove his worthiness to become a man of the Horse. He had killed a deer, and skinned it and butchered it alone. He had demonstrated his skill with spear and javelin and arrow, shooting at the targets that Huth had set for him. He had gone without food for three entire days. And now he was ready for the final test, when, at the bottom of the Sacred Well, he would be forced to confront the realities of his world. Pol would walk down the passageway that led to the Sacred Well a boy, and when he returned, he would be a man.

All of the men of the tribe were gathered within the main chamber of the sacred cave this second day of the Great Horse Ceremony, seated under the wild eyes and flaring nostrils of the bulls and the horses that were painted on its walls. Huth, dressed in his shaman's costume of long grass robe and horse-head mask, and holding in his hand the sacred staff of life, presided over the

initiation ceremony. On this day, the chief was but one
of the initiated men; this day belonged to the shaman.

Mar watched Pol's lamplight disappear down the long
dark passage, and remembered the day of his own initiation. How full of joy he had been! His father had been
the chief; Eva had been his promised wife; all had been
well with his world.

A man's initiation was a memory he carried with him
for all of his life. Mar remembered vividly that long silent walk behind Huth down the narrow passage filled
with engravings, he remembered the turn away from the
familiar painted gallery toward the mysterious darkness
of the corner wherein lay the Sacred Well, the place that
a man saw only twice in his life, once when he was initiated, and once when he was made a nirum.

After Pol, Mar would make that journey again.

The men waited within the great painted chamber, silent and solemn. They all wore about their throats the
carved horse-head beads of the initiated male, and they
carried only short javelins without spearthrowers, but
otherwise they were dressed as usual. Mar looked at the
great black bull on the wall across from him, and thought
of what was to come.

Finally, Huth returned with Pol. He led the boy into
the middle of the chamber and clasped about his neck a
string of wooden beads. "The Tribe of the Horse wel-
comes Pol," Huth said. "Now he is a man."

The men beat the shafts of their spears upon the ground
until the dirt floor throbbed like the skin of a drum.

"Now," Huth said. "The new nirum."

Four men were to be made nirum this day: Mar and
Tane and Bror and Melior. Each had to make the trip to
the Sacred Well alone, led only by Huth. Mar, as befitted
the chief, went first.

All the previous awe gripped Mar's throat as he followed Huth's great horse head out of the main chamber
and down the narrow passage whose walls were lined
with engravings. He could feel the skin prickle at the
back of his neck. As he left the passage, he looked up
quickly, toward the place where Tane had told him he
had done the picture of deer fording the river.

Mar's steps slowed as he saw it.

Tane, he thought.

Huth glanced around, as if he had sensed Mar's hesitation, and saw where Mar was looking.

The great horse head turned in the direction of the frieze of swimming deer. Both men stopped. In homage. Neither spoke. Then Huth went forward again, and Mar followed.

At the very end of the room there was a narrow, deep opening in the rock. The drop went thirty feet down into the earth. On the wall above the opening were engraved the holy signs of life and death. For this was the Sacred Well, the place that a man saw but two times in his life, and never forgot.

Huth stood in silence, his lamp held high, as Mar set his foot upon the rope ladder that would take him down to the very bottom of the deep drop. Holding his own lamp in one hand, Mar climbed slowly and carefully downward, until his feet were on the rough uneven floor, and he was looking at the heart of the mystery of initiation.

Near the floor of the shaft, on a flat protuberant rock, there was a drawing. It had been there for more generations of initiation ceremonies than anyone could remember. Unlike the rest of the engravings and paintings in the sacred cave, this particular drawing was of a scene that involved several different kinds of figures.

First, there was the picture of a buffalo, drawn in black onto a piece of yellow-stained rock. A great barbed-hook spear was depicted impaled in the hindquarters of the buffalo, and the animal also had a great tear in its belly from which its entrails were shown to be gushing forth. The buffalo's tail lashed the air in fury. Its head was turned, as though to look at its injury, and its terrible horns were directed toward the man who lay stretched out on the ground before him.

The painting was done with extraordinary realism, conveying a strong sense of the elemental power of the animal.

In front of the buffalo was the picture of a man, the only human figure in all of the teeming life that adorned

the walls of the sacred cave. The man had been carefully
drawn to avoid giving any clue of his identity; his arms
and legs were but straight lines, his head was in the image of a bird. The man was shown stretched supine on
the ground before the buffalo.

Under the feet of the man was a pole, with a bird
perched on the top of it.

To the left of the man and the buffalo was the picture
of a two-horned rhinoceros, drawn in thick black outline.
This was the only picture of a rhinoceros in the sacred
cave. The rhinoceros was shown as trotting away from
both the man and the injured buffalo.

Mar stared in dry-mouthed awe at the great mystery
revealed on the wall of the Sacred Well.

Death.

Death to the animals, so that man could live.

Death to the man, so that his spirit could fly like the
bird on the shaman's stick, to dwell in the World Beyond
where all men went when the spirit left their bodies.

Life was good. But, for the greater good, all life must
end with death.

To understand that was to understand what it meant to
be a hunter. What it meant to be an initiated male of the
Tribe of the Horse.

The men did not return to the cliffside caverns for the
night, but slept near the cave so they would not need to
make a return journey in the morning.

Mar and Tane spread their sleeping rolls side by side
and lay on their backs, looking up at the stars. The full
moon was in the morning side of the sky, beginning its
climb toward the top of the heavens, from whence it
would decline into the west.

"Your picture of the deer is wonderful," Mar said.

"Sa." Tane's voice was grave. "I am satisfied with it
also."

A peaceful silence fell between them.

"Tomorrow," Tane said at last, "you will lead the
men in the Sacred Dance."

"Sa." Mar's voice was as full of grave satisfaction as
Tane's had been.

"It goes well for us, my brother," Tane said softly.

Mar blew out through his nose. "We must get through Spring Fires," he said. He turned his head a little, so he could see Tane's profile in the moonlight. "Once the girls have made their choices, and the mating is done, then will I feel safe."

"So you still think the Red Deer tribe will come?"

There was a long silence. Then Mar said, "Sa. I do. I am thinking they will come for Alin."

Tane's face was looking upward, his eyes were on the stars. He said quietly, "Two days ago, Jes showed my father a picture she had painted on a slab of rock by the river." He turned his peaceful eyes toward Mar, and said, "My father has said that Jes may join the painters in the sacred cave."

Mar's breath caught in the back of his throat. "Huth said that a girl may paint the sacred pictures?"

"Sa." Tane's eyes were looking directly into Mar's. "My father said that such skill as Jes has is a gift from the gods. He said that it must be used for the good of the tribe. He drummed his drum, and went into a trance, and in the trance he saw a long-haired girl drinking from a stream. A chestnut horse stood beside her, tame as a dog. She lifted the water into her hands, and poured it over the head of the horse, and he bowed his head before her."

Another long silence fell.

"Huth says that the dream means that Jes should paint the sacred pictures," Mar said. It was not a question.

"Sa."

"Then Jes will stay with you, Tane, whether her tribe comes or no."

Tane nodded gravely. "Sa. I believe she will stay." His green eyes glimmered in the moonlight. "And what," he asked, "of Alin?"

Mar turned over on his back and put his hands behind his head. "Once I mate with Alin, I think she will stay," he said. "But not if they come before."

Tane looked at his friend's clean, strong profile. There had been no arrogance in Mar's voice. He spoke as a man who is simply stating facts.

"We are halfway through the Moon of the Great Horse," Tane said. "Soon it will be Salmon Moon. And Spring Fires is at the beginning of Salmon Moon."

"Sa," said Mar. "I know."

The following day was the day of the Sacred Dance.

The men arose, as usual, with the dawn. First came the ceremony of the new fire, which was kindled in the stone hearthplace the tribe had built near the opening to the sacred cave. Mar made the fire, expertly stacking kindling around the single log that had been kept from the previous year's fire and stored in the sacred cave for just this occasion. Once the fire was burning high, the men chanted the "Thanksgiving for the Fire" prayer to Sky God that was always made at this particular ceremony. Then Mar lit all the stone lamps from the new fire, and the men prepared to descend once more into the depths of the sacred cave. They took no food the morning of the Sacred Dance; they would feast after it was over.

Once in the cave, the men dressed themselves in the costumes of the ceremony: horse-head beads at their throats; horsehair cloaks around their shoulders; belts with a hanging tail clasped about their waists.

Mar stripped off his clothes and dressed like the rest of the men. Once he had finished, however, he alone took the great horsemane cap and fit it over his head, until his bright hair was covered by the erect bushy black mane of a stallion.

Huth, wearing his god-face not his man-face, took his position of power. In his hands he held his drum. Seated before him on the ground, also holding a drum, was Arn, his apprentice. When all the dancers had assembled, Huth raised the staff of life and gave the signal.

In the flickering light of the sacred cave, watched by their shaman, by the painted animals on the walls, and by their gods, the men of the Horse danced to the beat of the buffalo skin drums, an intricate dance pattern of prancing and leaping steps that mimicked the movements of horses running free on the plains.

The powerful life of the horse surged in the hearts of

the dancing men; the tide of the renewed life of the spring flooded into their blood.

"Nayeeh, nayeeh!" they cried. The drums pounded. The horse-men, naked save for their ceremonial ornaments, cantered and leaped and called. In the midst of them, Mar's stallion head lifted and swung, searching the wind, protecting the herd. The spirit of their totem was strong in them. The Horse God was proud of them. Sky God looked with favor upon them. They were the men of the Horse. They would survive.

Later in the day, the men cooked a deer over the new fire, and ate its winter-lean meat hungrily. A log was carefully extracted from the hearthplace, and stored in the sacred cave, to be used to begin the new fire of the following year.

Then the men of the Horse returned to the cliffside caves that were their home, tired but exhilarated by the three-day festival that was the religious high point of their year.

Two days after the Great Horse Ceremony had concluded, Alin sought out Mar to speak to him about Fali and Mora. She found him a little way upriver, helping the men to make fishing nets on the widest part of the beach. She came to stand beside him and silently watched as he finished tying a knot in the vine that he had woven through the whip-thin branches that formed the long part of the net. When the knot was done, he stood up and came a little way apart to speak to her privately.

Alin told him that she did not want Fali to be forced to choose a mate, and he surprised her by saying that he had already reached that decision himself.

"Poor little minnow," Mar said sympathetically. "Does she still cry for her mother?"

"Not so much anymore," Alin replied honestly. "She is much happier than she was, Mar. But I do not think she is ready yet to mate. Her spirit is still the spirit of a child. She was only at Winter Fires for the dancing. My mother did not wish Fali to mate, either. Or Dara, for that matter. But Dara has grown up over the winter. Fali has not.''

Mar leaned his shoulders against the cliff behind him, and smiled down at her genially. ''Dara has found Arn, you mean,'' he said.

Alin did not respond to either the comment or the smile. Instead, she broached the second thing she had come to say: ''I do not want Mora to have to choose a mate, either.''

The genial look left Mar's face abruptly. ''Why not?''

''She is still pining for the boy she was promised to at home.'' Alin strove to make her voice softly persuasive. ''It would be cruel, Mar, to force her to take another man just now.''

She stood before him, waiting for his reply. He was so powerful, she found herself thinking. Not just big, but powerful. It was inside of him, the power, not just outside.

This was the first time she had approached him in his position as chief.

''Is Mora intact?'' Mar asked at last.

Alin was surprised by the question. She hesitated, wondering which would be the better answer. She decided on the truth. ''Na,'' she said. ''She and Nial mated at Spring Fires last year. They would have wed, but there was a question of whether or no their kinship was too close. My mother finally decided that it was not, but before they could wed, Mora was taken.''

Mar straightened away from the cliff, a movement that brought him closer to Alin. ''If she has mated before, it will not be so difficult for her to choose a new man,'' he said reasonably.

Alin stood as tall as she could. Even so, he towered over her. She had chosen the wrong reply, she thought.

''Sa,'' she said to him firmly. ''It would be.''

Mar's thick golden brows rose. ''I do not understand you,'' he said. ''*You* do not seem to flinch at the thought of taking a new man each time you mate. Why then should Mora object to taking just one?''

Alin could feel her temper beginning to rise. I will not let him anger me, she thought. He is doing this deliberately. She answered him coldly, "My situation is entirely different from Mora's."

"Obviously." His voice was unusually heavy with sarcasm.

It was not just the words and the tone, but the almost contemptuous look on his face that overcame Alin's resolution. Suddenly, she was furious. "Hear me, man of the Horse," she said, narrowing her eyes so that they glittered at him from between her long, dark lashes. "If you are willing to honor the child in Fali's spirit, then you must honor the love that is in Mora's. If I thought that there was no chance of Mora ever seeing her Nial again, then I might say differently. But she will see him again, when the men of my tribe come to fetch us, and I do not want her to meet him with another tribe's babe growing in her belly."

Mar's face was unreadable. He did not answer.

Alin's narrow delicate nostrils flared. "Mora is no Nel, to turn her back on her man because things have gone ill for him," she said. Then, trying to speak more reasonably, knowing that anger never got her anywhere with him, "None of the other girls of the Red Deer have the kind of attachment Mora has. All of the other girls will choose a man." She took a deep steadying breath. "Mar. Leave Mora be."

Still no reply.

With difficulty, Alin refrained from stamping her foot. "Well?"

"I am waiting for you to tell me that the Mother will be angry if I do not give in to your demand," he said. "Have you forgotten that part of your speech?"

"You are blasphemous," Alin said between her teeth.

"Not at all," he replied with exaggerated surprise. "It was such a standard part of all your previous demands that I was waiting for you to bring it forth now."

They looked at each other through a long hard moment of silence. It was obvious now that they both were angry.

Mar finally said, "I cannot leave Mora out. It is unreasonable of you to ask it of me. The men of the tribe

have been patient for many moons. I cannot withdraw
two of the women from them now, and Fali's need is
greater than Mora's.''

Alin stared at him. He looked back, his eyes cold. ''It
will not be so terrible a fate for her,'' he said. ''She
might even come to like her new man better than the
old.''

Alin itched to smash her hand across that arrogant face
of his, but she knew well how fruitless an endeavor that
would be. They were still staring at each other, both bitter at what they considered the other's unreasonableness,
when a shout of alarm came from downriver. Without a
word, Mar pushed past Alin and began to run. Alin was
right behind him, with the men who had been working
on the nets following.

As Alin came around the curve of the river, she was
just in time to see Mar reach Bror, who was standing on
the gravel with a man's body thrown across his shoulder.
From the color of the man's hair, Alin knew it must be
Dale.

Mar was lifting the boy from Bror when Alin came
running up. ''What happened?'' Mar asked Bror as he
cradled the boy's body like a babe in his arms.

''A leopard got him,'' Bror answered.

Dale's clothes were soaked through with blood. Alin
thought, sickly, that the boy's entrails must be hanging
out. But when Bror pushed back the vest and shirt to
show Mar, there were great raking claw marks on Dale's
chest and shoulder, but no sign that a vital organ had
been touched.

''You cut the scratches open?'' Mar asked Bror, his
eyes on Dale's blood-covered front.

''Sa. As soon as I could.''

''Dale.'' Mar's voice was so gentle. Absurdly, Alin
felt tears sting at the back of her throat at its sound.
''How goes it with you?''

Dale's lashes lifted. Blue eyes, dark with pain, looked
into Mar's. ''He was up a tree,'' Dale said in a strange
thin voice. ''I didn't see him. Bror got him with his
spear.''

''You are home now,'' Mar said, still in that heartbreakingly gentle voice. "Huth will take care of you, Dale. Huth and Arn. I am going to carry you to their cave now. All right?"

"Sa," came the thin voice. "All right."

Dale might have been a child, so easily did Mar hold the boy in his arms. Alin looked from Dale's white face to Mar's, and saw the grim lines at the corners of the chief's mouth. Without another word, Mar turned and began to walk toward the path that led up to the first level of caves in the cliffside. Dale's head had fallen on his shoulder, the moonbeam-colored hair mingling with Mar's own sunny locks.

The men who had come up behind Alin began to talk among themselves. Alin turned to Bror. He looked exhausted, she thought. And sick.

"The scratches are ugly," she said, "but only the skin was broken."

"That may be enough," Bror answered bleakly. "I cut them open and let them bleed, but . . ." He too was covered with blood, Dale's blood, and now he put one of his blood-encrusted hands to his forehead, leaving a rusty red stain upon the smooth brown flesh. "Dhu, Alin! Just one scratch from a leopard can bring a man to the brink of death. And Dale has so many!"

A little silence fell. They both knew that the poison that lurked under a leopard's claws could be just as deadly to a man as the unsheathed claws themselves.

"But you got to him quickly," Alin said. "You opened the wounds. The poison may not have had time to get into Dale."

"Let us hope that that is so," Bror replied.

Huth did what he could for Dale. He soaked the deep scratches with herb water, and said all the proper healing prayers. Bror went wearily back to the place where the dead leopard lay, and cut out its heart and buried it, to propitiate Leopard God for the death of one of his children.

Dale was awake when Elen went to see him, and even managed to make a joke about being perfectly strong by the time of Spring Fires. But by the morning, he was in a fever.

A pall of quiet lay over the initiates' cave all day. When word came that Huth was making the journey to the Other World in search of help for Dale, the quiet became even heavier. If Huth had to make that kind of a seance, then things were very serious indeed.

"Zel recovered," Cort said again. He had been repeating those two words all day long, as if they were a talisman.

"Sa," the rest of the boys answered, as they had been answering him all day. "That is so."

What none of them said was that Zel had not been clawed by a leopard.

Bror, though he was technically supposed to be with the nirum, spent the day with his old friends in the initiates' cave. Never, he thought, would he forget the moment when the leopard leaped from the tree onto Dale's back. The scene played itself over and over in his mind. Again and again he saw the flashing figure of the cat, arching out of the shadows above, saw the dull-white talons raking their deadly way along Dale's shoulder.

"It was sheer luck that I had my spear in my right hand," he told the others. "I had just shifted it to wipe my left hand on my shirt, so I had only to lift it and throw. Another few seconds, and the leopard would have ripped Dale apart."

"Lucky indeed," the boys replied. "If Bror had not been so quick, Dale would certainly have died."

But it seemed, after all, that the leopard had done enough. After two days of raging fever, and despite all of Huth's brave exhortations to his friendly spirits for help, Dale died.

The Tribe of the Horse was accustomed to death. They were even accustomed to the death of the young. Even so, Dale's death was a bitter blow. He had been such a light-spirited boy, so full of jokes and good humor. He would be sorely missed.

Arn, his brother, mourned him. Elen, the girl he had loved, mourned him. His fellows of the initiates' cave mourned him. But the one who mourned him most was Cort.

The sky was overcast and gray on the day that they buried Dale. The men had dug a grave in the depths of a nearby cave, where they had buried others of their tribe before. They made the deep hole with sharpened wooden digging sticks, and with mattocks made from antler. The digging sticks and mattocks broke up the earth, which was then removed by means of an oval-shaped shovel. The scoop of the shovel had been made from elk antler, which Rom had split along its interior spongy matter to give it its ladlelike shape. The handle of the shovel was wood.

Huth and Arn dressed Dale for his burial. Together they decked the dead boy in his finest clothing and put upon him all of his ornaments, as well as the gift ornaments of his bereaved friends. Dale was carried to his grave wearing necklaces and bracelets of pierced shells, of deer's teeth, of fish vertebrae, and of ivory beads. He wore a headband decorated with small bone discs and around his waist was a belt inlaid with golden shells. The men of the tribe laid his body on its back in the grave, and at his side they placed his spear and javelin, along with several of Rom's finest flint spearheads. Dale would travel to the Other World with the finest accoutrements his tribe could provide. Around his body they placed funeral offerings of meat and deer bladders filed with fresh water so that Dale would not go hungry or thirsty on his journey.

After all of this had been done, Huth took shovelfuls of ochre and, watched by the sorrowful eyes of the tribe, he lined the grave and covered Dale's body with the red-brown clay. To the Tribe of the Horse, the ochre was symbolic of blood, and its purpose in the grave was to impart life to the corpse and to the grave offerings, so that they would keep their living quality in the Other World to which Dale's spirit was going.

Then Dale's friends came forward and placed a layer of stones around and over the grave, to protect the body from marauding animals. After that, they filled in the rest of the grave with dirt.

The buoyant mood of the tribe, engendered by the successful Great Horse Ceremony and the coming Spring

Fires, was broken by Dale's death. Sorrow hung thick in the caves and shelters of the Tribe of the Horse. It hung as well in the cave where the Red Deer girls dwelled. They had all come to like Dale.

Late in the afternoon of the day Dale was buried, Elen got to her feet. "I am going to go for a walk up the river," she said quietly.

"Do you want company?" Alin asked.

Elen shook her head.

"Take a dog," Alin said, and gestured to the rest of the girls to let Elen go.

Mar and Tane saw Elen's distinctive red-gold head as soon as she stepped away from the cliff path and began to walk slowly up the beach, a dog at her heels.

"Should someone go with her?" Tane asked.

Mar shook his head. "Let her be. She is safe enough with Roc, and I think she needs to be alone."

Tane nodded. Then he sighed. "We have not lost a man to a leopard since the year before we were initiated."

"Sa. We have grown careless, perhaps. When the leaves are on the trees, it is hard to see them, but at this time of the year . . . Dale should not have been caught so unaware."

"I am thinking that his mind was on other things," Tane said, his eyes on the girl walking away from them up the beach.

"Sa," said Mar bleakly. "That is so."

Elen walked slowly, her eyes on the gravel at her feet. The gray skies of the morning had not lifted, and all the world looked as dim and as bleak as she felt.

Dale, she thought painfully. She could not believe that she would never again see that mischievous smile, that mop of silver-blond hair . . . *Dale,* she thought, I will miss you so.

She saw the boy sitting on the large rock as soon as she came around the bend of the river. His back was to her, his head was bent, his shoulders were shaking. It was Cort.

Elen stopped, and the dog at her heels stopped also.

Would it be better for Cort, or worse, if she went up to him now?

Before Elen could make up her mind, Cort's head lifted, turned, and he saw her. She had not thought she had made a sound, but the men of the Horse all had the supersensitive hearing of the hunter.

Once he had seen her, she had no choice but to go forward.

Cort's face was streaked and wet with the tears he was making no attempt to hide. He did not stand up, and Elen halted before him. "Oh, Cort," she said with aching sympathy. "I am so sorry."

"I will miss him so," the boy said, his words echoing her own thoughts of the moment before. His lashes were spiked with wet, his warm brown eyes red-rimmed with sorrow and lack of sleep. He said in a rush, "Dhu, Elen, I would relinquish you even, if only he would come back again!"

Elen was wise enough not to take offense. "I know," she said sadly. "I miss him too." Then, when Cort's mouth began to quiver, she took another step forward and reached out her arms.

He flung himself against her, his arms going around her waist to clutch her close. He pressed his wet face against her breast, as if he could hide there from the anguish of his loss. His whole slim young body shuddered with his grief.

Elen held him tenderly, and rested her cheek against his soft hair. A strong, protective, almost maternal emotion swelled in her heart. Poor boy, she thought, cradling him closer. A picture of Dale's face came into her mind: the moon-colored hair, the crystal blue eyes, the mischievous smile.

He had been a lovely boy, Dale. But she had been going to choose Cort.

Like Alin, Elen was convinced that Lana would come for her children. And Dale would never have followed her back to the Tribe of the Red Deer. His spirit was too strongly tied to his own people for him to be able to do that.

Cort would follow. That was why Elen had chosen him

even before Dale's death, and as she held Cort now, cradled so closely in her arms, she made her choice again.

When the time came to name a husband, she would
name Cort. And when the time came to go back home,
she would take her husband with her.

Twenty-five

There were to be no marriages until after the matings of
Spring Fires. This custom was the custom of the Tribe
of the Red Deer, not of the Tribe of the Horse.

"How can a woman know if she will like a man if she
has not yet lain with him?" Alin asked Mar reasonably
when she realized he was assuming that they would have
the marriages first. She and some of the girls had been
practicing shooting their bows at a target of stretched
hide, but when Mar appeared and asked to speak to her,
Alin had slung her bow over her shoulder and walked a
little aside with him. Lugh stayed to watch the shooting.

"Are you saying that if the man does not . . . measure
up in mating . . . then the woman will not have him?"
Mar asked incredulously.

"The choice goes both ways," Alin replied, in an even
more reasonable tone than before. "The man can change
his mind also."

Mar looked at her. Then he shrugged. "I do not think
you will find the men of the Horse lacking, but if that is
how you wish to do it . . ." He frowned a little. "I am
thinking, though, that the women of my tribe will not
approve of this way of doing things."

"They think it is an excellent way of doing things,"
Alin replied, and tried not to smile at his astonished expression.

"They do?"

"Certainly."

"But if they get with child and have no husband, who will care for them, shelter them, hunt for them?"

He was not being arrogant, Alin saw. He was truly concerned.

"Mar. With all of the men in this tribe, no woman will have any difficulty in finding a husband."

Behind the screen of trees that separated them from the girls, Alin heard a shout of triumph. She cocked her head a little to listen better. Someone had made a particularly good shot. Alin looked at Mar's feet and then frowned. "Will Lugh be all right? He won't chase the arrows?"

"Lugh is safe enough." Mar ran his hand through the thick hair on his forehead. "It is true that the girls of the Red Deer will have no trouble finding a husband, but the women of the Horse do not have so wide a choice. There is the degree of kinship to be considered; many of the men in the tribe are too close in kinship to marry them. And it is not easy to trade out a woman who is with child."

A little silence fell between them.

"It seems to me that the men of the Tribe of the Horse hunt for the whole tribe, not just for their individual families," Alin finally said slowly. "Are you saying that if a woman was unable to hunt for herself, and had no man to hunt for her, then she would be allowed to starve?"

"Of course I am not saying that!"

"Well then, where is the worry?"

Mar blew air out of his nose. "I do not know. It is just . . . different. It makes me uneasy."

Two moons ago, Alin would have snapped at him, would have said something nasty about his regarding women as men's property. She knew him better now.

"No woman in this tribe will be unprotected so long as you are the chief," she said, looking into his troubled blue eyes. "And it is not good for either the man or the woman when one of them does not like the other. Discontent such as that breeds trouble."

He thought for a minute. Then he said, "The men of the tribe will say I am letting the women have the rule."

Alin made a small, exasperated sound. "What I am

saying, Mar, is that *neither* should have the rule." She pushed her bow further back on her shoulder and the gesture gave her a thought. "A marriage should be like a hunting fellowship. On the hunting trail, all goes better when all work together in harmony, when one is not constantly trying to impose his will upon the others. Is it not so?"

His head came up in a characteristic gesture. "But there must always be a leader," he said.

"Sa." Her perfectly arched eyebrows rose faintly higher. "But how does a good leader lead? Does he lead because his men fear him? Or does he lead because they love and trust him?"

They looked at each other. His mouth quirked humorously. "You are good with words, Alin."

She smiled faintly in return. "It is because I am also a good thinker."

His blue eyes glinted.

Alin said quickly, "I have something I must ask you, Mar. It is about Lian."

All the humor left his face. "What of Lian?"

"Is it possible for her to join with the rest of the women at Spring Fires, and make her choice?"

He frowned. "The law says it takes one year for her to be purified."

"It is almost one year," Alin pointed out. "And the men of the Horse need women."

His frown lifted and a thoughtful silence fell.

At last, "It is all right with me," Mar said slowly. "But the one who must judge this is not me but Huth."

"I will speak to Huth, then."

"Did Lian ask you to be her voice in this?" Mar asked curiously.

"Sa."

"Then will you tell her that if Huth grants her request, she is not to choose me." He looked disgusted. "I will not wed with Lian, but I do not wish to humiliate her by having to say so to her face."

Alin could not keep the smile from pulling at the corners of her mouth. "I will tell her," she said.

He noticed the smile. "If a woman feels about a man

the way I feel about Lian," he said, his own good humor
restored, "then I can understand what you were saying
earlier about such a marriage not being good for either
party." He shook his head. "I cannot look upon her
without thinking of death."

"Mar . . ." All the mischievous pleasure had left Alin's
face. She looked at him now out of large, grave eyes.

"Sa?"

"You know that I cannot wed with you. I told you that
before."

"I did not know you had a choice," he said.

The arrogance of his reply did not even stir her temper. "Na," she said. "I do not have a choice. I was born
the only Daughter of the Mistress. I have been dedicated
to the Mother. No man can be my husband. That was
decided for me long ago." Her voice was quiet. "I will
lie with you at Spring Fires. I will make the Sacred Marriage with you for the propagation of your tribe. But I
cannot marry you."

He searched her face. "You will not say the words of
binding with me," he said at last. "I understand that.
But, after Spring Fires, will you continue to lie with me?
You have told me that your mother has men. Why cannot
it be the same for you?"

His eyes were deeply, intensely blue. The early spring
sun slanting through the bare trees was striking sparks of
gold from his hair. Standing there before her, he seemed
the very embodiment of Sky God himself, radiating the
life-giving warmth and light of the sun.

"Alin?" he said softly, took a step closer, and put his
arms loosely around her, linking his hands together at
the small of her back. His big strong body was so warm,
she thought. He seemed to carry the warmth of the sunlight inside of him. She rested her cheek against his chest
and closed her eyes. The sound of his heart beating was
the pulse that brought light and life to the earth. In him
was more warmth and strength and peace than she had
ever found anywhere else.

So must the Mother have felt when she mated with Sky
God to make the world.

It was right that she make the Sacred Marriage with

one such as he, Alin thought. He was a true son of Sky
God, and she a true daughter of Earth Mother. Together
they would make a powerful ritual.

"Alin," he said again, this time in a different tone.
She lifted her face to look at him. His arms did not
tighten; the bow she wore was in his way. But he bent
his head and kissed her, tonguing her lips open, breathing the warmth and sweetness of his breath into her. Like
sunlight.

Finally, he lifted his mouth. "Well?" he asked, smiling a little. He already knew her answer.

She gave it to him anyway. "Sa. I will lie with you,
Mar." The pause before she said the next words was
infinitesimal. "Until my mother comes."

Spring Fires! Spring Fires!

The Moon of the Great Horse disappeared under the
rim of the earth, and for three long dark days no moon
at all shone in the sky. Then, watched breathlessly by all
the tribe, a small silvery sliver appeared over the sunset
on the western horizon.

Salmon Moon, the moon of Spring Fires.

The girls had already made their choices of men, an-
nouncing them to the tribe during the period of the
moon's dark.

The choices produced few surprises. Elen had taken
Cort. Nel, Altan's former wife, had named Finn, and
Lian had named Baird. Mora, forced to choose someone,
had named Bror. Those were the ones no one had been
certain of. The rest of the girls had chosen as expected,
with the exception of Fali, who had been excused.

The ceremony of Spring Fires was to be held in a large
cave located a little way downriver from the cliffside
home of the Horse Tribe. Both Alin and Huth had ruled
against using the sacred cave of the Tribe of the Horse.
Even though it might have been used for fertility rites
long ago, presently it was dedicated solely to male gods.
Alin wanted a site that would belong exclusively to the
Mother, and when she had first seen the big downriver
cave, with its larger outside and smaller inside chambers,

she had decreed that it would be most appropriate for her purposes.

For the past moon, Jes had been busy making engravings on the cave walls. Chiefly, she had drawn the ancient fertility symbols associated with the Mother's rites: the triangles that signified the vulva, the long loop that signified the phallus, the *P* signs that signified pregnancy.

There were no statues of mating deer in the inner chamber of this new cave, and Alin had asked Jes to draw something appropriate on the walls to take their place.

Jes had chosen a smooth section of limestone wall, and on it she had drawn the picture of a woman obviously in the last stages of pregnancy. The woman was lying on her back, looking upward. Above her towered a stallion, with its phallus prominently displayed. The woman's face was blank except for two lines denoting the eyes, but her raised hands signified her identity as the Mother Goddess. The great maned stallion standing over her protruding belly was obviously Horse God, totem of the tribe for whose benefit this fertility rite of Spring Fires was being held.

Closely attuned as they were to the animal world, the tribes of the Kindred had long understood the connection between the mating of male and female, and pregnancy. For centuries they had watched the animals mate in the late summer or early fall; for centuries they had seen the late spring and early summer dropping of the foals and fawns and calves. Male and female; phallus and vulva; both were needed to bring forth life. Life for the tribe, life for the herds, life for the world of men.

Spring Fires.

The ceremony began the day after the first moon was sighted, when the unmarried women of both tribes went out to the newly sanctified cave for the rites of preparation. This new cave did not require a long underground journey to reach its sanctuary, as had the sacred cave of the Red Deer tribe. The inner chamber, wherein Jes had drawn the picture of Earth Mother and Horse God, was reached by means of a narrow but relatively short passage. However, when the women filed in and saw Jes's powerful picture for the first time, the shock of reverence and awe it produced was almost as great as that generated by the statues of the deer at home.

The women of the Horse Tribe, who were joining in this ceremony for the first time, imitated the Red Deer girls and danced the dance of the drumming heels with growing confidence and abandon. Then the girls cooked their supper on the rocky ledge that led from the cave down to the river, and spread their sleeping rolls outside the first chamber of the cave to sleep.

Alin was awakened by the sound of a bird, a shrill screaming sound that drew her up from the depths of sleep into the world of the breaking day. She had been lying on her back and so she opened her eyes directly onto the misty morning gray of the sky and saw the hawk wheeling above her.

Alin lay perfectly still and remembered what day this was. She remembered too the last time she had awakened to such a day, only to find the quiet of the morning torn apart by men and dogs erupting out of the woods.

This morning there was no such desecration. This morning there was only the hawk, circling and crying above her in the clearing morning sky. Alin lay still in her sleeping roll, one arm crooked under her head, watching the hawk. A good omen, she thought. Then, beside her, she heard Jes beginning to stir.

The day was beginning. The day she was to make the Sacred Marriage with Mar.

After breakfast, the girls washed in the river. The water was freezing cold, but the ritual washing was part of the ceremony, and they gritted their teeth and splashed gamely away.

Next, they laid the wood for the seven small fires that would be the life force of the ritual. The fires were built within the outer chamber of the cave and arranged to form the feminine symbol of the triangle.

The men arrived shortly after midday, accompanied by the married women of the Horse.

The first thing Mar noted, as he looked around the group of girls who were awaiting them outside the cave

entrance, was that Alin was nowhere to be seen. Next he
looked for Jes, to ask her where Alin was, and saw that
Jes was missing too. He started to ask Elen, and then
stopped himself. Better just to wait and see, he thought.

Not all of the men of the tribe were present, only those
who had been chosen by the women. When the ritual had
been celebrated in the Red Deer tribe, Alin had told Mar,
all of the men had participated. But here a large number
of men would have been left mateless at the end of the
ceremony.

"That could breed trouble," Alin had said to Mar
frankly. "The drums and flutes of Spring Fires bring a fire
to the blood. To leave all of those men unsatisfied . . ."
She had shaken her head.

So Mar had told his tribe that the ritual called only for
those men who had already been chosen, and though there
had been a great deal of grumbling from those left behind, he thought the grumbling was probably safer than
the alternative. Besides, the men who had not been chosen were not happy about anything these days.

I would not mind losing a few of the nirum, Mar
thought to himself as he sat before the cave with the rest
of the men, slowly chewing the assortment of greens that
had accompanied his reindeer meat. I cannot possibly
find enough women for all of the men, and a large number of unmarried men is not good for the harmony of the
tribe. He crunched some lettuce between his teeth and
thought: If some of the nirum decide they want to leave,
I will not discourage them.

They finished eating, and the girls disappeared inside
the cave. The men and women outside could see fires
being lit within. In a little while, Mar heard the high
piping sound of music being blown on a bird-bone flute.
Elen appeared at the entrance of the cave and beckoned
them to come in.

The men and the married women advanced slowly,
wonderingly, into the cave. Inside, the girls of the Red
Deer, and the three unmarried women of the Horse, were
beginning a dance around the fires. The girls all wore
bell-shaped skirts that reached to just below their knees.
Otherwise they were naked, save for the shell necklaces

that hung around their necks and the loose hair that flowed over their shoulders and down their backs. Mar sat on his heels, leaned his back against the cave wall, and watched the girls weaving in and out among the fires.

Elen began a chant, and the rest of the girls picked it up after her.

There was still no sign of Alin. Or of Jes. Elen was leading the dancers, her hair as bright as the flames of the fires, and Sana and Iva were playing the flutes.

Mar watched appreciatively as Elen wove in and out among the flames using an intricate dance pattern of swaying and sliding steps. He looked with pleasure at Elen's breasts: high and pearly white and perfectly pink-tipped in the firelight.

Poor Dale, he thought with a sudden stabbing sorrow.

The flutes sang higher. The dancers' chants lifted with the flutes, as they swayed ever closer to the flames. Mar's head felt light and he began to feel the singing in his own blood.

Where was Alin?

The smoke from the fires was heavy now in the cave and the air was warm. Mar blinked, trying to clear his vision. When he opened his eyes, Jes was standing before him.

"Come with me," she said. Her face and her voice were expressionless.

Obediently, Mar rose to his feet and followed her into the passageway that connected the outer to the inner chamber of the cave. They did not go into the next room, however, but stopped in the passage. Then Mar saw that his chief's costume was there, piled on a buffalo robe on the floor.

He looked questioningly at Jes.

"You must put it on," she said.

"Over my clothes?"

Jes shook her head. She herself was wearing one of the skirts, and her breasts and her feet and lower legs were bare. He thought she was lovely. "You are the god," she said expressionlessly.

Mar nodded. He had danced naked in tribal rituals since his initiation, so nothing here was strange to him.

Quickly he stripped off his clothes, tying the horse-hide cloak over his broad shoulders, the belt with the hanging tail around his waist, putting on the ornaments. Lastly, he took the great headdress of stallion mane, and fitted it over his own bright hair.

He said to Jes, "I am ready."

A cry went up from the girls when they saw him arrive in the passage opening. Elen left the dance floor to come and take his hand, drawing him into the dance with her.

Jes went to sit by Sana and Iva and took up a drum.

The girls began to dance again, only now they were joined by Mar and by the men and women who had been sitting on the sides. The music of the pipes, a mesmerizing high birdlike flute, drew the dancers into it, while the heartbeat of the drums drove them on.

Suddenly, standing within the arched passageway that led to the inner chamber, was the figure of a girl. She wore the same bell-shaped skirt as the other girls, but her face and her bare breasts were marked with signs painted in red-brown ochre. Her hair was loose to her waist, but around her brow she wore a headband of leather set with white shells. Her ankles and arms were encircled with bracelets of the same white shells as the headband.

A breathless intake of awe ran through the group in the cave. The music stopped. Silence reigned.

Earth Mother was among them.

The girl moved forward into the firelight. Mar held his ground and watched. She was coming toward him.

Quietly, the rest of the dancers began to fade away toward the cave walls, leaving the triangular floor between the fires empty, save for Mar.

The girl reached him, and Alin's eyes looked out at him from the face of the goddess.

The flutes began to play again, a high piping sound that Mar felt thrilling along the blood in his veins. Then came the drum, played now by someone other than Jes.

Alin began to dance, and he followed.

To the others watching from beyond the fires, the dancing figures were more than human. There, before the eyes of the tribe, was being enacted the mating dance

that signified the beginning of the world. The girls of the
Red Deer had seen it before, and still they were amazed
at the power of it. The men and women of the Horse
were utterly awed.

Mar had never seen this dance before, let alone participated in it, yet he was perfect. He wore the stallion mane
of Horse God, but he was Sky God this day. No one who
watched him doubted that. Sky God, the engenderer of
the world. And Alin was the Great Goddess, the Earth,
the Mother of all that lived.

Suddenly, Jes grabbed Tane's hand and pulled him into the
space between the fires with her. Then Elen and Cort came,
and Dara and Arn, and all the others.

The bodies whirled and leaped together in a rising
frenzy of sexual passion. Then all of a sudden, Mar
looked around and Alin was gone.

He stood for a moment, the only still figure on the
floor, breathing heavily, searching for her among the
dancers. His blood was pounding. His phallus was erect.
Where was she?

Abruptly, the music stopped. The high chanting that
had been accompanying the music stopped also. The
dancers stood, alert, aroused, chests heaving, sweat
beading on bare skin.

"It is time to put out the fires," a female voice that
was not Alin's said.

The girls ran to douse the flames. The men stood
poised, full of potency. Waiting.

Then, obedient to a signal that Mar did not see, the
others began to leave the cave. Outside, Mar could see
the girls picking up fur tunics to cover their nakedness.
Then, arms twined about each other, the couples began
walking back along the river to the cliffside caves, and
bed.

Jes and Tane were the last to leave.

"In there," Jes said to Mar as she went past him toward the door. He watched the two of them for a moment, as they went out the opening of the cave into the
darkening day. He saw how they paused just outside, saw
how their bodies melted together. He saw how Tane's
hand caressed Jes's naked breast.

Mar turned and strode down the passage and into the inner chamber.

There was a very small fire near the opening of the passage. Otherwise the chamber was dimly lit with several stone lamps. Mar noticed the bedplace immediately, a pile of buffalo robes in the exact center of the room.

Alin was not lying there. Instead, she was standing before one of the walls. Her head turned when he came in. "Come," she said to him, "and look."

He began to stride across the room.

Alin stood very still and watched him come. He seemed immense to her in the flickering light of the fire and the lamps. The shadow he cast covered half the width of the floor.

This is Sky God coming toward me, Alin thought, taking in the great black crest of stallion's mane, the erect phallus, the eyes burning with intense, impersonal desire. Sky God. This is not Mar at all.

The thought brought with it a great sense of safety.

He had reached her now, and she turned and pointed silently to the picture on the wall that Jes had drawn. She heard the intake of his breath as he saw the gravid goddess with the great potent stallion towering above her.

Alin nodded with satisfaction, then looked back at him again. Under the great black horse mane, his eyes were glittering. She started to speak, but he surprised her utterly by bending a little and scooping her up in his arms. He lifted her easily, as if she were a child, and carried her to the pile of buffalo robes that was to be their bed.

Alin opened her lips to say his name, then shut them again.

This was not Mar.

Still holding her, he knelt, and laid her back upon the soft robes. His shoulders looming over her were so wide they blocked her view of the room. Then, straightening a little, he reached up and tore off the maned headdress, baring his own damp blond hair to the lamplight and the fire.

He dropped the headdress on the floor beside him and shook his head, as if to clear it.

Alin did not want that, did not want him clearheaded and Mar. She wanted him as he was: burning, impersonal, godlike.

She halted him by reaching up and placing her fingers upon his bare forearm. Under the short golden hairs, his skin was warm. She closed her whole hand around that arm hard as stone and tugged, drawing him down.

For a brief moment he drew back against her, raising a hand to pull off the cloak that was tied around his shoulders. Then he was down on the buffalo robes with her. One of his hands cupped an ochre-marked breast, the other settled on the curve of her hip. He bent his head and his mouth came down on hers, hard.

Alin reached up and gripped his shoulders between her hands, feeling the great muscles under her fingers. He was quivering.

His kiss was bruising hard.

At last he tore his mouth from hers, and looked down. His eyes were narrow blue-black slits. He was breathing as if he had been running for hours.

Alin stretched her back in answer to that look, arching upward a little, toward him.

His hand went instantly to the bottom of her skirt. He pushed it up.

Alin felt his touch, and felt the response in her own body. Sa, she thought triumphantly. This is the way.

When he moved between her knees, she was ready. He drew her closer, lifted her, and then he was in.

She felt him pause, hesitate, as he hit the barrier of her maidenhood. She dug her nails into the flesh of his shoulders, urging him on. He reared back, and drove.

Pain seared through her, but it was the pain she wanted, and she did not flinch from it.

He drove into her again and again. She set her hands upon his muscled shoulders and held on tightly, caught up in the irresistible, powerful vibration of the act of creation.

Sa, she thought through the pain. This is how it is done, this is how life comes into the womb: life for the tribe, life for the herds, life for the world of men.

Twenty-six

Mar and Alin slept deeply that night, warm under the buffalo robes of the bedplace. Alin awoke first. Only the smoldering embers of the fire remained to give light to the cave chamber, and one very dim stone lamp. It was a moment before she remembered where she was. Then she remembered who was sleeping beside her.

She turned her head to look at him.

Mar was lying on his stomach, the way Alin had seen Ware sleep sometimes, and all she could see of him at the moment was a muscular shoulder and a tousled blond head. One big hand was lying beside his head, loosely curled into a fist.

Alin remembered last night.

Slowly, cautiously, she slid out from under the buffalo robes. She got quietly to her feet, took one careful step away from the bedplace, and felt a hand close around her ankle. She stopped and looked down.

He was lying propped up on one elbow. His other hand was holding her ankle. His eyes were very blue.

"Where are you going?" he asked.

She answered him calmly. "I am going to wash in the river, Mar."

After a moment, his fingers loosened from her ankle and he nodded. She went to pick up her clothes, which had been left piled in the corner, and he said, "I will build up the fire for you." He sat up.

Without looking at him again, Alin left the chamber. Outside, the sun was fully up. The river water was shining invitingly in the morning light, but when Alin poked in a cautious toe, it was freezing. There was blood on her thighs, however, as well as the ochre markings on her face and chest, and Alin grimly waded into the icy water until she was up to her waist. She lathered the soapwort she had brought with her, and washed quickly but thoroughly. Then, shivering almost uncontrollably, she waded out of the river and picked up her clothes.

Once dressed, she stood irresolutely before the cave entrance, feeling the warmth of the sun on her head and shoulders, not wanting to go back in.

She was afraid.

Do not be a fool, she told herself. She crossed her arms over her breasts and looked up at the brilliant blue sky. The color of Mar's eyes, she thought. The mark of Sky God.

It was not Sky God who was waiting for her now inside that cave, though. It was Mar.

She was afraid.

As she stood there before the entrance, shivering in the sunshine, she saw him come out of the passage and into the far side of the first chamber. She turned her back on the cave, took a few steps toward the river, and halted.

His voice came from behind her. "You are shivering. Come back into the cave. I have built up the fire."

She was afraid to go. "The sun feels good," she told him. "I think I'll stay here. We must be going back to the others shortly."

As she felt his hand touch her shoulder, she pulled away from him, the first time she had ever done that. When she had put some steps between them, she spun around to face him.

He had put on his trousers and pulled his reindeer fur vest over his naked upper body. His feet were bare. His thick blond hair was tangled and fell over his forehead, completely covering his eyebrows. He was watching her. He looked troubled.

He said, "I did not know there was a need for us to return so quickly. I imagine the rest of the tribe will be otherwise occupied this morning." He reached up to push the hair off his forehead. "Alin," he said. "Come back into the cave with me."

She shivered again, and this time it was not from the cold. If she took him now, she thought, it would be the man she would lie with, not the god. And it was the man who frightened her.

He saw her fright, and misinterpreted its cause. He thrust his hand through his hair once more. "About last night," he said, his voice strangely uncertain. "I am sorry, Alin. I knew it was the first time for you. I knew it is always painful for a woman the first time. I never meant to be so . . . rough."

She was looking at the ground between them, in particular at a large smooth gray stone in the shape of an egg. He cleared his throat. "It was the flutes," he said. "And the drums. Dhu! I just . . . lost control."

She answered, her eyes still on the rock, "You did not hurt me beyond what I had anticipated, Mar. Nor was that you yourself last night. That was the god. You cannot control a god."

After a moment he answered thoughtfully, "Sa. Perhaps you are right. Perhaps there was a god in me." His voice changed, regained its usual confident tone. "But this morning it is only Alin and Mar standing here. This morning will be different."

That, of course, was exactly what she feared.

She shook her head. "I do not think it would be wise."

"Why not?" When she did not reply, he pressed her further. "You said that you would lie with me after Spring Fires, Alin. Do you not remember?"

She remembered. And she wanted to. Perhaps that was what frightened her most. How much she wanted to.

"I do not think you understand," she said, and finally raised her glance from the egg-shaped stone.

"Tell me," he said.

"I have told you and told you." She ran her tongue around her suddenly dry lips. "I cannot be your wife, Mar. Nor can I be your woman. I belong . . ."

"Sa," he cut in impatiently. "I know. You have told me and told me. You belong to the Mother. But how can you betray the Mother by lying with me, Alin? That is what I do not understand.''

How could she tell him? How could she say: You are dangerous to me, Mar. I want you too much. It would be too easy for me to forget other things lying in your arms.

It would not be at all wise to tell him those things.

He took a step toward her. "Last night, we mated for the sake of the tribe," he said. His voice was huskier than usual. He took another step forward. "This morning, it will be for us." He reached out a hand, curled it around her shoulder. "I won't hurt you again, Alin. I swear it." He began to draw her toward him and she let him do it. His other arm came up and he gathered her close. "I am so sorry I hurt you," he murmured. "Alin. I am so sorry."

The air came out of her lungs in a long, shuddering sigh. She rested her cheek against his broad, fur-clad shoulder. Her eyes closed. He bent his head and she felt his lips touch her hair.

After a long moment thus, they turned and went back into the cave together.

The marriages were held two days after Spring Fires. The only couple who had not agreed were Bror and Mora.

"She cried the whole time," Bror said disgustedly to Mar when he asked to be released from the proposed marriage. "Perhaps another man would not mind, but I could not bear a constantly wailing woman in my sleeping roll. Let her choose someone else."

The two were the only men in the nirum's cave at the moment. Most of the other men were working on fishing gear, as the salmon would be coming up the river shortly.

Mar was not pleased with Bror's request. "She will come around," he told Bror. "You must give her time. You only lay with her once."

Bror snorted. "Mar. This girl was not a maiden. What I did did not shock her. She just did not want to do it with me." He shrugged. "There is some boy in her own tribe to whom she is attached. She told me they were to wed."

Mar's thick golden brows drew together. He looked at Bror and said nothing.

Bror's face set. "I am not a man who enjoys taking a woman by force," he told his chief. "It is one thing on the night of the Fires, with the drums pounding hot in your blood. It is another thing to do it when the blood is cold and the mind is clear. Find someone else for her. I am withdrawing."

"I doubt if I will be able to get you another woman if you reject this one, Bror," Mar warned. "Any woman I am able to trade for will have to go to the older men first."

"I understand that."

Mar's frown deepened. "I do not understand you. We have had unwilling women before come into this tribe. You know that. And you know that the homesickness goes away when once they have made some friends and had their own babes. You must just give her time, Bror."

Bror stood for a moment, head a little bent, deep in thought. "What you say is so. But this is . . . different."

"How?"

Bror shook his head slightly from side to side. "I do not know. I do not know if it is Mora that is different, or if I am." His head lifted and his brown eyes met Mar's. "I do know this. None of the rest of the girls of the Red Deer appear to feel as Mora does."

Mar moved one foot a little restlessly. "That is so," he admitted.

"Let her remain with Fali and the young girls for a little while longer," Bror said unexpectedly. "Don't force her to choose a husband yet, Mar."

The frown did not lift from Mar's face. At last he said, "That is what Alin said."

"I would listen to Alin, if I were you."

Mar's forehead cleared and he looked thoughtfully at Bror. "You will take some rough handling from the nirum over this, Bror," he warned.

Bror shrugged. "I can take a little taunting better than I can take Mora weeping her eyes out in my arms."

Faint amusement glinted in Mar's eyes. "It does sound a little . . . daunting."

Bror grinned wryly.

Both men began to move toward the door of the cave. The day was chill, but the sun was shining. They stood for a moment, watching Alin coming up the beach, Ware trotting at her side, Lugh and Roc racing in circles around the two of them.

"The girls of the Red Deer are different from our women," Bror said suddenly. "One thinks of them as companions as well as women."

There was a thoughtful silence as both men continued to watch Alin. Then, "All right," Mar said resignedly. "I will give Mora some time."

Tane stood beside Jes and listened to his father reciting the opening words of the marriage ceremony. Around them stood seventeen other couples, the men all from the Tribe of the Horse, the women mainly from the Tribe of the Red Deer.

The long-awaited day that would save the tribe from extinction was here.

Huth was not wearing his usual shaman's costume this day. For marriages he wore a great buffalo hide cloak instead of his grass one, and his face was unmasked. He carried his shaman's staff of life, however, and upon his face were drawn the *S* and *P* marks that signified fertility to the Tribe of the Horse.

Huth would be marrying two of his sons this day, Tane thought, his eyes on his father. Himself and Arn.

Not Mar.

As Huth began to chant the second blessing, Tane's eyes moved from the figure of the shaman to the tall, powerful figure of his foster brother standing on Huth's right.

Mar had not seemed to be disturbed that Alin would not marry him.

"It is not the custom in her tribe for the Daughter of the Mistress to wed," he had said to Tane with an easy shrug. "It is no matter. She has moved her things into my shelter and she sleeps by my fire. That is all that matters to me."

Perhaps, Tane thought now, his gaze roving from Mar

to the slender brown-haired girl who was standing on Huth's other side. Alin was very still. Tane had never known anyone who could be as still as Alin.

He wished she had agreed to marry Mar.

It was interesting that Mar had not felt he could compel her.

Tane felt Jes looking at him, and he turned his head a little to give her a faint smile. Her wide-set blue-gray eyes seemed almost somber. He moved his hand a little, to touch hers, and was startled by the shock that leaped instantly between them.

Dhu! This was not the place or the time for that.

Apparently Jes felt the same, for he felt her hand withdraw, saw her step ever so slightly away from him.

Later, Tane thought with intense satisfaction. Later, they would be alone.

He had thought nothing could ever match the fiery passion that had sprung between them on the night of the Fires, but the times since had been just as good. Better, perhaps, because not so frenzied.

He had never dreamed he could feel about a woman the way he felt about Jes. But then, there was not another woman like Jes in all the living world.

She had the gift of the artist. One day she would be almost as good as he was. There was no one else in the tribe to equal her. Even Huth had seen that at last.

Dhu, Tane thought with sudden interest, what would their children be like!

He realized abruptly that Huth was beginning the words of binding. They were going before him couple by couple, and Tane began to listen so that he would not forget his part.

"What will you bring to the woman?" Huth was asking Cort now. Arn felt his eyes suddenly prick, and stretched them wide to force back the threatening tears. This was not the time to cry, he told himself sternly.

Oh, but Dale. Dale.

It should be you here, Arn thought, listening to Cort's low-voiced reply: "I bring my fire for her warmth, my kill for her food, my spear for her protection, my body for her shelter. These are the things that I bring to the woman.''

Cort's voice faltered a little on the last words, and Arn knew that he too was thinking of Dale.

Oh my brother, Arn thought achingly. How I miss you.

A small, warm hand stole into his. Arn's own long slender fingers closed about it, gripped it hard.

Dara. How lucky he was to have Dara. He had never felt as close to anyone as he felt to her. Not even Dale, not even his brother, had been as close to him as was this small, dark-haired girl with the great gray eyes.

Now Elen was answering Huth's question. There had been a little controversy about the ceremony, and Huth and Alin had finally settled on a combination of the ceremonies of both tribes. The question posed to the men was from the marriage ceremony of the Tribe of the Horse. The question posed to the women was from the ceremony of the Tribe of the Red Deer.

Elen's voice was low and clear and perfectly steady. ''This is the man I take for myself,'' she said to Huth. ''This is Cort, the mate that I choose for the life of the tribe.''

Now no one would ever say, ''This is Dale.'' There was such a pain in the back of Arn's throat that he doubted he would be able to answer at all when Huth spoke the words of binding to him.

''Dara and Arn,'' Huth said.

Dara looked up at him. Arn swallowed, kept his grip on her hand, and stepped forward.

Alin stood beside Huth and listened to the words of binding being said, again and again. The last ones to come before the shaman were Tane and Jes.

They looked well together, Alin thought, as the two stepped forward into the circle of firelight. Both so slim, so intense, so . . . so concentrated looking. Tane's hair shone black as a raven's wing, and his green eyes were fixed gravely and steadily upon his father.

For a brief moment, Jes looked at Alin.

Never again would it be just the two of them. Now

there would always be a man between them. There was regret in the look that they exchanged, and acceptance.

There had been a man between them for quite a while, Alin thought, as she watched Jes turn her attention to Huth and the ceremony. It had been so ever since Jes had first seen Tane pick up a graver and draw.

Nor, Alin admitted to herself, was Tane the only man whose shadow fell between her and Jes. She did not look at Mar, standing on the other side of Huth, but she felt his presence. She always felt his presence, as she knew he always felt hers.

The old fellowship between herself and Jes had not been breached by one man, but by two.

But it was so for the men also, Alin continued to think, as she listened to the now-familiar words being recited by Tane. The fellowship of Mar and Tane would never be the same either now that she and Jes had come along.

Perhaps it was meant to be thus, Alin thought, her eyes on Tane's serious dark face. After all, were not male and female fashioned so as to complete each other? Was there any other fellowship that was so close as that one was?

Perhaps, she thought wonderingly, perhaps that was what marriage was about.

Now Jes began to speak. "This is Tane. This is the mate that I choose for the life of the tribe."

Sa, Alin thought. Perhaps this is the most important rite of the Mother, after all. A man and a woman, coming together for the life of the tribe. Staying together for the life of the tribe.

She remembered Mar's words to her when they had first discussed delaying the marriages until after Spring Fires. "But if a woman gets with child and has no husband, who will care for her, shelter her, hunt for her?" he had asked.

Perhaps after all he had been right. Perhaps that was marriage: the man to give shelter and food and protection; the woman to give life. One could not exist without the other.

Neither should have the rule, she had told Mar. Both to bear their proper part.

*I give my fire for her warmth, my kill for her food, my
spear for her protection, my body for her shelter.*

*This is the man I take for myself, the mate that I choose
for the life of the tribe.*

If this is so, Alin thought, then where does that leave
me?

Dangerous thinking.

What is true for other women is not true for me. I am
not as the others are. I am the daughter of the Mistress,
the Chosen One.

Why does that mean I cannot marry? Mar can marry,
and he is the chief. Arn can marry, and he will be the
shaman.

Dangerous thinking.

Jes and Tane were stepping back into the circle of the
others. Huth said something, and all of the couples began
to smile. Then Mar was moving forward, clapping Tane
on the shoulder.

The girls of the Red Deer were married. But not Alin.

Twenty-seven

At the full of the moon, the salmon appeared in the river.

Mar made the first kill with a harpoon. The weapon he used had a shaft made of wood, but the barb point on the end of it was carved out of bone. A barb was very useful on a harpoon, as it held the fish after it had been speared.

The first salmon, a male with jaws just beginning to hook, was buried on the shore, its head turned toward the river in respect for its craving for water.

Then the men got out the nets. They manned small canoes of birch bark sewn over wooden frames and made watertight with plant gums. There were two men to a canoe, one to row with the wooden paddles, one to manage the net.

The women of the Red Deer were familiar with the ways of salmon, having seen the fish every year make a similar run up the Greatfish River. When the nets full of the red-brown catch were dumped on the shore, there were delighted smiles everywhere. After a long winter's diet of reindeer meat and smoked buffalo, the prospect of fresh salmon was very appetizing.

The feast of the first salmon was held that night. The tribe made a big fire and cooked the salmon on the beach, near the river that had given so generously of its fruits. Huth drummed his drum and there was dancing and laughter and general rejoicing.

Winter was over. The reindeer had gone back to the mountains, and the salmon had come. Soon buds would appear on the trees, and the deer foals would begin to drop. The hunting season for deer and aurochs and ibex and salmon was upon them.

It was spring.

The full moon had made half of its journey from the morning to the afternoon side of the sky when the feast of the first salmon began to disperse. In small groups, the men and women and children of the tribe left the moonlit beach to return to their shelters. By the time the moon had reached its apex, the only two left by the fire were Mar and Huth. Alin had gone earlier, to walk with Ware and Rom and Mada back to their cave in order to put Ware to bed.

"It goes well, my son," Huth said to Mar, who was standing at a little distance from the dying fire, his eyes on the river. Mar had shaved off his winter beard on the first day of Salmon Moon, and the chief's profile was cleanly etched in the bright moonlight.

"Does it?" Mar replied, still staring at the moonlit water. "There are some very dissatisfied men in this tribe, Huth." The line of his mouth was grim. "And there is little I can do about it."

Huth sighed. "How many men are without women now?"

"Three handfuls of nirum. The boys of the initiates' cave won most of the Red Deer girls."

"That could have come as no surprise to the nirum. It was clear almost from the first whom the girls would choose."

"Sa."

"There will be a Spring Gathering at the full of the next moon. Perhaps there will be some women available there."

At last Mar turned to look at his foster father. "Huth, we have exhausted the supply of extra women in the local tribes. If we want any more women, we are going to have to trade our women for them."

"We do not have any women to trade."

"I know."

A short silence fell. A splash came from the river, as a fish jumped out of the water and fell back again. Then,

"Are you planning another kidnapping raid, my son?" Huth asked mildly.

Mar's head came up. "Na." He smiled wryly. "I have learned that it is not so simple as it seems, to kidnap women and make them part of your tribe."

"It worked, though," Huth said unexpectedly. "Look at all the marriages I presided over recently."

Mar did not reply. Another silence fell. Neither man made any move to leave the beach. "Huth." Mar said finally, "I am thinking that I must drive the unwed nirum out."

This time the silence was uncomfortable.

"You cannot," Huth said at last.

"I cannot have the situation I have presently. There will be trouble. While the girls were still uncommitted, it was tolerable. A man could always hope he had a chance. But now . . . now it could get ugly." Mar's eyes were somber. "We could have the tragedy of Davin and Bard played over once again."

"Surely not, Mar!"

"The men have been too long without a woman. And now they must look every day at other men who have a woman."

"But this is their tribe. The people of the Horse are their people. You are their chief, Mar! You cannot tell men like Iver and Zel and Cal to leave!"

"The stallion is the head of the herd," Mar said. "And a good stallion will drive out his own sons. If he does not, there will be fighting. There will be death." Mar's eyes glittered between his lashes, deeply blue in the moonlight. "You know this as well as I."

Huth was silent.

"I do not like this, Huth," Mar said at last, his voice raw with a mixture of anger and despair. "If there is any other way, I would be glad to hear of it."

"Do not act too quickly, Mar," Huth advised after a moment. "Wait until after the Gathering. Perhaps we will be lucky, perhaps there will be women for us there."

"Perhaps," Mar answered, though he did not sound as if he believed it.

* * *

Alin was sitting cross-legged by the fire when Mar came into their shelter, Lugh at his heels as usual. He gave her a quick smile. "A good feast," he said, and came to sit beside her.

"Sa." She looked at him thoughtfully. When he was comfortably settled next to her on the buffalo robe, "What are you going to do about all the unwed nirum?" she asked.

He blew out of his nose like a startled horse, turned his head and stared at her. "It is in my heart that you can hear how I think."

She smiled faintly. "You think like a chief. So do I. And all those unwed men are a problem."

"I know." His expression became grim. "I was just talking about it to Huth. I think he expected me to kidnap another tribe of women."

"What!"

He grinned at her expression and then his eyes darkened. He stared into the fire. "The only answer I can find is that I must drive the unwed nirum out of the tribe, Alin."

"That is a . . . drastic step."

"I know." His voice was deeply bitter.

"Mar," Alin said. "What about those tribeless women down the river?"

His nostrils flared. "They are unclean," he said. "Faithless. Are you suggesting that we take them into our tribe?"

"They are women," she pointed out. "Perhaps their husbands were cruel to them. Perhaps they simply loved another man. Perhaps they would be happy to be taken into a tribe, to have one man of their own to hunt for them, take care of them."

There was a long silence.

"I had not thought of them," he said. "Some of them . . ." he frowned in thought. "Some of them might do."

Alin opened her mouth to ask him how he knew that, then decided she did not want to know the answer.

Mar was shaking his head. "The nirum would not take them, Alin. It would be a matter of honor. They have slept with many men, you see." He made a gesture of dismissal. "They are unclean."

"I will have a ceremony for them," Alin said. "I will purify them, make them swear sacred vows to be faithful to their new husbands."

"You will?"

"Sa."

He sat for a moment deep in thought. "We could tell the nirum that the ceremony washes away all that went before. I am thinking that they will not be too fastidious, will be happy to find a way to take the women and still keep their honor."

"Sa," said Alin with faint irony.

He missed the irony, grinned at her. "This is a wonderful idea," he said enthusiastically. "I have been thinking and thinking and thinking about this problem, wondering where I could possibly find more women. . . ."

"Anything to keep you from the kidnapping trail again," Alin said, and this time Mar caught the irony.

"It will be a better life for those women than the one they are leading now," he said to her very seriously. "And they will be treated well. I will swear that to you if you like."

She sighed. "There is no need for swearing. I know that it will be a better life, Mar. That is why I made the suggestion." She pushed her braid off of her shoulder. "It is not good for anyone to be without a tribe."

"It is not good for a woman to be without one man, or for a man to be without one woman." His voice had deepened in the way she was coming to know well. "I have found that out, Alin, these days since Spring Fires."

That voice of his . . . it was frightening what that voice of his could make her feel.

He was rising to his knees, was reaching out for her hands, was drawing her up toward him.

She had found that out too, Alin thought, as she felt the clasp of his big warm hands around hers, as she let him raise her up to kneel before him. Living with him like this, sharing the same hearth, the same bed; even, as he had said before, the same thoughts, she was conscious always of how her spirit reached for him, looked to him for its peace.

It had been a mistake to move into his shelter. In her heart she had always known that, and she had done it anyway.

It had been a mistake. Every day she grew closer to him, more entwined with him. Body and spirit, both. A mistake.

There was nothing she could do. She knew that with certainty as his hands came up to cup and hold her face, and his mouth came down to rest upon hers. On her own, she could not leave him. Her mother must come for her. Her future lay now in the hands of the Mistress.

There was darkness in the corners of the cave, but here by the small fire there was brightness and warmth. As Mar laid her back on the buffalo robe, Alin could hear the soft rustle of Lugh settling down on his bed for the night. Then Mar was leaning over her, his fair hair gilded with the firelight, his eyes narrowed to glittering slits.

Sky God, Alin thought, reaching up to run her fingers through that thick bright hair. But almost instantly she knew that she could fool herself no longer with thinking that it was Sky God who stirred such feelings in her blood, woke such a longing in her womb. It was not Sky God she longed to lie with. It was Mar.

But he was like the sun when he came to her like this, so hot, so fierce, so relentless. And yet so gentle. His hands under her clothes, he touched her and kissed her, and she felt welling up within herself the moist hot juice of fecundity. She lie beneath him and quivered and quivered, like a tightly strung bow that has been pulled by the strong hand of a hunter. His mouth covered hers again, he kissed her, and she felt as if the blazing heat of him would surely destroy her.

"A-lin. A-lin. A-lin." He was saying her name again and again, as if it were an incantation in a ritual. The small part of her that had yet held separate from him gave way at the sound of her name. The thinking part of her flickered briefly, and then went dark.

There was nothing left of her but the A-lin he had called to. As the flower opens itself to the warmth of the sun, so did Alin answer to his hands and his mouth, responding completely, utterly.

She wanted nothing but him, nothing but this, the warmth and the heat and the pure sensation as the two of them entered together into the source of creation and became not two separate beings but one.

Neither Altan nor Sauk had been on the kidnapping raid with Mar, and so they did not know the precise location of the home caves of the Tribe of the Red Deer. It was a full moon's time before the deposed chief and his companion located the Greatfish River, and another few days before finally they came upon the valley that was home to the tribe they sought.

As Altan and Sauk came around the bend of the river, they saw a group of men and women fishing with nets very like the ones made by the Tribe of the Horse. Altan halted when he saw them, and Sauk stopped also. Then one of the women on the shore turned her head and saw them.

She said something to the others, and then Altan heard her call out to the men in the boats. The rest of the women on the shore turned to look at the strange men. One of the small dugout canoes on the river began to return to land.

Altan stood silently, Sauk by his side, waiting.

The boat reached the shore and a man jumped out. Altan waited as the man crossed the rocky ground that separated them. The man reached them, halted, and said, "May we help you, strangers?"

Altan did not immediately reply, taking time to look at the man before him. He was tall, this Red Deer man, with striking long-lashed brown eyes. Eyes that Altan recognized instantly. He smiled.

"I am thinking rather that it is we who can help you," he said to Alin's father.

"Sa?" The man looked politely skeptical.

"Did your tribe perhaps lose some women during the time of Stag-Fighting Moon?"

The man's expression sharpened. Hardened. "Sa." His voice had hardened too. "We did."

Sauk spoke for the first time, saying harshly, "We know where they are."

Tor took them immediately to Lana.

Thus far, the Tribe of the Red Deer had been unsuccessful in its hunt for the kidnapped girls. Tor had returned only two days since from a long sortie, to report to Lana that the particular Tribe of the Horse they were seeking was not to be found in the west.

"A few tribes had heard rumors, but no one could say for certain where this particular tribe was located," he had said to the Mistress grimly.

Bitterly disappointed, Lana had made plans to send to the various Spring Gatherings that would be held at the next full moon, in hopes of learning something more definite.

Then Altan and Sauk had walked into their valley.

"Can we believe them?" Tor asked Lana when the two of them were sitting alone in her hut after Altan and Sauk had been dismissed to the custody of the men's cave.

"I think so," Lana replied. "What would they have to gain by lying?"

"That is so," Tor said slowly. He looked at her over the small fire. "But, if what they say is true, Lana, what kind of men are they? To turn traitor to their own people?"

Lana lifted her right hand in a characteristic gesture of dismissal. "They are followers of Sky God, sons of sons. They have forgotten the Mother. There is nothing that binds such men to their people."

"It seems not," Tor said wonderingly.

"Men like that," the contempt was plain on Lana's face, "seek only power for themselves. They have no understanding of the responsibility of being the leader. They want all of the privileges and none of the burdens."

Tor was silent, looking at the woman who understood better than any what those burdens were. Then he said, "It is to our benefit, however, that these are as they are. Because of that, we know where Alin has been taken."

Lana leaned a little forward, bringing her face more fully into the light of the fire. There was slightly more gray in her fair hair than there had been at Winter Fires, but the long, cool, blue-gray eyes were the same, as was the wide-browed cat's face. The golden shells of her necklace glimmered in the firelight.

"I have been thinking, Tor, and I tell you now that when we go to claim the girls, I do not want a fight."

"It is in my heart," Tor replied with a faint lift of his brows, "that this tribe will not give back our girls merely for the asking."

"I know that. But we have an advantage, Tor. We know exactly where our girls are. And not only that," Lana sat back again, "we now have someone who knows the kidnappers' territory."

Tor nodded thoughtfully. "That is so."

"This is what we will do," Lana said. "I will get a message to Alin telling her to pretend to gather the girls for a ritual of some sort. Away from the men."

A slow appreciative smile spread across Tor's face. "You mean to kidnap them back."

Lana looked at him. She did not return his smile. "Sa," she said coolly. "Why not?"

Twenty-eight

At the full of Salmon Moon, Mar and Alin together made the two-day trek downriver to the caves of the tribeless women. There they found seventeen women and five children dwelling within two great limestone caves that had been hollowed out of a cliff on the shore of the Wand.

At first Alin was surprised by the small number of children.

"They expose the new ones when they're born," Mar told her briefly. And in truth, when Alin saw the end-of-winter emaciation of most of the women, she understood that they would have no extra nourishment to offer an infant.

Alin had been appalled by the whole situation of the tribeless women. Appalled by their inability to hunt for themselves, by the way they were forced to get the food they lived by. Most of all, she was appalled that a tribe would condemn a woman to such a fate for any reason, let alone for such a transgression as marital infidelity.

"If she has been unfaithful, then let her husband leave her hearth!" she said passionately to Mar when they were alone together at the campsite they had pitched a little distance from the women's caves. Alin had spread out their sleeping skins and now she sat cross-legged on her own and looked at Mar with flashing eyes.

"I agree that he should not be forced to continue to live with a woman he can no longer trust," she continued. "Let him turn his back on her, find a new wife. But not this, Mar! This is . . . intolerable."

Busying himself with building up the fire, Mar did not immediately reply. "They are a sad sight," he said finally. "But, Alin, they brought it on themselves."

"That is no answer!"

He turned to look at her, his eyebrows cocked.

"Think about it, Mar," she said to him, striving to moderate her voice, to speak reasonably. "These are women who were raised in the Way of Sky God, who were never taught to hunt for themselves. They worked for the tribe and the men of the tribe the way the women of the Horse work: they made the clothes and baskets; they gathered fruits and nuts and grains and berries and eggs in their proper seasons; they cooked; they bore children and nursed them and reared them."

The fire was blazing up now, and Mar sat back on his heels in front of it, facing Alin. She went on, "I am thinking that the men of the Horse have come to know well what it is that a woman brings to a tribe, and what it is to be without her."

"Sa." He made an impatient gesture. "I know all this, Alin. But these are women who betrayed their tribes. . . ."

She shook her head sadly. "Na, Mar. These women did not betray their tribes, their tribes betrayed them."

He opened his mouth to interrupt and she held up a hand, leaning toward him, speaking with great intensity. "There is a covenant made between a woman and her tribe, Mar. If the tribe does not teach a woman to hunt for herself, if the tribe expects her to bear and to nurture the tribe's children, then the woman has the right to expect that the tribe will shelter her. That the men of her tribe will hunt for her, feed her and the children that she bears to them." She straightened up a little, lifting her chin. "Is that not so, Mar?"

"Sa," he said evenly. "That is so."

Alin picked up a stick, and as she spoke she stabbed it into the ground. "What kind of chiefs do these tribes have, that they could so disregard such a covenant?" she asked.

"You are forgetting, Alin, that it was these women who broke the covenant first."

Alin's hand stilled. "I am not speaking of the covenant that is called marriage." She shrugged. "What is that, after all? One man, one woman. If they disagree, let them separate. What I am talking about, Mar, is the covenant between the *tribe* and the woman. 'Give up your self-sufficiency,' the tribe says to the woman. 'Do not hunt. Rely on the tribe to hunt for you. Keep at home and rear our children.' "

She put down the stick and said, "Is that not so, Mar? Is that not how it is for a woman who lives under the Way of Sky God?"

"Sa." He dragged the word out, seeming unwilling to pronounce it.

"This is a great and serious thing, Mar, this covenant made between the woman and the tribe. I do not say it is wrong to make such a covenant. The Way of the Mother teaches that nothing stands alone, that each thing is a part of something else. Life is a part of death. Man is a part of woman. But it is wrong when the covenant is not understood as being between the woman and the tribe, but between the woman and one man."

He looked both puzzled and irritated. "But that is what marriage is!"

Her mouth curled with disdain. "And what if the man is bad, Mar? What if the man hurts his wife? Starves his children?" She flipped her braid back over her shoulder and regarded him. "Where does the woman turn, Mar? Who is there to protect her welfare if her husband will not?"

Silence.

"The tribe should be there," Alin said. "The tribe should be there for protection. The tribe should be there for justice. The chief of the tribe should be there to see that the covenant between the woman and the tribe is kept." Her brown eyes were no longer indignant. Now they were grave. "That is what it means to be a chief, Mar, to see that the protection of the tribe is given to all, even to the smallest and lowest of its members. To the children. To the simpleminded. And to unfaithful husbands and wives also. That is what I learned from my mother, and she is a very great chief."

The indignation that had died in Alin seemed now to catch fire in Mar. "But suppose the man is *not* bad, Alin?" he said forcefully. "Suppose it is the woman who is bad, the woman who for . . . excitement . . . wants to lie with another man?" He thrust his fingers through the hair at his brow. "That happens, you know," he said.

"I am not saying that unfaithfulness is an acceptable thing," Alin replied. "It is not. It is very bad. It disturbs the harmony of the tribe. A woman such as the one you just described should be punished." She spread out her hands. "In your own tribe, Mar, is that not how you handled Lian? She was punished, and you were right to punish her. But you did not cast her out, and she was guilty of a much greater crime than simply lying with a man who was not her husband. From what you say, Lian was responsible for a man's death."

Mar thrust his hand through his hair once again. His eyes suddenly blazed. "Dhu, Alin, but I hate to argue with you!"

She smiled.

"Is that why you learned to hunt?" he asked her curiously. "So that you would never have to depend upon a man?"

"Na." The smile spread to her eyes. "I learned to hunt because it was fun."

He grinned.

"The girls of my tribe have always learned to hunt," she explained, linking her arms comfortably around her knees as he came to sit beside her. "Any woman of the Red Deer left in the position of those women," she gestured toward the caves, "would be able to get herself food in the winter. But until I formed our hunting companionship, the girls of the tribe learned only the very basic skills of hunting. They learned how to throw a spear and a javelin, they learned how to shoot an arrow, they learned how to skin a deer. But after the training they rarely went out on the hunting trail."

"Why so?"

She sighed. "Because of the covenant I spoke of before. A man cannot bear and nurse a child. If the women are out on the hunting trail, then who will care for the children?'' His eyes on her face remained grave and attentive. She went on, ''And if the women are not to be the hunters of the tribe, then why should they spend their time perfecting a skill they will never use?''

''That is so.''

''Those women in the caves could have used such a skill,'' she said dryly. ''They would have some flesh on their bones now if they had once learned how to hunt.''

''That is so, too.'' He smiled at her. Lugh trotted out of the woods, where he had been investigating, and came to curl up before the fire.

''Why is it so hard for me to stay angry with you?'' Alin demanded with mock exasperation.

''I am too reasonable a man,'' he replied.

Alin began to laugh.

He looked thoughtful. ''All this talk of hunting has made me hungry.''

''Shall I get you your dinner?'' she asked.

He looked horrified. Then he saw her amusement. He reached over, gave her braid a pull, and got to his feet. ''I will get us some meat,'' he said, bending over to pick up his spearthrower.

Alin watched him go off into the woods, Lugh at his heels. Then she set about making a roasting spit for the fire.

The following day, Alin talked to the tribeless women. Then Mar talked to them. The result of both discussions was that all of the seventeen women said that they wanted to join the Tribe of the Horse.

Alin insisted Mar agree to one condition before she would consider holding a ceremony to purify the women and make them acceptable to the men of the tribe. Mar had to take all of the women who wished to come, even those who were older and less attractive than some of the others.

When Mar protested that these women might not find husbands, she replied, ''If they do not find a husband, then they can live in the women's cave.''

''From a situation where I have too many men, now I

am going to find myself burdened with too many
women,'' he grumbled.

"The men of the Horse are fine hunters," Alin said
sweetly. "You will have no difficulty in feeding a few
extra mouths. And I refuse to leave any woman in this
place who does not freely choose to stay." Faced with
such a stand, Mar had been forced to agree.

For his own part, Mar had made one stipulation to
Alin. "If the men of the Horse do not agree to take these
women, if the purifying ceremony is not enough for them,
then the women stay where they are. The last thing I need
at the moment is an unattached group of women such as
these living in my own caves!"

Alin had seen that this was a point upon which he was
adamant, and she in turn had reluctantly accepted his
condition.

So the situation stood as the two of them returned upriver to present their suggestion to the tribe. If the single
men agreed to accept the tribeless women as wives, all
of the women would be taken into the Tribe of the Horse.
If the men did not agree, then the women would stay as
they were.

The men agreed. They had been too long without a
woman, and now that the Red Deer girls had been wed,
there was no prospect of more women for them. As Mar
had foreseen, they were not in a mood to be fastidious.

Mar sent Alin back downriver again, along with some
of the tribe's women, to perform whatever ceremony she
deemed was needful to make the tribeless women clean
again. When Mar himself, with a handful of the men,
went downriver two days later to escort the women home,
they found a very different scene from the one he and
Alin had encountered the previous week.

"The purifying ceremony must have been physical as
well as spiritual," Mar said to Alin in a low voice, when
first he beheld the clean faces and shining hair of the
tribeless women.

Her large eyes were full of laughter though her mouth
was grave. "Sa," she said. "They will look better to the
men, so."

"They certainly will," Mar said fervently. They were standing at a little distance from the group and now he regarded the women with amazement. "Even the older ones look decent!"

"How will you make these matches?" Alin asked next. "That is not something we have discussed."

His blue gaze became wary. "I hope you are not going to ask me to give these women time to make their own choices."

"Would you?"

"Na." His tone was uncompromising. "The men have waited too long, Alin. Nor have these women been kidnapped. In fact, I am thinking it is just the opposite. They are grateful for the chance to be taken into our tribe. It is in my heart that they will be satisfied with any of our men."

"Perhaps," Alin admitted after a little. "Will you let the men make the choice, then?"

He shook his head. "*I* will make the choice, Alin. The men will have a woman, the women will have a man. They must all be satisfied with that."

"I suppose so," Alin said, her eyes on the women as they gathered their meager belongings.

"Alin!" It was Dara coming toward them. "I think we are ready to leave."

"All right, Dara," Alin said. "Let us go."

Mar gave out the women solely on the basis of age. The oldest women went to the oldest men and so on downward. The result of the pairings was that all of the nirum got wives, as well as two of the boys from the initiates' cave. At long last, the Tribe of the Horse was in balance.

On the night of the marriages, Alin and Mar returned together to their shelter well pleased with a good day's work.

"At last," Mar said, turning toward her as he dropped the buffalo skins in place over the entranceway, effectively shutting out the world. "At last we are a tribe again!"

He grinned, and then he reached out his hand for her.

They had not yet made up the fire so the shelter was lit only by two of the stone lamps. Alin moved toward him in answer to his touch and his arms came around her. Alin rested her cheek against his shoulder and put her arms around his waist. She could feel the exuberance that was pumping all through his big powerful body.

"All those women," he said exultantly.

"Sa." Her own voice was very soft. "All those women."

She closed her eyes and turned her face toward him. He smelled so good. He smelled like Mar. She would know him anywhere, she thought, just by his smell.

He was so full of happiness. It had glowed in his eyes all day, it had crackled in his hair.

She rubbed her cheek against his buckskin shoulder, inhaled his scent, and thought about her menstrual calendar. Her bleeding should have started at the full of the moon. It was now the first of the Moon of the New Fawns, and still the bleeding had not begun.

She had never been more than a few days late before. It would take a little more time before she could be certain, but in her heart she knew that she was with child.

For the first time since the kidnapping, Alin seriously contemplated the possibility of never returning to the Tribe of the Red Deer.

". . . could not have done it without you," Mar was saying. "Even if I had thought of the tribeless women, I never would have been able to get the men to accept them if it had not been for you. You and your ceremony." He loosened his arms so he could look down at her. Reluctantly, she took her face out of his shoulder and looked up.

It was true what he had said, she thought. He would not have been able to do it without her. He was smiling down at her. He was happy.

Perhaps Lana had not been able to discover their whereabouts after all, Alin thought. Perhaps the Tribe of the Red Deer would never come after its girls.

She was shocked by the joy that seared through her at this prospect.

"What is it?" Mar asked. His smile had been replaced

by a look of concern. He reached a finger up to smooth between her brows, as if he would wipe away whatever trouble was there.

"What do you mean?" she replied, trying to keep her voice unreadable. Her face, it seemed, had been too clear.

"You looked . . . frightened."

"Did I?" She managed a smile. "You are imagining things."

"Perhaps." He sounded doubtful. He looked worried. "You must never be frightened of me, Alin. I would die before I would hurt one single hair of your head." His eyes were no longer the unclouded blue of a summer sky. They were darker. She could always tell his mood by the color of his eyes. "It is in my heart that you must know that," he said.

"Sa," she answered quietly. "I know that."

But I am frightened of you, she thought, looking up into that splendid face, that beloved face. I have forsaken my mother for you, Mar. And I am afraid.

"You are . . . part of me," he was saying. "There, all the time, in my mind, in my heart. I never have to look for you, Alin, you are always there."

"How did this happen to us?" she whispered.

He shook his head slowly. Then he bent it, and his mouth covered hers.

Twenty-nine

It was a lovely morning when Alin received the message from her mother. The tribe was planning to make a great deer hunt within the week, and Alin and some of the women had been spreading baskets on the beach to air in the sun, when a slim dark man came out onto the beach from the path that ran between the cliffs.

"Who is that?" Elexa asked, rising and looking with curiosity at the slender figure coming toward them across the gravel.

Alin turned to look also, but it was Jes who first recognized the stranger.

"Dhu!" she said in a low, vibrant voice to Alin. "It is Ban!"

Alin felt her heart skip a beat, and then begin to slam within her chest. It *was* Ban, she saw. He had cut off his braid, was wearing his hair like the men of the Horse, but still, unmistakably, it was Ban.

He came up to the watching women and stopped. "Greetings," he said. He looked directly at Alin, but he did not acknowledge her. "I have become separated from the people I was traveling with," he said. "I would be grateful for some directions before I go on my way again."

"We will be glad to help you if we can," Alin said, speaking as he did, as if to a stranger. She glanced around quickly. The girls of the Red Deer had all recognized Ban, she could see that from the way they had averted their eyes. The women of the Horse were regarding him curiously. Alin felt sweat spring up on her forehead. She managed to say calmly, "Come with me, stranger, and if I cannot answer your questions, I will take you to someone who can."

Lian said, "What is your tribe, stranger? And how is it that you have become separated from your companions?"

Alin flashed the girl a stern look. "Go back to your work, Lian. I will see to this man."

Lian flushed angrily. As Alin walked away, Ban at her side, she heard Jes saying to Lian soothingly, "Alin is right, Lian. Best not to get too friendly with strangers until we learn more about them."

"How can we learn more about them if we don't ask them questions?" Lian snapped in return. Then Alin was out of their range of hearing.

"Where is my mother?" she asked Ban immediately.

"But a morning's walk away," Ban replied. "She and Tor and a moon's number of men."

"So many!"

"Sa." His young mouth set. "We have been searching and searching for you, Alin. If it had not been for the men who came to us with news of you, we might never have found you, so far to the north of us is this Tribe of the Horse."

"Men? What men?" Alin asked sharply.

"One's name is Altan," Ban replied. "The other is called Sauk."

Alin halted in stunned surprise. "Altan and Sauk found their way to the Tribe of the Red Deer?"

"Sa. Altan said he had been the chief here, but the tribe had driven him and his companion out. They came to us seeking revenge." Ban's voice was full of contempt. "They are like hyenas, preying upon their own people, but they were useful to us."

Alin did not reply, just continued to stare blankly at Ban. He glanced around, checking to see that no one was within earshot, then took a step closer to her. "Alin. Hear me. The Mistress says you must bring the girls to an agreed-upon place. The Mistress says to tell these kidnappers that you are holding a solemn vigil to the Mother,

that it is a rite only the women of your tribe can participate in. We will meet you there," he smiled, "and take
you home."

Alin continued to stare at him, saying nothing.

He looked bewildered. "Do you understand me, Alin?
We have heard the story of how this tribe lost its women.
We know they will not give you up simply at our asking. You must escape in secret." Then, when still she
did not answer, "Do not worry about them coming after
you. There are enough of us to protect you if we must."

"Ban." Alin too glanced around. "Things are not as
simple as they might seem. I must speak to my mother
before I do anything. There are things she does not understand."

Alin could tell from Ban's face that he wanted to ask
her what those things were, and she was surprised when
he did not. She had forgotten how unquestioned was her
voice to the men of the Tribe of the Red Deer.

"All right," he said slowly. "I will tell her so."

"Tell her I will meet her tomorrow at midday at the
place of the blasted tree. Altan is with you?" At his nod,
she continued, "He will know what place I mean."

As she spoke, Alin looked up at the cliff above them.
Apparently they had been seen, for even as she looked,
Bror came out of the carver's cave, peered directly down
at them, and moved purposefully toward the ladder.

"This is their home?" Ban asked incredulously, his
head thrown back also to look up. "This eagle's aerie?"

Alin remembered that they were the very same words
she had used when first she had seen the cliffside home
of the Tribe of the Horse. "Sa," she said softly. "This
is their home."

Bror had reached the third terrace and was moving to
the ladder that would take him down to the second. "I
think you ought to leave now, Ban," Alin said. "It is
important that you get this message to my mother."

"All right," he said again obediently.

By the time Bror reached Alin, Ban had once more
disappeared between the cliffs.

* * *

Bror was puzzled by the way Alin had dismissed the stranger, and she was certain he would take the tale to Mar. She spent the remainder of the afternoon planning what she would tell Mar when he confronted her with Bror's story. She did not want to tell him the truth until she had spoken to her mother.

But Mar was surprisingly disinterested in the stranger who had appeared so briefly and mysteriously on his beach. It was unlike him to accept her explanation so easily, and Alin knew that she had benefited from his preoccupation with the controversy over the upcoming deer hunt.

The nirum had wanted to make a fire hunt, and Mar had forbidden it. Alin had heard the whole of the story from Jes, who had gotten it from Tane. There had been an ugly argument between Mar and Heno over the subject of the hunt. Evidently, in the absence of Altan and Sauk, Heno was the new spokesman for those of Altan's discontented companions who were still in residence. And Heno had chosen to take his stand against Mar's prohibition of the fire hunt, a prohibition that was extremely unpopular with the more traditional nirum.

"All of the men were sitting around the hearth in the nirum's cave," Jes had told Alin, "when Heno began to argue with Mar about the fire hunt. Tane said Heno went on and on, until finally Mar said to him, '*Enough.*' Then Mar stood up. You know how big he is, Alin. Well, he stood up and looked at the nirum. Looked around the whole hearth, from face to face. Finally he looked at Heno. He said, emphasizing each word, '*I am the chief and I say there will be no fire hunt.*' "

Jes had paused, had looked at Alin significantly before going on, "Tane said the cave was deathly silent. Mar and Heno stared at each other. Then Heno looked away."

So there was to be no fire hunt of the deer, but Mar was very anxious that the spear hunt be a successful one, and that was the subject preoccupying his mind to the exclusion of all else. That was the reason Alin found herself spared a quiz about the mysterious stranger.

She slept fitfully that night, running again and again through her mind the words she would use to describe to her mother what had happened over the winter between the girls of the Red Deer and the men of the Tribe of the Horse.

Alin did not think about the decision she herself would soon be forced to make. She blanked that out of her mind, thought only of the problem of bringing the two tribes to the sort of compromise that would be necessary if they were to avoid conflict.

Mar awoke with the dawn. Alin lay quietly, pretending to sleep, and watched him from under lowered lashes as he built up the fire and set the tea to warm on the stones. He raised the hides so that Lugh could go out and then stood at the shelter entrance, looking out at the dawning day.

Alin sat up slowly, feeling heavy-headed from lack of sleep. Mar heard her move, and turned with a smile and a greeting.

She heard herself answer him.

"Are you all right?" he asked.

"Sa. I did not sleep so well, that is all." She smiled at his suddenly anxious face, trying to hide the fact that as she sat up she felt very sick to her stomach.

Apparently she was successful, for Mar went about his usual morning routine without seeming to notice anything different in her. Alin sat by the fire and concentrated all her attention on keeping the nausea under control.

Mar left shortly after he had drunk his tea; he had a full day before him of making certain that all of the equipment for the hunt was ready. Alin watched the hides fall into place behind his broad back and felt a sense of relief at the removal of his too-knowing eyes.

Alin knew all about pregnancy, which was one of the main businesses of the Mother. She went back to her sleeping roll and waited until the worst of the sickness had passed. Then she got up and drank some of the tea Mar had left. She felt distinctly better and was smothering the shelter fire when Jes appeared, her spearthrower in her hand.

"Are you ready to go, Alin?" Jes said. "Most of the

men appear to be well occupied. We should be able to get away with few questions asked.''

"Sa,'' Alin said, rising to her feet and going to fetch her own spearthrower. The two girls made their way down the path that led from the first terrace to the beach. A pack of dogs was sleeping under the place where a part of the cliff overhung the beach, and Alin called for Roc. The big dog came trotting over to her, tail wagging, and followed happily as the two girls headed for the path between the cliffs.

"I didn't sleep at all last night,'' Jes said, as the two of them turned toward the hunting track that would take them to the place of the blasted tree. She gave Alin a wry look. "I suppose I had given up thinking that the Mistress would ever find us.''

Alin sighed. "It was the same with me.''

"Did Mar say anything about Ban's appearance?''

"Very little. He is too preoccupied with this hunt.''

Jes said, "Tane says that if they have a good hunt without the fire, then that will make Mar's edict more acceptable to the nirum.''

Alin nodded.

They walked in silence for a while, both wrapped in their own thoughts, Roc trailing faithfully at their heels. The sun was bright and the day was growing steadily warmer. The trees of the forest through which they were traveling were beginning to show the first shoots of pale spring green.

When Alin and Jes reached the place of the blasted tree, Lana had not yet come. The two girls sat on the great felled oak that had given the place its name, and looked around the little clearing that surrounded it.

As they watched, a small group of deer came bounding along the trees at the edge of the clearing: a stag, three does, and three fawns. Alin spoke to Roc, and the dog remained by her side, reluctant but obedient.

From within the dappled sunlight of the trees, the graceful animals turned to look at the strangers in the clearing. One of the fawns began to suckle. A small breeze blew up, the branches of the budding tree swayed, and the deer were gone.

Half an hour later, Lana arrived.

Roc smelled the new arrivals to the clearing before ever the girls heard their steps. As soon as the dog raised his voice in warning, both Alin and Jes jumped to their feet and stared with rigid attention at the game track that had attracted Roc's notice.

The party of nine men and one woman came out of the forest and into the sunlight of the clearing.

Lana was a small woman, and she was surrounded by tall men, but hers was the figure the girls' eyes flew to, clung to, as they watched their would-be rescuers approach.

Then Alin said, "Mother," and ran on light feet across the clearing to throw herself into Lana's arms.

"Alin." The well-remembered voice was vibrant with emotion. "Oh, my daughter, how glad I am to see you again!" Lana's arms closed around the tall girl with fierce possessiveness.

Alin felt keen surprise when she realized how far her mother had to reach up to embrace her. She had remembered Lana as being taller, more robust. But the round, wide-browed cat face was exactly the same as Alin remembered, as were the unusual long, slightly slanted blue-gray eyes. There was the brightness of unshed tears in those eyes as they looked up into Alin's face, and Alin could feel a reciprocal wetness springing in her own.

"You haven't changed at all, Mother," she managed to say.

Lana laughed huskily. "Why should I have changed? You are the one who was kidnapped, my daughter."

Then Lana turned to Jes, holding out her arms to her daughter's friend. "My heart rejoices to see you, Jes."

They embraced. Then Lana stepped away from Jes and regarded both girls with possessive satisfaction.

Alin did not look back. Her eyes had moved to the man standing at Lana's right.

Tor looked back at his daughter gravely, although his brown eyes were luminous with emotion.

"Tor," Alin said softly. "It is good to see you."

"It is good for me to see you, Alin," the man replied. "We have missed you sorely."

She bowed her head. Next she looked to the big buffalo of a man who was standing on Lana's other side.

"So," she said, and now her voice was icy cold. "Altan."

His return gaze managed to look both dogged and defiant at once.

"Where is your companion in treachery?" Alin asked the deposed chief.

"I left the other one behind," Lana said. "Safer not to keep them together."

Alin nodded in perfect agreement. Then she said to her mother, "Mistress, we must talk."

"So Ban has told me, my daughter. That is why I am here." Lana's face was serene. "Have you come to tell me that it is not possible for you to separate out our girls from the rest of the tribe? If that is indeed so, we must make other plans."

Alin was shaking her head. "Na. It is not so simple as that, Mother. It is . . . I must tell you all that has happened to us in this tribe. That is the only way you will be able to understand."

"I shall build a fire, Mistress," Tor said quietly. "Then you can be comfortable."

While the humans were talking, the dogs had been establishing their own tribal hierarchy. As soon as the Red Deer party had entered the clearing, the five dogs accompanying it had objected to Roc. Now, as the humans began to talk, they flattened their ears and rushed forward to drive the strange dog away. For his part, Roc was not impressed, but stood his ground, head and tail erect. He bared his teeth in a warning snarl.

The attacking dogs were checked by Roc's surprisingly authoritative stance. For a moment there was a standoff, as the dogs considered their options. Then, as Alin and Lana were speaking together behind the Red Deer dogs, Roc decided he would rejoin his mistress.

He gathered himself haughtily. He stalked forward, right between the astonished Red Deer dogs. Reaching Alin, Roc took his accustomed place at her heels.

The out-faced newcomers dropped their tails, and answered to the call of an amused Tor.

When finally Alin took a place around the fire with Lana and Jes, Roc curled himself up behind her, his back snug against her back, and watched the doings in the clearing out of hooded eyes. When the men and dogs disappeared into the woods to find food for the midday meal, Roc rested his chin on his paws, closed his eyes, and slept.

As soon as the men had disappeared into the forest, Alin smoothed the buckskin of her trousers over her knees and commenced the telling of her tale.

"You must have learned from Altan and Sauk of the tragedy of the poisoned water." Lana nodded, and Alin went on. "The men of the Horse told us that tale on the very first night of the kidnapping. It made the reason for their actions very clear." She paused, and smoothed the buckskin over her knees again. "I do not know if Altan told you that they had already tried to trade for women with the other tribes of the Kindred, but of course it was impossible to replace the number that they had lost. They resorted to kidnapping out of desperation." Alin frowned faintly at her knee. "At the time, it seemed to them a good idea."

A small silence fell, and then she looked at Lana. "There was always one great flaw in the kidnapping scheme, however."

"And what was that, my daughter?" Lana asked calmly.

"The men wanted wives. Willing wives. They wanted women who would become part of their tribe." A beat of silence. "That was the thing I used against them."

Lana looked interested. "How?"

Alin told her the whole story, from her persuading Huth to agree to wait until Spring Fires to the marriages made between the girls of the Red Deer and the men of the Tribe of the Horse. But she told her scarcely anything of Mar.

A tense silence fell when Alin had finished speaking. Then Lana said, focusing on the one part Alin wanted her to leave alone, "You are telling me that you made the Sacred Marriage for this tribe?"

"Sa," Alin replied, keeping her eyes steady and grave. "I did."

"Why?" Lana asked sharply.

"This was a tribe that was dying, Mistress," Alin answered quietly. "It was with them as if the swift-flowing mountain stream that feeds into the lake had dried up." Alin gestured gracefully with her hand and then was still again. "Thus was the Tribe of the Horse when once it had cut itself off from worship of the Mother. Dry and dead, like the lake. The people of the tribe worshipped Sky God. They worshipped all the gods of the hunt. But what good are any of these without the Mother?"

Alin looked away from Lana and into the fire. "When the girls of the Red Deer came to this place, the men and women of the Tribe of the Horse did not understand any of this." She looked up, met her mother's gaze. Held it. "Now they do."

"If what you have told me is true, Alin, then I do not understand why you cannot simply collect our girls as if for a ceremony and bring them away."

Alin said soberly, "I can do that, Mother. But the girls are married, and not all of them will wish to leave their husbands."

Lana was stunned. Jes sat very still. "You are saying that our girls will want to stay in this place? With these impious men?" Lana asked at last. Incredulity vied with anger in her voice.

"Sa," Alin said. "That is what I am saying."

"Who?" Lana demanded. "Which of the girls of the Red Deer would be so suborned?"

"Dara," Alin returned. "Sana."

"Me," said Jes.

Lana stared at the girl who was sitting beside Alin. "You, Jes?" she asked. "You would choose to remain with such a tribe?"

Jes went pale at Lana's tone, but her voice remained firm. "Sa, Mistress. I would choose to stay with Tane."

"You would desert Alin?"

Jes's pallor was livid. Before she could reply, however, Alin put a hand over her friend's where it was clasped tensely around her knee. "No need to answer, Jes," she said softly.

After a moment Jes nodded, clearly unable to speak.

"This is what I propose we do, Mistress," Alin said with brisk authority as she removed her hand from Jes's and turned back to her mother. "I propose to tell Mar that you have come to take back to the Tribe of the Red Deer those girls who wish to return. I believe he will agree to give the girls their choice."

"Why should he do that?" Lana asked coldly, her eyes still on Jes.

"I am thinking that he will expect most of the girls to choose to stay. But that will not happen, Mother. I am guessing that half will choose to stay and half will choose to return home with you."

Lana moved her gaze to Alin. "And if *I* do not agree to this?"

"You cannot take all the girls home, Mother," came the devastatingly simple reply. "They will not go."

Lana lifted her hands and then let them fall once more to her lap. "It is hard for me to understand how girls who were brought up in the Way of the Mother could forsake her to follow male gods."

"We have not forsaken the Mother!" It was Jes's passionate voice that answered Lana's accusation. "Never, Mistress, will a woman of the Red Deer cease to follow the Way of the Goddess. It is not we who have learned to worship new gods, but the men of the Horse who have learned to worship the Mother!"

There was a pause as Lana regarded Jes coolly. "Who rules this Tribe of the Horse?" Lana asked the girl, her voice as cold as her eyes.

"Mar," Jes answered steadily. "Mar is the chief."

"And who is the shaman?"

"Huth is the shaman."

"Men," said Lana disdainfully. "Sons of sons. Na, Jes." The small, imperious head shook from side to side. "There is no hope of following the Way of the Mother while men rule the tribe."

"Why do you say that, Mother?" Alin asked.

"It is their nature," Lana said. "Men are useful. Men

are even necessary. Without men there would be no children. But once a man gets a taste of power, then he is ruined.''

Lana's eyes went sharply from Alin to Jes and then back again to Alin. "Look at this Altan," she said. "There is a man who was a chief, who held the welfare of his tribe in sacred trust. Then his power was taken away and he sought revenge."

Lana paused, letting the words sink in. Then she went on. "That is why the Mother decrees that a woman must rule the tribe," Lana said. "The people of the Tribe of the Red Deer are my children. I am not just chief, I am Mistress and Mother. No man can understand that. No man feels for his children as a mother does." Her cat's face was perfectly calm as she added, "Nothing my tribe could do would make me do aught to bring it harm. Nothing."

Alin and Jes knew she spoke the simple truth, and they bowed their heads in acknowledgment.

Two hours later, the girls were on their way back to the Tribe of the Horse to speak to Mar.

Thirty

There was little conversation between Alin and Jes on their way back to the caves by the Wand.

"You will speak to Mar?" Jes asked Alin.

"Sa. I will speak to Mar," Alin replied. And then the two girls lapsed into the silence of their own thoughts.

Lana had never once doubted that her daughter would be one of those returning home, Alin thought, as she walked silently beside Jes through the newly budding forest. Well, why should she doubt? Alin had said naught that would incline her mother to think there might be a reason for her to choose to remain.

I will not think of Mar and me, Alin thought. I will think of what I must say to Mar in order to get him to agree to give the girls their choice.

Mar would not want a conflict with the men of the Red Deer. His chieftainship was new, his hand on the tribe not yet secure. He would listen to the words of compromise.

It would not hurt that he was likely to think that most of the girls would choose to stay with their husbands. Nor would Alin say anything to dissuade him from that notion.

Once Mar had agreed to give the girls their choice, then, no matter what the outcome, he would have to bide by it. Alin knew she could trust him for that. Mar was not a man to go back on his word.

* * *

By the time they reached home, Alin felt leaden with fatigue. There was no reason, she thought, for such an easy walk to tire her so. No reason save one.

She parted from Jes on the beach and climbed the cliff-side path to the shelter that she shared with Mar. It was empty, and there was no sign of Mar in the vicinity of the cliff.

Alin lay down on her sleeping skins, to rest a little and to think, and promptly fell asleep.

She awoke to find Lugh nuzzling her cheek. She opened her eyes in time to see Mar ducking under the hides at the door. She was surprised to see that outside it was almost dark, and raining.

"Dhu!" Alin sat up. "I must have gone to sleep."

He did not answer, but dropped the hides and turned to look at her. There was no fire going and it was too dark for her to see the expression on his face. After a minute, "Are you well, Alin?" he said.

"Sa. I am fine." She forced a smile. "I did not sleep well last night, that is why I am so tired today."

"You seemed to me to have slept well," he answered. "When I got up to let Lugh out, you never stirred."

She said nothing.

He came across the shelter to her sleeping roll, and sat on his heels beside her. His hair was damp from the rain. She could smell the wet fur of his vest. "Do you think perhaps you are with child?" he asked gently.

She felt how her eyes widened as she stared at him. "Why do you ask that?"

"This is not the first day you have been tired." He reached out and smoothed the forefinger of his right hand along her cheek. "Nor have you bled. Not since we mated at Spring Fires, Alin, and that was over one full moon ago."

When she did not answer, but continued to look at him in wide-eyed amazement, "I have been married before," he said. "I have lived with a woman who carried a child."

That was not something she ever thought about. She never wanted to picture him with any woman other than herself.

She looked away from him, looked at the stones of the

cold hearth. "Perhaps I am with child," she said. "It is too soon to be certain."

"This Spring Fires is a powerful rite, indeed," Mar said. She could hear the humor and pride in his voice. He grasped her chin between his fingers and turned her face toward him. She looked up into his eyes.

"Mar," she said. "My mother has come."

He went utterly still, his fingers still holding her chin. Then, "The stranger on the beach," he said.

"Sa. It was one of the men from my tribe. There are a moon's number of them with my mother."

He dropped his hand. "How did they find you?"

Her mouth thinned. "I am thinking you will find this hard to believe," she said. "It was Altan and Sauk."

"Altan and Sauk!"

"Sa. After you drove them out of the tribe, they sought out the Tribe of the Red Deer. For revenge, Mar. It was Altan who guided my mother's party here."

"He is with them now?"

"He is with them now. I saw him myself."

"Sauk too?"

Alin shook her head. "My mother separated them, left Sauk behind."

Mar nodded grimly. "When did you see her?"

"Today. Jes and I met my mother at the place of the blasted tree this noontide."

He blew out through his nose. "Dhu! And I had begun to think she would never find us. I had begun to think we were safe."

So had I, Alin thought sadly. So had I.

Mar rose easily to his feet from his squatting position, and stood, head bent, staring down into the empty hearth. His thick hair slipped forward over his brow, and absently he pushed it back. Alin sat on her sleeping skins and watched him, an ache she had never before felt tightening the muscles at the back of her throat.

He said, "What did you and your mother talk about?"

Alin too looked into the hearth. It was becoming too painful to look at him. "My mother wanted me to separate out our girls, to pretend that there was a rite of Earth Mother we must celebrate. Then I was to meet her and the men, and they were to take us home.'' She rested her forehead on her updrawn knees for a moment, then lifted her head again. Mar had not moved. She said, ''I told my mother of all that had happened to us here, Mar. I told her that the girls were happy with their husbands, would not want to leave them.''

''Sa?'' At that he turned his head to look at her. ''What did she say to that?''

''At first she could not believe it. Jes was with me. Jes told her she would not return to the Red Deer tribe, but would stay with Tane. It was hard for my mother to understand.''

He nodded gravely. ''And what did you say, Alin?''

She deliberately misunderstood him. ''I said that I would speak to you, Mar. I said that I wanted the girls to be given their choice whether to go or whether to stay. I do not want there to be any fighting. Let the girls choose.''

''Did your mother agree to this?''

''She did.''

Within the shelter it had grown too dark for her to see his face clearly; it was merely a shadow under the lighter halo of his hair. ''Will *you* agree to it?'' she asked.

''Let me understand you,'' he said. ''Once again you are asking me to give the girls their choice. Those who wish to go with your mother are to be free to go.''

His voice was expressionless, unreadable.

''That is right,'' Alin said.

He said next, ''How many do you think will go?''

This was a question she did not want to answer. ''I do not know,'' she said.

''Guess.''

''I cannot guess, Mar,'' she said irritably. ''I do not know.''

Pause. ''More than I might think, then,'' he said.

He was too clever. He knew her too well.

''About half, I think,'' she said. ''Half to go and half to stay.''

He shook his head decisively. Even in the dimness she could see the crispness of the movement. ''That is too many.''

Silence fell. Alin frowned. Mar was not the one she had anticipated would make difficulties over this compromise.

Without speaking, Mar went to the corner where a small supply of wood was stacked. He began to lay the fire. Alin sat on her sleeping skins and watched him.

"You will not agree?" she said, when finally the kindling had caught from the hot coal Mar had used as a fire starter.

"I will not agree to let half the girls go and leave half of the men without women again." The fire flamed up suddenly, lighting the shelter. He turned to her, and now she could see the blue of his eyes. "Dhu, Alin! I have finally got the tribe in balance. If I let the girls go, then it is all to do again!"

"My mother has brought many men with her, Mar. They will not give us over without a fight."

"Then they will have a fight," he replied grimly. "There are more of us than there are of them."

"That is a fine way to bring harmony to a marriage, harmony to a tribe," Alin said with palpable irony.

He did not rise to her bait. "I cannot ask the men to let go of their wives," he said quietly. "Not when there is no hope of replacing them."

It was the quietness that told her that her arguments would fall upon deaf ears. Anger she could have played with. Not this.

There must be some way of resolving this impasse, Alin thought, as she cast about for a solution. The answer came to her as she watched Mar shrug out of his fur vest and toss it onto a buffalo robe on the floor.

"What if the men should choose to go with their wives?"

Silence. Then, "What do you mean?" he asked cautiously.

"That is the way things are done in my tribe. I have told you that before. The woman does not go to the tribe of her husband; the husband comes to her kindred. That is the Way of the Goddess." Alin fingered the pendant she wore about her neck. "If the men are desperate enough to keep their wives, let them return with the women to the Tribe of the Red Deer.''

"The Tribe of the Red Deer is ruled by your mother. No man of the Horse would ever put himself under the rule of a woman," Mar answered immediately.

"Why not?"

He threw up his head. "It is just not something we would ever do, Alin. It is not . . . natural.'' His nostrils flared. "The stallion rules the herd," he said. "Not the mares."

Alin could feel her temper starting to rise. "Sa. And the stallion drives all the other male horses out of the herd," she replied. "He tolerates no rivals. I don't think I'd choose the stallion as my model for a good chief, Mar."

The fire-lit side of his face was perfectly clear, and Alin could see a muscle twitch near the corner of his mouth.

She would gain nothing by making him angry, she thought. It was better to appeal to his reason.

"Is it not wiser to offer both husband and wife a choice than to risk lives in a fight, Mar?'' She folded her legs under her and got to her feet. He was too far above her; she was at a disadvantage sitting. When she was standing, "The men of the Red Deer are hunters," she said. "Their lives are none so different from the lives of the men of the Horse."

"They have a woman for a chief."

"My mother is a good chief," Alin said. "She is just. She is generous. The people of the tribe are her children, and she is their mother. The tribe's welfare is as dear to her as is her own heart's blood.'' Alin held out her hands. "Who could wish for a better chief than that?"

This time the silence went on for quite a while. She dropped her hands. Finally, "Which of the girls do you think would want to go?" he asked.

"Fali and Mora, of course.'' She frowned slightly. "Elen," she said.

"Elen?" He was surprised.

"I think so."

Mar frowned also. "Cort would go with Elen," he said.

Alin nodded, then named some of the other girls she thought would choose to go with Lana. After she had given him the names, Mar said nothing, just turned and went to the shelter door. Alin watched as he opened the hides and stood there looking out at the rain.

From the corner, Lugh gave a little questioning bark, and started to get up.

"Na, Lugh," Mar said over his shoulder. "I am not going out. Stay." The dog subsided back onto his buffalo skin.

Alin looked from Mar to Lugh. The dog's intelligence never ceased to amaze her. It was almost like living with another person, she thought.

The rain had begun to come down harder. Slowly Alin walked across the shelter until she was standing behind and a little to the side of Mar. Outside of the shelter door, beyond and below them, was darkness with a slanting fall of rain. The fresh wet smell of the night drifted to her nostrils.

Mar said without turning around, "I would like to kill Altan. All was going so well for us. . . . ." His voice was quiet but full of a fierce intensity.

"I know." She slid her arms around his waist and laid her face against his back. The buckskin shirt under her cheek was warm and dry. She closed her eyes, not thinking, just feeling.

Under her arms, the breath went out of his lungs in a long release. "You are right," he said. "I do not really want a fight."

She did not open her eyes, just rubbed her cheek gently against his back. "Let the men choose. I am thinking that at least half will choose to go with their wives. That will leave you less than a handful who will lose their women."

"Alin," he said, and now his voice held a great weariness. "I am sick unto death about thinking of finding women for the tribe. Will it ever end?"

"It is ending now," she said.

Silence fell. Outside were the rain and the dark. Be-

hind them the fire flared and crackled with warmth and
light.

Alin felt his fingers on the hands she had clasped together at the front of his waist. Gently, he broke her grip,
releasing himself so he could turn and face her. She
opened her eyes. The door hides were still partially raised
and were resting against his shoulder.

"You will get wet," she said softly.

He shrugged the shoulder and stepped forward, closing out the night and the rain. "And what will you choose
to do, Alin?" he asked.

She looked up into his eyes. They were not at all worried looking.

She did not answer him directly. "I love you," she
said instead. "I love you more than anyone else in the
world."

The hands he put on her shoulders were hard, almost
hurting. He bent so that his body was looming over hers,
and pulled her into him. With a little sob—of longing, of
desperation, of desire—Alin went.

She lay awake for most of the night, pressed against
his big body, her heart filled with despair.

She would have to leave him. Training, duty, honor:
all those things she lived by told her that she would have
to leave him. She was the Chosen One. It was not possible for her to desert her people.

Lana had known that.

Mar had not.

He thought she would stay. He had asked her, but he
had been satisfied with an evasive reply simply because
he did not doubt.

What would he do when she told him she must return
with her mother? Would he renege on his promise? Would
it come to a fight, after all?

She had better not tell him until after he had spoken to the
tribe. Then it would be impossible for him to go back on his
promise, whereas if he knew beforehand of her decision, he
might not give the girls their choice after all.

Alin lay still and listened to his quiet, even breathing.
Outside the rain beat against the closed skins of the shel-

ter door. She thought, I might never lie beside him like this again, and the thought brought with it acute anguish and grief.

How had this happened? she thought. I used to hate him.

How long ago that seemed. That had been a different girl, the girl who had cursed the outlander who had kidnapped her. That girl and that man seemed like different beings from the Alin and Mar who lay here tonight, with their bodies fitting so familiarly into each other's.

He was sleeping on his side, holding her cradled in the curve of his body. One big hand was resting on her breast. She bent her head and touched his fingers lightly with her lips. Mar, she thought. Grief closed up her throat. Mar.

He stirred slightly, as if he felt her disturbance. His fingers on her breast moved a little, tightened slightly. She lay very still. Tears began to run down her face, but she made no sound.

The night was very long.

She was sick in the morning, and this time she could not hide it from him. Nor could she hide the significance from herself.

She was with child.

Mar did not fuss over her, for which she was profoundly grateful. He got her what she needed, and then let her be.

Finally, when she was resting on her sleeping skins, "What did you tell your mother you would do if I agreed to the choice?" he asked her gently, needing to know so he could make his plans.

"I was to collect the girls who wanted to come, and meet her before dark at the place of the blasted tree," Alin returned.

Mar nodded. "I had better gather the tribe on the beach, then. Rest here, Alin. Jes can speak for you. No need for you to be there."

"There is need for me to be there," Alin replied. "I shall be all right, Mar. The sickness does not last long."

He quirked an eyebrow. "You do not want to be sick in front of the tribe."

She shook her head a little. That was a mistake. She shut her eyes and fought down the rising nausea. When she opened them again, he was sitting on his heels beside her. "Dhu!" he said. "You went white as snow."

She looked into his concerned face, and knew she could not wait until they were on the beach in front of all the others to tell him she was leaving. No matter what his reaction, she had to tell him now. She owed that to him, to what had been between them.

"Mar," she said, swallowing.

"Sa?"

"Mar, I am one of those who must leave. I am going back with my mother."

He said nothing. He didn't move. The only change was in his eyes.

"Why?" he said at last.

"I must. I am the Chosen One, the future Mistress." She swallowed again, and the taste in her mouth was sour. "The Mistress of the Red Deer Tribe is not like the chief of the Horse. The successor to the Mistress is chosen by the Mother. I have known since before I can remember that I was Chosen." She looked away from him, and then back. "I am who I am, Mar. I cannot change it."

He was still perfectly immobile. "You said last night that you loved me."

"I do. I can imagine no greater happiness than living out my life with you, here in the Tribe of the Horse. But that life, that happiness, is not for me, Mar." A beat of silence as they looked at each other. She said again, quietly, "I am who I am."

He had seemed even to cease breathing, but now he inhaled, long and shuddering. He let the breath out carefully, and said, "I am who I am also, Alin. I cannot come with you."

"I know that. I would not ask it of you. You are the chief, as one day I will be the Mistress. We both of us belong to our tribes."

He broke his stillness, flung up his head. "What if I do not agree to this choice? What if I say we shall fight to keep our women? What then, Alin?"

"It is as I said before," she replied. "That is no way

to keep harmony in a tribe.'' She closed her eyes for a moment, gathering her energy. "My father is with the men of the Red Deer,'' she said. "How do you think I will feel if you kill him?''

She looked at him steadily. His eyes were glittering in a face that was as white as hers.

"You have never once mentioned your father to me,'' he said. "It has always been your mother.''

"I have never lived with my father, but I know who he is. And I like him. If you kill him, I will not like you.''

"You cannot leave,'' he said next. "You are carrying a child for me.''

She did not shake her head again, but she made a faint, negative gesture with her eyes. "Not for you, Mar,'' she said. "For the tribe.'' Then, "You need not fear. My child will be sacred to the Tribe of the Red Deer.''

His mouth curled in a grimace that was not a smile. "Sacred if it is a girl,'' he said. "You have no use for sons in your tribe, Alin.''

Alin thought for a moment of her half brothers, brought up by foster mothers at a distance from Lana. Alin had seen more of Ware in the few moons she had spent with the Tribe of the Horse than ever she had seen of her half brothers. She did not know how to answer him.

He was watching her face. With an abrupt, angry movement, he got to his feet. Alin watched as he walked to the door of the shelter, raised the hides, and stood looking out. The rain had stopped overnight and the day outside was sunny.

"If it is a boy, send him to me,'' he said over his shoulder to her. "I do not want my son brought up thinking he is unwanted.''

Hot tears stung Alin's eyes. Tears of relief. Tears of sorrow. He was going to let her go.

"Do you hear me?'' He swung around to face her. The sun slanting in through the opened hides gilded his hair from behind. "If the child is a boy, Alin, send him to me.''

Alin thought once again of her phantom half brothers. "All right, Mar,'' she said unsteadily. "I will.''

PART THREE

End of Winter, One Year Later

Thirty-one

Alin stood outside her hut and watched the full of Shadow Moon rise in the sky. In one moon's time, she thought, the men of the Tribe of the Horse will sacrifice a stallion for the Ceremony of the Great Horse.

The men of the Red Deer had no such ceremony. In truth, as Alin had come to realize during the time she had been back at home, the men of the Red Deer were as cut off from their gods as once the women of the Horse had been from Earth Mother.

It was not right, Alin now thought. All of humankind needed to feel connected to the world beyond. The spirit thirsted for such a connection, was unfulfilled without it.

The men of the Red Deer should have some religious ceremonies of their own.

Alin looked across the space that separated her hut from her mother's. Lana would be watching the sky also, watching and making the appropriate notch on her calendar to signify the full of Shadow Moon.

The next new moon but one to rise would be the moon of Spring Fires.

Alin felt suddenly cold in the chill evening air, and crossed her arms over her chest. She was to make the Sacred Marriage at Spring Fires this year. She had been great with child during Winter Fires, and so had not participated. But now that her son was near three moons old and she was slim again, it was time for her to assume her proper role.

She felt no joy at the thought, only a strange kind of

reluctance. She did not want to mate with another man. Even though she knew that the drums and pipes would fire her blood, even though she knew it was her destiny, still she did not want to mate with another man.

She was beginning to fear that she would bring bad luck on the tribe if she made the Sacred Marriage with such a feeling in her heart.

How could she explain this thing to her mother?

She had not missed Mar so much during her pregnancy. She had been numb, as if the baby growing within her had dulled all her senses. She had eaten and slept, and eaten and slept.

Then he had been born. A boy with blue eyes and a cap of pale silky hair. Every time she looked at him, her heart ached.

Lana was disappointed. She had wanted a girl.

"You are young," she consoled Alin as she gave the baby back. "We shall find him a foster mother, and you will be free to conceive again."

Alin had refused. No foster mother, she had told Lana. I will nurse my child myself.

It was the first falling out they had ever had.

"It is hard with your first," Lana had said. "I remember well that it is hard. But if you nurse this child, it will be even harder to give him up when the time comes. Best to do it now, before you grow too attached."

Give him up. The words had fallen like stones into Alin's heart. She had looked down at the silky-headed baby nuzzling against her breast, tightened her arms, and known that she could never give up this child.

"I will nurse him myself," she had said.

Short of taking the baby from her by force, there had been nothing Lana could do.

Now the time was coming for Spring Fires, and desolation was growing in Alin's soul. Now it was truly coming home to her, what she had lost, and what her future would be.

She was so lonely. Nursing the baby, holding the baby, helped somewhat. But then he would look up into her face with those familiar blue eyes, or the faintest wisp of a grin would curl his mouth, and pain would engulf her.

As she lay alone in her sleeping skins at night, she felt as if she were sliding into a great dark pit, with no help, no hope, no chance of ever climbing out again into the light.

She tried so hard not to think of him, and the very effort was an admission of her need.

I am no good to the tribe like this, she thought this night as she stood outside her hut in the cold starry night watching the full moon rise in the sky.

Perhaps if I make the Sacred Marriage at Spring Fires, the power of the Mother will enter into me and heal me, she thought.

Whom would she choose to be her mate?

There was no one she wanted.

She must choose someone.

Ban, she thought. She and Ban had become good friends this past winter. More than anyone in the tribe, he had helped that weary time to pass. Ban would not be so intolerable.

A sharp wail came from within the hut. Tardith was awake and hungry. It was always better when Tardith was awake. Alin turned with relief to go in and feed the baby.

Mar too was watching the moon rise that night, standing alone at the door of his shelter in the cliff above the River Wand.

The next full moon to rise would signal the beginning of the Ceremony of the Great Horse, he thought.

Last year at this time, he had been waiting to challenge the chief.

Last year at this time, Alin had been here.

He shook his head at the thought, like a stallion bedeviled by flies.

No use in thinking of Alin. She had left him of her own choice. He shook his head again. No use in thinking of her.

She would have had the baby sometime during Reindeer Moon. Was it a boy or a girl? Mar wondered. Was Alin safe?

Jes had said she would go south once the weather had grown warmer to visit her old tribe and see Alin. Mar knew he had to wait. Jes herself had given birth but one moon since. She would not wish to travel with her babe until the Moon of the New Fawns, at least.

As if he sensed his master's distress, Lugh came and pressed his head against Mar's knee. Mar dropped his hand to caress the dog's expressive black ears. Then he lowered the hides and turned to bank his fire for the night.

Two days after the full of Shadow Moon, Mar and a group of the men of the Horse went out together to hunt reindeer. They had located a herd and had killed two good-sized bucks when Lugh spotted a boar in the trees.

Lugh, in every other way a highly intelligent dog, had one weakness. He hated pigs with a mindless, passionate hatred. Without a moment's hesitation, he launched himself after the boar, yipping madly.

"LUGH!" Mar yelled after him, but for once Lugh paid no attention to his master's voice.

Mar turned to Tane. "I am going to go after him. You and the rest of the men take the reindeer meat back home."

"I will come with you," Tane said. Mar nodded, and after giving orders to Bror, both men plunged into the trees on the track of the dog.

The men ran steadily forward, dodging through the trees, following the sound of Lugh's yipping in the distance.

"Dhu," Mar grunted as they went up a small wooded hill, "I hope we can get there before the boar turns. I had a glimpse of it before Lugh took off. It was big. Big tusks. Lugh could get himself killed tangling with a boar that size."

Ahead of them, the yipping stopped. Mar set his jaw and increased the pace, Tane right behind him.

The winter day was closing in on night. It was growing dark under the trees. Dark and cold. Mar gripped his spear tightly and ran on, fear mounting in his heart at the silence before him.

Somewhere to their left, a hyena screeched.

The boar had turned on Lugh in a small clearing. The first thing Mar and Tane saw as they came running up was the bleeding body of the big tusked pig, sitting on its haunches at the edge of the trees and looking at a heap of black and silver fur on the ground in the midst of the clearing.

It was Lugh.

"Kill the boar," Mar said to Tane, and he strode forward to kneel beside Lugh.

The dog was ripped apart. There was blood everywhere, and exposed bone, but he was still breathing.

"Lugh," Mar said, taking the dog's uninjured head into his arms. "Lugh."

The dog's ear twitched at the sound of Mar's voice.

"Why?" Mar asked despairingly. "Why did you chase after the boar?"

Once more the only sign of life was the faintly twitching ear.

Mar looked at Tane. "Make a litter out of branches and my tunic," he said. "We'll carry him home."

Tane opened his mouth to say that the dog would never survive the journey, looked at Mar, changed his mind, and silently picked up the fur jacket Mar had shrugged out of.

While Tane cut branches to make the litter, Mar began to talk softly to the dog he held cradled in his arms. He could tell by the occasional twitching of the black ear that Lugh heard, and so he talked on, trying desperately to keep his dog alive by the sound of his voice.

"Do you remember," he said, "do you remember the time when you were a pup and we two went hunting for antelope?"

It was growing colder. Without his fur, the cold was seeping into Mar's bones, stiffening his muscles and his joints. Lugh must be cold, he thought, and sought to gather the dog closer into his arms for warmth. Blood had poured into the ground and had soaked Mar's shirt and his trousers. He scarcely noticed. He kept talking.

Lugh's breath was coming slower, was more and more shallow.

He can't die, Mar thought desperately.

"Lugh," he said. He bent his head until his mouth

was right beside the dog's ear. He spoke into the ear and the ear twitched.

"I have the litter made," Tane said.

Mar looked around. "Good." He turned back to Lugh. The dog was no longer breathing.

"Lugh," Mar said. The ear no longer twitched.

There was silence in the forest. Tane said nothing. Mar knelt there beside his dog, his face bent. Finally he said softly into the now-motionless ear, "Go well on your journey." He straightened up and stared sightlessly at Tane.

"We'll carry him home anyway," Tane said gently. "You can bury him. A heart like his deserves all the honor we can give it."

"Sa," Mar said. His voice sounded hollow. He stood up, then pressed his hands over his eyes. Tane said nothing, just stood there waiting. Mar dropped his hands. "I will lift him onto the litter," he said. "And we will carry him home."

Mar buried Lugh on the gravel beach a little way up the Wand, with rocks heaped over the grave so that the scavengers could not get at it.

At the full moon, the men of the tribe held the Ceremony of the Great Horse. The stallion was caught and sacrificed, the initiates and new nirum were made, the new fire was lit, and the Sacred Dance performed. All seemed well with the Tribe of the Horse.

Two days after the Great Horse Ceremony had concluded, Jes sought out Mar. He and the men were out in the woods to the east of the caves, cutting long thin branches to make new fishing nets. The salmon would be starting their run up the river soon. Mar left the men, however, and came to Jes when she appeared on the edge of the clearing and spoke his name.

"This is the farthest you have been from home in quite some time," he said with good humor as he propped his shoulders against an oak to lessen his height.

"Sa." She gave him a brief, rueful smile. "I never knew how much trouble one small child could be."

He nodded, and waited for her to go on.

"Mar," she began. "At the start of the new moon we must hold Spring Fires."

He nodded again.

"What I have come to discuss with you," she said, "is who is to make the Sacred Marriage."

He looked surprised. "I was thinking it would be you and Tane."

Jes's blue-gray eyes, the color of the day's sky, looked at his face, from his forehead to his chin, then back up to his forehead again. She said, "I think it should be Dara and Arn."

He shrugged easily. "That is for you to decide, Jes. I have no wish to meddle in things that belong to the women."

She did not immediately reply, but continued to look at his face. Then her gaze flicked to his feet, and she said, "I cannot get used to seeing you without Lugh. I keep finding myself looking for him."

His expression changed faintly. "Sa," he said. "I look for him also."

"You should get another dog, Mar. There will be pups soon. Choose one and take it into your shelter."

He shook his head. "There will never be another Lugh."

"This would be a new dog, a different dog. You will never replace Lugh. He was unique."

"Sa. He was. Alin used to say it was like living with another person, living with Lugh."

Silence fell between them at the mention of her name.

"It will be Spring Fires in the Tribe of the Red Deer also," Jes said.

Mar's face tightened.

"Since Alin left us, no woman has stepped forward to take her place as Mistress," Jes said. "Without her, the women of the Horse are cut off from the Mother."

"I thought you had taken her place," Mar said.

Jes shook her head. "I do not want to do it. I want to paint."

"Is that why you want Dara to make the Sacred Marriage?" he asked.

"Sa. Arn will be the next shaman, so he and Dara are

the most fitting. But it should be you, Mar. The chief of
the hunters should be the god. Not the shaman.''

Mar raised his brows in irony. ''I do not think Arn
would agree. Or Dara, either.''

''That is not what I meant,'' Jes said.

A silence fell.

Jes was the one to break it. ''You have not taken another woman,'' she said. ''You gave out the two new
women you traded for at the Fall Gathering.'' Her eyes
were steady on his face. ''It is not right that the chief
should be without a woman.''

Mar's face was closed and faintly hostile. He stood up,
moving his shoulders away from the oak, straightening
to his full height. ''I do not wish to discuss this matter
with you, Jes,'' he said.

She said, ''If that is how you feel, imagine how Alin
must be faring.''

He did not reply, merely looked down at her, his jaw
set, his face very white, his eyes very blue.

''Lana will expect her to make the Sacred Marriage
this time,'' Jes said. ''She would have been exempt from
Winter Fires. She would have been too far gone with
child to have been able to make the journey into the cave's
sanctuary. But now . . . now she will have to do it.'' A
beat of silence. ''Think, Mar, how she must be feeling.''

''She left me,'' Mar said. His face was still very white.
''She knew the life she was returning to.''

''I am thinking, that to know it and to experience it
are two different things,'' Jes said.

Mar shrugged, the movement looking stiff, not easy.
''It was her choice.''

''I am thinking, Mar, that you are like Lugh,'' Jes said.
''He was a dog for one man, and you are a man for one
woman. And I believe it is the same for Alin, that she is
a woman for one man.''

The set of Mar's jaw became more noticeable. He did
not reply.

''Mar,'' Jes said. ''Why do you not go south to the
Tribe of the Red Deer and make the Sacred Marriage
with Alin?''

He had appeared to be standing perfectly still, but now

he went even more still. It seemed to Jes that even his
breathing had stopped.

"I do not understand you," he said after a minute.
His lips scarcely moved.

"Alin will be the one making the Sacred Marriage for
the Tribe of the Red Deer," Jes said. "And she has the
right to choose the man who will play the god. You should
go south so that she can choose you."

"I am not a man of her tribe," Mar said. His voice
sounded oddly off its usual timbre. A muscle jumped
along the line of his hard-set jaw.

Jes raised her hands. "That will not matter. There is
nothing to say that the man must be born to our tribe."

"She made her choice," Mar said again. But he did
not sound certain.

"There was no choice for her, Mar," Jes said. "She
had to go back."

"What will be different now?" Mar asked.

"I will give you a message to take to her," Jes said.
"The message might make a difference."

"What is the message?"

Jes straightened her slim shoulders, raised her chin.
"This is what I would have you say:

" 'Alin. We have need of you in this tribe. Since your
going there has been no Mistress for the women. Without
you we are separated from the Mother. There is no one
here who can take your place.

" 'The Tribe of the Red Deer has many young girls
upon whom the Mother may lay her hand. The Tribe of
the Horse has none.

" 'If you cannot return to us, we will understand. We
will not hold your going against you. But if it is in your
heart to come back to the Tribe of the Horse, you are
needed.' "

There was silence as Mar considered the message.

"She knew that before she left," he said.

Jes shook her head. "I do not think she did. And there
will be one more thing that will make it difficult for her
to deny my request."

"And what is that?" Mar asked.

Jes said, "You."

* * *

When darkness began to fall, Mar returned with the men to the cliffside caves, and went by himself to his shelter.

Since Lugh's death, he had dreaded going into the shelter. It had been awful without Alin. Now that Lugh was gone, it was almost intolerable.

He pushed up the hides, entered into the dim, cold room, looked around, and was overwhelmed by desperate loneliness. It caught at his throat and ached in his gut.

He would have given everything he possessed to see Alin sitting there by his hearth, gazing at him with her big luminous brown eyes, a smile curling her delicate lips, caressing a black-and-silver bundle of fur.

He sank down on his heels beside his cold fire and pressed his hands against his eyes. Everything ached in him. Nothing had any meaning for him anymore. He had gone through the Ceremony of the Great Horse with joyless precision.

It was not good for the tribe to have the chief thus.

Jes was right. He would go south to see Alin. If she were faring as ill as he was, perhaps he would have a chance of persuading her to come back to him.

He would tell her he had come to see his child, to discover whether it was a boy or a girl. He would give her Jes's message. Then he would see.

Thirty-two

Lana sat before the small stone hearthplace in her hut, staring into the glowing embers of last night's fire. The Mistress had slept but restlessly, and now, with the dawning day, she was fully awake, brooding on what had kept her from sleeping for most of the night.

Alin had not been the same since she had returned from her sojourn among that tribe of kidnappers.

At first Lana had blamed pregnancy for the change in Alin. Once the babe is born, she had told herself, then will Alin be herself again.

It had not happened. If anything, Alin had become more withdrawn. Then she had refused to relinquish the child to a foster mother.

That was when Lana had known for certain the cause of the change in Alin.

It was the chief the girls called Mar. That was the man with whom Alin had made the Sacred Marriage, the father of this boy-child she would not relinquish. His name scarcely passed her lips, though it seemed ever to be on the lips of the other girls who had returned.

Lana raised her hands to her temples and pushed back the soft, gray-streaked hair.

What was to be done?

This was her successor. Lana had known that from the time Alin was but a very small child. It was not just that she was Lana's only daughter. That was important, but there was something more to Alin than that: a power, a force that other people immediately apprehended and responded to. Even when she had been a small girl, that power had been there. Lana had recognized in it the mirror image of her own.

The power was still in Alin. But it had dimmed, was banked and smouldering, like the fire into which Lana stared this dark and chilly morning. All the brightness had gone.

She was grieving for this son of Sky God with whom she had mated.

Her first man. Taken in the heat of the Fires. A chief, a man of power himself.

That was all it was, Lana thought. Let Alin take another man. Let her discover that more than one man was able to bring the heat to her blood, the sap to her womb. Let her take another man at Spring Fires, and the image of this man of the Horse will be erased from her mind.

Rushing Stream Moon was at its end. In two days' time, the First Moon of Spring Fires would rise in the west.

Alin must name the man with whom she will make the Sacred Marriage, Lana thought. She had said she would choose at the dark of the moon. This night, no moon would rise in the sky. Alin could delay no longer.

I will go to see her after I have broken my fast, Lana thought. Let her name the man. Then will all be well with Alin once more.

Lana summoned two girls from the women's cave to bring her fresh water and food to eat. She splashed the cold river water on her face, feeling the weariness of the sleepless night imprinted in her skin. She had one of the girls comb her hair, braid it, and knot it at the back of her head. When the last bone hairpin had been thrust into place, she rose to her feet and shook out her long buckskin skirt.

"I am going to see my daughter," she said to the girls, and pushed open the skins at the door of her hut. Alin's hut was close by, on the other side of the entrance to the women's cave. Lana had had it built for her when first she had come home last spring.

Lana stepped outside and looked up at the sky. The

sun was fully up now, and the day was clear. The air was crisp and cold and pure. Lana looked around the home-site for a moment, surveying her domain.

There was movement by the river, and Lana turned her head to look. A man was walking along the riverbank, coming from the north, a dog at his heels, a spear in his hand, a bow slung over his shoulder. Lana narrowed her eyes to see more clearly.

It was not a man of her tribe. No man of the Red Deer had hair of that color.

He turned away from the river, began to come up the path that led into the tribal homesite.

It was then that she recognized him. It was the man who had kidnapped Alin.

Lana's heart began to slam. She had seen him but once, on that terrible morning when he and his men had fallen upon her and her women outside their sacred cave, but he was not someone she would ever forget.

She looked around quickly, searching for some of her own men. They had to take him before Alin saw him!

From the opposite hut, the skins covering the entrance opened.

"Mother," Alin said with surprise. "You are awake early."

Lana stared at her daughter. "I want to talk to you, Alin," she said. Her voice sounded perfectly normal. "Come back into your hut with me."

Alin nodded. "All right." She turned to go back inside. There came the sound of dogs barking, and Alin looked toward the source of the noise.

"Come inside," Lana said loudly.

A single dog came tearing up beside the two women, barking with obvious delight. Alin looked with astonishment. "Roc!" she said. "What are you doing here?" And then she looked in the direction from which Roc had come.

Lana saw all the color drain from her face. "Mar." Her lips formed the word, although no sound came.

The golden-haired man had seen them, was coming onward, his long legs making the ground disappear beneath them. Alin took one step forward, stopped, then began to walk forward once more.

Too late now, Lana thought bitterly. She stood in silence and watched as her daughter and the man met.

The two stood together for a moment, looking at each other. Lana could see that they spoke. Alin's back was to her, but the man seemed to be responding to a question he had been asked.

A group of dogs came tearing up to the pair, noisily objecting to the presence of the new dog. Roc laid back his ears and growled. Lana could see the Red Deer dogs recognize his scent from their previous meeting in the forest. They stopped barking, backed off, and began to circle each other, as if they had other, more important things on their minds than this strange dog in their midst.

When Lana looked away from the dogs, she saw Alin and the man advancing toward her.

"Mistress," Alin said formally when they had halted. "This is the chief of the Tribe of the Horse. This is Mar. He has come to see his son."

Lana looked up and up, into the man's face. She had not realized how big he was. His blue eyes were hard as they scanned her from her smooth head to the moccasin-clad toes that peeped out from under her soft buckskin skirt. Her own eyes narrowed, making her look even more catlike than usual. She said coldly, "Greetings."

He inclined his bright head. His hair was too short, Lana thought critically, cut off before it could even touch his shoulders. A thick fringe had fallen over his forehead. "Greetings, Mistress," he said. He sounded as friendly as she had.

"And is that all you came for, man of the Horse?" Lana asked. "Your son?"

"I came for that," he answered. The expression in his eyes as they held her own was not pleasant. This is my enemy, Lana thought. He knows it as well as I. "And I came also for Spring Fires."

"Spring Fires?" It was Alin's slightly breathless voice.

He looked away from Lana, looked at Alin. "Sa," he said, a different note in his voice. "I was not needed at home. Dara is to make the Sacred Marriage with Arn.

So I thought I would come here, to the Tribe of the Red Deer, to make the Sacred Marriage with you.''

It was the look on Alin's face that told Lana how truly dangerous this man was. More dangerous even than she had thought.

"Have you named the man yet?" he was asking Alin.

"Na." She shook her head, staring at him, wide-eyed.

"You can name him now," he said.

"Sa," said Alin. She smiled, and it was as if a knife twisted in Lana's heart. "I can name him now."

Alin led him into the small hut that had housed her since she had returned to the Red Deer tribe nearly one year earlier. The room had never been large, but with Mar inside it, it seemed smaller still.

"Dhu!" Alin heard herself saying with a shaky laugh. "I had forgot how big you are."

"I have not forgot you." Alin had built up the fire for the baby as soon as she had awakened. It was bright enough to see his face, see his eyes. "I have not forgot anything about you, Alin," he was saying. He reached out a hand, touched her cheek. "Not anything."

She could feel the color flare under her skin where his finger touched. "Come," she said, still in that same shaky voice. "Here is your son." And she pointed to the fur-lined basket that lay beside her own rumpled mound of sleeping skins.

One long stride and he was at the basket. Alin followed more slowly, stood beside him, and looked as well.

The baby was awake, his blue eyes raised to the faces that had come to lean over his basket. When he saw Alin he made a little cooing sound and began to wiggle.

"He looks like me," said Mar in absolute wonder.

"Sa." Alin's voice was very soft.

"What have you called him?"

"His name is Tardith."

Mar's head swung around. He stared at her. He said, "Tardith was my father's name."

Alin said, "I know."

The baby, outraged when he was not immediately picked up, began to scream.

"Dhu!" Mar jumped. "Is he always this loud?"

Alin laughed at him. "Only when he is hungry. Which is often." She reached into the basket and lifted out the baby. Tardith immediately began to nuzzle at his mother's front. "Softly, softly," Alin said. She sat down on her sleeping skins, lifted her deerskin shirt, and put the baby to her breast.

Silence descended.

"Sit," Alin said into the quiet, gesturing to a place before her. The dirt floor of the hut had been fully covered by deerskins, so it was possible to sit anywhere and keep warm and dry.

A whine came from without. "You do not want Roc in here," Mar said, his voice holding a note of inquiry.

"He can come in. Tardith is used to dogs."

Mar nodded, went to the door hides, and lifted them. Roc came in. Mar ordered him to stay by the door, and the dog flopped down, his nose propped on his feet. He gazed bemusedly at Alin.

Alin looked at the dog and frowned in puzzlement. "But why do you have Roc with you, Mar?" she said. "Was it because he knows me?" She frowned harder, looked again toward the door. "And where is Lugh?"

Alin looked back at Mar. He was staring intently into her small fire. He said nothing.

"Mar," she said a little more loudly. "Has something happened to Lugh?"

No answer again, but this time he nodded.

Alin shivered. Tardith lost the nipple and screeched. She reached to give it to him again. Then she looked once more at Mar, waiting until he was able to speak.

"He died," Mar said hoarsely at last. He shut his eyes.

Alin looked at him and felt as if her heart would break. She could not imagine him without Lugh. "Oh, Mar." The ache in her heart sounded in her voice. "I am so sorry. He was such a wonderful dog. You will never find his like again."

He nodded. He said, still in that thick, hoarse voice, "It was a boar."

She ached to comfort him, to take him in her arms and

hold his head against her breast, as now she held his son. But she did not have the right to do that. She had left him to bear this sorrow alone. She did not have the right to touch him now.

"He was so faithful to you," she said. "Such a loyal friend." The baby's sucking was lessening. "When did it happen?"

"At the beginning of the Moon of the Great Horse."

The baby had finished. Alin lifted him to her shoulder, patted his back.

Tardith belched.

Mar looked up. The ghost of a smile flickered across his strained face. "Dhu," he said. "That is one loud baby."

She smiled at him, hoping he would not notice the tears in her eyes. "Sa," she said, "he is."

He said, "Jes told me that if the child was a boy you would give him to a foster mother."

She felt her arms tighten around the damp warm bundle of baby upon her shoulder. She shook her head. "My mother wanted me to," she said. "It is true that it is the way of the Mistress to give over her sons. But I would not."

"Why not, Alin?" His voice was quiet.

"I am not the Mistress yet," she said.

"And if you were?"

She swallowed. "My mother says that it is hard to give over the first, easier with the others." A beat of silence. "But I do not believe her."

He sighed, pulled up his knees, and rested his chin on them, much in the manner of Roc. He said, "Jes has given me a message for you."

"What is it?"

He repeated it to her, word for word.

There was a long silence when he had finished.

Mar looked around the room, his gaze roving over all the small items that made the place distinctly Alin's: the baskets where she kept her extra clothing, her large spear and spearthrower leaned against a wall, a small beautifully woven basket where she kept her ornaments. A pile of clean swaddling clothes lay beside the baby's basket.

Finally, his gaze returned to Alin's face. He said into the silence, "It is good to be together again like this."

"Sa." Her face was white. "It is."

"I want you to come back with me, Alin," he said. "I need you. The women of the tribe need you. Come back to me."

"I do not know," she said.

He blew air out of his nose. "That is better than I feared."

"I do not know, Mar," she repeated. "I want to. I have missed you . . . so much. But I do not know where my loyalty should lie. It is not so simple for me as it was for Lugh." She swallowed. "I cannot tell you now."

He nodded. "That is all right. I will not press you, Alin. But I wanted you to know why I have come."

She nodded back. She smiled. "I am so glad to see you!"

"I will tell you something else that Jes said to me," he said.

She looked an inquiry.

"She said that I was like Lugh, that as he was a dog for one man, so was I a man for one woman. I think she was right."

She could not disguise the rush of joy his words gave her. She had spent too many sleepless nights envisioning him in the arms of another woman.

"And you?" His voice was hard, abrupt. "Did you take a man at Winter Fires?"

She shook her head. "At Winter Fires I was far gone with child, Mar. There was no man for me." Something flickered in his eyes, something that made her add softly, "There has been no man for me but you, Mar. Nor have I wished for one."

His eyes narrowed. He leaned a little forward, his slitted eyes seeming to devour her face. "Is it necessary to wait until Spring Fires?"

Her mouth curved downward. "Sa. It is taboo to mate during the dark of the moon before the Fires. And today is the dark of the moon."

He remained leaning forward, toward her. "Today,"

he said. "And tomorrow. And then it will be Spring Fires?"

"Sa. In two days' time it will be Spring Fires."

"So." He stretched out his hand to her. "I can wait."

She leaned forward herself, stretched out the hand that was not holding the baby to her shoulder. She felt his big warm clasp envelop her fingers. "I can wait also," she said. She smiled. "Just."

For the first time in her life, Lana found herself out-maneuvered. The man named Mar had surprised her almost as completely as he had that first time. Now he had appeared on the very eve of Spring Fires, and Alin had said she would make the Sacred Marriage with him.

He had acted so quickly that Lana had not had a chance to react. Nor was the Mistress accustomed to situations that required instant reaction on her part. She was one to plan carefully, to look for future consequences. She was the leader of a tribe, not a mere hunter who must rely on his reflexes to survive.

There was nothing she could do to stop the Sacred Marriage from going forward, not without provoking Alin into refusing to make the Sacred Marriage at all. That would not be good for the tribe. The only objection Lana could reasonably have made was that Mar's shoulders were too wide to allow him to climb up the chimney into the higher passage that led to the cave's sanctuary.

But Alin was not going to make the Sacred Marriage in the sanctuary this year. She was nursing a child, which, Lana thought angrily, she should not be doing, and so she could not be out of reach of the baby for the day and night it would take to complete Spring Fires.

Lana had refused to allow a male child to be brought into the sanctuary. "I brought you when I was nursing you," she had told Alin, "but you were the Chosen One. It was right that you should accompany me. But not a boy-child. That I will not allow." Especially *this* boy-child she thought, but did not say.

Alin had refused to leave Tardith with another nursing mother. "*I* will be in great discomfort if I do not nurse for a day and a night," she said to Lana. "And that is not the proper state in which to make the Sacred Marriage.''

They had come to a compromise. Alin would make the Sacred Marriage in one of the chambers near the opening of the cave, and the baby would be brought to her there.

So Lana had been outmaneuvered. She would have to allow Alin to mate with the man. Her only comfort was the thought that there was little likelihood of another pregnancy, not while Alin was still nursing that child. One son of a son of Sky God in the tribe was quite enough, Lana thought.

But after Spring Fires . . . after . . . she had to get rid of the man. He had come for Alin. Lana had seen that immediately. That did not frighten her, however. Many men wanted Alin. What frightened her was the thought that Alin wanted him too.

Alin was the Chosen One. No girl had ever shown more clearly that she was Earth Mother's choice than had Alin. And then she had been kidnapped. Then this man had got his hands upon her. And nothing had been the same since.

The man must die. Alive, he was a danger: a danger to Lana, a danger to Alin, a danger to the tribe.

That could not be allowed.

The man must die.

Thirty-three

The girls of the Red Deer who had been kidnapped with Alin and had since returned to their own tribe greeted Mar like an old friend. Even Mora had a smile for him. And Fali was patently thrilled at his coming.

"It is good to see you, minnow," he said to her with his disarming good humor. "I am thinking you have grown some fingers since last we met."

"Sa," Fali had returned, her small face glowing. "That is so, Mar."

Cort and the handful of men of the Horse who had chosen to join the tribe of their wives went hunting with Mar the day after he arrived.

"Tell me," Mar said to them as they sat around the fire they had built to cook their midday meal, "what is it like to live in a tribe that is led by a woman?"

"It is none so bad," Russ said practically. "In most ways she is a good chief, Mar. The tribe lives well here. The hunting is good. The water is fresh. The huts are warm." He grinned. "And it is good to reach out your hand at night and feel a woman sleeping there beside you."

"Sa. That is so," said the rest of the men with similar grins.

Mar looked thoughtfully from face to face. Then he looked back to Russ. "In most ways?" he said.

Russ looked to Cort, and it was Cort who answered. "In all ways really. Save one." Cort frowned. "The men of this tribe are hunters, as we are, but they have no hunting ceremonies, Mar. There is no sacred cave for the men, only for the women." His frown deepened. "It is a strange feeling. I do not like it. It shows a lack of . . . respect . . . for the animals one kills, not to make a prayer to the gods before a big hunt."

"That is so," Russ said. "They have hunting songs. All hunters everywhere have hunting songs. But no hunting ceremonies."

Mar stirred the fire under the cooking rabbits with a stick. "What are the ceremonies of this tribe?" he asked.

"The Fires, of course. Spring Fires and Winter Fires. Those are the two ceremonies that involve the men. The rest are private, for the women only. I do not know what they do," Cort said. "Elen will not tell me."

Mar looked up from poking the fire. "Elen is more beautiful than ever," he said to her husband. "Pregnancy becomes her well."

Cort smiled with pride. "Sa."

"What kind of men are these men of the Red Deer?" Mar asked next. He put the stick on the ground between himself and the fire. "Are they any kind of men at all?"

Cort answered soberly, "Some of them are good men. Good hunters. Good companions. They care for their families, the same as we do. They care for the tribe."

Mar nodded. Silence fell.

"It is hard to explain, Mar," Cort said finally. "All of these things are true. And yet they are . . . diminished somehow. They do not have their own sacred world. No man can be truly a man if he does not have that."

Mar nodded again.

"We have found a cave up in the mountains," Russ said softly. "We, the men of the Horse. We had our own ceremony there at the full of the last moon."

"That is good," Mar said.

"We did not tell the Mistress," Cort said. "But I told Alin."

"What did Alin say?"

"She said it was a good thing. She said as it had not been good for the women of the Horse to be without ceremonies to Earth Mother, so it was not good for the men of the Red Deer to be without their own sacred rites."

Mar looked thoughtful. Then he asked. "Did you bring any of the men of the Red Deer to your ceremony?"

"A few of them only. The ones we could trust to keep silent."

Mar smiled ironically. "I am thinking the Mistress would not be happy if she learned of that."

"Na." Cort smiled in the same manner. "She would not be."

A companionable silence fell. Then Russ said, "It is good to see you, Mar. It is good to have you here."

"It is good to be here," Mar replied.

"Alin has missed you," Cort said.

Mar looked at him.

"There was great talking among the women when she would not give over her child to a foster mother to nurse," Cort said. "The Mistress never keeps a boy-child."

"Alin is not the Mistress," Mar said.

"She is the Chosen One. The same rules apply to her as to the Mistress."

Mar said, "Tane was Huth's only son, and yet Huth had to look elsewhere for a successor. Perhaps Lana will have to do the same."

Cort's eyes were troubled. "I don't think she will give up Alin easily, Mar. She is a soft-looking woman, and her rule is light, but I would not care to cross her. There is that in her that says she would make a dangerous enemy."

"She is a little thing," Mar said mildly. "Little, with the face of a kitten."

"Not a kitten," Cort said. He met Mar's eyes straight on. "A lioness. And the lioness is the most dangerous animal in the world when her cub is threatened."

Mar looked serenely back. "I will not make the mistake of underestimating Lana," he said.

Cort looked unconvinced.

"She will have the tribe behind her, whatever she may do," one of the older men cautioned. "The men revere her. I have not seen the like in any of the other tribes of the Kindred. They will do as she says.''

''They fear her?''

Russ was the one to answer. ''It is more that they are in awe of her. She is Earth Mother to them, Mar. She is a powerful leader. More powerful in this tribe than the chief is in ours.''

''So that is the Way of the Mother,'' Mar said thoughtfully.

Russ nodded. ''And that is why they will none of them give up Alin easily. If it is as I think, that you have come to take Alin back with you, you will not do it easily.''

''And what if it is Alin's choice to come with me?''

''Is it?'' Cort asked bluntly.

Mar turned his eyes once more to the fire. ''The rabbits are done.'' He leaned forward, as if to reach for the spit that held the cooked meat. Then he stopped, said over his shoulder, ''I do not know. She does not know. She must think, she said.''

Cort puffed out his cheeks. ''I would not turn my back on Lana,'' he said frankly.

At that Mar looked around. He smiled. ''I will be careful,'' he said. And with that they had to be content.

Cort had insisted that Mar sleep in his hut, not in the men's cave with the unmarried men of the Red Deer. It was not possible for Mar to sleep in Alin's hut; the law said that the two who were to make the Sacred Marriage must keep apart until the day of Spring Fires. It was a law that the Mistress was strongly enforcing this year.

''You will not be disturbing me and Elen,'' Cort assured his old chief when he issued the invitation. ''Elen is in no mood these days for me, and even if she were, the taboo against mating at the dark of Spring Fires Moon would keep us apart as surely as it is keeping you from Alin.'' So Mar had unrolled his sleeping skins at Cort's door, and the two nights had passed. Then it was the day that the women went up to the Sacred Cave for the Purification Ceremonies.

Elen did not go, being too near her time.

''I was not planning to join in the Fires this year either,'' Cort said to Mar as they shot arrows at a target they had set up near the river. ''I was planning to stay here with Elen. But I think I will come, after all.''

Mar raised his thick golden brows. ''Are you coming to protect me, Cort?''

''You have few friends in this tribe, Mar,'' Cort replied soberly. ''It will be as well for the friends that you do have to be present.''

''The Mistress will not do anything to compromise Spring Fires,'' Mar said.

Cort gazed at a pointed bone arrowhead and thought for a few moments. ''That is probably true.''

''You see shadows where there are none, my friend,'' Mar said genially. ''Stay at home with Elen. She is more in need of you than I am.''

''I do not know about that,'' Cort responded with a rueful smile. ''She seems to be as content without me as with me these days. But it is true that *I* will feel better if I am near.''

And so they left it.

Dusk was falling on the final day before the Fires and Mar was standing by the river watching the sun set, when the tall slim man he had noticed at various times around the camp sought him out.

''Greetings, man of the Horse,'' Tor said as he approached Mar from the direction of the huts.

''Greetings,'' Mar returned pleasantly. He stood his ground and watched as the other man came up beside him. Tor was tall for a Red Deer man, but he was not nearly as tall as Mar. ''You are Tor,'' Mar said in the same pleasant voice he had used before. He added softly, ''Alin's father.''

He would have known it even had Alin not told him, Mar thought as he looked into Tor's grave face. Strange, he would not have supposed those huge brown eyes of hers would suit a masculine face. Somehow they did. Dhu! Even the way the man's braid fell between his shoulder blades looked familiar.

''It is a very peculiar feeling,'' Mar said honestly, ''to look into a man's face and see Alin.''

The man smiled briefly. It was not Alin's smile. "The daughter of the Mistress has no father," he said in his deep, soft voice. "She is the Chosen One. No man may claim her."

So that is how it is, Mar thought.

He said nothing, just continued to look steadily into the brown eyes that were Alin's and were not Alin's. The man's nose was different from hers, he noticed: full-boned and arrogant. Tor did not look like a man who would put his head under a woman's foot.

Tor's eyes did not flinch away from Mar's look. He spoke: "We drove away the other men of your tribe who came here," he said. "The ones who came seeking revenge."

"Altan? Sauk?"

"Sa. Altan and Sauk." Brown eyes and blue still held in an odd kind of battle. "There is no faith in men like that," Tor said contemptuously. "No loyalty to the tribe."

"That is so," Mar agreed. "That is why I drove them out. Altan was not fit to be a chief."

Tor's lips thinned in the exact way Alin's did when something had angered her. Then, "They were useful to us, though," Tor said.

"To you, perhaps. Not to me," Mar returned.

Silence fell. The men continued to stare at each other. Again it was Tor who spoke first. By unspoken accord, they both understood that he was the one who had sought out Mar, and so the burden of the exchange lay with him.

"Why have you come here, man of the Horse?" Tor asked.

"I came to see how the men of my tribe were faring," Mar said. "I came to see my son."

"The Mistress does not want your son here. He bears the mark of Sky God, as do you yourself. Your son is not a child of the Tribe of the Red Deer."

"If Alin will give him up, I will take him back with me to my own tribe," Mar said, "where we value boy-children who are marked by Sky God."

For the first time, Tor's gaze wavered. He turned away

from Mar, looked out across the river. "Alin will not give him up."

"That is what I have heard."

Silence fell again. Tor continued to look across the river. Mar watched his profile and said thoughtfully, "We have a shaman in my tribe, Tor. His name is Huth. He is an important man in the Tribe of the Horse. He is the link between us and our sacred world. This shaman has only one son, and for many years he thought the son would succeed him as shaman. But then it became clear that this was not the son's calling. The gods had other plans for him. And so Huth looked elsewhere for his successor. Huth took a young boy into his cave, a boy who dreams as shamans must, and now Arn is learning to be the next shaman of our tribe in the place of Huth's son."

Tor looked at Mar out of the side of his eyes. "Why do you tell me this story, man of the Horse?"

"I believe you know the answer to that question, man of the Red Deer."

Tor folded his arms across his chest. He said, "There is no one in this tribe who can take Alin's place."

The wind had shifted in the last few minutes, had begun to come from another direction. Mar pushed his blowing hair away from his cheek. "I am thinking that there is."

Tor's nose lifted, became still more arrogant looking. "Who?"

"Elen," Mar said.

Tor lifted his brows and looked skeptical.

"Elen could be your next Mistress," Mar repeated. "She has the . . . ruthlessness that the chief of a tribe needs to have."

"Elen is wed to one of your men, man of the Horse. The Mistress does not wed."

"Cort is a good man," Mar said. "He is young, but he is a fine hunter, a man other men would be glad to follow. He understands the sacred things of the hunt. But he is not ruthless. He would never try to stand beside Elen. He would be content to serve her."

"They are wed," Tor said again, shaking his head.

"That is not how we do things in the Tribe of the Red Deer."

"I am thinking that you will have to change how you do things in the Tribe of the Red Deer, Tor. I think you will have no choice."

Silence again. Mar reached down, picked up a handful of pebbles, and began to throw them into the water, one by one.

"You want Alin to go back with you," Tor said at last. It was not an accusation or a question.

Mar agreed with it. "Sa, that is what I want."

"Why did you not try to keep her in the first place?" The Red Deer man sounded truly curious.

Mar closed his fist around the pebbles. They were smooth and cold to the touch. He said, "I will tell you what Alin said to me, Tor, when she told me that she was going back home with her tribe and I said that perhaps I would fight to keep her. She said that her father was with the men of the Red Deer, and that if there was a fight and her father died, she would be unhappy."

Tor said nothing. Mar turned back to the river and threw a few more stones. Tor watched him and then asked, "You would not consider staying here with her?"

Mar shot him a quick glance. "I do not think the Mistress would allow it.'

"But if she would?"

Mar blew out out through his nose and threw the last stone. It sailed far out into the river and fell with a plunk into the moving water. "Sa," he said grimly. "I would consider it."

"You would?" Tor sounded surprised. He stared at Mar's profile. "Why?"

"Nothing is any good for me without her," Mar said. "Nothing. I have found that out this last year. I do not like it, but it is so."

Tor continued to stare at that strong, clean-planed profile. "You are right," he said at last in a low voice. "The Mistress would never allow you to stay."

"I would not fit into Alin's tribe, but Alin will fit into mine." Mar continued to stare at the place where the last pebble had disappeared "I am not the only one who is missing her. The women of the tribe have sent a message with me, begging her to return.''

''And you have given her this message?''

''Sa.''

''What did she say?''

''That she must think about it.''

Tor turned so that he too was staring out at the river. The setting sun splashed it with colors of red and gold. ''I believe it is the same for Alin as it is for you, Mar,'' he said sadly. ''Nothing is any good for her either, without you.''

''It must be so,'' said Mar. ''The thing that is between us has touched us both.''

''Elen,'' said Tor thoughtfully, and relapsed into silence.

''She likes to rule,'' Mar said.

Tor nodded abstractedly. ''And if Alin chooses to go with you?'' he said. ''Will she serve you as you have said that Cort will serve Elen?''

Mar grinned crookedly and turned to look at Tor. ''Alin?'' he said. ''Serve me? You must be speaking of another woman, Tor.''

Unexpectedly, almost reluctantly, Tor smiled back.

''She will not serve me,'' Mar said. ''She will help me. Alin has much understanding. The two of us together will bring fine leadership to the Tribe of the Horse. We did it before, and we can do it again.''

''And you would not stand in the path of her serving the Mother?''

''Na.''

Tor sighed. ''It is the babe that has complicated things.'' He spoke almost to himself. ''She cannot give up the babe.'' His attention came back to the man beside him. ''I am thinking that she will go with you, Mar. Because of the things that you have said, and because of the babe.''

''It is in my heart to hope that you are right.''

''I do not know what I hope for. The Mistress will be heartsore to lose Alin. The tribe will be heartsore. But I have enough fondness for Alin not to wish to see her as

she has been since she returned from being with you."
He sighed again. "It will have to be Alin's choice."

Mar said, with a painful attempt at humor, "I have
discovered in the last year and some, Tor, that it always
comes down to the woman's choice. It is a humbling
truth for a man to learn. But it is so."

Tor gave him a long level look. "Perhaps it is the
Mother's wish that Alin stay with you, Mar," he said
very softly. "There is much she has taught you already,
and much she has yet to teach."

Alin's father nodded, turned, and was gone.

Thirty-four

Alin awoke to the sounds of soft footfalls as someone stepped beside her sleeping skins on her way to the stream. Then, clarion clear in the misty dawn air. Tardith screamed with sudden, fierce hunger.

"Shhh, my babe. Shhh," Alin murmured, as she reached for the child lying by her side and put him to her breast. Tardith fell immediately quiet, but his cry had done its work well. The girls and women sleeping around the fire began to stir.

Alin held her son close against her and looked at the place where Mar had once stood, her hated kidnapper. She shook her head and a small, secret smile touched her mouth. How long ago that seemed.

"Alin." It was Lana's voice, edged with irritation. "When you have finished with that child, I need you."

Alin's smile disappeared. She nodded. "I hear you, Mother," she said mildly, not betraying by either voice or look her own annoyance.

Lana never referred to Tardith as other than "that child," any more than Mar was ever other than "that man."

I cannot blame her, Alin told herself, as she had told herself time and again before. She has devoted the last three-handful years of her life to training me to be her successor, and now she fears it will all go for naught. I cannot blame her for not loving Mar or Tardith. They are the ones who have got in the way of her plans.

When Tardith had finished nursing, Alin gave him over

to the woman who would look after him for the day and
went to help Lana and the rest of the women with the
preparations for the ceremony: bringing the costumes into
the cave to put in their proper places, arranging the bed
of skins in the side chamber wherein she was to make
the Sacred Marriage with Mar, laying the wood for the
seven fires that gave the ceremony its name.

There was no great black-maned cap for Mar to wear
this day over his hair, nor any other of the familiar em-
blems of the Tribe of the Horse to provide for its chief.
Today would Mar wear on his head the great branching
antlers of a stag, emblem of the Tribe of the Red Deer.
The antlers, and a long deerskin cloak hanging from his
shoulders: this was the god costume they placed in the
passage for Mar to assume sometime during the course
of the dance of the Fires.

Alin would wear the bell skirt of the dancers, and a
headband and bracelets of white shells, far more intricate
and beautiful than the makeshift ones she had worn at
Spring Fires one year earlier, when the Red Deer girls
had been forced to improvise for the ceremony they performed for the Tribe of the Horse.

Alin's mind was full of memories as she went about
her tasks this cool spring morning in the mountain cave
her tribe held sacred to the rites of Earth Mother. She
cherished the memories, used them to block the excitement she could feel pounding ever stronger in her blood
as the hours passed and the moment when the men would
arrive at the cave came ever closer.

She could not think of Mar without desire stabbing
through her like a burning brand.

Think of the mammoth hunt, she told herself, as she
arranged the skins for her bed in the small side chamber
she had chosen to use this year. Think of the moment
when we saw the two young mammoths wrestling in the
forest clearing. Remember the mammoth mother we saw
that morning on the game trail. I was sure she was going
to charge us, sure we were too close to her calf for us to
be safe.

When Lana spoke to her, Alin almost started, so intently had she fixed her mind upon the past.

When all the arrangements were in order, the woman who was looking after Tardith brought him by boat into the first chamber of the cave, and Alin nursed him. Then Tardith and the nurse left once again, and there was nothing for Alin to do but wait until the arrival of the men.

Custom said she must wait alone. When Lana beckoned to her, Alin followed her mother out of the room where the seven fires were laid, triangle-shaped as was proper, and down the small passage that led into the White Chamber. There Alin's costume was laid out; there she would await the moment when Lana would come back to lead her into the throbbing drums and high piping flutes of the Fires.

Lana had brought ochre with her, and with her finger she drew the proper signs on Alin's face and on her breasts. Then she left. Time passed. The women in the outer chamber were quiet in deference to the coming ritual. Finally the ever-present sound of the river was overlaid by the sound of voices in the outer chamber. The men and the remaining women of the tribe were coming into the cave, boatload after boatload of them. It would take a while; there were only two small boats to carry over two moon-fuls of people.

After what seemed to her a very long time, Alin could hear the sound of the flutes beginning.

At last.

She felt her breathing begin to quicken, but it was not because of the sound of the flutes. It was because of the picture of a man that had formed in her mind.

She thought of him as she had seen him at the last Spring Fires, dressed in his chief's regalia, splendid and powerful as the stallion he embodied.

He would not be the stallion this time, she remembered. This time he would be the stag.

Any man could play the stallion or the stag. What mattered to Alin was that he would be Mar.

In the outer chamber, the flutes had been joined by the beat of the drums. Soon the sound of voices drifted down the passage to Alin's waiting ears; voices raised in the sacred chant.

Within the White Chamber all was silent. Alin stood

at the opening that led into the passage, and listened intently to the sounds that were coming from the dancing chamber at the passage's other end.

Suddenly, the music changed. The drums beat more quickly, more intensely. A high cry came floating down the passage to fill the silence of the White Chamber.

Mar must have left the chamber, Alin thought. Lana would be taking him into the other passage, where they had stored his costume.

Alin could not see them, but she closed her eyes and pictured what was happening in her mind. He would be stripping naked, she thought, tying the antlers onto his head with the new sinew strings they had attached earlier in the week. He would be putting the long cloak over his shoulders.

It swept the floor when worn by the men of the Red Deer, Alin thought, but it would clear the floor easily when worn by Mar.

A sharp cry of welcome and of excitement came echoing down the passage. The drumbeat intensified.

The God! The God! the dancers cried.

Mar had returned to join the dance.

It was the signal for Alin to begin to strip off her own clothes. She had put her shirt back on over the sacred signs drawn on her throat and breasts so she would keep warm while she waited. Now she folded her clothes, laid them on the pure white floor of the White Chamber, put on her bell skirt and her white shell ornaments. She went back to the end of the passage, and waited again.

After what seemed a very long time, she heard the sound of her mother's footsteps approaching up the passage. Alin backed into the White Chamber and watched as Lana appeared in the passage opening. The Mistress wore the same bell skirt as the rest of the women, her hair hung loose to her waist, and her necklaces were made of golden shells. Her breasts were no longer firm and high as once they had been, but her face looked young in the dim lighting of the cave.

"Come," she said to Alin. "It is time."

Alin nodded without speaking, crossed to the passage,

and went before her mother down the short hall that led into the dancing chamber.

The dancers nearest the passage saw her first, and halted behind their barrier of fire, awestruck, breaths catching in their throats. Then the others began to realize what was happening: one after the other the men and women in the chamber halted and turned toward the passageway opening and the slender figure that was framed within. The drums and the flutes fell silent. Soon the only sounds in all the great chamber were the sounds made by hard breathing and by the river as it dropped down into the depths of the mountain on its dark subterranean course.

Alin did not see the river. She did not see the seven burning fires, or the mass of sweaty half-naked dancers packed within them. Out of all that vast expanse of staring eyes, Alin saw only two, blazing blue under a towering headdress of stag antlers.

The eyes were waiting for her. Slowly Alin began to walk toward the fires, moving through the mass of dancers on a straight line toward the place where Mar stood awaiting her in the midst of the floor. The rest of the dancers fell away from her as she walked, backed outside the perimeter of the fires, leaving the dancing space open for Earth Mother and her mate.

The flutes began to play.

Alin stood before him, her eyes still locked with his. They had scarcely looked at each other directly these last two days. Now they looked their fill.

Soon, Mar, Alin thought, reading the message in those blazing eyes. It will be soon.

She began to dance. It was the same dance they had done together at Spring Fires the previous year, and after a moment Mar followed her lead with the same effortless ease he had then. The flutes trilled through the air, and soon the beat of the drums joined in under the flutes, to boost the tempo and drive the dancers onward. In a little, the other dancers began to come back into the space between the fires. Couple by couple they came, until the entire floor was filled with people dancing, as were Alin and Mar, the most ancient of all the Mother's dances, the fertility dance of the mating beasts.

The bodies on the floor leaped and spun. The music grew in its intensity. Alin felt all the pulses in her body pounding in rhythm with the drums. She was aware of nothing save the beat of the drums. And Mar dancing beside her.

Suddenly, out of nowhere it seemed, Lana's voice sounded in her ear.

"It is time."

It was a moment before Alin understood that Lana meant it was time for her to leave the chamber.

She inhaled deeply to steady herself, nodded, and began to turn away.

Mar's hand shot out, closed hard on her wrist.

She swung back around, met his eyes. She shook her head. "I must go," she said to him. He could not possibly have heard, but he must have read her lips. His fingers loosened, and once more Alin turned away. Not to the passage that led to the White Chamber this time, but to a smaller passage that led away from the dance chamber's left wall.

It was dark in the passage, but the small room that lay at the end of it was lit by the two stone lamps that Alin had placed there earlier. In the center of the room was the pile of skins that was to be the bed for the Sacred Marriage. Near the door of the passage, wood for a small fire was laid, with a live coal tucked in an antler horn to light it with.

Alin halted halfway to the pile of skins and turned to look back at the door. She was breathing quickly, though only partly from exertion. The stone floor was cold under her bare feet, but her long loose hair fell around her like a cloak and the rest of her was warm. There was even a faint misting of sweat between her breasts.

She looked around. The room was so empty. She was so empty. Empty and aching.

Would he never come?

It seemed to Alin that the drums in the outer chamber were beginning to slow their rhythm. It would take a while for the dancers to leave the cave; they had to use the boats to get out. Some would not bother to wait for the boats; some would melt away into a dark corner of the cave to be more swiftly about the Mother's business.

Alin crossed her arms over her breasts. She shivered, though not with cold.

Would he never come?

There was no revealing sound in the passageway—he had always moved as silently as a spirit—but suddenly he was there in the chamber with her. He was naked except for the deerskin robe and the antlers attached to his proud golden head. He was naked, his white skin gleamed in the dimness of the room, he was full of a terrible, potent beauty, and she did not think he was the god at all.

"Mar," she said. "Mar."

They moved at precisely the same time. She felt his arms come around her. She pressed the whole length of her half-naked body along his, locked her arms around his waist, and pressed her mouth to his shoulder. Then, for some reason she could not possibly explain, great shuddering sobs began to rack her body.

"Na," he said huskily, his mouth buried in her hair. "Do not. Alin, do not."

At the sound of that A-lin, her sobs increased.

He crushed her against him even harder. He said, "If you keep this up, you will start me crying also."

"I don't know why I am crying," she said into his shoulder. She loved the familiar taste of his skin against her mouth. "I should not be crying. I am happy." She licked his skin with her tongue, savoring the taste of him mixed with the salty flavor of his sweat and her tears.

"A-lin," he said. His voice had gone from husky to hoarse. "A-lin. Look up."

She took her face out of his shoulder, tipped it up to look at him. He bent his head and put his mouth hard against hers.

The drums began to beat once more in her blood. She opened her mouth for his tongue. Her head bent back and her long hair streamed down over his arm nearly to the floor. Her hands moved under his cloak, up and down his bare back, greedily caressing the smooth flesh and strong muscles they found there.

Her flesh had lived since she had left him, but within all had been winter. Now was come the spring. Now was come the heart of her being, the power that to her was life itself.

Mar, she thought to herself. Mar.

He lifted her, laid her down upon the skins of their bed. She looked up at him out of enormous, dilated eyes.

"Take off the antlers," she said.

He pulled at the sinew strings that held the headdress secure, loosened them, and put it aside. He undid the ties that held the robe together at his throat, and let it fall to the ground.

She watched him.

He was so beautiful.

She reached up her arms, and he came to her. He stretched out beside her, put his hands upon her, and with his coming all the desolation of the long empty year without him began to dissolve. The cave wherein they lay seemed to dissolve as well, until there was nothing left of the world save they two, alone together in the bright dark. They were a part of the mystery, part of the star-filled night, the heat of the earth. They lay together at the rocking, pulsing heart of the world and in their coming together was not only great hunger and passion, but also a great and heart-healing peace.

Alin awoke to the weight of his arm across her back. They had lit the fire before going to sleep, and it was still giving off enough light and heat to make the chamber comfortable.

Mar must have got up to tend it sometime during the night, Alin realized. She had not felt him move.

I was weary, she thought. I did not know how weary I was. She felt vaguely uncomfortable, and shifted her position slightly, seeking relief.

"Awake?" His voice was soft but not even faintly slurred with sleep. He always awoke to total clarity.

"Sa." She turned her head toward him so that their noses were but a hand's span apart. They lay with their cheeks pillowed against the warm deerskins of their bed and regarded each other gravely. He had not removed his arm.

"Since you left me," he said at last, "it has been winter in my heart."

She sighed. A soft, acquiescent sound. "Sa. It has been the same for me."

They regarded each other some more, content with what they saw.

"I spoke to Tor," he said after a while. "Did you know that?"

Very faintly she shook her head. "What did you say to him?"

"He asked me if I would consider staying here in the Red Deer Tribe with you."

Mar was so close to her that he could see the pupils of her eyes dilate in surprise. "He did?" she said.

Mar nodded.

"And what did you answer him?"

"I said that I did not think the Mistress would allow it, but that if she would, I would consider it."

Alin's pupils enlarged noticeably, making her eyes look even darker than usual. "You said that?" A single strand of hair had caught in one of her lashes. Mar blew gently to dislodge it. He smiled faintly and nodded.

His soft breath had made her blink. "What did Tor say then?"

"He said that he did not think the Mistress would allow it either."

"Na," Alin said sadly. "I do not think she would."

Mar's hand moved in a brief caressing gesture on her back. "I told him about Huth and Tane," Mar said. "I told him how Huth had been forced to look elsewhere for a successor when it became clear that Tane was not the one."

Alin lay quietly, looking into his eyes. Finally she moved her hand, raised it to smooth the hair off his brow. He had bathed in the river yestermorning, to purify himself for the ritual, and his hair was soft and feathery from the soapwort. Some strands of it clung to her fingers as she brushed it back, circled them like rings of gold.

She looked at her gold-spangled hand. "It would be a

terrible thing for me, Mar,' she said, "to desert my people."

"I know," he replied. "Neither do I belittle the seriousness of it. But it is as I told Tor, Alin. It is possible for you to fit into my tribe; it is not possible for me to fit into yours."

Silence.

"I know that," she said at last. She freed her fingers from his clinging hair and rested them on the deerskin between them. "I know." She was looking at her naked hand, and not at him.

"Tor said to me that there was no one in the tribe to take your place," Mar said to her. "I told him there was Elen."

Alin looked up from her hand. "I have thought of Elen," she said in faint surprise.

He smiled. "I knew you would have."

They looked at each other in silence. Then she sighed, rolled over on her back, and stared up at the high undecorated limestone ceiling. "Tane would paint bulls on that ceiling," she said.

"Sa. Or horses."

Alin suddenly realized the source of her discomfort. She sat up. "My breasts hurt, Mar. I need my baby."

"Is he still outside the cave?"

"Sa. We pitched a tent. Mela is keeping him there for me." Alin was looking around as if for her clothes.

Mar reached out a hand to keep her from rising. "Stay. I will bring him to you."

"It will be easier for me to go out to Mela than it will be to bring her and Tardith in here, Mar," Alin said.

"I said nothing about bringing Mela," he replied. "I said I would bring Tardith. Mela can stay where she is."

Alin's stared at him in astonishment, her eyes great dark pools of brown in the dim light of the dying fire. "You will bring Tardith by yourself?" She had never seen Mar hold a baby, nor had the strain between them these last two days been conducive to his becoming more closely acquainted with his son.

He grinned at her. "I have got you to myself at last,"

he said. "I am not yet ready to let you go." He stood up, splendidly naked. "I will get the baby."

"All right," Alin said a little dazedly. Then, with amusement, "I am thinking you ought to put some clothes on first, Mar. Mela will think Sky God is descending on her else."

He gave her a very blue look. "My clothes are probably still in the passage here. Don't move. I will be back shortly."

Alin listened to him moving around as he dressed in the passage. Then there was silence until she heard the splash of the oars in the water of the river. She thought about going to fetch her own clothes from the White Chamber, then changed her mind. She did not feel like moving. Besides, from what Mar had said, she suspected she was not going to need the clothes again for quite some time.

She did get up to put more wood on the fire, then went immediately back to her warm sleeping skins to wait for Mar and Tardith to return.

She had expected to hear Tardith long before she saw him, but in fact the baby was sleeping in his father's arms when Mar once more stepped silently from the dimness of the passage into the light of the fire-lit room.

Alin sat up. "Dhu," she said in dismay, regarding her peaceful son. "Did Mela feed him?"

"Sa. But she said he should be hungry still. She did not give him all he wanted." Mar came to kneel before her. He was holding the baby with surprising confidence for so new a father.

"He certainly seems content," Alin said dubiously, and reached out her arms.

"He was screaming when I first arrived," Mar said. "He quieted when I began to walk with him to the boat, and then he fell asleep." Mar looked very pleased with himself as he handed the baby over to Alin. "I must have a touch with babies," he said.

Alin grinned. "I will remember that."

Once Tardith felt the trickle of milk on his lips, he woke up, and soon he was sucking in earnest. Alin sighed with relief.

Mar sat down cross-legged next to her and, fascinated, watched his son. Alin looked up from the silky baby head and caught Mar's look.

Her heart swelled with tenderness.

This is the first time we have been together as a family, she thought.

Tardith squirmed, hiccoughed, and began to suck again. Mar grinned.

Is that too much for me to ask? To have my husband and my son beside me?

It was more than Lana had ever asked.

The Mistress belonged to the Mother. The Mistress belonged to the tribe. She could not belong to any one man. That was the rule.

Alin had known that since she was a very small child.

I cannot give them up.

The thought formed in Alin's mind as she sat there in the profound morning silence of the sacred cave, Tardith at her breast and Mar at her side. The thought formed, and she knew it was the truth. It was not in her to give them up.

Perhaps one day she would be called to account for such a decision. Perhaps she was wrong. She did not know. She only knew this one thing.

I cannot give them up.

Mar's voice was soft. "He is falling asleep again."

Alin cradled her warm and milky baby. "Sa. He is."

"Good," said Mar. "Now it is time for me."

Thirty-five

Lana awoke the morning after Spring Fires with Jus still sleeping heavily by her side. Last night had been good, she thought. It had not been the Sacred Marriage, but it had been good. The Mistress stretched with all the lazy satisfaction of the cat that she often so uncannily resembled, then lay back again and looked thoughtfully at the muscular back of the man lying next to her.

Jus was the instrument Lana had chosen to effect the disposal of Mar. He was a big man, Jus, and a fine hunter. He worshipped Lana. He would do as she said, and ask no questions.

Tor was also a fine hunter. An even better hunter than Jus, to speak true. Tor also adored Lana. But Tor would ask questions.

Tor had a tenderness for Alin that could prove to be the undoing of Lana's plans. It would be best to keep Tor out of the way when Jus was about his business, Lana thought. She stretched again and felt surging through her body the renewed energy that always came to her after the fierce mating of the Fires.

She looked once more at Jus's recumbent form. Men were always somewhat torpid after the Fires, she thought with a faint flicker of contempt. Lana herself always felt renewed.

Tor had never been torpid.

Tor was of the same breed of man as was this chief of the Horse, Lana thought now. Such men were attractive. Attractive and dangerous.

Lana had seen the danger early, and she had been strong enough to turn away from it.

Not for the Mistress the domestic contentment of other women. One could not lead the tribe and be a wife. It was the most fundamental rule of the matriarchy of the Tribe of the Red Deer. The Mistress must stand alone.

Alin knew that. But it seemed that Alin had forgot.

It was not Alin's fault, Lana told herself, defending her daughter from her own critical thoughts. Alin had been kidnapped. It was while she was being held against her will that Alin had been brought under the sway of that man.

That man.

Lana stared, narrow-eyed, at a slanting ray of sun that was coming in through the place where the door hides did not fully overlap and thought about Mar. He had kept Alin just long enough, Lana thought bitterly. Alin was caught.

Lana had seen that clearly enough last night, though she had certainly suspected it before. She had seen last night that Alin would not be able to send the man away. Alin was helpless in the grip of her own desire.

Lana would have to act for her.

At her side, Jus began to stir.

Good, Lana thought. The sooner this whole business was accomplished, the better it would be for the tribe.

The day after Spring Fires, Jus proposed to the men of his tribe that they hold a great deer hunt to impress Mar.

"Let us show to this son of a son what fine hunters those who are the sons of mothers can be," he said to the men gathered together in the men's cave late in the afternoon. "These men of the Horse think that because we do not draw hunting pictures in our cave, we are somehow less skilled than they. Let us make a great hunt out by Stone Lake and show them how a tribe that hunts with spears, not pictures, can win much flesh for its fires."

The men of the Red Deer agreed with enthusiasm and the hunt was set for the following day.

Alin was surprised when she heard of a hunt being organized so quickly, but no suspicion of possible danger crossed her mind. "I will speak to my mother while you are gone," she told Mar. "I will tell her that I am taking Tardith and returning to the Tribe of the Horse with you." Alin's face had been pale and strained, but her voice was steady. "It will be as well if you are not around when I tell her such a thing, Mar. She must have a chance to come to terms with my decision."

Cort was not so unsuspicious.

"The men of the Horse will have to cover your back for you this day," he said to Mar grimly when they discussed the invitation. "This hunt has come about too quickly. I mistrust it."

"You see shadows where there are none, Cort," Mar returned good humoredly. He was so full of happiness since Alin had made her decision that he would not have recognized a shadow if it had covered the sun. "This is a peaceful tribe," Mar continued. "You must remember how horrified the girls were when we told them we would fight if anyone invaded our hunting grounds. This is not a tribe to raise its hand against aught but the game it needs to live upon."

Cort remained unconvinced, however, and he and the five other men of the Horse resolved to keep as close to Mar as possible during the course of the day.

The hunters set out early in the morning, singing a hunting song as they went. There was no more preparation than that. Mar, like the rest of the men of the Horse, was shocked by the lack of reverence shown to the gods of the animals they were going forth to slay.

Most of the initiated men of the tribe had come on the hunt. Only Tor and one other man had remained behind at Lana's request, to perform some duty for her.

Their destination was a small lake that nestled in a long and gently sloping section of the mountainside a morning's walk from the homesite of the Tribe of the Red Deer. On the far side of the lake was a mountain meadow, covered now with wildflowers and the newly sprung nutritious grass of early spring. Beyond the meadow the ground dropped away steeply down into a gorge.

When the hunting party appeared at the lake, they saw a large herd of red deer grazing on the meadow beyond.

Mar and the men of the Horse looked to Jus for their directions.

"Stone Lake is a good place to take a herd of deer," the hunt leader told Mar. "See you how the lake and the steep drop of the hillside form two sides of a trap?" Mar nodded. "We will set up a line of men on both of the open sides," Jus said, "and drive the deer back and forth between us until we have slain as many as we can carry home with us again."

The men of the Red Deer made their dispositions quickly. It was apparent to Mar that this was a place they had hunted often. Mar and the men of the Horse went with Jus's group, to the eastern side of the meadow. There they took up a line at right angles to the lake, spreading themselves all the way across the meadow to where the hillside dropped off steeply below.

Opposite them, the other half of the hunting party was waiting to do the same thing. As the wind was blowing from west to east, the deer would pick up the scent of the men making the western line first, and so they waited to be certain that the men on the east were in place before taking up their own positions. It did not matter so much if the deer saw the men; it was the scent that would spook them.

Behind Jus's group was a stand of mountain pines, and beyond the pines the mountain slope rose gently upward.

As soon as Jus's group was in position, the rest of the men began to run forward to form the opposing line.

The deer picked up their scent almost immediately and began to flee toward the safety of the pines.

The hunters, who had been crouching in the grass before the stand of trees, rose and rained a hail of spears and arrows among the fleeing animals, turning them back in the other direction. In the meantime, the opposing line of hunters had got into position, and as the deer reached them, more spears and arrows rained into the panicked herd, and more animals fell. The terror-stricken deer swung around again and began to stampede back toward the first group of hunters.

A few of the deer fled into the lake and swam to safety. The rest were three times driven back and forth between the hunters before the survivors finally broke through the human lines and got away.

Mar was impressed by the efficiency of the Red Deer hunters. However different their Way might be, there was no denying these men's skill as hunters. The men of the Horse could not have used the geography of the lake more cleverly or been more effective with their weapons.

He said as much to Jus, who looked pleased. "We are a large tribe," he told Mar. "There are many mouths to feed. We have learned to hunt with our thoughts as well as our hands."

The men had begun the work of butchering the fallen deer when Jus put a hand upon Mar's arm and invited him to come and look at a small cave that lay just up the mountainside. "There are some drawings in it," Jus said. "Perhaps you can tell me what they signify."

Mar had no choice but to accept the invitation. To refuse would have been a grave insult. He nodded pleasantly and went to the lake to wash the blood from his hands and arms. Then he picked up his spear and spear-thrower.

"You will not need your spear," Jus said.

"It is a rule in my tribe never to venture forth without a spear," Mar replied in the same pleasant voice he had used to accept the invitation.

As the two men were standing there regarding each other, Cort came up to them. "Where are you going, Mar?" he asked his old chief, utterly ignoring Jus.

Mar told him.

"I shall come also," Cort said immediately.

Jus's strongly marked brows drew together. "Your help is needed with the deer," he said to Cort.

Cort set his jaw. "I will come with Mar."

Jus's brows met over the bridge of his nose. "You are no longer under the leadership of the chief of the Tribe of the Horse," he told Cort angrily. "You have chosen to join the tribe of your wife. I am the leader of this hunting party, and I tell you that you are to remain here and help with the butchering of the deer. If we are to return home on the morrow, there is no time to be wasted.''

Cort opened his mouth to protest, but Mar cut in. ''Jus is right, Cort. I would say the same if I were in his place.''

Cort looked furiously at his old chief. Mar's face was grave. ''Of your own will you chose to join this tribe,'' he said. ''You must follow its leader's commands.'' Then, when it appeared that Cort would continue to protest, Mar faintly shook his head.

With ill-concealed reluctance, Cort went back to his butchering.

Mar and Jus left the meadow together, heading for the pines that were on its eastern side. They both carried spears in their right hands.

When they reached the place where the mountain began to climb more steeply upward, Jus said, ''The cave is halfway up this part of the hill. As you can see, there is a track that ibex use. I will go first and you can follow.''

Mar nodded, and Jus began to scramble up the goat track. Mar came behind.

There was indeed a cave, lying in the rock of the mountain face at a place where the ground leveled off. Its opening was too low for Mar to enter without ducking his head.

''The pictures are of animals,'' Jus said. ''Do you want me to go first?''

''Sa,'' Mar said. ''That would be best. You are the one who knows the cave.''

Jus grunted. ''I must relieve myself first. Wait you here until I get back.''

Mar nodded, and Jus went off into the pines to the left of the cave opening.

Mar balanced his spear between his fingers and leaned his back against the rock wall beside the cave. He narrowed his eyes a little and scanned the entire area in front of him. There was no sign of any unwelcome presence. Mar did not think anyone else had left the camp before himself and Jus. He had been watching. And if anyone had left the camp after them, Cort and the men of the Horse would have seen and followed also.

Somewhere a bird called to its mate.

Jus appeared at the edge of the pines and began to walk toward Mar, who immediately stepped away from the wall of rock to face him.

What if they had sent men up before the hunt? What if there were men already in place inside the cave?

It was that thought, not any telltale sound, that made Mar swing suddenly around. The movement saved his life. The spear that had been throw at the center of his back went through his arm instead. Blood gushed immediately forth and Mar's own spear dropped from his fingers. With scarcely an instant's pause, he ran forward and threw himself on his attacker. The force of their meeting dislodged the spear that had been stuck in Mar's arm.

There was only one man. And of course Jus, who was coming behind. With a tremendous effort, Mar grappled with the man beneath him, and rolled. Neither of them had a spear, but the fight was hardly fair. Mar had only one working arm. And there was Jus.

Jus would not be able to use his spear while the two of them were thrashing around, Mar thought. Jus could not be certain of whom he might hit. Mar must not get on top to finish the fight. To be on top was to be vulnerable to Jus's spear.

He rolled again, and all his weight went over his injured arm. The world went red before his eyes. He heard the man on top of him grunt, felt him shift his weight. Two hands grasped Mar's shoulders, pinning him to the ground. The pain in his arm was making him dizzy and sick.

"Now, Jus!" the man panted. "I have him! Now!"

With a tremendous effort of body and will, Mar arched his back and pushed off with his legs. The grip of the man on top of him was broken, and the man fell crashing to the ground. He rolled out of Mar's reach.

A good move, Mar thought, as he lay for a moment, every muscle trembling from the effort he had just made. Now he was open for Jus.

Sweat was pouring down his face and into his eyes. He was close to losing consciousness from the pain in his arm. In the blur of spots that was his vision, he thought he saw Jus raising his spear.

Instinctively, Mar rolled onto his good side, gained his feet, and began to run toward the cave opening, weaving left and right so as not to present an easy target for Jus.

Jus threw. The spear hit the side of Mar's right thigh. It lodged in the flesh and held. The shaft sunk low, forcing the spearhead up, tearing through more flesh. Mar reached over, put his left hand to it, and yanked it out.

He had a weapon.

He turned to face the men who had attacked him, the spear in his left hand. Not his throwing hand, but it couldn't be helped. His right arm was dangling uselessly at his side.

The two men were bending to pick up the fallen spears. Mar sighted the man nearest to him, and threw.

Thump. It was the sound of a spear that had landed true. The man grunted, and fell.

Now there was only Jus.

But Mar had lost his spear.

"You are dead, man of the Horse." He heard the words dimly, coming as though from far off through the roaring in his head. Blood was pouring from the wounds in his arm and his thigh.

Even in this extreme condition, Mar wondered why the man took the time to make such a foolish announcement.

I must get to the cave, Mar thought. But his legs were not obeying the command of his brain. He took one faltering step. He saw Jus raising his spear. He gathered his strength to leap aside.

"*Stop, Jus!*"

The words froze both Jus and Mar into immobility. They came from within the pines.

"*Stop or I will kill you.*"

Cort, Mar thought, dazed. Cort must have followed

after all. He shook his head a little, trying to clear his vision.

But it was not Cort who stepped out from the shadows of the pines. It was a man of the Red Deer. A boy, really, slim and dark-haired. He was holding a strung bow in his raised hands; its flint-tipped arrow was pointed directly at Jus's chest.

"Ban," Jus said, in utter surprise. "What are you doing here?"

"I followed you," the boy said.

"You do not understand," Jus told him. "I am acting at the command of the Mistress. Now go away, before I tell her how you have interfered."

"It is you who do not understand," Ban said. His voice was quiet and calm. "This is Alin's man. I am not going to let you kill him."

Mar backed up toward the rock wall, reached it, and leaned against it heavily. He blinked, blinked again, and looked around for a weapon.

He could try to get into the cave, but he did not know how big it was. He did not at all like the idea of being cornered in a small cave. There would be more room to maneuver outside.

The boy called Ban was saying, "At this distance, Jus, I can kill you easily. Put down your spear."

"You would not dare to kill me," Jus said.

The dark-haired boy's voice was very soft. "Would I not?"

It was very still in the clearing around the cave. Not even the birds were calling.

It was not a bird before, Mar thought with sudden clarity. It was Jus. The call was his signal to the man in the cave.

Jus was laying down his spear.

"You will regret this," Mar heard him saying to the boy. "The Mistress will be very angry with you."

The boy did not reply, nor did his drawn bow waver.

The wound in Mar's thigh was burning like fire, but that did not worry him so much as did the wound in his arm. He could not move the arm.

"Mar." It was Ban's voice, coming as if from very far away. "Can you hear me?"

"Sa." He said the word through clenched teeth.

"I am thinking it is not safe for you to return to the camp."

"Sa," Mar said again.

"You are sorely wounded. I do not know what to do with you." Ban sounded distinctly worried.

"First, bind Jus," Mar said. "You cannot do anything while you are holding that bow."

"Sa," said Ban on a note of enlightenment. "I have extra sinew for my bow tied around my waist. I will bind Jus with that."

"Good," said Mar. His knees buckled slightly and he braced his feet, willing himself to remain upright. "First bring me the spears," he said to the boy. Ban collected the spears that were in the clearing and came to lean them against the mountain rock. One he gave to Mar. Then the boy proceeded to tie up an infuriated Jus.

"I need help, Ban," Mar said when the boy came back to stand before him. "You must return to the camp and bring Cort and the other men of the Horse here to me. Do it quietly."

"You want me to leave you here with Jus?"

"He is tied up. You have done a good job?"

"I have done a good job."

"Then I am safe. Go now. Quickly, boy. I have lost much blood. I do not know how much longer I can stay awake."

"All right. I will go, but first I will tie up your wounds to stop the bleeding."

Ban took off his shirt, ripped it at the seams, folded it, and tied the buckskin around both of Mar's wounds, using the sinew from his bow. Mar shut his eyes and remained perfectly silent during the whole procedure. If he had not been on his feet, Ban would have thought he had fainted.

When Ban had finished, Mar opened his eyes. "Now go."

Ban went.

Mar was still standing propped against the mountain

wall when the boy returned, bringing with him Cort and the other men of the Horse.

"Mar!" Cort said in horror as he ran across the clearing to stand before the blood-covered figure of his old chief. "Are you all right?"

"I am glad to see you, Cort," Mar said, pitched forward on his face, and lay still as a stone.

Thirty-six

It was after midday the day of the deer hunt when Alin sought out Lana to tell the Mistress of her decision to leave the tribe. She left Tardith sleeping in her hut, and crossed the wide, open space before the women's cave to the hut that belonged to her mother.

Lana was not there.

Relief surged in Alin's heart, and immediately she was angry with herself. Putting off the moment would not help. She turned away from Lana's empty hut, walked briskly up to the women's cave, and asked the girls if they knew where the Mistress had gone.

"She went to the sacred cave this morning," one of the girls replied.

Alin frowned. "Why would she be going there?"

"She said one of the boats was leaking. She took Tor and Kar with her to mend it."

Alin thought for a moment. "I have left Tardith sleeping in my hut," she said. "Will you watch him until I return? I have something I must say to the Mistress."

"Surely," the girls replied. "We will watch him for you, Alin."

Alin smiled briefly and turned toward the river and the familiar path up into the mountain.

Lana was sitting on a deerskin robe she had spread in the sun when Alin finally arrived at the clearing before the sacred cave. Tor and another man had one of the boats turned upside down on the shore beside the river and were working on it with the glue that they made out of plant saps. Lana was watching them, but her head turned when her daughter came around the bend in the river.

"Alin!" she said in surprise.

Alin came up to stand beside her mother. "The girls at the women's cave told me you were here, Mother. I must speak with you."

Lana smiled and patted the robe beside her.

Alin glanced at the men, decided they were sufficiently out of earshot, and sat down.

Alin held her face up to the sun. "It is nice here to-day," she murmured. "You can feel the warmth of spring in the sun."

"Sa," was all Lana said in reply. She waited.

Alin sighed with resignation. "Mother, I do not know how to say this to you, but it must be said." She stared straight ahead of her at the water of the small river, sparkling now in the bright afternoon sunshine. She said, "I am going back to the Tribe of the Horse with Mar."

Silence.

After a few moments, Alin made herself turn to look at Lana's face. Her mother was watching her. Meeting the familiar slanting blue-gray eyes, Alin felt a sharp pang, compounded of guilt and sorrow and frustration. "I cannot live without him, Mother," she said. "Nor can I live without my son."

"This is a selfish decision," Lana said.

"Perhaps it is." Alin's lips set. "But I am no good to the tribe the way I am now, Mother."

"I do not agree."

Alin pulled up her knees, bent her head forward and rested her forehead on them. "Elen can take my place," she said, her voice a little muffled, projected, as it was, downward. "Elen has the strength to stand alone. I do not."

"That man has cast a spell upon you," Lana said coldly.

"No spell," Alin said. "It is just that"—she raised her face from her knees—"I love him."

"You have no right to love him," Lana's voice was

growing colder with each word. "You are the Chosen One. Your love must be for the tribe."

"But it is not for the tribe, Mother. Not any longer. That is why I must leave."

Lana's face was set hard. "I am thinking that this is how Sky God came to rule so many of the tribes of the Kindred," she said. "Fools of women, like you, Alin, gave over their powers to men."

Alin straightened her shoulders. "I am giving over my rule of the Tribe of the Red Deer to another woman, not to a man," she said. "Nor have I given over my allegiance to Earth Mother. Mar knows that. He does not wish me to be other than I am."

"You are the Chosen One. He wishes you to be other than that."

Alin said, "Would you allow him to remain here with me? Allow him to be my husband? Allow me to keep my son?" Her voice made clear that the question was in the nature of a challenge.

Lana's reply was impatient. "That is impossible," she said, an adult speaking to a child. "The Mistress can belong to no one man, and the tribe is her child. You know that, Alin."

"Sa, I know that. But in Mar's tribe, the chief can have a wife. The chief can belong to one woman, can have his family around him in his shelter. In Mar's tribe we can be together. That is why I am going back with him, Mother. It is as simple as that."

"He will not belong to you, Alin," Lana said. "When they hold power, men belong only to themselves."

Alin's chin came up. She looked at her mother, a long level look. "It is true that he belongs to himself. He belongs also to the tribe. And he belongs to me."

Silence fell as the two women regarded each other unflinchingly.

"This is a test for you, Alin," Lana said finally. "Earth Mother has put this man into your path to test your strength. To test your devotion. Never did I think you would fail such a test, my daughter. I would have staked my life upon your steadfastness. It is hard for me to believe that I was so wrong."

As her mother spoke, Alin began to grow very pale. She felt as if Lana's words struck directly at her heart. She could not answer.

Lana, seeing this, pressed her advantage. "This Mar is the only man you have ever lain with," she said. "You do not understand that he is not the only man who can make your blood run with fire. Take another man, my daughter. See if what I say is not true. You have lain with this Mar at the Fires, and he is as the god to you. But there are other men who can fill you that way, Alin. From long experience, I can assure you of that."

Very slowly, Alin shook her head. "It is not just that, Mother," she said. She lowered her eyes, to hide them while she said things that would lay naked her most private feelings. "It is that . . . it is that when I am with him, I am happy." She gazed with absorption at a wrinkle in the deerskin robe upon which she sat. Her voice had grown soft. "I am happy when he throws his head up, the way a stallion does; I am happy when he smiles at me and looks like a little boy; I am happy when his hair falls over his brow and he pushes it back. . . ." She gazed hard at the wrinkle, refusing to look up. "That is the way it is, Mother. It is not just the fire in the blood— though," she added honestly, "it is that too."

There was a deep sharp line between Lana's brows as she stared at her daughter's averted face and sealed eyes. "It is not your business to be happy," Lana said at last.

Alin's head bent even lower. "Perhaps that is so. Perhaps if I had never known it, I could live without it," Alin replied. "But I cannot turn my back on it now."

"I did," Lana said. "And you can, too."

At that, Alin's head lifted. She looked at her mother. "Tor?" Alin said at last, in the same soft voice she had used when she had spoken of Mar.

"Tor." Lana's cat face was unusually strained. "I saw the danger, and I turned away."

"Perhaps I could have also, at the beginning," Alin answered. "But now I cannot. It is not in me, Mother, to give them up."

There was a long, reverberating silence. Then Lana said, "All right, Alin. You may keep your son."

Alin's face went as white as snow. She did not reply.

"Keep the boy," Lana said. "And send the man away."

Alin shuddered. She drew a long rasping breath, and shuddered again. Then she said, "I cannot."

Lana said, "You are a fool."

Alin's lashes lowered, fanning out across her cheeks. She said, "Look to Elen for your successor, Mother. Elen has it in her to do what I cannot."

"Will Elen put away this man of the Horse that she has taken?"

"If she must, she will." Alin's lashes still screened the pain in her eyes. "I am thinking that Elen is not a woman for one man."

Lana said bitterly, "And you think you are."

At last Alin looked up. She said, "The first day he came here to find me again, Mar said to me that he was like his old dog. 'Lugh was a dog for one man,' he said, 'and I am a man for one woman.' I am like Lugh also, Mother. I am a woman for one man, and that man is Mar."

Slowly, deliberately, Lana turned her face away. "I cannot keep you against your will, Alin. You are no good to the tribe unless you serve it willingly."

"I am sorry, Mother." Alin rose slowly to her feet. "I have failed you, and I am sorry."

"It is not I whom you have failed, Alin," Lana said, her face and her voice adamant. "It is Earth Mother. She called you, and you have turned your back."

Alin bowed her head. She could offer no defense. It was true. She turned away from Lana and went back toward the path, her heart laden with sorrow and guilt.

Alin returned along the well-trodden path to the tribe's homesite, and it was for her as if the sun-filled afternoon did not exist, so bleak was her outlook.

What did you expect her to say? she asked herself, as she sat within the confines of her small hut. Did you expect her to give you a blessing? She but named you what you are: Deserter.

No way out for me, Alin thought. No way to turn that was not fraught with betrayal.

Lana returned from the sacred cave, and the girls in the women's cave began to build the cooking fire. Soon the delicious scent of fennel drifted through the air. As if he had smelled the cooking food, Tardith woke from his afternoon nap and cried to eat. Alin had finished feeding him and was thinking of eating her own supper, when she was startled and alarmed by Ban's sudden appearance at the door of her hut.

"Ban!" She stared at him. He was breathing hard and covered in sweat. Fear smote her. "What has happened?"

"It is Mar," Ban said.

Na, Alin thought. It cannot be Mar. I will not believe it. She stared at Ban, her face white, her eyes enormous, and said nothing.

"He is hurt," Ban said.

Alin began to breathe again.

"Come in," she said. "How hurt? What happened?"

"Badly hurt," Ban said, coming all the way into the hut. He wiped his sweaty face with his sleeve. "We did what we could for him, but his wounds will need sewing. You will have to come and see to him, Alin."

"Of course I will come. But how did it happen, Ban? You were on a deer hunt!"

"Not just a deer hunt. Jus went hunting for Mar," Ban said. "They are spear wounds that he bears, Alin. They are not the work of any beast."

Alin stared. "Jus attacked Mar?"

"Sa." Ban's breath was beginning to come more slowly. "While the rest of us were butchering the deer we had taken, Jus asked Mar to go with him to see the pictures in a nearby mountain cave. Cort wanted to go also, but Jus would not let him. I heard this, Alin, and I wondered. I followed them. It is my sorrow that I did not come in time to save Mar from injury."

Alin said, "Jus could not best Mar in a fair fight."

"It was not a fair fight. Gul was already concealed within the cave, waiting for them."

There was a small silence as Alin digested this information. "It was planned before the hunt then," she said slowly.

"Sa."

"The Mistress."

"Sa," said Ban once again. "Jus told me he was acting on the Mistress's command."

"I will come with you," Alin said. "What do I need besides my needle box?"

"Some skins to stanch the flow of blood."

"How badly is he hurt, Ban?"

"He has lost much blood, Alin. But he is strong."

"The wounds?"

"The leg wound is mainly through the flesh. But the wound to the arm is serious. He cannot move it."

"Which arm?"

"The right."

Alin closed her eyes. "I will gather my things," she said. "Sit you down, Ban, and rest." She gestured. "There is water over there." She frowned, thinking, making plans. "I will leave Tardith with Mela."

"We must take Mar's sleeping skins," Ban said. "And yours."

Alin nodded. She knelt and began to put together a package for herself to carry as Ban went to take a long drink out of the bladder of water she had indicated.

"Is Mar in the hunting camp?" she asked Ban over her shoulder.

Ban shook his head. "We did not think it was safe. We hid him away on the mountainside, in another cave that we knew about."

"We? Who is with him?"

"Cort, and the men of the Horse."

"And Jus?"

"We left Jus tied up in front of the cave. The men in the camp will have sent someone to seek out Jus by now. I do not think he will come to harm."

"I do not care if he comes to harm," Alin said bitterly. "I am thinking that if he is eaten by a cave bear, I will rejoice."

Ban grunted.

"Wait here," Alin said. "I will take Tardith to Mela, and then we can be on our way."

The cave where Mar was hidden was the cave the men of the Horse had found and used for their secret hunting ritual. It was dark by the time Alin and Ban arrived, and so Alin did not have a clear view of the cave's situation. Cort had clearly been watching for them, for he met them holding high a torch in his right hand.

"How is he?" Alin asked immediately.

"He breathes but he is deeply asleep. We cannot wake him," Cort replied. His voice sounded worried. "Dhu! I wish Huth were here."

"I will look at him," Alin said, her own voice calmer than she felt.

"This way," Cort said, and he led her into the first chamber of the cave.

They had built a fire to keep Mar warm and spread a pile of their own fur vests under him to warm and soften his resting place. Almost the first thing Alin saw was the blood. It was all over his clothes, all over the furs on which he was lying. She dropped to her knees beside him. Roc whined a little from Mar's other side. Mar's eyes remained shut.

Alin looked at the blood. He had lost so much. She shut her own eyes for a moment, swallowed, opened them again. Then she looked at the blood-soaked deerskin tied around his upper arm.

"I shall need the water we brought," she said to Ban. She set her teeth, took out a sharp-edged flint knife, and cut the sinew binding the deerskin to his arm. Gently she began to pull the deerskin away. As she did so, the wound commenced to bleed again.

Alin never knew how long she worked over Mar that night, painstakingly washing and then sewing the wounds in his arm and in his thigh. It was as Ban had told her, the leg wound was not of great concern. But the wound in the arm had gone deep, had torn through the sinews that connected the muscles to the bones of the arm. Even if the wound healed, Alin was not certain that Mar would ever have the full use of the arm again.

For now, though, she could not worry about that. Her concern was that he would fall into a fever and his soul would go wandering and never return.

Cort and Russ and the other men of the Horse feared the same. "If only Huth were here!" they said again and again. But there was no Huth to summon his helping spirits, to make the journey to the Other World in case Mar's spirit failed to return to his body in the morning.

Alin longed for Huth's presence almost as deeply as did the men. In her deepest heart, she harbored an icy fear that Mar's injury was Earth Mother's punishment. The Goddess, Alin thought with grim honesty, had no cause to love Mar.

Ban had carried Mar's sleeping skins from Alin's hut to the cave, but in the end they did not try to move him from where he lay. "Use them yourselves to keep warm," Alin said to the seven men who were sharing the cave with her. "You have given him your furs and you are cold. I will lie beside him and pull my sleeping skins over us both."

And so she did, lying down carefully on Mar's left side and spreading her skins over the two of them. He was so big, he took up far more than half of the coverings. Alin lay close against him on her side and pressed her nose against his uninjured arm. She shut her eyes tightly.

This was her mother's doing. Lana had seen that she was losing Alin, and so she had acted. When Alin had spoken to her this afternoon, Lana had already set in motion this plot to remove Mar from Alin's path forever.

I will never forgive her for this, Alin thought bitterly, lying in the semidarkness of the fire-lit cave and listening to Mar's slow breathing.

She thought back once again to the afternoon's scene with her mother. "You can keep the boy," Lana had said. "Keep the boy, and send away the man." And all that time she had known that Mar was likely dead.

Her mother's doing.

What of her other mother? What of the Goddess?

Earth Mother, Alin thought. What is your will?

All the things of the earth were part of the Mother. They were born of her body and, at death, they returned to her once again. This was true for Mar as it was true for all living things. Ultimately, there was no escaping that.

Let him live, Alin thought. Mother. Let him live.

She was a great and terrible Goddess, full of love and full of pain. I have always served you, Alin thought now, lying with her nose pressed up against Mar's sound bare arm. And I shall serve you better if Mar lives.

One of the men had begun to snore softly. Otherwise the cave was quiet.

Earth Mother, Alin prayed, her silent words going out in anguish on the cold night air to the Goddess who had formed the whole of her moral being. Mother, this is my man. He is to rule the things of men, I am to rule the affairs of women. Neither greater than the other; both needful to the life of the world. Save him for me, Mother. If it is Your will that I should do your work, save him for me.

Mar moved a little, murmured something indistinguishable, then lapsed back into his deep sleep.

If Mar's injury were indeed Earth Mother's punishment on her, he would die, and the best part of her would die with him. But if he should live, then she would go with him to the Tribe of the Horse, and there she would lead and instruct their women so that when the women of the Horse went in marriage to new tribes, proper respect for the Goddess would return there also.

Mother, Alin thought with a sigh that was almost peaceful, it is in your hands.

Thirty-seven

When the morning light came, Mar's skin was hot. But he opened his eyes and recognized Alin.

"My arm?" It was the first thing he said to her. "I cannot move my arm."

"It will be fine," she told him. She smiled. "You must give it time to heal. Rest now, and regain your strength."

He frowned, looked around the cave, as if trying to determine where he was, and saw Ban. His blue eyes stopped on the boy's face. Then he said, "You are Ban."

The boy took a few steps forward, looked back at Mar out of grave dark eyes. "Sa," he said. "I am Ban."

Mar was bloodstained, feverish, and flat on his back. But he said, with great dignity, "I thank you for my life."

Ban bowed his dark and graceful head.

Alin said softly, "Drink some water, Mar. You are hot."

Mar looked back at her and then he nodded. Cort came forward with the water bag to help him drink.

"I am so tired," Mar said, when he had managed to get some of the liquid down, spilling half of it in the attempt. He frowned again in frustrated puzzlement. "Where are we? What is happening?"

"Nothing is happening," Alin said firmly. "You are not to fret. You are safe. We are all safe. If you are tired, then go to sleep."

"Where is the baby?" he asked her, looking around the cave as if he were seeking something.

"Safe with Mela. Do not worry about Tardith. Do not worry about anything. Just rest, Mar. Rest and get well."

She could see that he had other questions but was too weak to form them. After a minute his eyes did indeed close, and he went to sleep.

Toward nightfall, the fever worsened. Alin sat beside him, holding his sound hand, too exhausted herself even to think. She just sat there with her eyes fastened on his face, which was illuminated by the fire they had built to keep the cave warm.

His hair was filthy and matted with blood. He must have run his hand through it, Alin thought. He had no head wound. He had been clean shaven when he had left her the morning of the deer hunt, but now his cheeks and chin were covered with golden stubble. Most of the time he was still, but sometimes he would toss his head restlessly, as if he were having bad dreams, and sometimes he spoke.

"Lugh," he said once, very clearly. And for the first time since she had seen him lying there, so ill and badly hurt, Alin felt tears well up in her eyes.

"How is he, Alin?" Cort asked softly, coming to sit on his heels beside her.

"I think he will be all right, Cort," she answered, blinking away the tears. Her voice sounded odd and she cleared her throat. "He is very ill, but I have seen men more ill than Mar who have lived. And Mar is very strong. If it does not get worse than this, he will be all right."

"You have been as good as Huth, Alin," Cort said.

Alin smiled faintly and shook her head.

"I have been wondering how long we will be able to lie here safely," Cort said next. "The men of the tribe will have found Jus. The Mistress will know what has happened. Will they come looking for us, do you think?"

Alin turned her head, looked into Cort's kind and worried brown eyes. "If Mar is better in the morning," she said, "I will return to the Tribe of the Red Deer. I will get Tardith. And I will speak to the Mistress."

Ban's soft voice came from behind her. "I will go with you," he said.

Alin looked over her shoulder, to the face of the man who had saved Mar for her. "Sa," she said, "You should come with me, Ban. You too must face the Mistress."

Ban nodded, his dark eyes grave.

"Alin . . ." Cort said. "You will see Elen?"

Alin managed a smile. "I will see Elen."

"Tell her I must remain here with Mar for now. He is not well enough for the men of his tribe to leave him alone."

"I will tell her."

"Elen will understand. She has always admired Mar."

Alin nodded but did not reply.

In the morning, Mar was still sliding in and out of sleep, but he did not seem as hot as he had been. Alin decided she would indeed make a trip back to the Red Deer homesite. Her breasts had become painfully full, reminding her continually of her need for her baby.

The cave where they had hidden Mar was warm and dry. She would be able to take care of Tardith in the cave. She would bring him, and some of his things, and never again in her life would she return to the place where her mother dwelled.

"Ban," she said later in the day to the boy who was traveling so lightly beside her through the forest. "I believe you will be welcome in the Tribe of the Horse."

"You are going back there, then?"

"Sa. You knew that."

A soft sigh. "Sa."

They were walking swiftly along a deer track, in and out of sunlight as they went through the trees. After a few minutes, Alin said, "The Mistress will be angry with you."

"Jus will certainly be angry with me," the boy said. Alin could hear from his voice that he was smiling.

"Why did you do it?" she asked him, slowing her pace slightly so she could turn to look at him. "Was it for me, Ban?"

"For you," he said. "And there was another reason, too."

"Sa?" she said encouragingly.

The sun shone through an opening in the trees onto the soft brown of Ban's hair. He was like a deer himself, Alin thought, watching him, so slim and brown and graceful as he slipped through the forest. He said, "Alin, do you remember how you told me this winter of the painted cave of the men of the Horse, and the hunting ceremonies the men of the tribe hold?"

"Sa," Alin said. "I remember."

"And do you remember that the men of the Horse who now dwell with us held such a ceremony? It was held in the very cave where Mar is now lying."

"Sa," Alin said again. "Cort told me."

"I went to that ceremony," Ban said. "It was . . . it made me feel . . ." His straight brows drew together slightly as he searched for the right word. "Significant," he said.

Alin watched his face. Then she said softly, "It is right that a hunter should speak to his gods."

"Sa." Ban's voice was eager. "I do not speak against the Way of the Mother, Alin. Never would I so speak. But there are other gods as well as the Mother, and these we have neglected in the Tribe of the Red Deer."

"That is so," Alin said. She smiled at him. "There are sacred things for women and there are sacred things for men. Each should be revered by the other."

"Is that how it is in the Tribe of the Horse?"

"That is how it will be," Alin said.

"Then I am thinking that I will come with you," said Ban. "I am thinking that it would be an honor to join such a tribe as that."

All seemed quiet in the homesite of the Red Deer when Alin and Ban came walking up the river path in the late morning sun. The girls who were scraping skins before the women's cave saw them first. Then some of the children who were playing in front of the huts spied them and cried out, "It's Alin! It's Alin!" At the words, five men came striding out of the men's cave to stare at the new arrivals.

Alin said to Ban, "We shall go first to the Mistress."

Ban nodded, and the two walked on, taking no notice of the excitement their sudden appearance had occasioned.

Lana was standing at the door of her hut when they approached; obviously she too had heard the cries of the children. Her face impassive, she watched Alin and Ban as they came up to her.

"So," she said when they had halted. Her eyes flicked over Alin and lighted on Ban. "You have come back." It was the boy to whom she spoke.

"I have come back with Alin, Mistress," Ban said in his gentle way. That gentleness was deceptive, Alin thought, watching the boy's finely featured face as he answered Lana with superb composure.

"You disobeyed my wishes," Lana said to him.

"I had not been told of your wishes, Mistress," Ban replied. "What I saw was Jus attacking an unarmed man. This was not something I thought was done by the men of the Red Deer."

Lana's eyes narrowed. "Jus told you he was acting on my command."

"Sa," said Ban softly. "He did."

"Did you believe him, Ban?"

"Sa," said Ban even more softly. "I did."

The two of them looked at each other. Then Lana said, "You may leave me now. I wish to speak to Alin."

Ban's eyes flicked toward Alin. She gave him a faint smile. "Wait for me," she said.

Ban melted away.

"Come into the hut," Lana said, and turned to push open the hides. Alin followed.

"I suppose he is alive," Lana said when once they were inside. They both remained standing, facing each other. Alin was half a head taller than her mother, but lack of height had never caused the Mistress to lose her authority.

"He is still alive."

"I am sorry to hear that," Lana's voice was cold and

flat. The hut was cold too, an unusual occurrence for the warmth-loving Mistress.

"I have come to get my baby," Alin said. Her heart felt like a stone in her breast. "I will be going back to the Tribe of the Horse, Mother. Even if Mar were dead, I would still be going back to the Tribe of the Horse. You lost me forever when you sent Gul and Jus out after Mar on a mission of murder."

"I had lost you before that," Lana said. "I hoped that if that man were dead, you would return to your true vocation."

"His name," Alin said, her voice as hard and as cold as Lana's, "is Mar."

There was a silence. Then Lana shrugged wearily. "You may go, Alin," she said. She looked suddenly very old. "Your man will be safe from me. I understand well that I have lost you. Take your baby, and go." Lana folded her arms across her breast and looked away from Alin to the cold ash-strewn hearth.

Thus dismissed, Alin suddenly found herself strangely reluctant to leave. For a reason she could not fathom, her anger had begun to dissipate the moment her mother had said Mar was safe.

"Why did you do it, Mother?" she asked now in bewilderment. "It is so unlike you to resort to violence."

"It is as I said, I wanted to keep you for the tribe."

But Alin was shaking her head. "If I had made the sacrifice voluntarily, if I had given Mar up, then would I have been a fitting Mistress. But not that other way. The Mother would not have wanted me made an unwilling Mistress over the dead body of my man. I would be no good to the tribe like that." Alin stopped shaking her head and frowned in puzzlement. "Surely you knew that, Mother? Surely you, of all people, knew that?"

Lana sighed, uncrossed her arms, raised her hands to her eyes, and rubbed them as if they were burning her. For the first time, Alin realized how small her mother was. "Perhaps I did," Lana said.

Alin looked down into Lana's shielded face. "Then why?"

Lana dropped her hands, so they lay, opened-palmed,

by her sides. She raised her chin and looked at Alin. "Nine children have I borne, Alin, and only you was I able to keep. Think of how you feel for Tardith, Alin, and then perhaps you will understand what it meant to me when finally I was able to keep my child. All of the love that I could not give to the others, I gave to you." She gestured with her open hands, a strange, heartbreakingly vulnerable gesture. "I could not bear to lose you, Alin. That is why I sent Jus after Mar."

There was silence in the hut. Alin's throat had begun to ache. "I am sorry, Mother," she finally managed to say. "This is not the road either of us ever thought our lives would follow. But I think it is the will of Earth Mother that I go to the Tribe of the Horse. There are other girls in the Tribe of the Red Deer who are fit to be Mistress after you. There is no one in the Tribe of the Horse to take my place. That was Jes's message to me, and Jes would not lie."

"No," Lana said dully. "I suppose she would not."

Alin forced words around the ache in her throat. "It is not so great a distance between the Tribe of the Horse and the Tribe of the Red Deer, Mother."

Lana looked up in surprise. Then she said slowly, "Na. It is not."

"Mar is not one to bear a grudge," Alin said.

"He will be all right?"

Alin thought of his torn arm, refused to contemplate the possibility that it would not mend. "He will be all right," she said.

Lana nodded.

Alin looked at her mother's face for a moment. She sighed and said, "You have the heart of a chief, Mother. I am not your equal."

"You are," Lana said. As strongly as Alin had spoken before. "It is just that your way is not my way, Alin." For the first time in this meeting, she smiled. "I am thinking that the Tribe of the Horse will not be the same for your coming."

Alin smiled back. "Na, It will not." She reached forward, and then mother and daughter were in each other's arms.

It was Lana who broke the embrace first. "Go find your son," she said brusquely. "Find your son, and go."

"Ban is coming with me also," Alin said hesitantly.

"So I thought."

Alin turned away to the door, halted, turned back. "Who will you choose to take my place?" she asked her mother curiously.

"I do not know as yet," Lana replied. "I have several likely girls in mind. I will have to see."

Alin smiled faintly. It was a good sign, she thought, that Lana had been thinking of several likely girls. With a decisive gesture, she put her hand upon the hides, pushed them aside, and went out into the sun.

Alin stopped to see Elen before she went to collect Tardith.

"Cort is with Mar," Alin said. "But I am certain that you guessed that."

"Sa." Elen smiled and shifted a little on her deerskin robe. She was great with child. Alin marveled at how well she looked, considering how close she was to her time. "When I heard the story about Jus and Gul, then I knew where Cort would likely be."

"We were afraid that Mar was still in danger," Alin said. "I have spoken to the Mistress, however, and now I know that he is not. I will send Cort back to you, Elen. You must miss him sorely at such a time."

Elen nodded. "He is good to me, is Cort. I am not so able to get up and down as once I was." She gave Alin a rueful look. "You remember how it is, Alin."

"You still look beautiful," Alin said sincerely.

"I wish it were over," Elen said. "This last half moon, I have been wishing it were over."

Alin laughed. "I remember."

"You are going back to the Tribe of the Horse, then?" Elen asked.

"Sa."

"With Mar?"

"With Mar."

Elen nodded. "I am not surprised."

"Have you ever wished that you had chosen to remain, Elen?" Alin asked curiously.

Without hesitation, Elen shook her red-gold head. "It was fun, those moons we spent in the Tribe of the Horse. But this is home," she said. "This is my world."

Alin nodded. "Good-bye," she said softly.

"Good-bye," Elen grinned. "Give my greetings to Mar."

Alin pushed back the hides and went out.

Tor was waiting for her when she came out of Mela's hut carrying Tardith in a backpack. He was holding his spear and spearthrower.

"I will come with you to see you and the babe safe," he said.

"Ban is coming with me," she said to him.

"I know. But it will be better if there are two of us. It will be growing dark by the time you reach the cave."

Alin smiled. "It will be good to have you by my side."

"Papa!" A small boy of perhaps three years was running toward them over the hard-packed dirt of the clearing. "Where are you going?' he asked stopping in front of Tor and raising up his arms. His big brown eyes were shining.

The man laughed, bent, and lifted the child up to sit on his shoulder. "I am going somewhere with Alin, minnow."

"Can I come?"

"Na. But you can come with me as far as the river. Then you must return to your mother."

"All right," the child said, disappointed but obedient. He shrieked with glee as Tor began to move off swiftly, and grasped his father's hair with his hands for balance.

Alin stood for a moment and watched her father and her half brother as they trotted down to the river. A pang of regret pierced her heart, that she had grown up without the companionship of a father. Then she felt guilty that she should have such a regret, she who had had all of Lana's love. She shifted the backpack with which she was carrying Tardith to a place a little higher between her shoulders and began to walk after Tor and his child.

Thirty-eight

The Moon of the New Fawns was in its first quarter by the time Alin, Mar, and Ban reached the River Wand and the home of the Tribe of the Horse. They were escorted by Tane and Huth and Bror, whom Cort and Russ had fetched before returning, somewhat grimly, to their new home with the Tribe of the Red Deer.

Alin experienced a sensation she had never expected to feel as she came out between the towering cliffs onto the familiar beach and looked up at the great cliff face studded with its caves and shelters.

She felt as if she had come home.

"Alin!" The cry came from the first terrace, and Alin looked up to see Jes, standing poised in front of the shaman's cave. As Alin watched, Jes began to run along the terrace to the cliff path; then she tore precipitously downward, to the beach. Alin ran forward at the same time to meet her. The two girls fell into each other's arms, crying loud each other's name.

At last they separated, and gazed into each other's face.

"And who is this?" Jes said at last, peering over Alin's shoulder to the baby, reposing in unusual silence in his mother's backpack.

"This is Tardith," Alin said.

"Dhu!" said Jes with a laugh. "He is a small picture of Mar."

Tane's voice sounded from behind Alin. "Greetings, Jes. Remember me? I am your husband."

"Greetings, Tane," Jes said pleasantly. Then she grinned.

"She has seen you much more recently than she has seen me," Alin said with a smile. Then to Jes, "Tane tells me you have a son also."

"Sa. He is like his father, wanting constant attention."

Tane made a protesting noise.

Alin laughed. "Mine is like that too."

As they stood together, talking, the beach had been filling up with people, Alin gradually becoming surrounded by women, Mar by men. Alin cast one quick sideways glance in Mar's direction before she turned to her own followers.

"He will be all right," Tane said in her ear.

The frown smoothed from between her brows. "I know. It is not that. . . ."

It was Tane's turn to say, "I know."

They looked at each other, then looked away.

"Alin!" It was Dara, her small face lit with joy. "It is so good to have you home again!"

The smile came back to Alin's face. "Sa," she said. "It is good to be here."

It was really like coming home to walk into Mar's small shelter off the first terrace and see the familiar buffalo robes thrown around on the floor.

Automatically, Alin looked in the corner. She compressed her lips. "We must get another dog," she said to Mar. "Otherwise I will always be looking for Lugh."

"We can take Roc," Mar said, his face impassive. "Roc has always followed you, Alin."

Alin did not want a dog for herself. She wanted a dog for him. "Roc is one of the lead hunting dogs," she said. "He belongs to the tribe. We need a dog that belongs just to us."

"There have been puppies this spring," Mar said after a minute. "You can take one of those if you like."

She nodded. "Good. We will look at them in the morning."

Mar shrugged and looked around. "What do you need for the baby?"

"Nothing at the moment. He is asleep." Alin untied her backpack and carefully lowered Tardith to one of the buffalo robes. She did not want him to wake now. She wanted to focus all her attention on Mar.

"It is too cold in here for him," Mar was saying. "We need a fire." He went to the small pile of wood he kept in the corner, and lifted a log in his right hand. He crooked his left arm, so he could pile a few logs to bring them to the fire. Alin watched as he began the slow, painful process of raising the right arm, elbow-high, to put the log in his other arm. She could see how the sweat stood out on his forehead as he strained to lift the arm.

He managed it. Bent for another log, and began the whole painful process once again.

Alin turned away. He wouldn't allow her to help him, and she couldn't bear to watch him. Mar, whose strength was legendary among the men of the tribe, struggling to lift a small log.

Not for the first time, she thought, What will he do if he can never lift that arm again?

How could a man hunt, if he could not raise his arm?

How could a man be chief, if he could not hunt?

And if he could neither hunt nor be chief, how could Mar be himself.

The leg injury had completely healed. The external wounds of the arm injury had healed. But the inside of the arm was not the same. Alin was beginning to be afraid that it never would be.

It did not matter to her. It mattered only in that she could not bear to see him hurt, bear to see him struggle, bear to see him less than he thought he should be. But nothing in her feelings for him would change whether his arm healed or no.

No use in telling him that. It mattered to him.

She began to unpack the other things she had carried in her backpack, fussing with them to avoid watching him work. Then, when finally the fire was going, she looked up. She smiled. "Do you know," she said, "ever since we came out on the beach, I have had the oddest feeling that I have come home.''

He had been standing staring down into the new-made fire, but now he turned his head to look at her. "Have you? I have been thinking that I never will be home again.''

The day after his return, Mar went to the cave where the dogs slept and picked one of the puppies that had just been weaned. When Alin had suggested getting a new dog, he had placated her by agreeing, but he had been planning to leave the choosing up to her. This puppy would be her dog. He could not bear the thought of having a dog that was not Lugh. But as they were about to leave the shelter, Jes had come along with something that Alin had to see to, and she had insisted that he go alone.

He had not wanted to confess to her that he could not bear to choose a puppy. So he had gone. And he had found Cam. Or, to be more precise, Cam had found him. He had scarcely walked in the door of the cave, before the puppy had come walking over to him, parked its little rump neatly on his toe, and stared up into his face.

Mar leaned over. The puppy gazed intelligently back. He made no sound. Mar hated dogs who did not know when to be quiet. He reached out and took the puppy's muzzle gently into his hand. The dog's tail began to wag.

Cam was his.

Later in the day, while the men were out hunting, Mar took the puppy and went for a walk up the beach.

He spent a little time teaching Cam how to come when he was called, and then he sat down on the large rock that all the tribe used at one time or another, and stared blindly at the river.

He was beginning to be mortally afraid that he would never have the full use of his right arm again. Alin said he must be patient, but he could see that she too was coming to fear that the arm would not come back.

What kind of a man would he be without his right arm?

Oh, it had come back partway. He could hold it almost straight out now. But he could not get it further. He had tried and tried, but he could not.

No such thing as could not. His father had said that to him once, when he was a small boy complaining about something he was not able to do.

Fine words to say to a small boy. Words he would say to his own son someday, no doubt. But he was not a small boy any longer, and he knew that sometimes *could not* was true.

Mar bent, picked up a stone in his right hand, and thought about trying to throw it into the river. Then, slowly, thoughtfully, he shifted the stone into his left hand, drew back his arm, and threw.

The stone arched out over the sparkling water, then fell with a satisfying *plunk*. A fish jumped out of the water near where the stone had gone in, arched also in the sun, and sank once again beneath the river, making no sound at all.

A sign, Mar thought.

The stone had not gone as far as it would have if he had thrown it with a sound right arm. But . . .

I killed Gul with a left-handed throw, he thought. I have yet one good arm left to me.

So, Mar thought. What I must do is teach myself to throw a spear with my left hand.

Until the sun began to slip lower in the sky, Mar stood on the bank of the river and threw rocks with his left hand. Finally he turned away, looked up and down the beach, then whistled. A furry brown ball began to tear toward him across the gravel. Mar smiled.

It was good to have a dog again.

Alin waited until the end of the Moon of the New Fawns before she asked Mar, "When shall we be wed?"

He looked at her, startled. He had been playing with Cam in the corner of the shelter.

"Wed?" he said blankly. "You once said that you would never wed me."

"That," Alin said, "was before."

"Oh." Even more blankly than before.

Alin finished folding Tardith's clean swaddling clothes. "Now that I have come to live with the Tribe of the Horse for good, I think we should wed."

"Alin?" His voice sounded faintly strained. "I do not know if I will ever use this arm again."

She looked at him. "I would sorrow for you if that were so, Mar. But I do not see what that has to do with us."

He said, "You do not want to wed a man who is a cripple."

Cam heard the new note that had come into his master's voice, and leaped to his feet, growling softly, searching the shelter as if for an enemy.

Alin said, "Whether you can lift your arm or no, I want to wed you. It is you I love, not your arm."

"It is not so simple as that," he said, and turned away.

Na, she thought sadly. For him, it was not so simple as that.

"I cannot even make the dance of the Fires," he said viciously, "if I cannot raise my arm!"

"You can make the dance well enough," she said. "More important is what comes after the dance. And that you can still do very well indeed." She rose to her feet and went over to where he was standing, his back to her. She put her arms around his waist and laid her cheek against his back. She could feel his muscles tense under her touch.

"Mar," she said, and softly she rubbed her cheek against the deerskin shirt that covered his back. "Even with one arm, you are more man than anyone else in the Tribe of the Horse. The tribe knows that. I know that. Even Cam knows that. He is a chief's dog if ever I saw one, and he knew you right away."

She felt his muscles bunch. For one dreadful moment, she thought he was going to pull away from her and plunge out the door. But he didn't. Instead he turned, pulled her hard against him, and bent his mouth to cover hers. In a moment they were down together on the buffalo robe upon which Alin had just carefully piled Tardith's clothes.

He made love to her, but he said nothing about them being wed.

The Moon of the New Fawns died and the Moon of the New Year rose in the sky. Mar confided in Tane, and every day the two men went by themselves into the forest, and Mar practiced throwing a spear with his left arm.

"Do not give up on the right arm," Tane advised. "My father says you must keep working it. He has made all the proper ceremonials, and he says that now the curing work is yours to finish."

And work Mar did, day after day. And little by little, as his dexterity with his left hand and arm began to improve, so did the mobility of his right.

"You have time," Tane would tell him when it seemed to him as if Mar would work himself into a state of collapse, so intensely did he drive himself.

But Mar knew that in fact his time was running out. Thus far the nirum had expressed no doubts about Mar's right to be chief, but how much longer could he expect the men of the tribe to forgo the hunting leadership of their chief? How much longer before they started to say out loud what all must be thinking now in their hearts: will Mar ever have the full use of his right arm again?

Within the next half moon the tribe would be moving to its summer camp, a site farther up the river. There they would pitch their tents, and live in them for the three moons of summer, not returning home until the sun was once more setting early in the evening sky. There was good hunting in the area surrounding the summer camp. There were still aurochs to be had in that part of the tribe's hunting territory, and ibex and antelope as well.

One way or another, Mar was determined to be a hunter by the time he got to summer camp.

The women of the tribe were packing for the move to summer camp. As Alin was discovering, this yearly journey was no easy chore. The men would carry the tents and the weapons. The women were responsible for transporting the sleeping gear, all the spare clothing, and the cooking utensils. Even the small children would be given something to carry. With everyone laboring under burdens that weighed almost as much as they did, the tribe would need as much as four days to reach the summer camp.

It was past supper time two days before the scheduled move when Mar and Tane came walking down the beach together, a deer slung between them on two poles. They were both carrying their spears.

Under normal circumstances, the arrival of Mar and Tane with spears and a deer would not have provoked much notice. But these were not normal circumstances. No one in the tribe had seen Mar with a spear since he'd come back from fetching Alin and Tardith. He had hidden his weapon in the forest clearing where he was practicing, and no one but Tane had seen him with a spear in his hand for many moons.

"A man should not carry a spear unless he can use it," Mar had said to Tane, when his foster brother had queried him about his reason for going so obviously weaponless. And Tane had understood the profound humiliation his disability was causing Mar, and had not pursued the subject further.

But now, on this golden evening during the last half of the Moon of the New Year, Mar was carrying his spear as he came down the beach toward the cliffside caves that were his tribe's permanent home.

Melior and Bror were on the beach before the cliff, rolling fishing nets. They both looked up from their work, stopped, put the nets down, and rose to their feet.

Mar and Tane stopped a few feet away, and lowered the carcass of the deer to the gravel.

Melior and Bror looked at the deer. "Good," Bror said with elaborate offhandedness. "The dogs could use more meat tonight." He looked from the deer up into Mar's face, and raised his eyebrows in Mar's own gesture.

Mar grinned.

It is all right, Bror thought in profound relief. He looked at his chief's lit-up smile, at his blazing blue eyes. He grinned back. It is going to be all right.

The four of them did a quick job of butchering the deer, and Mar took a hunk of the haunch for Cam's supper. Then he climbed the cliff path and went along the terrace to his own shelter.

As he paused for a moment outside the lowered hides,

he thought back to those bleak moons of the past winter, when he had dreaded going in here, dreaded the emptiness that awaited him behind the snugly drawn hides. He put his hand upon the hides, then paused again, deliberately prolonging the moment, savoring it.

Cam looked up inquiringly, and gave a short bark. He was hungry, Mar was carrying his supper, and he could not understand the delay. Mar smiled, pushed aside the hides, and went in.

Tardith was lying on a buffalo robe in front of the fire, his little rump sticking up in the air as he tried to push himself up on his knees. Lately this had become an occupation that commanded a great deal of Tardith's time and attention.

Alin was kneeling in front of a roll of clothing, frowning direfully. She scarcely glanced at Mar as he came in. "I cannot understand how Mada got so many clothes rolled and packed so neatly," she said crossly as she jerked viciously at a sinew tie. "Every time I tie down one place, another place bulges out."

"Mada has been packing for summer camp for more years than you have been alive," Mar answered. He tossed the meat into the corner for Cam to work on, and turned back to Alin. "Leave it. It looks fine to me."

"You aren't going to have to carry it," Alin said even more crossly than before. She sat back on her heels, and looked up at him. He watched her face change.

"What happened?" she asked. Her voice sounded suddenly breathless.

He could scarcely contain the surge of joy that ran all through his entire body. "Why should you think something has happened?" he asked, trying to appear nonchalant and failing dismally.

"You look . . . all lit up," she said.

He didn't answer, but came over to regard her bundle. It did look lumpy. He said, "Do not worry, Alin. I will carry your bundle for you."

She didn't answer. He looked down into her upturned face. "I was standing outside the hides before I came in here tonight," he said. "I was remembering how much I dreaded coming into this shelter after you had left me.

I used to think up any excuse I could, to keep from having to come back in here.''

She rose slowly upward, until she was standing before him. She said, ''Mar, if you do not tell me what has happened, I will hit you with this wretched bundle.''

He grinned. Joy pumped through him as he said, ''I have been teaching myself to throw a spear with my left hand, Alin. That is what I have been doing for almost two moons now.''

Her lips parted slightly. Her large eyes grew luminous. No one else in the world had eyes like Alin.

''I knew you would not be defeated,'' she said.

''Tane has been helping me. All day long, we would work. And today,'' the grin broke out again, ''today I killed a deer.''

The expression on her face . . . it was wonderful, the expression on her face. ''Oh, Mar,'' she said.

He felt like the chief of all the tribes of the Kindred combined.

''You killed a deer with your left hand?''

The joy was so intense he was feeling dizzy. ''Last week I killed a deer with my left hand,'' he said. ''Today, Alin I threw the spear with my right.''

Her eyes were enormous.

''Look,'' he said. And raised his right arm over his head.

It was an effort still. He tried to make it look easy, but he could feel the sweat beading on his forehead and between his shoulder blades. He could not keep it aloft for long. But he would. Today, when he had thrown the spear and the deer had fallen, he had known in his heart that his arm would be his again.

Alin was smiling at him. ''Now it is you who look all lit up,'' he said.

Her voice sounded shaky. ''I should be furious with you for keeping this from me. But I am too happy to be furious.'' She stepped forward, into his arms.

''I wanted to surprise you,'' he said. ''I wanted you to look at me just the way you did. It is what I have been working for, these last moons. That look on your face.''

Her arms around his waist tightened. She said something into his shoulder that he couldn't understand. It didn't matter. He knew what she meant.

"Did you hear me?" she asked, taking her face away from him and looking up.

"Na." He looked at her in a little surprise.

"I wanted to know when we could be wed."

He looked at her in more surprise. "Whenever you wish," he said. "Tomorrow."

"Good." She smiled at the expression on his face. "It is the custom of your tribe that men and women should not live together if they are not wed," she explained. "I have been thinking that if the chief does not follow the customs of the tribe, then he cannot expect the rest of the tribe to do so."

"That is so," he agreed. He put his hands on either side of her face, his thumbs meeting under her chin. "Have you been worrying about this?" he asked softly.

"Not worrying. But . . . it has been on my mind," she said.

"We will wed tomorrow."

She smiled. "That will be well."

He moved his thumbs to touch her mouth. "Do you know what I want to do now?" he asked.

Her brown eyes glimmered. "What?"

He glanced aside, toward the buffalo robe where Tardith lay. The baby was asleep, worn out from all his efforts. Mar looked back to Alin.

"Guess," he said softly.

"Are you hungry?" she asked, with great innocence. "I have kept your supper for you."

"I am hungry," he replied. "Very hungry indeed. But it is not for my supper."

Alin raised her hands, slid them under his shirt, and ran them up and down the bare skin of his back. "That is very good," she said with great satisfaction.

He did eventually eat, and Alin fed Tardith, and they retied her bundle into some semblance of tidiness.

Then they rolled themselves up in their sleeping skins, and he drew Alin's body into the curve of his own. His eyes closed. It had been a day he would never forget, but he was tired.

"Mar?" Her voice was soft, almost wistful.

"Sa?" He answered her without opening his eyes.

"If one day we should have a daughter, will you carry her around on your shoulders?" she asked. "The way you did with Ware that day on the beach?"

He opened his eyes. He bent his head, touched his lips to the shining brown crown of her head that was tucked into his shoulder. "Sa," he said. "I will." He smiled. "I will even teach her to hunt."

He could hear the return smile in Alin's voice. "Oh, that will not be necessary, Mar," Alin said. "She will have a mother who can do that."

Joan Wolf is the author of several outstanding historical novels. Her books include *The Road to Avalon*, *Born of the Sun*, and *The Edge of Light*. She lives in Milford, Connecticut.